BEST NEW AMERICAN VOICES 2009

BEST NEW AMERICAN VOICES 2009

GUEST EDITOR
Mary Gaitskill

SERIES EDITORS
John Kulka and Natalie Danford

A Harvest Original • Harcourt, Inc.
Orlando   Austin   New York   San Diego   London

CONTENTS

PREFACE

The Best New American Voices series, now in its ninth year, promotes short fiction by emerging writers. Its focus is the writing workshop. Why the workshop? Because writing workshops are (have been for decades, really, since the Second World War and the GI Bill) an important part of American literary culture. Or, more to the point, because the workshop happens to be a place (*the* place) to which young, talented writers gravitate. Saul Bellow's New York has disappeared along with the subway token, and Hemingway's Paris has faded. Of course, writers will always be attracted to the big cities, but they are no longer first destinations. Younger writers seek out established writers, who, more often than not, can be found somewhere on a college or university campus, where they find employment as instructors.

As long as there have been workshops, there have been those who want to blame the workshop for many real or perceived ills, from the homogenization of American fiction and society to the failure of our collective political imagination. But these prophets of gloom seem not to understand the first thing about creativity. They confuse the workshop (craft) and influence. It is not particularly illuminating, when reading the stories of Flannery O'Connor, for example, to know that she was a graduate of the Iowa workshop and that other famous Iowa alums happen to include Wallace Stegner, John Gardner, Gail Godwin, Andre Dubus, and T. C. Boyle. On the other hand, we gain a deeper appreciation of O'Connor's fiction when we see it in relation to the work of her precursors: Hawthorne, Poe, and Nathanael West. These are the writers who sparked O'Connor's imagination and with whom she is engaged in creative dialogue (or, as Harold Bloom would insist, struggle).

The Best New American Voices series has become recognized as a rite of passage for American fiction writers and an important stepping stone in their careers. Joshua Ferris (*Then We Came to the End*), Rebecca Barry (*Later, at the Bar*), William Gay (*Provinces of the Night* and *I Hate to See That Evening Sun Go Down*), Julie Orringer (*How to Breathe Underwater*), Ana Menéndez (*In Cuba I Was a German Shepherd*), Frances Hwang (*Transparency*), Adam Johnson (*Emporium*), David Benioff (*25th Hour*), Eric Puchner (*Music Through the Floor*), Kaui Hart Hemmings (*House of Thieves*), John Murray (*A Few Short Notes on Tropical Butterflies*), Maile Meloy (*Half in Love* and *Liars and Saints*), Jennifer Vanderbes (*Easter Island*), the late Amanda Davis (*Circling the Drain* and *Wonder When You'll Miss Me*), and Rattawut Lapcharoensap (*Sightseeing*) are just some of the acclaimed authors whose early work has appeared in Best New American Voices since its launch in 2000. This is far from a complete list.

How does the Best New American Voices competition work? Each year we invite workshop directors and instructors to nominate stories for consideration. We ask them to send on to us what, in their judgment, were the best stories workshopped during the past year. We do not accept submissions from writers. Participants include MA and MFA programs (such as Brown and Iowa), fellowship programs (such as Stegner and the Wisconsin Institute for Creative Writing), and summer writing conferences (such as the Wesleyan Writers Conference, Sewanee, Bread Loaf, and the New York State Summer Writers Institute). A directory at the back of the anthology lists all of the U.S. and Canadian institutions that participated in this year's competition. After we receive the nominations we read them all at least once, grade them, and debate their merits. From a much larger group we pass on a few dozen finalists to our guest editor, who then makes the selections for the book.

Guest editor Mary Gaitskill has chosen fourteen stories for inclusion in *Best New American Voices 2009.* If the authors of these stories are not as familiar as those mentioned earlier, strong evidence suggests that will soon change. Of course the raison d'être of the anthology is that they *are* unknown. Here then is an opportunity for the reader to discover a promising group of writers perhaps at the same time they are first encountered by agents, editors, and publishers. Some of the contributors have previously published fiction in literary journals or magazines. Others make their publishing debuts here. They are, generally speaking, young or young*ish,* though age is not a criterion for eligibility. They seem to have little in common other than the fact that they were recently enrolled in a writing workshop. The stories must speak for themselves.

We thank Mary Gaitskill for her editorial suggestions, for her perspicacity and professionalism, and for her general support for the Best New American Voices series. We extend thanks, too, to all of the teachers, administrators, and workshop directors who nominated stories for this volume. Without their continuing support, this anthology would not be possible. We must thank and congratulate all of the contributors, whose book this really is. To name some others:

We thank Andrea Schulz at Harcourt for her ongoing support; our editor, Adrienne Brodeur; Lisa Lucas in the Harcourt contracts department; Kathi George for her careful copyediting; and our families and friends for their love and support.

—John Kulka and Natalie Danford

INTRODUCTION

Mary Gaitskill

The short story is a primitive art form; any written art form is primitive. Consider the dominant mode of modern storytelling: technically complex methods of film amped up with sophisticated editing, special effects, and music, then compare this to black-and-white words on a page. By filming on a city street, a director gets the whole world as a backdrop free of monetary or artistic charge. With the voices, body language, and facial expressiveness of great or even good actors, overlaid by music and underlaid by the subtle use of scenery and how it is shot, a talented director can viscerally accomplish in a flash what an author must labor for an entire page or even pages to produce, using a method that, while purely symbolic, must mimic the visceral so closely that it almost achieves its same effects in the mind of the reader.

This is the limitation of the form: Writing is about words, but life is not about words. This is the transcendent potential of the form: Great writing uses words in such a way that they evoke images, feelings, associations, and ideas that come together, line by black-and-white line, to create complex pictures that represent not just life, but something truer than what we think of as "life" on a day-to-day basis. The limits of the short story are even more stringent; a short story is, well, shorter. The great potential of a short story is linked with its limits; it may create a small moment that acts as a secret door to a great house that turns out to be not a house at all, but the illusion of an understandable structure in a vast sea of forces that we live with every day without seeing.

One of my favorite short stories is by Vladimir Nabokov. It is called "Signs and Symbols" and it is six pages long. It is about an old married couple who are going to visit their son in an institution for the mentally ill. He is ill with "Referential Mania," a condition that causes him to see outrageous metaphorical meanings in all physical phenomena, each of which concerns him in the most malevolent possible way. On arriving at the institution, the old couple are told that they can't see their son because he has just tried to kill himself; that evening they are tormented by wrong-number phone calls. The story ends with a call that may or may not be from the hospital saying that the son is dead. On the face of it, it's an almost pointlessly cruel little piece of work. But the cruel story line, if it can even be called that, is only the surface of it. The story is about the hidden and complexly coded nature of things, which is sometimes comic, sometimes vicious, and always unknowable. Even more, it is about what gets expressed as the thoughts of the boy's mother as she sits on the stairs of their miserable tenement waiting for her husband to come back with their dinner:

> This and much more, she accepted—for after all living did mean accepting the loss of one joy after another, not even joys in her case—mere possibilities of improvement. She thought of the endless waves of pain that for some reason or other she and her husband had to endure; of the invisible giants hurting her boy in some unimaginable fashion; of the incalculable

amount of tenderness in the world; of the fate of this tenderness, which is either crushed, or wasted, or transformed into madness; of neglected children humming to themselves in unswept corners; of beautiful weeds that cannot hide from the farmer and helplessly have to watch the shadow of his simian stoop leave mangled flowers in its wake, as the monstrous darkness approaches.

This "story" is a narrow door, a trapdoor, through which one falls into the sorrow of the world, against which even the cleverest of human minds is completely inadequate. It is a cruel story because it is about reality. It is a transcendent story because it is about compassion so big it goes beyond compassion to an unnameable something redemptive beyond hope. How do you go, in a few lines, from an old woman sitting on tenement stairs to all the sorrow of the world—only in the inmost realm of the mind, a place that connects down the spine to the deepest forces of destruction and creation.

This is an exceptional story, a great story. But it is not the only one that may be described as a small entry to a great conundrum or experience. Think of Saul Bellow, Alice Munro, Gogol, Haruki Murakami, Chekhov, Katherine Anne Porter—Porter, who wrote in "Pale Horse, Pale Rider" of the death of an unknown man tended to by hospital orderlies:

It had been an entrancing and leisurely spectacle, but now it was over. A pallid white fog rose in their wake insinuatingly and floated before Miranda's eyes, a fog in which was concealed all terror and all weariness, all the wrung faces and twisted backs and broken feet of abused, outraged living things, all the shapes of their confused pain and their estranged hearts . . . the fog parted and two executioners, white clad, moved towards her pushing between them with marvelously deft and practiced hands the misshapen figure of an old man in filthy rags whose scanty beard waggled under his open mouth as he bowed his back and braced his feet to resist and delay the fate they had prepared for him. In a high weeping voice he was trying to explain to them that the crime of which he was accused did not merit the punishment he was about to receive; and except for his whining cry there was silence as they advanced.

What is remarkable here is the emergence of a single figure out of an implacable storm of suffering, a specific figure who has nothing to do with the story, who is not really even a character, but a random being who isn't actually headed for execution in the real world of the plot, but who, in some parallel world evoked by Porter for just an instant, has been chosen as Victim by some complex system the son in "Signs and Symbols" might understand perfectly. Film, both movies and television, may accomplish something like this, or try to. But it is precisely that medium's felicity to the seen world that so often make its attempts to portray the unseen world buffoonish.

In *Best New American Voices 2008*, Richard Bausch prefaced his introduction of said new voices with an eloquent and elegant argument that, conventional wisdom to the contrary, the short story is not dead, and likely never will be. Given the great examples I have just quoted, and their perceived advantage over film, I might be expected to do the same. However, I am not as optimistic as Mr. Bausch. I would not say the short story is exactly dead, but it looks to me pallid and ill from neglect, volumes like this one to the contrary. Even its most ardent students seem disinterested in its greatest powers; students of mine, sometimes even those of whom I am especially fond, find "Signs" depressing and "Pale Horse" weird. They complain about the use of dreams—they've been told they aren't supposed to depict them—and they don't like not knowing what happens at the end. They sometimes seem to want stories to function as television shows. And these are the ardent ones, the lovers of stories, the ones who want to write them. The rest, most of them, I mean the population, just don't read them at all. Even if they read novels. They don't read stories at all.

So. When I went to speak at a high school in Portland, Oregon, last year, I quoted Shelley, who said that "poets are the unacknowledged legislators of the world"; I said while this may once have been true, it is now more accurate to say that writers are the unacknowledged beatific taxi drivers and janitors of the world. I went on to explain that sometimes when one is feeling hounded and beset on all sides, one might get into a cab and have the driver turn around and say something totally unexpected that changes the course of one's day. It doesn't have to be a taxi driver, it could be any strange person who turns to you and says that unexpected thing. It could be a janitor who works in the halls of the legislature; he could have one of those moments with an actual legislator on the way up in the elevator. And the unseen force of his words could have their secret effect.

It is a humble concept, perhaps a desperate one. I did not mean it negatively, but the students took it that way. At the end of my talk, one of them raised his hand. He had a bad stutter, so it took him a long time to get it out, but he was absolutely determined to do so. "I totally disagree," he said. "Writers are not just like taxi drivers or janitors. When you read a book it affects you in a way a movie can't. It can take you into the minds of people you wouldn't normally know. It changes how you think. And if enough people are changed it changes the world."

"Young man," I said, "I have never been so happy to be disagreed with in my life."

It is on this note that I would like to introduce the stories in this volume. I don't know if the writers are taxi drivers, janitors, or legislators, but their stories spoke to me in unexpected ways. They affected me in ways a movie can't. Suzanne Rivecca ("Look Ma, I'm Breathing") writes about a young woman writer stalked by an older man who, with his inappropriate, creepy, crazy attentions, sees her—with "peerless and unforgivable" clarity—better than anyone else ever will; Larry N. Mayer ("Love for Miss Dottie"), about a beatific cleaning lady named Ruby who in some special pocket of the true universe has every right to believe she will receive an inheritance from the great and ridiculous Dorothy Parker, but who is instead led off in handcuffs on the evening news, one eye rolling "like some crazy Roman candle"; Nam Le ("Love and Honor and Pity and Pride and Compassion and Sacrifice"), about the layers of mystery between one set of perceptions and another, in this case coded first as "cultural differences," then "generational differences," and the absurd smugness that thinks such mystery can be quickly understood; Mehdi Tavana Okasi ("Salvation Army"), about how a boy is taken from a soccer field and transported to war and death while, thousands of miles away, the teacher whose fatal error sent him there hopelessly tries to make amends through her own sons, who will never know of the connection.

Like the best of the genre, these stories take you through a small door to a place that is huge, idiotic, tragic, crass, numinous, and mysterious all at once. Several of the stories drop outsiders into foreign locales, like the rock climbers of "The *Fantôme* of Fatma" and the grateful parents of "Mules," who hope to make an offering of prescription drugs in an African country. The teenage girl in "Wintering," sent away to her grandfather in the Russian countryside while her mother serves out a jail sentence, becomes a foreigner in her own country. Other characters discover they simply can't go home again. The surviving brother in "Weather Enough" finds he has become one of the Chicago "flatlanders" his father derides, the returning soldier in "Welcome Home" is deflated because he was never able to fire his weapon in Iraq, and the carnival worker in "The Still Point" is made homeless by his own restlessness. The teenaged son of divorced parents in "Statehood" and the victim of the Khmer Rouge who narrates "The Monkey King" are nothing alike, but each is testing his limits and trying to eke out a safe spot for himself. As is the protagonist of "Yellowstone," who, while waiting for an earthquake to subside so that he can bury his lover, makes the acquaintance of a neglected little girl, or the musicians of "Little Stones, Little Pistols, Little Clash," who stumble on a magical word that makes them superstars of a nightmare variety.

Like the best of the genre, all of these stories use their primitive black-and-white symbols to conjure the low, fleeting voices of angels and demons expressed in human words. Will they last? Will the short story last? I've no idea. Very little lasts long, and perhaps nothing human will last forever. Art doesn't have to last to touch the people who see it, who read it or hear it before getting out of the taxi and heading on their way.

BEST NEW AMERICAN VOICES 2009

BAIRD HARPER

The School of the Art Institute of Chicago

YELLOWSTONE

Hurst struggled to keep up with the van transporting Emily's casket. He rarely drove at night anymore, and the way the oncoming headlights painted his hands the color of bone made him feel frail and hesitant, too old to attend the simple ceremonies of a death. At the American border, her body passed through easily—an unfolding of papers and a wave of the guard's long metal flashlight—and Hurst could only watch as the van sped off into the darkness while an officer searched his Buick. The border guard rifled through the trunk, clicking his tongue. "I'm awful sorry about your girlfriend, mister."

"We were more like longtime bridge partners," Hurst said, leaning over the young man's shoulder to see what he was finding in the trunk. "But we lived together, too."

The border officer's smile extinguished as he clicked off his flashlight. "All right, mister, you can go through now."

The sun lifted, turning white hot as it rose over the high plains. Hours of scorched Montana hissed by. South of Billings, Hurst's car skidded off the highway and plunged into the shore of burnt grass along the roadside. He turned off the engine, slapped his cheeks, took one of Emily's half-smoked cigarettes out of the ashtray, and put it to his lips. It was sour, and he could not taste the lipstick she'd kissed onto the filter.

In nine years living together Hurst had barely heard Emily speak of Wyoming, but as he pulled into her childhood home—a place east of Yellowstone called Carson—the loneliness of the little dirt-patch town made his heart slow. She'd admitted once it had been a decent place to grow up, before the new highway brought in the drug addicts and prostitutes, but she'd been clear about not wanting to go back until it was time to return for good.

The motel was a seedy row of closed doors. Each had a concrete stoop with a tin bucket of sand and spent cigarettes. The front office was empty. A shoe box with a hole cut in the top and CHECKS markered onto the side sat on the counter. Beside it, an envelope labeled *Mr. Hurst* held his room key. The windows to number seven were open and the rotten bleach odor of the motel hot tub had attached itself to everything inside. The trash cans told of protected sex and chocolate bingeing, a bedside table was strewn with a dozen brochures for Yellowstone Park. COME SEE THE ERUPTING GEYSERS!

He walked around the corner to a diner called Runny's Grill. There were no other customers except for a plump little girl, no older than ten, sitting alone in a large semicircle booth, rolling an empty milk-shake glass between her palms. Hurst winked at her in the friendly manner that he figured old men were supposed to use when winking at children. The girl's eyes narrowed and she raised her middle finger at him. He ordered a BLT, to go.

When he got back to his room, rock music ached through the wall. He spread his dinner on the table and did his best to enjoy it, until he realized that what he'd thought to be the music's bass beat was actually number eight's headboard thumping against the other side of his wall. The radio went to commercial and the yaklike sounds of a man's determined grunting could be heard more clearly. Occasionally, a female voice offered guidance ("Slower, Victor! Slower!"). Though the couple's cadence spread itself thinly, it continued so long that the constraints of endurance seemed no longer to apply. Finally it wound down—an uncoiling rhythm, a decelerating engine.

Later, the headboard struck its final thump, the radio quit, and a door slammed the place quiet. Hurst had brought some of Emily's things. He took them out: her favorite silver earrings, her old yellow robe. He set these things on a chair and watched them turn gray as the fading hour licked away the last rims of daylight.

Sleep led him into dreams of hellish sulfur pools, of falling in and sucking boiling liquid into his chest. He gasped awake and rolled over to see the clock radio surge 2:41 before blinking out. The streetlamp outside fluttered, then died. A rattling din like the hooves of an approaching herd rose up and set the whole room trembling. Coffee mugs clattered against the tile counter in the bathroom. Something fell off the wall and shattered behind the television. Hurst's suitcase slumped over in the dead light of the corner. As the shaking subsided, the concrete parking lot cracked and moaned like a frozen lake shouldering against its banks.

In the morning, Hurst parked a half-block short of the cemetery entrance on account of a two-foot-high buckle in the asphalt. A front-yard water main sprayed a rooster tail onto the sidewalk as a whole family looked on from their porch while eating breakfast.

At the front gate of the cemetery hung a cardboard sign reading, CEMETERY CLOSED—EARTHQUAKE, but the gate itself was not locked. Beyond the circular drive, a green backhoe lay on its side, leaking oil into a bed of morning glories. From the base of a tree, a crevice had opened in the earth and snaked up over a hill toward the burial grounds. It was as wide as a sidewalk and deep enough for a grown man to disappear into. Hurst walked along the crevice until he reached the crest of the hill and the cemetery grounds spread out below him. The fissure carried on for another few hundred yards, yawning open in places as wide as a car lane. Scores of gravestones lay on their faces. A ways off, a short-haired woman in dark slacks and suspenders gave orders to a man in overalls. Nearer, two workmen stood looking into the crack in the earth.

Hurst passed a row of gravestones that bowed forward reverently. Then he saw them—dozens of coffins peeking up from inside the fissure, rusted metal domes and rotting wood boxes. A few had been thrust upward, almost breaching the surface. One had splintered open and was perhaps showing its contents to a different vantage point. The earth, he thought, was giving them back.

"Sir!" shouted a man's voice. The woman with suspenders was a man, a petite fellow with sloped shoulders and a thin cap of black hair gelled against his skull. He hustled closer on little legs. "Please, sir. The cemetery is closed."

"My friend is supposed to be buried this morning."

"I'm sorry." Beads of sweat shimmered on the man's temples. "As you can see, sir, we have a bit of an emergency."

"But I drove all the way down from Calgary."

"Please." The man took Hurst by the elbow. "You'll have to wait until tomorrow."

Hurst let himself be walked to the entrance, where the petite man locked the gate behind him. "Does this happen often?" asked Hurst, but the man was already scrambling away.

Again, the shoe box manned the counter of the motel office. Thinking he'd wait for the manager to return, Hurst took his time writing a check to pay for a second night's stay. He thought how Emily's name should be removed from the checks. They'd combined bank accounts to simplify their lives, moved in together for the same reason, but now it seemed insulting to have her name on things. It wasn't right for her to be paying bills, for her name to be jammed into a shoe box at some awful motel. It was important to get her into the ground and off their checks sooner rather than later. He folded the check into his pocket and went back to the room to read the Yellowstone brochures. The pictures of the park were supposed to be beautiful, but he found them hectic, ominous even. So much volcanic disorder. The whole place seemed a cancerous pock on the earth's surface.

Through the window, a little girl approached with a wooden crate in her arms. She was a rotund creature with straight yellow hair and a green uniform full of unflattering angles and colorful badges. The uniform looked to have been made from a single piece of fabric fastened recklessly around her like a knee-length toga.

He swung open his door. "Yes?"

The girl stopped along his walkway. She leaned the crate forward to show him its contents, bright boxes of something edible.

"You're the little brat from the diner, aren't you?"

"I'm a Girl Scout," she replied.

"No, you're not. I've *seen* Girl Scouts. You're the girl who gave me the finger."

She idled patiently, chewing the cud of her cheek. "I'm really poor," she finally said. "We hardly have enough to eat. I couldn't afford a real uniform, so my mother made this one."

He looked her over. Her pudginess belied the claims of hunger. "Well, I'm sorry for that," he said. "Your mother's not much of a seamstress. In the army they taught me how to sew better than that."

She stepped closer. "Would you like to buy some cookies?"

He did not. But the girl's resolve intrigued him, unmoved as she was by his meanness. She advanced to the bottom of his stoop, placing a foot on the first step, the crate of cookies coming to rest on her thigh. As her knee rose, the coarse green fabric of the uniform lifted off her shoulders.

"This is a motel," he said. "Not a house."

She rattled the crate. "If you buy some, I'll get out of your face."

The offer was tempting. There was a loose bill in the pocket of his slacks, a tissue-soft ten he'd found in the dryer some days before. He'd been learning to do his own laundry for the first time in his life, and the appearance of coins and wadded Kleenexes came as a regular reminder of his ineptitude. But the ten-dollar bill—fatigued and clinging to a blouse of hers—had foretold something worse than simple incompetence, something cheerless and permanent, a new life on his own beset with these kinds of small disheartening moments.

The girl huffed, suddenly impatient, and wiped her nose on the sash hanging diagonally across her torso. What were supposed to be merit badges on the sash were actually political buttons and a dull antique brooch probably stolen off her mother's dresser. And up close he saw her uniform was not sewn at all, but clipped together with dozens of safety pins along one side of her body. Between the sutures, little lobes of pink skin peeked out.

"This is ridiculous," he said, wincing at the visage of Ronald Reagan. "Let me fix that sheet you're wearing."

He stepped down off the stoop and she followed him to the Buick parked on the curb.

"Where are we going?" she asked.

He leaned into the passenger seat and drew a small olive green box from the glove compartment. "We aren't going anywhere." He shut the door and led her into his room. The girl parked herself on a chair beside the bed. He set the green box on the comforter and handed her Emily's yellow bathrobe. "Now take that thing off." He pointed toward the bathroom, but already she was pulling the uniform over her head. He spun away and made for the front window, dragging the drapes almost shut, catching her reflection off the glass. With the uniform tangling her arms, she looked as plump and fleshy as a seal.

"Your robe smells funny." Her fists jammed around inside the deep plush pockets. One hand emerged with a key on a length of blue thread. She gave a repellent frown and tugged at it, finding the other end of the thread fastened securely to the inside of the pocket.

"My friend," he said, feeling a smile move across his face, "she used to lock herself out of the house when she went out to get the morning paper."

The girl sniffed the key. "You're weird." She gave it one last tug and dropped it back into the robe pocket.

"Why don't you open one of your boxes and have a cookie," he said, "on me." He put on eyeglasses and pulled a needle and spool of thread from the olive green box.

"Can't," she said. "My mom says I'm too fat."

He looked up over the top of his glasses and nodded. "My doctor says I'm too thin. And now I don't eat anything because Emily was the cook, and she's recently died."

The girl pulled an orange box out of the crate and laid it on the bed. "These have the most fat," she said, petting the top of the box. "They're my favorite."

He pulled the ten-dollar bill out of his pocket and set it on the bed out of her reach. "I'll need you to make change," he said, pushing the needle into the cloth. His hands began to remember how much he enjoyed sewing. The arthritis had ended his model car building years ago and kept him from fishing on account of the knots, but the new medicine he'd begun taking had pumped some life back into his hands. It was a small measure of good that came out of Emily's plunge into infirmity. He'd begun to see his own doctor again, and, as Emily slid into the throes of disease, he'd found himself improving.

"Why's your wife dead?" the girl asked.

"We weren't married," said Hurst. "She was more like..." He thought how the girl might best understand. "Like a girlfriend."

"But she's dead," said the girl. "Why?"

"Because she smoked. You don't smoke, do you?"

"I'm only ten. But my mom smokes cigars."

"You mean she smokes ciga*rettes*."

The girl itched her chapped lips.

"Well, if she smokes," he said, "then she's going to die, too."

The girl absorbed his remark without argument. She began to hum and swing her legs, and Hurst found a rhythm in the idle commotion as he moved the needle through the fabric.

He explained to her that during the war he'd been known for his talent with a sewing kit. Every company needed men skilled at such things: giving a good haircut with surgical scissors, cooking a Thanksgiving dinner out of K rations and snared pigeons. Hurst's company had called him "Seamster." It became his call sign, gave his hands some worth outside of pulling a trigger. He kept his company looking dapper as they charged across Normandy. French women, Hurst explained to the little girl, were terribly interested in their handsome American liberators.

A knock came at the door. His hands stalled above the folds of green cloth. The girl's humming petered out and her legs froze. As Hurst moved to the door, he heard her get up and make for the bathroom. He opened the door to a woman on his stoop wearing a leather skirt and a neon orange tube top, her makeup too heavy for the daytime. The overdarkened eyes and lips made her face look as though holes had been shot through it.

"This is a motel, not a house," he said.

The woman scratched her armpit. "I'm looking for my daughter, Monica."

"Is that her name? Monica?" Hurst waited to see if the girl would respond. "She came to my door selling cookies a while ago." Watching the cavernous, bruised eyes, he worried that a woman such as this could actually be someone's mother. "I bought some of the orange ones."

The woman was already clopping down his steps, waving a *thank you* over her shoulder. She stopped at the curb, dug through her purse, then unrolled a narrow dark cigar the size of a pinkie finger from a leaf of tinfoil. She lit it, mouthing a series of quick puffs, and then stood in the cloud it formed around her.

"Are you waiting for something?" he asked.

The woman held a hand above her eyes, scanning down the street, ignoring him.

He turned back inside to discover the cookies and the ten-dollar bill gone from the bed. There was no answer when he knocked at the bathroom door. The window was open, a footprint stamped onto the top of the toilet tank.

———

Hurst trolled the neighborhood in his Buick. The postquake disorder played out in peculiar scenes through town: Men with hard hats buttressed a leaning telephone pole with two-by-fours; a woman ran *X*'s of duct tape across her windowpanes; children rode bikes through water main cesspools. The girl's uniform lay bunched on the passenger seat—currency toward a trade-back. Nearly a decade of Emily was in that robe—countless Sunday mornings with coffee cake and the newspaper, her long freckled legs crossed over the leather ottoman.

Something yellow moved into a backyard. He left the car running in the street, got out, shuffled along the side of a house. The backyard was full of bikes and deflated basketballs. Unmowed grass poked through an overturned trampoline.

"I'm leaving!" he shouted. "I'm leaving town, so I need that robe back."

Little heads appeared from behind a row of bushes: two heads, then a third, then a fourth, popping up like mushrooms, the same dirty bowl haircut on each one. They were hovering over something on the ground that he couldn't see. As he moved toward them, they went frantic, grabbing things up into their arms, then scattering just as he descended upon their position. The clear plastic rib cage from a cookie box lay empty at his feet. "Those are *my* goddamn cookies." He pivoted, locating each child, their jittery creature-eyes watching him from points around the yard, their dirty little hands clutching the other boxes. "Which way did she go?" he demanded.

The smallest one, who crouched behind a punching bag, pointed into the next yard.

When Hurst pulled up to the motel, the girl's mother had her hands cupped against the front window of his room. She rose up onto her tiptoes, the backs of her legs bulbous and dusty like potatoes fresh from the ground. There were parts of her, underneath the soot and makeup, which seemed to belong to a more sincere woman, but the outer layers of clinging smoke and tight clothing made her look desperate for vulgar attention.

Hurst swept the little green uniform onto the floor mat. "I told you," he said, getting out and approaching the woman directly, "she's not in there."

"It's not that." She lifted her purse off his doorknob, rifled through it for another of her miniature cigars. "The earthquake," she said, thumbing her lighter. "My toilet bowl is cracked and they turned off my water." She motioned to the room next to his. "Can I use your bathroom?"

"*You're* staying in number eight?"

She lit a flame and puffed, her nodding chin chopping the bulbs of smoke. The cigar smelled sweet and earthy.

"Do those earthquakes happen often?" Hurst unlocked his door and held it open for her.

Slow gray ribbons snaked from her mouth and wrapped around her shoulders. "We're not from around here." She stepped inside, carrying with her the shawl of smoke.

He stared at one of the Yellowstone brochures, listened to the sound of her skirt dropping onto the bathroom tile, the flush of the toilet. "A working toilet," she called out. "You must have to pay extra to get one of these. Only the rich, I guess."

"What? Oh, yes, the bathroom isn't very nice. I wasn't expecting a guest." He could hear her tearing the wrapper off a new bar of soap, the faucet running.

"At least yours works," she said.

"What?"

When she came out, Hurst stood for her, pulling open one of the huge glossy Yellowstone brochures. *The bubbling volcanic mud!*

"Are you okay, buddy?" She stood by the bathroom door putting her hair into a ponytail. Her makeup had washed away and the dark holes in her face were filled in with tired human flesh. "You look kind of shitty."

"I'm not comfortable with this," he said.

"With what?"

"With having you here in my room like this."

"I'm not 'in your room.' I just needed to use your bathroom." She looked at his black suit hanging in the closet. "Jeez, you're so up-tight." She moved to the bed stand, fingered Emily's silver earrings.

"I'm really not comfortable having you here."

She flicked one of the earrings, and it settled beneath the clock radio. "I just needed to use the toilet, asshole." She thumbed her purse onto her shoulder and made for the door.

"I don't mean to offend you." Hurst wanted to explain about Emily, about the cemetery and the robe. "My friend just passed on," he finally said. "I suppose it's got to do with that."

"How sad," said the woman, angling toward the door.

Hurst suddenly wanted to keep her there in his room. As she brushed past him, he was seized with the desire to grab her bare shoulders with his fingernails and squeeze some of the pain into her. He wondered if you could pay a woman for just that.

The sullen wet smell of the cigar lingered after she'd gone. The late afternoon set the windows ablaze and the fearful shadows of magpies swooping across the curtains sank a slow, looming feeling into his chest. Hurst went walking for some air, taking his check down to the front office. A man with long sideburns sat behind the counter reading a Jacuzzi repair manual.

"A second night, please," said Hurst, laying his check on the counter. "But do you have another room available?"

"Is it a real problem?" asked the man. He wore a denim shirt with VICTOR sewn into the lapel. The stitching to the *r* was coming undone, and the man's name would soon be VICTO.

"It's the people in number eight," said Hurst. "A woman and her daughter."

"Oh, sure, *them,*" said the man. "Don't give them anything. They're trouble for everyone, especially me. I won't even tell you how hard it is to get that woman to pay up."

"So you'll get me a new room then?"

The man held the check up to the light, swiveling on his stool. "How come you crossed out the other name?" He touched sets of keys hanging from hooks on a board.

"I guess I shouldn't have." Against the light, Hurst could see too clearly the heavy black pen strike through Emily's name.

"Oh, wait," the man said, remembering. "Plumbing's turned off in that room, too." He hung a key back onto its hook. "Sorry, mister. No can do."

Hurst retrieved Monica's uniform from the car and took it back to his room. Needing the distraction, he finished sewing it, taking extra care to double-stitch where the child's girth threatened to add pressure. The controlled stabbing motion of needle into cloth cast a trancelike calm over him, and he began to believe that he'd actually get to leave this place eventually.

Outside, footsteps scraped the concrete and the doorknob jiggled against the lock. He stashed the uniform under a pillow before opening up. Monica, shivering beneath the soaked yellow robe, stood shouldering the weight of her mother's hands.

"She needs to use your shower," said the woman. "Or she'll catch hypothermia."

Tar and soil clung in streaks to the terry cloth. The girl moved past him without making eye contact and disappeared into his bathroom.

Her mother guarded the door. "She won't say where her clothes went."

"I'm sorry about before," said Hurst. "I don't know how to talk to people lately."

She swung her purse forward until it settled like a codpiece over the front of her skirt. "I need a hundred and forty dollars. That asshole's trying to kick us out onto the street."

"Which asshole?"

"Victor," she said. "He's worthless. Trust me. We've been here a month and the hot tub has been broken the whole time."

The television returned from a commercial. It was a show about a man who drank snake venom to build up an immunity. It showed the man drawing cobra's venom into a glass beaker, putting the beaker into a special refrigerator, and, later, diluting it and drinking some.

"I bet he's not really even drinking the stuff," said Monica's mother.

The water in the bathroom shut off; wet feet padded on the tile floor. Monica came out with one of Hurst's towels wrapped around her, corkscrewing a tissue up her nose. At the door, her mother put her hands on Monica's shoulders, her nails like talons clenching the little girl's pink skin. "What do you say to the nice man?"

"Did he give us any money?" asked Monica.

"No. He didn't." The mother's fingers squeezed little white marks into the girl's skin. "He isn't going to give us anything."

They left him there with the TV on. The man teased a rattlesnake with a bamboo cane. He said he believed drinking snake venom would allow him to live to be a hundred years old.

In the bathroom, Emily's sodden robe bled gray into the tile crevices. Hurst filled the tub with warm, soapy water, dropped the robe in, and stirred it with his foot. But then, getting down onto his knees, he scrubbed the stains with a coarse hand towel, wearing down a new bar of soap against the ruined fabric, twisting the dirty water out of the terry cloth, and hanging it on the back of the door. It was better, he thought, but still ruined. When this was done, Hurst called the cemetery and left a message on the caretaker's machine warning that he'd be coming by at ten in the morning expecting a burial.

When he hung up, the phone rang.

A woman's voice could be heard at a tinny distance from the receiver. *"Do it!"* the woman's voice hissed. *"Say it!"* A man's gravelly twang rasped loudly onto the line. "The lady here wants me to tell you 'this is what a hunderd 'n forty dollars gits you,'" and then they hung up. A woman's laughter peeled off from the other side of the wall, and the radio came on at a volume that made the wallpaper seem to detach and levitate from the plaster.

Hurst jammed the uniform into his fist and burst out onto the stoop. He paced around the corner, sucking the parched night air into his lungs. The girl sat in the front window of Runny's, stabbing a glass of Coke with a straw. He stood there, waiting for her to notice him on the sidewalk. His heart was racing now, so fast he mistrusted it. He stood, angling forward, arms straight and blunt as pipes, fists shaking. When she finally saw him, he unfolded her uniform like a banner between his hands, and then he threw it down onto the sidewalk and kicked it into the garden of pumice rocks and dead bush roots below the window.

He stalked away for what felt like miles in only minutes, until he came to a bar with no windows, where he ate a fried steak and drank scotch from a juice glass until he could barely imagine making it home.

———

In the morning, Hurst woke with the feeling of a damaged nerve running through his entire body. He showered quickly and put on his suit, which felt clammy and stretched as clothes do when they've already been worn. He packed his things, put the damp robe into a plastic grocery bag, and dragged his suitcase outside.

From the backseat of his car, Monica's eyes watched him approach. "Where are we going?" she asked, rolling down her window. She was wearing her uniform.

Hurst stepped closer, admiring the job he'd done with the stitching. She looked clean and determined, ready to support some important cause, like a soldier. "You don't look quite so ridiculous anymore," he said.

"Where are we going?"

Monica's eyes floated in the rearview as they wove through town. The same CLOSED sign still hung from the cemetery entrance. Hurst pushed the gate, which seemed loose at first, but then would not open.

"I can squeeze through," she said, and as she tried to press herself through a gap in the wrought iron bars, the petite man appeared. He wore a dirty blue jumpsuit that was too large for him. "Mr. Hurst, we're ready for you," he said, putting a key to the lock. "Take the road to the left until you see the casket." He bowed and fed a warm smile to the girl. "It'll be the only clean one."

They rode the winding gravel path through the cemetery grounds. Workmen with backhoes toiled at the far end, filling in the long gaping fissure. Strips of new sod lay like stitching over the earth's wounds. Three mud-covered coffins sat in a row beside the edge, waiting patiently to go back into the ground, and there were rectangular dirt outlines where others had been. Monica breathed against the glass in the backseat, whispering words of amazement. They paused at a spot where a small crane lowered a dirt-crusted coffin into the crevice. A man poked the coffin with a shovel, chanting, "slow-er...slow-er..." When the crane cable went slack the man turned to them and shouted, "You aren't supposed to be here."

Monica pressed her swear finger to the window, leaving the imprint in the fogged glass.

They came to the place where Emily's casket lay, saddled with a bouquet of lilies, above a newly dug grave collared by AstroTurf rugs. The sun, which had been burning through a high haze all morning, now blazed upon them and seemed to be sucking the mist of the sprinklers straight up into the sky. There were prayers from his childhood he tried to remember, but eventually he decided that it didn't matter. He looked around at the graves of Emily's family. Some of them were people he'd met—her older brother, Wayne, her cousin, Marva—and some of them he'd never heard of.

"That one died when it was my age," said Monica, pointing to a stone that read OUR DEAR PATTY 1929–1939. There was a cracking sound from far away and the man with the shovel screamed, "No, no, back up!"

"There's supposed to be people here to lower the casket while we watch," said Hurst. "I paid for them to do that." They stood and waited, watching the sun suck the moisture off the fields of dead. After more time had passed, he said, "I don't suppose anyone's coming to do it."

"Maybe," said Monica, "if we walk backward really slowly, it'll be the same."

It was an odd idea, but without thinking Hurst began inching backward toward the Buick. This is absurd, he told himself, but as he watched the casket shrinking away, he felt as if he were moving for the first time in months, as though the gears of the world had started again. Their heels crunched backward through the grass and he felt himself floating away from her. Monica brought her hand to her brow, saluting the dead, humming a dim version of "taps." He cuffed her gently on the side of the head. She kept humming. They drifted back.

They drove west. Sudden pioneers, exploring how far away an hour on the gas pedal could get them. The baked landscape of Wyoming turned greener as stands of pine forest populated the hills more and more fully, until the arid tumbleweed plain had been left behind and a robust forest walled them in on both sides. The highway relented to a local road channeling them into the east entrance of Yellowstone. As Hurst handed money to the ranger, Monica announced, "He's stealing me!"

The ranger looked bored. "Exercise caution everywhere," he said in a monotone. "And don't harass the wildlife."

They drove on, into the center of the park. Green pools steamed into the atmosphere, reeking clouds of sulfur rose like the menacing flags of untended fires. The seams of the earth gaped open. Hurst could feel his heartbeat slowing before the volatile grandeur of things. They pulled over to where a single buffalo grazed in a field of tall grass. The animal walked in circles, bristling its hide at some unseen distraction.

A man in a khaki outfit snapped photos by the dozen from a tripod set up along the shoulder. "You rarely get to see them like this," the photographer said in an Australian accent.

Monica smoothed her uniform against her hips and stepped off the shoulder into the field.

The photographer stopped taking pictures. "Stay back," he warned her. "It's something to be feared."

The buffalo swung its head through the grass, one of its horns hung with a purple beaded necklace. The animal blinked and snorted at the string of beads bumping against the side of its face.

"Stay back," repeated the Australian. "When they're alone like that, it means they've lost control of themselves."

They watched her step up onto a flat rock a few yards short of the buffalo. The girl didn't look at all afraid as she stood hovering above the grasses, watching, waiting to be noticed. When it finally saw her, it raised its massive head and squared itself to her, grazing a few steps closer.

Hurst could feel the photographer's eyes urging him. "Come back, Monica," he called in a weak, choked voice. What would it be like to drive back to Carson and tell the mother that the girl had been gored to death? What an awful thing to have to say, to have to be told. There were sad connections in the possibilities for that moment, and no relief in any of it.

"Come back here." His voice was clear now, insistent. "Come back here *right now*."

She stepped to the rock's edge, lifting her back leg for balance, leaning into the space separating her from the buffalo. "You look ridiculous," she said, and lifted the string of beads off its horn.

WILL BOAST

University of Virginia

WEATHER ENOUGH

His younger brother died young. Late on a February evening, on a county road heading for Chicago, John and his best friend, Mason, plowed into the broadside of an eighteen-wheel truck at eighty miles an hour. The boys had been speeding toward a party in the north suburbs. Forty minutes outside of Lake Geneva, there were already five empty beer cans rolling around the floorboards of the BMW. Mason was driving, and John, when Tim tried to picture his brother in the moments before the accident, would have been handling the music and rolling joints with the little machine he always kept on him.

Tim had been living in the city the last three years, but hadn't known John was coming down from Wisconsin that night. When Tim put down the phone, he sat staring at the carpet for a long time. It wasn't until he got out of the taxi at Union Station that his father's words took any form: the lungs crushed, the sternum and all John's ribs shattered. Killed on impact. Tim missed the last train on the Northwest line and sat all night in the dim, high-ceilinged station waiting for the first.

The Saturday following, Tim stood with his father in the lobby of the funeral home. The guests came in red-cheeked from the wind outside, and when they shook hands, their hands were cold. They kept filing in. Parents, well-wishers from the community. High school boys in their junior and senior years looking circumspect and uneasy in dressed-up clothes. Pretty girls, still tanned in the winter months, some of them old girlfriends of John's. The high school soccer coach—John had played a season and a half with him. Mrs. Stevens, who taught American history and had been Tim's favorite teacher. Bill Tompkins, the town president. The local orthodontist, his wife and children.

Tim reached out automatically to take the next hand—it was warm, oily—and then he recognized Hayden Kersch, Mason's older brother.

"Hey, Tim. Hey, buddy," Hayden said. "You holding up okay?"

It had been maybe five years since he'd last seen Hayden, around the time John first fell in with Mason and Mason's circle of friends. Hayden was tagging along, wearing his hair long like the younger boys, dressing in baggy khakis, polo shirts, a sun-bleached ball cap. He was two or three years older than Tim, which put him in his midtwenties. His hair was the same butter blond it had always been, but cut short on top and buzzed on the sides. He wore dark blue trousers and a blazer with golden, anchor-shaped buttons.

"We're okay," Tim said. "We're doing okay. I'm sorry about Mason, too."

The Kersch family had held a private service for Mason the day before.

"How you like it down in Chicago?" Hayden said.

Tim hesitated. "I might be coming back a while. Back to Lake Geneva."

Hayden smiled a big, uninhibited smile. "That'd be nice, buddy. That'd be real nice. Me and John were close, Tim. We were real close."

"I know," Tim said gently. In high school, he'd heard the rumors about Hayden—that he was slow, a little unstable, that he'd got into trouble after graduation for lurking around the girls' locker room. But Tim had ingested enough small-town gossip during his years in Lake Geneva to make him loathe rumors, especially cruel ones. For his part, Tim had always thought Hayden was just a stoner.

A frigid draft swung through the entryway; the line of people trying to get in was backing up and keeping the door open. "You like basketball, Tim?" Hayden said. "You ever watch the Bulls? I'll have you over some time."

Tim's father leaned over from where he'd been talking with another of John's teachers. He rested a hand on Tim's shoulder. "We'd better keep things moving," his father said.

"If you guys need anything," Hayden began, "I really want...I want to..." He didn't finish, or couldn't, and, still smiling, he went to take a seat in the next room, where, surrounded by flowers, photos, and mementos, the clean, smooth, brass-fitted casket sat like an altar.

Tim asked for leave from his job. Maybe a few weeks, he told them. He was going home to be some comfort and company for his father. It took half a day to pack the contents of his efficiency on the far north side. Most of the furniture he just put out on the curb.

The first week back in Lake Geneva, Tim spent his days restlessly thumbing through the *Popular Mechanics* and sci-fi novels stacked in boxes in his old room. He helped his father clean and did odd jobs around the house. It snowed heavily two days in a row, and they rose early to shovel the drive together. Tim felt better getting his blood moving, the heat of the labor building under his thick coat and sweater until he couldn't wait to get inside, strip off, get a cup of hot coffee, a hot shower. At night he sat up listening to his father's Neil Young and Procol Harum LPs on low volume. Sometimes the arm of the record player bumping back to its cradle woke him from dozing and he would startle, confused for a moment about where he was, missing the clamor of traffic on Kedzie Avenue.

After that first week, his father went back to work. He worked half of Tuesday and Wednesday, then all of Thursday and Friday. His father needed the distraction—Tim understood that well enough.

When he had the house to himself, Tim went upstairs to John's room. He couldn't bring himself to do more than sit there on the bed and let his gaze wander over the X-Men and Chicago Cubs posters, the page-sized photographs of Cindy Crawford that John had torn out of magazines and tacked to the walls. The room was a museum now. The clothes hanging in the closet already seemed like relics. Tim picked up a Little League trophy from the dresser—not more than a few pennies' worth of plastic and wood, yet he couldn't bear the thought of throwing it away.

When she was still alive, Tim's mother had had the little room downstairs, at the back of the house, for her knitting things and gardening books. She had died from cancer when both Tim and John were young. John had hardly remembered her at all, but Tim bore the image of her wasting away in the hospital bed, folding into herself, deflating, through several very quiet years in grade school. His father eventually converted the little back room into a home office, but even then Tim was reluctant to enter it. Now the house had two museum rooms.

At the end of the second week, Tim walked into town and read the newspaper in a corner of the public library. The next morning he had breakfast at a little place known for its Scandinavian-style pancakes. Lake Geneva was the sort of town that appeared in brochures—full-color brochures with photos of gleaming condominiums, sprawling lakefront mansions, the town square with its ice-cream parlors and crafts and antique shops trading in old Coca-Cola signs and decorative butter churns. The weekenders from Chicago tripled the town's population during summer, but come Labor Day most of the houses on Tim's street sat vacant. The previous owners of Tim's house—summer people—had nailed up a wooden plaque above the front door that read THE CABIN.

At night Tim set off on long walks; three miles to the lake and up and down the path along the shore till his cheeks tingled, then went numb, and he went on walking, eyes following only the progress of his feet, with the moon, on cloudless nights, shining above the ice like a polished shield.

When the phone calls started, Tim barely noticed. A dull, stunned mood had descended on the house. He concentrated on one thing at a time. His father had been misplacing things—his keys, wallet, gloves—and Tim searched until he found them, always in unlikely places: the drawer of the computer desk, on top of a basket of laundry, up in John's room. The phone rang around three or four in the afternoon. His father would answer on the first or second ring, then murmur a few brief replies and something that sounded like an apology before hanging up.

One evening, coming down the stairs, Tim heard his father say, "No, he's out. On a walk somewhere. I don't know where he goes." Halfway through dinner, his father pushed his plate away, fixed Tim with a hard, searching stare, and said, "Don't go getting mixed up with that Kersch boy. You got enough to think about without him adding to it."

For a moment, Tim saw Hayden's face before him. His memory briefly called up a picture of Mason, as well. On the social scale—

looks, charm, popularity—the two of them couldn't have been further apart. From what Tim knew their parents both came from money. They had split up, the father gone out to California to speculate on real estate, probably sending back checks every month. Neither boy had worried about a job; Hayden was probably too whacked-out to have ever looked for one. Talking about basketball at a funeral, Jesus. Tim took his plate to the sink and scraped it clean. "The guy's dealing with his own stuff," he said over the clatter of the garbage disposal.

Early the next afternoon, Hayden showed up on the doorstep.

"We could go down to the clubhouse. Go swimming, get some burgers. They got good burgers down there."

They'd been driving around for half an hour, down by the lake, out into the corn, soy, and mustard fields that hemmed in the town on all sides.

"Don't have any swim trunks," Tim said. "Guess I'm not hungry, either."

"That's cool," Hayden said. "No problem. Hey, Tim, what'd you like to do down there in Chicago?"

What had he done in the city? When Tim left Lake Geneva, it seemed he was proving himself better than the place—he was escaping, getting even somehow. But in Chicago he was just another face in the street, on the El, in the office, and the anonymous white classrooms that housed the handful of night school courses he'd managed to take.

"Museums," Tim said. "Concerts. Didn't get out much. Read a lot." Hayden turned to him and grinned a wide, mouth-open grin. There was something ragged about him, Tim thought, or rumpled, like he'd been left out to dry and never ironed. "Can we just go to your place?" Tim said. "Watch TV or something?"

Hayden had an apartment above a little gallery near the lake. Tim peered into a fogged-up window display filled with watercolors in elaborate frames—vistas across the lake, scenes of country living, a forest of maple trees. Hayden led them up through an adjacent door to a series of practically bare rooms. A corduroy couch and an armchair bulked against one wall in the first room; on the opposite stood a huge entertainment center, a large-screen TV, and several thousand dollars, easily, of stereo and video-game equipment. The middle room held nothing but a Ping-Pong table, and the kitchen was crowded with old cartons of Chinese takeout, soda cans, and pizza boxes.

Tim went back out to the living room, where Hayden was already sitting in front of a video game, something to do with martial-arts fighting. "Check it out, Tim," he said. "You can do all of the fatalities in this version." Tim sat watching him play. After a few minutes, he fell back into the couch. It smelled of dust and pepperoni pizza. He settled into the smell like a man sinking into dark, boggy water.

"You want to try, Tim?"

"I'll watch. I don't understand these things."

Hayden paused his game and turned around. "Everyone missed you around here," he said. "It's cool that you're back now."

"Sure," Tim said, not knowing how else to answer. "Sure."

Hayden went back to clicking away at his game, the sounds of two pretend people hitting and kicking each other on screen rumbling from large speakers flanking the TV. "I'm going down to the corner," Tim said. "Get some beer."

Outside it was already nearing dark; his father would be leaving work. Tim walked quickly up the street, hands jammed in his pockets. He bought a twelve-pack of Old Style at the liquor store at the end of the block. The man behind the counter tried to make conversation. "Sorry," Tim said, "I'm in a rush."

For an hour Tim drank beer on the couch. Hayden put on the satellite TV and they watched reruns of a cop show. Tim had finished six of the twelve beers. His father would have been home for two hours at least. "Listen," Tim said thickly, "I have to beat it. You can have the rest of this beer. I'm going to need a ride back."

Streams of their breath filled the car. It was a late-model Lexus, but the heater hardly worked. Hayden took the south-shore road, which ran straight alongside cornfields, then wound through low hills. Though the night was clear, the winter sky seemed close on top of them. Off to the right stood the darker mass of a large, flat-topped hill.

"Hey, Tim," Hayden said, "just let me show you this one thing. Just real quick."

Well, Tim thought, what was he rushing home for? The beer was finally warming him up. He had a long night ahead either way. "Okay. Real quick."

Hayden turned onto a B road, then another, and, closer to the flat hill, a farm track, gravel pocking against the undercarriage as they went. Halfway up the hill, sumac saplings and tall grass rising from the middle of the track brought them to a stop. They got out to walk, and as they did, Tim realized where they were. The high school kids came to camp here. John had talked about it all the time—bonfires, kegs of beer, weed, acid, making out with girls by firelight. The kids called the hill Spider. With the high-tension power lines angling over and down its sides like spindly legs, Tim could see why.

The snow was crusted with a thin layer of ice, and their boots left little craters as they climbed. By the time they reached the top, Tim's eyes were watering from the wind and the chaff off the dry grass. They came out into a large, square clearing—the onetime site for a little subdivision of luxury log cabins that had never gotten built. Lakeview, Oakview, something like that. Scrub and rose vine had taken it over again. From where they stood, they could make out the undulations of the Grand Geneva golf resort to the north.

"Look, Tim," Hayden said, pointing, "the Playboy Mansion!"

It was true. In its previous incarnation the resort had been the grounds of the Playboy Mansion. "Sure," Tim said. "Yeah, I know. I see it."

On the far side of the clearing, a stand of white birches swung their long, thin branches as if they were reaching out, feeling for something in the breeze. As Tim and Hayden crossed the clearing, something began to take shape—a curved triangle, more than ten feet high, standing in silhouette to the dark gray sky. It ran back into a blunt, dark mass maybe thirty or forty feet long. It took Tim a moment to realize that he was looking at a speedboat, the largest he'd seen out of water. It leaned on one side of its hull; part of the Fiberglas bottom had caved under the boat's weight.

"How the fuck did this get here?"

"Don't know," Hayden said happily. "Someone ditched it, I guess." Then with real reverence in his voice: "This is where we party, Tim. Once, everyone slept by the fire and John's shoes melted!"

The wind had quieted. Tim ran his hand along the smooth, cold hull. He could hardly picture John coming to this remote, deserted place. Well, but that was what kids did in small towns. In summer, they probably had a pretty good view from the hilltop—better than partying in a cornfield, though John had probably done that, too. Tim and John had been so close, right up until Tim left for Chicago. Tim's shyness had rubbed off on John. In middle school, the boys ate lunch together. On weekends, they walked into town just to look at comic books at the drugstore. They didn't talk to the lakefront kids, the kids who wore designer jeans and drove German cars to school.

But when Tim moved away, John seemed to come into his own. Suddenly, he was tall and slim and sure of himself. He was popular with girls. When Tim took the train home on weekends, John was always out, usually with Mason, who knew how to get his hands on drugs and beer. And somehow John had been able to get money out of their father for clothes, expensive shoes, trips to the Dells and the ski hill. John started smoking cigarettes; he and their father fought about that constantly—did John *want* to give himself cancer? Those weekends at home, eating dinner in silence, his father waiting up for John all night, grew fraught. Tim started staying away for months at a time.

A long, slow gust of wind swayed the grass. Tim hunched into his coat. His eyes had adjusted to the dark now, and he saw that the intact half of the hull was covered in graffiti. "Hey, buddy!" Hayden's voice rang out above him. "Hey, up here!" Hayden had gotten up into the cabin of the speedboat. He wedged himself into the driver's seat and began to spin the wheel one way and then the other.

Tim called up to him, "Got a lighter?"

Something thumped softly on the snow. A square, metal Zippo—he could feel the oily warmth of Hayden's hands still on it. By the light of its flame, he could just make out the graffiti. JESSIE N. GIVES HEAD. CLASS OF '93. DARE TO SAY NO. BITCH.

"I'm freezing," Tim said. "Let's go already."

They wove back down through the trees to the car. "Want to come over tomorrow and watch basketball?" Hayden said, driving away from Spider. "We could see a movie. There's a diner where they let you hang out if you just get coffee."

Tim didn't answer. When they turned onto his street, he told Hayden, "Don't pull in. My dad goes to bed early. I don't want the lights to wake him."

They sat on the side of the road with the engine idling.

"Well," Tim said, "take it easy then." But something, Hayden's silence maybe, held him in the car another moment. Tim looked down the road to where the corner of his iced-over porch and the icicles hanging from the gutter glowed faintly at the outer edge of the headlights. Suddenly, the thought that the night would end and he would have to go inside seemed unbearable.

Hayden spoke. The words were nearly lost under the rushing of the heater, but Tim heard. "Do you miss him?" Hayden said. "Remember how much John liked music?"

Anger flashed up inside him, a ridiculous, hot surge. He had to fight it down. "I'm not thinking about it," he said.

"Yeah," Hayden said softly. "I can't even think about it."

"I have to go."

"Want to watch the Bulls tomorrow?"

Tim looked again at his house. "Fine. Pick me up at five."

When he went inside, his father was sitting at the kitchen table staring at a half-eaten plate of pork chops and mashed potatoes. A napkin, neatly folded and perfectly white, lay beside the plate. His father seemed not to hear him come in. Tim stood there a moment considering him. He had always seen his father as a firm, unyielding man, but since the funeral he looked hollow, blasted out. He looked startled all the time, too, as if he were waking up every minute and still finding his younger son gone.

"I had to get out a while," Tim said. "Walked down and looked at those new condos they're putting up over on Button's Bay."

His father rose from the table, went to the counter, and folded the chop still sitting in the frying pan into a square of foil.

"I'm going up," Tim said. It wasn't yet nine o'clock. "Do a little reading."

"Sleep good," his father tried to say, but his voice caught.

He'd never watched so much basketball in his life. There were two games a night at least. When the Bulls came on, Hayden sat wringing his hands, calling out to the players on the screen—"Come on,

Cartwright, get that board. Get it, man! Come on! Offense, now. Offense. Let's go, Scottie. Let's go!

"You ever go and see them, buddy? When you were living down there?"

Tim hadn't.

"My dad and I went once. Saw Jordan play. Awesome. In the summer I'm going out to California. My dad says we'll all go see the Lakers sometime."

Tim opened another beer and rolled the cool bottle across his forehead. "Awesome," he said.

Mid-March, the last of the cards reading *condolences* and *our sympathies* arrived. Tim's father put them with the rest in a large Tupperware container and stowed it on a high shelf in the coat closet. The weather got warm, a brief thaw, and then it was brittle cold again— the streets and sidewalks etched with the quick-frozen crosshatch of tire treads and boot prints. Tim started growing a beard. Fewer people seemed to recognize him in the grocery line and at the gas station. A week later he had his hair cut short.

Tim and Hayden went to a movie. "Anything," Tim said. "I don't care. I'm up for anything." It was Monday night; there weren't more than a handful of people in the theater. The movie was loud and poorly acted, and the jokes it made about its Chinese villains were borderline offensive. Afterward, standing outside the theater, Hayden breathlessly recounted the most exciting scenes.

"So how could they have jumped off that building and survived?" Tim said, unable to resist a little mockery. "You think someone can strap on a parachute midfall? How tall could that building have been anyway?"

Hayden laughed. "You can do it," he protested. "I saw these guys on Discovery Channel. It was like they were *flying*."

"And where the hell did they get the parachutes? They were already wearing them under their clothes?"

"You don't know what kind of things they got. They got all *kinds* of stuff we never know about. The Stealth Fighter, Tim. Remember about the Stealth Fighter?"

"Shit," Tim said, "that didn't defy the laws of physics." He laughed out loud, for maybe the first time in weeks. For a moment, thinking about the movie, he was lost in its world, the same hyper-real place he'd imagined on the afternoons he and John spent reading comic books at the drugstore. He looked at Hayden, who was hopping up and down and rubbing his hands together to keep warm. "Shit," Tim said, and laughed again, "you don't understand a thing, do you?"

They went to the movies the next three nights.

Tim started waking late and staying out as long as he could. In the mornings, when his father called up to say good-bye, he lay sweating and turning under the heavy quilt. In sleep, he heard John's voice. He could see his face. John said something. It had the lightness of a joke. The two of them were just sitting around telling jokes as if nothing had happened, laughing, gentle, contented laughs. His dreams didn't feel like dreams. He seemed to wake into, not out of, them, tried to stay in that half-sleep as long as possible. The sound of the front door closing, the screen door banging shut behind, came like a shot. He was awake. The house was still again; he was alone. He sat at the foot of his bed wrapped in his quilt and watched the sun angling in through the frost-starred window.

The diner was small and brightly lit with nicotine-yellow Formica tables and bitter, scalding coffee. Parents in the community had been trying to have it shut down for years for selling cigarettes under the counter, literally, to minors. Tim and Hayden had been drinking coffee in the booth in the very back for half an hour, Hayden talking about California, about the Lakers, the beach, driving around in his dad's Porsche convertible.

Tim broke in. "Where's your dad live out there?"

"Santa Barbara. Me and Mason go see him when it starts getting nice out."

The woman who ran the place brought them plates of eggs, bacon, and corned beef hash, then went back into the kitchen. "Does your dad come out here much?"

It took Hayden a moment to answer. "Every once in a while." The clattering of an automatic dish scrubber started in the kitchen. "He came last year."

"When did your parents divorce?" Tim was trying to be interested now, concerned.

"I don't know," Hayden said.

"You don't know?"

"I guess it's been . . . maybe ten years. Me and Mason go out to California every summer."

The woman came out and refilled their coffee. Tim took another swallow. The coffee and fluorescent light were making him jumpy and tired. His own voice rang strangely metallic. He blinked heavily and had the dazed feeling of being outside his body, of sliding and rising out of himself at the same time. "Hayden," he said deliberately, "you're talking in the present tense."

A strained look crept over Hayden's face. He was sitting up stiffly, holding his coffee cup with both hands. "Hey," he said, "we still have to go swimming at the clubhouse sometime."

The bells tied to the door of the diner jangled, and a group of high school kids came pushing in from the cold.

There were three boys in khakis and puffy coats with ski hill passes pinned to the zippers and with them a tall girl of about seventeen with dark hair and very dark, almost glinting, brown eyes. They took a booth in the opposite corner, lighting up cigarettes as soon as they got their coffee. The girl recognized Hayden. He waved to her. She came over.

"What's going on, guys?" she said brightly.

She was very beautiful. Tim wondered if she knew who he was. She must have been six or seven years younger than the two of them, but she held herself with such confidence and self-possession that he felt trembling and small beside her. She wore a black peacoat and worn-out jeans and smelled of airy, expensive perfume. He had to look away. This was one of John's or Mason's girlfriends, he suddenly knew without a doubt.

"We were just talking about Mason," she went on, cautiously now, as if testing the words. "About how much we miss them."

"What are you guys doing, Jen?" Hayden said. "What are you up to tonight?"

"Getting some coffee. The boys just got done with hockey."

"Who won?" Hayden said.

"Oh, it was practice."

"Hey, you guys should..." He began again. "You guys should come up to my place. We got beer. We can get some beer."

She looked back at her friends. They were smoking and talking quietly and pointedly, Tim saw, not looking in their direction. "We have to go soon," she said. Tim looked up into her dark eyes—her expression didn't falter but only turned more reflective. "Thanks, though. I mean, thanks. It's a bad night. Those guys...we've been thinking about them a lot."

"Sure. No problem, Jen." Hayden smiled, but spoke very softly. "It's cool."

She looked back at her friends again. "I should go. Listen, we're thinking about you, okay? We're thinking about all you guys."

The dish scrubber had stopped in the kitchen. They could hear cars and trucks buzzing through the slush on the streets outside. Tim held her gaze a moment. He said simply, "Thanks." She smiled at him. *Thanks.* He had no idea what he meant by it.

After they paid, Hayden and Tim wandered the downtown in silence. They walked to the lake, a little inlet that served as a slip for putting in boats. They sat on the concrete boat ramp in a pool of light cast by a lamp at the end of the permanent pier, picked up stones from the gravelly beach, and tossed them out onto the ice. Forty feet out, a round orange buoy was bobbing in a little lagoon of free water. When the wind came up and the buoy swung back and forth, a distant, slapping sound carried over the water. They started aiming their throws at the buoy, but neither of them could hit it, and the stones skittered away on the ice. "Come on," Hayden said under his breath. Tim gave up, his fingers numb, but Hayden kept on. He stood to get a better throw—stone after stone, each one missing the target. "Come on. Come on."

And then Hayden was out on the ice, running toward the buoy, hurling stones as he went. As he brought back his arm again, he slipped, fell backward, and landed heavily. Even from a distance, Tim could hear the water in the slushy ice seething to the surface. In the darkness he couldn't see Hayden, didn't know if he'd gone through. He called out Hayden's name, listened for a reply, for movement or breathing, and heard nothing. Too early in the year for the ice to be really dangerous. The chances of Hayden going through...It occurred to Tim that he was panicking. No, he felt strangely calm. He tried to call Hayden's name again, but his lips wouldn't form the sound.

He stepped out onto the ice, went ten, fifteen feet out where he knew it would still be solid, then dropped to his belly and crawled. The glare from the pier light made it difficult to see more than a few feet ahead. The ice was hard and sharp despite being slushy, and he could numbly feel himself bruising and scraping his hands. If Hayden had gone through, he might not have enough sensation to get hold of him, let alone pull him up. He kept crawling, elbows first, belly, then legs—his coat soaked through and then his shirt.

He bumped something—with his foot, not his hand. He'd almost gone right by him. Hayden was lying on his back like he was gazing up at the stars. It was an odd, peaceful sight. Tim nudged him again with his foot. "Are you okay?" he shouted. "Hey! Wake up!" He twisted around, grabbed Hayden's shoulder, and shook him. Tim's hands were weights; he couldn't tell the fingers apart.

Hayden stirred. He pushed himself up to his knees. He grasped the back of his head and rubbed it. He started to stand. The ice squeaked and popped all around them.

"Don't," Tim said, so quietly he hardly heard himself.

Hayden rose. He looked down at Tim blankly. "It's fine," he said groggily. He felt the back of his head again. "It's fine." And without seeming to give it another thought, he reached to give Tim a hand up.

His father was already in bed snoring softly. Tim crept upstairs and went into John's room. He lay down on John's bed, on top of the checked bedspread that had remained untouched since the night of the accident.

Had it been five weeks? It might have been five days, five years. Watching his mother die had been no preparation. Or only preparation enough to harden him now, so that the things he felt—regret, anger, resentment, an almost giddy sense of release—seemed part of the same solid, unswayable block of grief. He lay there with his temples thumping. He thought that if he could just concentrate on his pulse, the streaming of blood inside him, he could slow it gradually, steadily, one fewer beat every minute. Maybe the line between living and dying wasn't so hard and fast. Maybe living and dying were simply acts of the imagination and his imagination was crippled while Hayden's worked on the edge of delusion. If he could concentrate... Feel it all emptying out of him—swing down into that gray and then indigo and then black place. One fewer beat. Gradually, steadily.

He merely fell asleep. In the morning he woke with the bedspread twisted in his arms. The sky was cloudless, his lips dry, the house very warm. His father was calling up that he was leaving for work. Tim went downstairs and ate the scrambled eggs left in the pan. He spent three days alone in his room reading and sleeping. He left the phone off the hook. On each day but the second, around three in the afternoon, he heard quiet knocking at the front door. It stopped after a minute. He didn't get up to answer, only fell back into sleep, too deep for dreaming.

When he woke on the third night, it was past ten. As Tim was putting on his coat his father came out of his bedroom and said, "Hold on a minute. Let me get my boots on. Take a breath of air if you don't mind company." They went out into the cold, his father in socks, boots in hand.

"I don't know how far I'm going," Tim said.

"Think your old dad can't keep up?" His father sat on the front step lacing his boots. His hair was greasy and tousled and there was a bit of fluff in his mustache.

At the shore, they walked in silence, cutting across the long, snow-covered lawns that ran up to the lakefront homes, past stacked-up boards from the piers taken out for winter, whitewashed boathouses and gazebos. They stopped to look at some new construction, their boots squeaking on the snow as they moved to keep warm. "They finally got that deck done," his father said. "Know the guy who did the work. He took those flatlanders for a real ride."

Tim looked at his father. "I guess I'm one of those flatlanders now."

"You just lived down there."

"Well," Tim said, and couldn't help the bitterness in his words, "that is the definition."

His father turned to look over the lake. A dusting of snow covered the ice. The night was still and mild, and they had pocketed their hats and gloves. "No need to get sharp with me," his father said.

"Are we keeping things light, or are we talking?"

His father huffed out a breath. It plumed, curled, then dissipated above him. He rubbed his hands together, clapped them softly to bring some blood back.

"The ground stores up heat," his father said. "Right around midnight is the best part of a cold day."

Tim went on: "I was trying to make a life down there. I wasn't trying to abandon the family."

"Never thought you were," his father said quietly. "Couldn't keep you boys on a leash. Never could. I don't know. They tell you not to even try. Let them go, right? Let them go. Your mother would've done better. I had dreams about it—some kind of accident. And it was always John. Slow-motion dreams, you know. Like I wanted it to happen. Just to show I was right."

His father turned to face him. He crossed his arms, put his hands under his armpits as if he were trying to keep them warm. But Tim saw his shoulders trembling, his whole body. "You don't have to answer anything to that. I'm just saying it. Your mother would've done better."

They climbed a set of wooden steps and came to another lookout. The lake opened out below them like a clouded eye. On the opposite shore, they saw the dark curves of the hills and three red lights crowning the top of a water tower.

"Only ones that are guilty," Tim said, "only ones that had *any-thing* to do with it, are that truck driver and that little shit Mason."

They stood looking across the lake. "It's no one's fault," his father said after a time. "Or it's everyone's. But don't ask me to answer that question."

On the walk back it began to rain.

"Great," Tim said, "now this."

His father was walking ahead. "I don't know." His voice floated back. "It feels okay. Anyway, it's weather enough for a breath of air."

The next morning the rain had eaten away half the snow. Tim watched through his bedroom window as the sun burned off the haze. He picked up the phone and dialed Hayden's number.

"Hey," Tim said, "there's a party tonight."

They walked up the hill through the sumac and the scrub, Hayden carrying a thirty-pack of Pabst under his arm. They came out into the clearing. The sight of the speedboat seemed no less strange, but in the gray evening Tim saw that it was an old, battered thing and had been there a long time. In the boat's lee were the remains of a fire pit. Tim turned up two hewn logs to sit on.

"We're early," Hayden said. He cracked a beer and took a sip. His expression was solemn, almost ruminative, as if he were saving himself for the excitement to come. The snow had been melting all day. The ground underfoot was muddy and the bite had gone out of the wind. Neither of them spoke. They sipped their beers.

"Bet it's eighty degrees in California," Tim finally said.

Hayden nodded. "Yeah, surf city."

Tim finished his beer. "I'll bet they're all on the fucking beach smoking joints." He tossed the empty can into the pit. "Come on," he said. "We need a fire."

At the base of a thick stand of pines, they found dry needles for kindling. They took up fallen logs, broke branches off saplings, pulled strips of papery bark from the birches. Hayden worked eagerly, nearly running back and forth between the woods and fire pit. When they had a good pile of wood and kindling built up, they sat down with fresh beers, sweating and red-cheeked. The beer felt good going down. Now Tim himself half-expected that at any minute teenagers would come clambering up the hill and into the clearing. He could almost hear shouting and laughing, the clatter and *shush* of ice sliding around in the coolers they carried between them. He could almost see the cherries of their cigarettes dancing up through the night. For an instant, a thrill of anticipation ran through him. Jesus, had he come for this, to try to live one night of John's life? He'd envied, even resented, that John didn't remember their mother, that he could party every night of the week, hang out with the worst, most careless people, never think twice about it. But what good were those kinds of feelings? He'd gone down one path, John another. Tim always fleeing, John wresting as much pleasure out of life as possible. No one could blame John for not wanting to be like his older brother. And that fact had taken John to his end. No, those were junk feelings. Lousy, self-important, nothing feelings.

He closed his eyes until his thoughts quieted, then reached into his pocket and felt for the cold metal of the Zippo. He opened his eyes, knelt, and touched the flame to the kindling. After a minute, the wet wood was hissing. The larger chunks began to catch. Hayden sat hunched over, staring into the heart of the growing fire, his eyes reflecting pinpricks of its light. Tim watched him. Hayden was in some other place—not on that hillside waiting for a party that would never happen, but in the past, years and years away. Mason was still there, not old enough yet to drive himself, needing rides from his older brother, taking him along wherever he went. His mother was there, his father. He still lived at home—there was still a home to live in—and he wasn't twenty-six, going on thirty, going on forty and always alone, no one left to look after what he did all day and night. They were still there. They stood all around him, waiting just past the reach of the firelight.

The underside of the boat glowed, the graffiti flickering in and out of darkness. Tim knelt again before the fire. For a moment, he saw himself flying into a rage, imagined putting his hands into the fire, hurling burning chunks of wood off into the night, hurling them against the boat, the hollow hull booming, the Fiberglas drooping and deforming as it, too, went alight. He could burn the thing down to a puddle. Torch the whole goddamn town if he wanted. He held out his hand, waved it before the flames. The fire was dying, the embers going dark—the wood too wet to burn long.

"You can make some other friends," he said softly. He didn't look at Hayden. He couldn't. "Someone who likes basketball and games. Someone more like you."

The crackle of the fire had quieted. "Me and John and Mason used to come up here all the time." By the waver in Hayden's voice, Tim knew he understood—he hadn't been brought up to Spider for a party. "I miss him. Me and John were real close, Tim."

"No, you weren't," Tim whispered. "No, you weren't." He rose from kneeling, looked off toward the dark undulations of the golf course and, beyond, the expanse of the flat prairie. "Come on," he said, "time to go."

With the toe of his boot, he scattered the fire.

He rented a smaller apartment in his old building and after a month of interviews got another job in the Loop. A parking spot came up for rent on his block, and he bought a cheap used car. He went on a few dates with an older woman from work who chided him for being so silent all the time. Life seemed something like it had been. He dreamed of John less, which saddened him. He felt relief, too.

They said that no one had heard from Hayden for weeks. He'd disappeared. When they brought his body back from Junction City, Kansas, they buried him alongside Mason. There had been a scuffle in a hotel parking lot—that was all anyone knew.

It took another week for the item to show up in a Milwaukee paper. He'd run into some rough guys outside the Greyhound station, the story said. They'd talked him into taking them along to the hotel, where they robbed him and kicked him around. One of the staff found him lying on his back in his hotel bed, the covers pulled over him like he was asleep. He'd died of his injuries early that morning. He had a bus ticket to Santa Barbara.

Tim went to a bar that night. He played several games of pool by himself and watched a baseball game on the big-screen TV. He dozed for a few minutes with his head on the bar. When he went to order another bourbon, the man working the door came up and said, "Time to go, chief." When Tim wouldn't budge, the man took him by the shoulder. Tim shoved him away. "Don't you tell me when to leave," he said in his haze.

When he found his car, he was a long time fumbling with his keys. It was late, he had no idea how late it was. His shoulder throbbed from the man yanking his arm behind his back. He tried to get the key in the lock but kept missing. He stabbed at the lock, missed again, and, with a squeal of metal on metal, scratched the key against the door. He cursed violently. A young couple coming down the street crossed to the other side. He made another scratch, scored it white through the paint. And then another. Another. Reeling in the street, key in hand, he set to it.

ANASTASIA KOLENDO

Boston University

WINTERING

For Varvara, Sochi would forever remain the land of summer. Every vacation season, the city's population tripled as tourists flocked to its pebble beaches, palm trees, and crumbling piers. Her mother delivered milk every morning to the pensions along the shore, and the girl played soccer barefoot with the visitors' children. Then, in 1999, Varvara's mother, having fallen asleep on her route, crushed a pedestrian with her truck on a gravel road north of Mountain Air Beach.

The sentence was three years in prison. Varvara's grandfather lived in a small village in the Western Urals, and in March the girl was told to buy warm boots and change to a bus at the train station in Perm.

After three thousand kilometers, Varvara arrived at Kliukovka around midnight. She had been afraid she would not recognize her grandfather when he came to meet her and had squinted for hours on the train trying to remember his face. Yet except for her, the station was empty. The bus creaked and puffed as it drove away. She shivered. Within minutes of arriving, she inhaled a snowflake the size of a peony bloom. The cold gripped the bridge of her nose like a vise.

She waited for an hour before she walked west, toward the loud bass of techno. To her horror, she discovered Kliukovka had a dance club—a hut with lights flashing in the windows and a banner that said DISCOTHEQUE! over the door. Around the entrance, next to the gray snowbanks topped with ice shards, five boys her age stood and smoked.

"You know where Faim Ulyanich lives?" she asked.

"Why on earth do you want Faim Ulyanich? He won't keep you warm at night, honey," the tallest one said. He was slurring his words.

"He's my grandfather," Varvara said.

The boys hooted. "Kostia, did you hear that? The Snow Maiden is Faim Ulyanich's granddaughter!"

"It's a little early for New Year, Snow Maiden. Go back to the forest."

"The devil had progeny? Aren't there laws against that?"

"Nice knapsack!"

"Yeah, like a hump on a camel."

For three days, Varvara had been carrying all of her things in three bags. One was a green cotton alpinist sack her mother had sewn for her thirteenth birthday. The bag might have been patched and faded, but it was still Varvara's favorite. She had stuffed it with books she was reading to prepare for the entrance exams to the Kuban University back south the next summer. All of her friends would apply, and the Kub. U. alpine team was the best. She started crying. Someone snorted. She turned and walked away.

"What, honey, can't take a joke?"

The music grew quieter as she got farther. Then she realized she was also hearing footsteps behind her. She turned around. One of the boys was following. He was close, only two or three steps behind.

"Help!" she yelled, and ran. She felt his hands tugging on one of her bags. "Help!"

"Quiet, you," the boy whispered. He was short. Clumps of ice hung from three curls of black hair that protruded from underneath his cap. "You'll wake the whole village."

"Let go of my bag," she said.

"I'm just trying to help you carry it, silly."

"Carry it straight to your house, you thief."

"Just let me—"

"I can manage."

"You have frozen snot on your face," he said.

She let go of the bag and wiped her nose with her sleeve. She decided he was short enough that, if she had to, she could take him.

"I'm Nikifor. Nikifor Uganov," he said. "Your grandfather's on the other side of the village. I'll take you."

"Won't your friends need you for their comedy troupe?"

"My friends are idiots. The village midwife dropped them on their heads. I was serious about the backpack though. Where'd you get it?"

"That was you?" she asked.

"Yes. I said 'nice knapsack.' Call the UN Commission of Human Rights."

She stopped and set down her other bags, rubbing her shoulders. He picked up her luggage. "I have one I take to the mountains, but mine doesn't have nearly as many pockets."

"You climb?" she asked.

"You don't believe me?"

She shrugged. "I just think it's easier when you live somewhere with summer."

"Right. Summer."

"So you've heard of it?"

"Once, but it was a vile rumor."

Varvara laughed.

"You going to tell me your name?" he asked.

She sighed. "Varvara."

"Well, Varvarochka." He stopped and pointed to a house across the street. "That's your grandfather. And this is as close as I come."

"This is the other side?"

"It's a small village. You want to go for a walk with me tomorrow?"

"So you and your friends can make more juvenile jokes?"

"No, so that you and I can go skiing. You want to?"

"About as much as I want to lose a toe to frostbite," she said, and took back her bags. She crossed the street. The snow crunched under her boots.

"Is it because I'm shorter?" he yelled. "'Cause I don't mind."

Varvara turned and waved, then closed the lattice gate behind her. The footpath to the *izba* was cleared, and she felt relieved not to have to wade through any more snowdrifts. Yet all the lights were out. No one was waiting for her. She pounded on the wooden door. A few minutes later, she heard footsteps.

"Who's there?" a hoarse voice asked.

"Varvara," she said.

The door opened. A thin old man towered over her with a kerosene lamp. He wore a striped terry-cloth robe and pilled wool slippers two sizes too large.

Varvara rushed in. "I thought you were meeting me at the bus station."

The man's toothless jaws moved, as if munching on something. "I didn't see you."

"Oh? It might have helped if you'd been there to look."

The old man squinted at her. "I was right. Your mother was a whore. Your skin's so dark I thought you were a Gypsy."

"It's a tan," Varvara said.

"A what?"

"A tan. Sun. Rays. Melanin. Tan." To demonstrate, she removed a
mitten and peeled a burnt patch of skin from her nose.

"There's pickled trout if you want it," the old man told her and
blew out his candle. "You can sleep with me on the stove. I'll heat another room for you tomorrow."

In the dark, Varvara could hear him shuffling away. The snow covering her coat was beginning to melt and drip. Slowly, she followed.
She'd always heard her mother say her entire family had slept on a
single furnace during the winter. When she was little she had nightmares about being put to bed on the stovetop and boiled in her sleep.
She discovered that the kiln was made of brick and that its surface
was wide enough to fit three adults. The embers from the logs inside
still glowed and crackled through the iron shutter. Varvara could see
little else. She removed her coat and lay under a sheepskin blanket.
By then, her grandfather was already snoring.

The rooster woke Varvara. Her grandfather was nowhere in sight,
and she went to look around. Faim had built the *izba* himself, and
the house had six rooms—large by village standards. Three con-
tained furnaces, three others were heated through the common walls.
Five were meticulously clean and shut. In the room used by Faim,
there was a stove in the corner, a rug, some benches, a broom, a
chest, and a table with two chairs and a teakettle.

The house itself was built of basswood logs rabbeted together.
From the outside, the corners looked like interlocked fingers. The
yard was fenced in by pickets of birch, which seemed to Varvara to
do little more than prop up the mounds of snow. By the front door,
in the icebox next to a birch bench, she finally found the promised
trout. She bit into a fish, ignoring its head. The eye glinted at her like
a soap bubble. She shivered and went back inside.

Faim had fathered seven children. One had died from cancer, two from cirrhosis of the liver, and one in a boating accident. Of the remaining three, two refused to speak to him, and one—the youngest, Varvara's mother—was in prison. All of their pictures hung above the table. Varvara studied them as she sucked on the fish.

Her grandfather reentered, stomping the snow off his boots in the anteroom. "I bought a box," he said. The container was made of recycled cedar, heavy and unfinished. Varvara thought that if she touched it, she'd have to pluck splinters out of her fingers for an hour. Faim continued, "It's for your mother. We ought to send her a package."

Faim set a few dried fish on the table and wrapped them in an old newspaper. Then he shuffled over to the chest and rummaged through it for three pairs of gray wool socks. Varvara smiled and approached him as he started to stack the things in the box. Reaching behind her neck, she untied her necklace of Sochi seashells and placed it on top of the trout.

Her grandfather looked in and took out the choker. "What's this?"

"Something to remind her of Sochi," Varvara said. "Maybe she'll look at it and feel like she's still in the sun, feel warm."

Faim slammed the shells into the table and ground a few of them with his thumb. "These are going to crumble in the box right over everything. They'll ruin it all." He rapped on Varvara's forehead with his knuckles. "Is there anything left in there, or did you have one too many heatstrokes? Now, sit down and write your mother a letter."

Varvara sulked in her chair as Faim fetched paper and two pens. She looked through her knapsack for something else to send. She found photos. In one, Varvara and her mother were sitting cross-legged on the beach and eating shrimp. Her fingers orange from the spice, Alla was dangling a crustacean over her mouth. Varvara was pointing and laughing. She smiled and slid the photo back into her Herodotus book.

The train ride was bumpy and cold, she wrote. *Grandfather's the abominable snowman. I'm going to start taking pictures and selling them to periodicals.* She smiled to herself and decided she'd have fit right in among Tolstoy's aristocrats with her bons mots. When she finished, she folded the letter and tried to slide it into the box, but Faim intercepted her hand. "My dearest *mamochka*," he read out loud. "Good, good." But he soon fell silent and lowered himself onto a chair.

"I ought to whip you."

"That was private."

"I ought to crack that forehead of yours."

"It's also a joke. Did your sense of humor freeze off?"

He crumpled the letter. "You think your mother's life isn't hard enough without worrying about you?" Then he shuffled off to the chest again—slower, Varvara thought. She sighed and started over. *The train ride was long. There's so much snow. Grandfather looks healthy.* She went over to show Faim, but he wouldn't look. "Just put it in," he said.

Life in Kliukovka had changed little since its founding three hundred years earlier. The residents ate the food they grew or gathered in the summers and heated their homes with wood. Many had left for the cities. Only twelve students and one classroom remained in the village school. Only two places still hired. Nikifor's parents, the Uganovs, sold *matreshkas* and wooden spoons to stores in Yekaterinburg, where foreign businessmen bought souvenirs during their trips to Siberia for oil and gas deals. Faim's neighbors ran a store in their home. The collective farm went bankrupt after being privatized, and its tractors rusted in the empty fields, like dinosaur skeletons.

Faim lived on his pension, which was enough to pay for electricity, a gallon of pressurized gas for the range, four loaves of bread, two gallons of milk, and an occasional kielbasa. With Varvara there, he had to dispense with the sausage and buy more of everything else instead. He had made all the things he owned with his hands, except for the nugget of malachite he had found in the mountains. A few days after their fight, he showed Varvara where he kept the gem—wrapped in panty hose at the bottom of the chest.

"Sell it when you need money for the coffin and the wake," he said.

Varvara did not answer. She did not make a single sarcastic remark that day because the old man had sniffed his dead wife's stockings as he talked.

Every day, Varvara walked to and from school. She still moved clumsily on the snow. The wind blew at, over, and under her, and no matter what she did, a stray flurry always wormed its way into her eye or mouth, or under her mitten, where it burned her the whole way. She skidded and fell and even lost a boot in a snowbank.

One afternoon, about a week after she arrived, she noticed Nikifor Uganov watching her from a hill as she stumbled home. In class, he sat a row over and said nothing, not even when the others teased her. Varvara had made no friends. The boys still remembered her crying at the discotheque. Varvara's chest was flat, her shoulders wide, her arms thick, and her thighs muscled. Dresses never flattered her, and she wore boys' jeans. She hadn't even spoken to the girls, who stalked through the school in miniskirts and fake eyelashes.

Just as she became aware that Nikifor was looking, she slid and fell, cursing. He ran to her and pulled her up.

"What happened to the skinny bully who walks you home?" she asked.

"You are welcome," he said. "And Kostia was drafted."

"I hope they send him to Chechnya."

He let go of her coat. "He's my brother."

"I'm sorry."

"Why are you always so angry?"

She shrugged. "I haven't had the warmest of welcomes."

"You might try being friendlier."

"Oh, it's my fault?"

"For example. Come for a walk with me."

She told him no. She said never. Yet Nikifor would not give up. He would follow her every day and ask her to go to the movies if the truck with the projector was around. And though Varvara refused every time, she began noticing how well-made the young man was, how the fabric of his shirt stretched and tautened like the skin on a tambourine every time he turned or twisted. Once, she caught herself wanting to pluck an ice crystal out of the bristles of his rabbit fur collar. She wanted to slip it into her mouth in secret and suck it and taste it as it dissolved. But by then, Nikifor stopped asking and talked to her about mountains instead.

Faim noticed they were becoming friends. Over dinner of potatoes and more fish, which Varvara had oversalted and overfried, he said, "That boy I see skulking around you, Nikifor. He's not good news, Varvara. You stay away from him, you hear?"

"He's all right."

"All boys like that want from ugly girls like you is something they can get easy. At least until they start wanting a real skilled woman around the house for a wife. You keep away."

"No one in this village except for him has said a kind word to me because they all hate you, you old, shriveled wretch."

He pounded on the table. The dishes jumped. "You little snot! I marched two thousand kilometers to Moscow and then another two thousand to Berlin for you. In the winter. In just one sock! You'd all be speaking German if it weren't for me, you guttersnipes!" He rose. His face was red, but the knuckles of his fists blanched.

Varvara ran outside without her coat and sat on the bench in front of the neighbors' house for an hour.

In the morning, the thaw began, but Varvara could not go out to look; she had pneumonia. After the doctor came and left antibiotics, she lay in her bed, which she preferred to the furnace, and listened to the ringing of the water drops on the metal top of the icebox. She wondered what it would be like to stand right under the roof and catch them with her tongue.

Her grandfather walked in around noon with a pine crate. It was squeaking. Her curiosity piqued, Varvara sat up.

"I thought you'd need something to do while I went hunting in the summer," Faim said. He set the box on the floor, reached into it, and lifted up a small bird. It was yellow, and it peeped as it pecked Faim's thumb with its rose beak. He brought it over to Varvara, and she petted it.

"There are a dozen in there," Faim said.

The gosling stepped out of Faim's calloused palm and onto Varvara's blanket, then squeaked and stumbled over her fingers, tickling her. It pecked at her wrist. She laughed, and, cupping it with her palms, rubbed its soft fuzz against her nose. It was May, and spring was finally coming. She would have freckles soon, she thought. She always looked prettier with freckles.

Two weeks later, Varvara woke feeling better and went outside to the bank of the Kama, where, after months of being caged in ice, the river resurged, roaring. Icebergs—racing, breaking, rumbling—floated southward. The snow was almost gone, and she galloped along the shore.

To the Volga! Varvara thought, her heart leaping. *To the sea!*

When she returned home, Nikifor was waiting in the common room with Faim. "There she is!" the boy exclaimed.

Glaring, Faim cleared his throat and left. Varvara sat down and elbowed Nikifor, who handed her a handmade get-well card. "You're just in time," he said. "Faim Ulyanich just finished with the questions about my immunizations and medical records."

She opened the front flap and realized that Nikifor had gotten the teacher and all their schoolmates to sign. The word *camel* had been written only once and crossed out with a marker. She smiled. "Is this what took you two weeks?"

"I also brought you your homework. I knew you'd just die if you didn't get it."

"Now I know you've got to be after something."

He told her he needed a tutor for the entrance exams in August. The army was worse than he had imagined, Kostia had written. The soldiers in the second year of their military obligation had kicked in his bunkmate's ribs. Another greenhorn was whipped with a leather belt because he stepped onto a floorboard in the barracks the army "grandfathers" had arbitrarily chosen as a no first-year zone. Nikifor would apply everywhere and anywhere to receive a draft deferment.

Varvara agreed to help. "Even though I have my own grandfather problem at home," she joked.

The June days were endless, the clear northern skies staying light until dawn. Varvara, Nikifor, and a dozen geese—all of them occasionally interrogated by Faim—spent the month together, in the forest. Every morning, she would rise with the first rooster to chase the birds out into the clearing where they feasted on baby grass. They would teeter from foot to foot, quack, peck at each other and at Varvara, and, in the afternoon, nap with their beaks tucked under their wings. She had a favorite—the small one—whom she fed bread crusts instead of barley.

Nikifor would join them after lunch and pretend to study. She brought him novels, choosing the ones with erotic scenes. She stopped him every hour to ask how far he'd gotten, and, as he approached the sexy parts, she'd ask him to read to her. Her head pillowed by moss, she listened as Pechorin seduced Bella and Ruslan waited keenly for his first night with Ludmila. She gave him *A Thousand and One Nights* and wondered if he had fallen in love with her yet. Like Scheherazade, she had plied him with stories.

At the end of July, Faim announced over breakfast that time had come to start slaughtering the geese. "I'll kill the lone gander tomorrow. He hasn't paired. There'll be no one to grieve."

Varvara was buttering her burnt toast. "But he's my favorite. I read Derrida to him."

"You ever see a goose grieve for its partner?" Faim asked. "It loses the will to live. Will put its neck right in a dog's jaws on its own. It'll break your heart to watch."

"Why do we have to kill them at all?"

"Be serious," Faim said. "We've got to send some food to your mother."

"Please?"

"And what are you going to eat in the winter?"

"I'll become a vegetarian!"

"A vegetarian! And you say you want to be treated like an adult."

That day, Nikifor tried to make her laugh. He juggled pinecones. He sang gibberish out of tune. Nothing worked. Then in the evening, after she fed the geese, the gander disappeared. How men underestimated beasts sometimes—the bird, whom Varvara had started calling Derrida, had sensed a threat and escaped. Her grandfather was unperturbed, and, despite her objections, killed another instead.

The next morning, she was sitting on her log and reading when Derrida stumbled up, quacking, with a red bow around his neck and a note. She opened the envelope. "Now will you come for a walk with me?" it said. She laughed and looked up to find Nikifor, squinting at her.

"You saved him!" she screamed.

He sauntered over. "Calm down. No need to have kittens."

"I could just kiss you."

"All right. If you want."

But her tongue was numb. Her feet and hands felt heavy, as if filled with lead. Everything about Nikifor was perfect. The crook of his nose was perfect. The scar on the left hill of his lip was perfect. Wanting to touch him felt perfect, too. She was terrified of spoiling something. After a minute, Nikifor sat down next to her and, from inside her book, removed the photo of her and her mother on the beach. He twirled it between his fingers. "What did you love most about Sochi?"

She smiled. "Sochi kisses."

"Because they are just so different?"

"If you have a real Sochi kiss, it is. You kiss on the beach, and you're covered in sand, and your lips are salty and wet, and you touch—"

Nikifor smiled. "Have you ever had one?"

Varvara shook her head.

Nikifor rummaged through her lunch sack and found the matchbox with the salt. He dipped his fingers into it and smothered the crystals over Varvara's lips. "Don't know what we'll do for sand," he whispered.

She could smell apricots on his breath. "It's all right."

Then he kissed her.

Faim's goose holocaust continued. He killed one every Saturday and expected Varvara to help with the plucking. The down sidled into her eyes, and, unlike the chickens her mother had bought, the geese were still warm when she tore off their feathers. At least Derrida, safe in the Uganovs' barn, was exempt.

Her grandfather hated her whining. "When I was your age, I lay in a wet trench for three months for the Fatherland and didn't complain a peep!"

"Was it because otherwise they'd starve you?"

"And there were bullets!" The grandfather drew his finger through the air and whistled.

Four dead geese and a mountain expedition later, in August, Nikifor went to Yekaterinburg to take his exams. He failed. He scored high on math but low on composition. After he told her, he sat on her bed as she paced across her room, reading the essay he'd written in response to the prompt "Some historians claim that Russia's God-intended destiny is to save our civilization. Discuss." He wrote ten pages and used no commas. When she pointed this out, he sighed and kissed her. His hands swept over her breasts.

"My grandfather will kill you," she whispered.

He chuckled. "Better than Chechnya."

That evening, after Faim had fallen asleep, Varvara grabbed an armful of blankets and went to meet Nikifor at the clearing. She watched him from the shadows of the trees. He had started a fire and was fiddling with the pack of condoms he'd brought from the city as she'd asked. He stretched the latex with his hands, seeing how far he could pull it. It snapped, and Varvara chuckled. He turned and smiled.

They undressed each other. Their mouths grazed and their fingers wandered. He was Varvara's first lover, and when he was halfway inside her, she yelped. He froze, moving neither forward nor back, whispering, "Did I hurt you?" His palms rested on the ground next to her shoulders as he held himself above her, and his arms were trembling—either from desire or from the effort, she could not tell.

Grabbing his buttocks, she pulled him inward. "Aah," she sighed, and he kissed her neck.

Afterward, as they lay beneath a camel-hair blanket, she said, "I feel like a witch. Sneaking out to the forest to be naked with you."

He chuckled. "All you need is a broom."

"Well, I know where to find the handle." She reached for his sex.

The first snow fell early, in October, but this time Nikifor, a true northman, showed Varvara how to winter. They went sledding. They skied. They sculpted obscene snowmen at night and skated across the Kama. They climbed trees and broke icicles off the tin shingles of the roofs. Varvara learned to love the pink fuzz of the snow at dawn, as Pushkin wrote she should. She loved that when she tapped the surface of a puddle with her boots, the ice crackled like a crème brûlée.

Meanwhile, the Uganovs exhausted their options. They could not afford a medical or a psychological diagnosis that would get Nikifor a deferment. No university had accepted him, and Nikifor's War Commission summons was served in December. He was to appear at the training center by January 20.

"How nice. They gave me some time to sober up after the holidays," he said. But his voice trembled and no one found the joke funny.

On Orthodox Christmas Eve, January 6, his parents went to Mass and Varvara sneaked into his bedroom. As they made love, the squealing of the mattress springs and Varvara's single moan melded into the choir of carolers singing outside. They laughed about it afterward and Varvara was still smiling when he asked, "Why don't we get married?"

"Ha."

"Seriously. I bet your grandfather's a funny drunk."

Varvara laughed. "Mmhm. Tempting. But then what?"

"We live together. Have babies. Grow old."

"Nikifor, I am sixteen!"

"So? Ma got married around then."

"You want to tell me what this is really about?"

Nikifor sighed. "Kostia wrote that a guy who was drafted with him got turned into a woman."

Varvara arched her eyebrow. "I'm sure having to wear a skirt's bad—"

"No, Varia. They cut his balls off. He's their woman." Nikifor smoothed a wisp of hair from Varvara's forehead. "I can get an extension if we get married."

She cupped his cheek with her hand. "Nikifor," she mumbled.

"I love you, Varia."

"What's a few months going to do?"

"I can get three years if we have a baby. And I'll never have to go if we have two."

It seemed to Varvara that the blood in her veins froze. "A baby?"

"We can live with Ma for now. I've already asked."

"I'm moving back south in the fall, Nikifor."

"Only if you get into a university. And I didn't."

"You jerk."

"Varvara—"

"No."

"You realize you might be killing me right now?"

"You manipulative ass! Get out!" She pulled the blanket off him.

"Technically, this being my place—"

She started crying. "Why did you have to ruin everything again?"

"I just want to get married," he whispered and started kissing her. She reached for his lips. There were dozens of things she wanted to believe but could not. She grimaced, as if she'd tasted curdled milk, then bit his nose, grabbed her clothes, and, still naked, ran out the door.

———

The next few days, Varvara stayed home and sat in front of the oven, poking the coals and watching the wood burn through the open shutter. She waited for Nikifor to apologize, but he did not come. He did not visit the next day or the day after. Faim gloated. "These boys are like dandelions now. Blow and they're gone. What did I tell you?"

But Varvara didn't answer, and after a while her grandfather stopped.

A week passed before, in the middle of the night, she realized she had forgotten about Derrida. He was still with Nikifor. Varvara threw a coat over her nightgown and snuck out. The door of the Uganovs' barn creaked and their cow bellowed at her from its stall. Shushing the animal, she petted its muzzle. She did not see Derrida anywhere and gabbled to summon him. He did not come. She called louder. Perhaps he was in the Uganovs' chicken coop, where he slept sometimes because it kept the smaller birds calm. She tiptoed into the picketed promenade and flinched as the ground, covered with a layer of snow and chicken droppings, squished underneath her boots. Then she saw the door of the henhouse was padlocked.

Varvara returned to ask about Derrida in the morning, wearing a ruby pendant and some blush. She found Kostia and Nikifor home alone, eating inside the *izba*. Kostia, she had heard, had been wounded in the left buttock during a firefight in Chechnya and had been discharged. The men rose when they saw her walk in.

She nodded instead of saying hello. Her mouth was dry. "When are you leaving?"

"Next Monday," Nikifor said and brought his right hand from the table to his mouth. He was eating a wing. Varvara froze. She watched as he, seeming unconscious of her gaze, gnawed on the meat. It was the fried wing of a bird. She wanted to bite his fat-glossed lip. She wanted to bite him until he bled.

"You murderer," she said. She had not moved.

He looked up at her in surprise.

"You killed him. You killed Derrida. I came to get him from the barn, but he wasn't there."

Nikifor looked at his hand, then at Varvara. He smiled. "Better me than your grandfather. He's tasty." He bit into the flesh so forcefully that the meat spurted juice, dotting his cheek.

Varvara bolted and ran home. On the way, she stopped to uproot a colony of snowdrops with the toes of her boots. Nikifor had brought her a bouquet of them once. The flowers' blossoms faced downward because of the weight of the melting snow, and, as they toppled, turned up toward the sky. Then she crushed their stems with her steel-tipped toes and stomped them into the ground.

Varvara did not speak to Nikifor again before he left. He did not write. She began watching Mexican soap operas, calling it her hour of comic relief. Faim's neighbors bought two cell phones and no longer had to walk to the post office like the other Kliukovkians to make calls. From then on, they shoveled snow and weeded with their behinds thrust up toward the sun and mobiles nestled between their shoulders and their ears.

Varvara blamed Nikifor most for forcing her to start paying attention to people. She'd spent six months getting used to thinking about him and anticipating everything he wanted. Paying attention had become a habit, and now that he no longer consumed her every thought, she found herself noticing things about others. She noticed that her teacher wanted to be left alone with the principal, that the mailman's coat needed a new lining, and that in the mornings, Faim needed a drink—his voice was hoarse. She offered the mailman hot tea and filled Faim's tin mug with water before he even said a word.

One day, her grandfather had entered the common room of the *izba* and started bathing his feet in a bucket as she studied on the bench. Faim's breeches were rolled up to his knees, and for the first time Varvara noticed that his soles were scarred and scaly. She went to the oven and put in a kettle. When it boiled, she offered it to Faim. "More hot water, Grandpa?"

"Hmm," he said and chewed on his cheeks.

She poured some into the bucket and handed him a towel.

He looked at it. "Stop being so lazy, Varia. Go fetch me a clean one."

"What, are you blind? That's just a pattern."

A week later, Kostia came to visit with a snow goose on a leash. He yanked it behind him, and the bird's neck jolted forward. It gaggled loudly to protest.

"We were eating chicken," Kostia told Varvara. "He'd hidden the goose in the henhouse so that you'd come and talk to him rather than sneak your pet out in the middle of the night."

Varvara hugged Derrida, who was impossibly fat now, almost unable to move, and the gander pecked at her earlobe, as if angry. "How is he?"

"As you can see, alive and obese."

"I meant Nikifor."

"Oh. He charmed some Arctic Fleet major into letting him become a sailor. Thank god Chechnya's landlocked."

Varvara laughed and nodded.

"The grandfathers took away his warm coat his first day on the ship, of course. That, and someone beat his nose to a pulp, so he may no longer be quite as pretty."

Varvara looked away from Kostia, kissing her goose on the beak.

"He tried to kill the bird after you called him a murderer, by the way. Just for your information, you don't get to start calling us names until after Chechnya."

"You called me a camel," Varvara said.

"Did I?" Kostia asked.

"Yes. On my first day here."

He nodded. "Sounds like me. Nikifor got a butcher knife and everything. Caught the fat bastard and held him between his knees, but he just couldn't cut its neck. He said he could hear the heart beating. Said he'd never heard anyone's but yours before."

He waited for Varvara to answer, but she felt stubborn. Eventually, Kostia saluted, turned on his heels, and, with small penguinlike steps, marched out the door.

Snows melted. Icebergs caved. Winds shook the glass in the windows of her grandfather's *izba,* and naked branches of the linden trees scratched it. Derrida became a changed bird. He turned lazy. It took him half an hour just to amble from his shed to the lattice gate of Faim's yard, and yet he still managed to run away every other day. Inevitably, she found him in Nikifor's barn, honking at her through the small vent in his orange beak. He bathed in puddles of mud, and she shuddered at the thought of washing him.

In May, thunderstorms tore the shutters off Varvara's windows. Soon the sunsets merged with dawns. The days were interminable. Spring and summer seemed to Varvara to be seasons of violence. They burned, melted, and transfigured everything. She had no curtains to shut out the light, and she lay awake missing the previous winter.

She reminded Faim to fix her windows for three days before he finally tried. As he started hammering the first nail into the rotted wood of the frame, he slipped in the mud and fell on his back. He lay in the muck for hours before Varvara returned from school and heard him calling and cursing everyone he could name. No bones were broken, but he'd bruised his back and thighs and needed weeks of bed rest. He could not eat unless Varvara cooked and served him his meal, and he lashed out at her with furor.

"When are you going to learn how to cook properly? There's too much salt."

She did not blame him. She, too, was angry because she needed someone.

Soon after, she wrote to the University of Perm for information on the entrance exams. She could make it back to Kliukovka in less than a day if her grandfather ever fell again. And, though she was afraid to admit it, she knew she wrote to them because in another year and a half Nikifor would return.

One day at the end of June, after Faim had recovered, she finally asked. "Grandpa?"

He looked up from his newspaper.

"When we send a package to Ma next Monday, can we send one to Nikifor as well?"

He smirked. "Ay. The girl's lost. That bad, eh?"

"Like a goose with its neck in the mouth of a bulldog," she said.

"Well, suit yourself. But all we've got is your beloved gander."

Varvara nodded. "C-could you? I'll can the meat Sunday."

The grandfather rose. "You stay inside, Varia. Put another kettle in."

"No, I'll help."

They dressed and went into the yard where she picked up Derrida. He was heavy and pecked at a strand of her hair with his beak, quacking in recognition. His webbed feet teetered on her hand, nipping her skin. She carried him to where the grandfather waited on a bench with a small ax. She set the bird down, bent his neck over an oak stump, and cupped the head with her palms so the goose would not see. Still, through the tips of her fingers, she could feel his pulse quickening. Glimmering, the ax came down.

Weeks passed without a word from Nikifor. Preparing for another winter, Faim went hunting and fishing for days at a time. Dirty, hungry, and mean, he'd return once in a while to sleep, then leave again. Varvara was alone. She wrote to her mother, but not too often—if Alla received letters daily, she would worry about why.

Then the mailman brought something with a military stamp. The paper sheet, folded into a soldier's triangle, served as its own envelope, and at first Varvara could not understand how to get inside. Her fingers trembled.

> *Varvara, so far, no one's tried to rape me. You didn't ask, but I knew, you'd be worried. Personally, I'm hurt. It makes me feel unpretty.*
>
> *My ship's captain's promised vacations to anyone, who kills ten rats, and I'm up to seven. I can hear them, scurrying in the walls, the varmints, so, there's plenty more, I just have to get them, all, before October, because otherwise we'll freeze solid, in the water, and have to wait weeks for the icebreaker to pull around. But I'll manage. I'm persistent, as you well know.*
>
> *Wherever you decide to apply, be it Yekaterinburg, be it Sochi, or be it the South Pole, is all kittens by me. I've been to one end of the geography, and I'm ready and willing to go to any other.*
>
> *Thank your grandfather for the socks. You didn't say they were from him. But I figured.*
>
> *Love,*
>
> *Nikifor.*
>
> *P.S. I hope you don't miss that goose more than you miss me. It was tasty.*

Varvara reread the letter a dozen times, went outside, and sprinted downstream along the bank. She hopped over the gnarled roots of the linden trees. She felt that her heart was beating faster than it should. She felt as strong as the river, carrying the riches of the north down into the Caspian Sea.

SHARON MAY

Stanford University

THE MONKEY KING

The people called him *sdaik swaa,* the monkey king, or *ta asay,* the hermit, because he was very old and had a white pointed beard like the hermit in folktales. He was different from the other gray monkeys I caught and killed in the forest—larger, more dignified. Unlike the rest, he had a ring of white hair surrounding his face. It resembled the halo of light that frames a lunar eclipse, when the serpent-god Rahu swallows the moon and women clang on cooking pots and soldiers fire guns into the air to frighten the snake into spitting the moon out again. I can't say Rahu is real—only that one bullet did not reach him and instead killed my five-year-old cousin in Phnom Penh during the lunar eclipse in late 1974, two years before I went into the jungle. It was a beautiful night, the moon washed red in Rahu's mouth. The *pop pop pop* of guns put me on edge even before my cousin was hit. Afterward, I held her, her slight body feeling far too heavy, blood soaking my shirt, smelling of bitter metal. I thought, why her and not me? What has this girl done? Only later did I realize what that bullet spared her, when after the new year the Khmer Rouge took over.

I was seventeen and therefore sent to work in a single men's mobile team, planting rice and building dirt dams that would wash away in the rain. Like the other "new people" evacuated from the cities, I starved and caught malaria. After a year and a half, the Khmer Rouge sent me to fish in the forest surrounding Lake Tonle Sap. I thought the Khmer Rouge meant to kill us, as they had those sent away "to cut bamboo." But my friend Darith—who was also chosen—told me not to worry, the jungle was the best place to be.

He was right. The Khmer Rouge leaders stayed in a compound nearer the villages, and came to check on our work fishing inside the forest only once in a while. I'd heard of this place but never seen it. For half the year, during the monsoon, the river flows into the lake, submerging the plain and the jungle. After the water peaks, the river reverses course and the lake empties back into the sea, leaving behind ponds full of fish trapped in depressions in the forest. Instead of fishing with nets, we drained the ponds. Two men stood facing each other on benches, holding ropes tied to buckets that we dipped and swung in unison. Afterward, the women gutted, dried, and smoked the fish left wriggling in the mud. It was hard work, swinging the buckets all day, especially when I arrived, skinny and weak.

My first day in the forest, sweating, I took off my shirt. That night my skin itched so badly I couldn't sleep. The "old people"—local villagers who had lived in the area before the Khmer Rouge took over—said it was from the dust. The lake leaves behind tiny shells and fragments of bone and rotted leaves, which stick to the trees. All that has accumulated and decomposed in the water coats the brush and dries into fine dust. Whenever you touch anything, this powder falls on you like white rain, mixing with your sweat and seeping into your skin.

Later, you become accustomed to the dust, just as the soles of your feet harden, and the muscles of your back and legs strengthen from the heavy work. You learn to walk quietly, to be aware, to distinguish between the shades of green, the variations of light and shadow. Your ears, once assaulted by the constant noise of the forest, learn to discern the sizes of fish by the popping sounds they make in the ponds.

Your body has been shaped by this place. And though the fear never quite leaves you, you have found freedom in entering a place that others fear. The forest conceals dangers: cobras, crocodiles, disease. It is isolated, so you can be killed easily and no one would know. Deeper in the lake, soldiers patrol in boats. But here on the vanishing shoreline, following the water's edge as the lake diminished, we lived in a narrow border of safety. We had enough food, more than in the villages outside. Our bodies grew strong. The Khmer Rouge leaders could not watch us all the time, so we had some freedom. A constrained freedom—careful, guarded.

I would have done anything to stay.

It was Comrade Peng—he liked us to call him Grandfather Peng— who came up with the idea of killing gray monkeys to increase "food production" for the villages. He called a special meeting to tell us his plan.

"The monkeys are the enemy of the revolution," he said, at the start of what was sure to be a very long speech. "They attack our farms. They eat our vegetables. They eat our corn. And so they must be destroyed."

No one said anything. The monkeys came only occasionally to the farms. The old people rarely killed them; they trapped them only when they were desperate for food, not as a regular practice. Sometimes boys played games of catching a monkey by hand, but then they would let it go.

"The monkeys are the enemy," Peng repeated. His speeches were the worst of the three village leaders. The other two, locals who had been promoted, tended to keep things shorter. One of them had once saved my life by secretly giving me quinine tablets for malaria, but this one, Peng, was out to show off and rise in the ranks. "If we kill the monkeys we don't have to worry about them eating our vegetables. Nothing wrong with killing them, because monkeys don't give us any benefit, only problems." This was a variation of the Khmer Rouge saying used to justify killing people: *To keep you is no benefit, to destroy you is no loss.*

"If we kill the monkeys we get two benefits," Peng continued. "One is that the farm is free from attack. The other is we get meat to send to the villages." I glanced at Darith, who wore a look of feigned interest. My other friend Arun—whom I'd met after arriving in the forest—was trying to keep his expression neutral and conceal his disgust. "The monkey is the enemy of the revolution," Peng said once again. "So you don't need to feel sorry for the monkey. You just organize and kill as many as you can."

Peng did not forget about his idea. A couple of days later he returned to check on our work and called another meeting before lunchtime. He had a small gray monkey, a juvenile. With one hand he held its elbows, which were tied behind its back.

"I have a monkey," he said, as if we couldn't see. "Can anyone take care of it?" The young monkey squirmed, kicking its legs as it hung suspended. Peng smiled. "Is there anyone here who can finish off this monkey and cook it?"

He laughed, lowering his arm. We were all scared to death to kill a monkey. He was testing us, because we were new people. The monkey's legs scrabbled in the mud, and Peng raised it off the ground so that it fought uselessly in the air.

"Who can take care of this monkey?" he asked again. He did not say "kill."

No one answered. I wondered what Peng would do if we refused. Someone had to do it, or the entire group would be in trouble. Maybe he would take one of us instead of the monkey.

"I'll do it," said Arun. He was a shy man, tall and dark-skinned. Perhaps in compensation for his height, he spoke softly. When we worked draining ponds, just three or four of us, he would sing. Sometimes I worked his shift to keep him singing longer. At night, as we lay in our hammocks, he entertained us by becoming the voice of an imaginary radio, singing songs from before the war, forbidden now. He could make you cry with that voice. The women who dried the fish often tried to sneak near our camp just to hear him. He was the gentlest man I knew. I couldn't believe he was offering to kill the monkey.

"I'll do it," Arun said again, more firmly. I thought he must be trying to prove himself to the Khmer Rouge. He took the monkey and an ax from Peng and walked away. You couldn't do a dirty job like that near the work compound, because it might smell. I followed to help him, hurrying to keep up with his long stride.

"What are you doing?" I asked. "Do you know what you're doing?"

Arun kept walking. As soon as we were out of sight, he turned to me, his face pale and his normally smooth voice shaking, "Brother, how can we kill it?"

"Why did you say yes?"

"I was upset with Peng."

Arun stopped at a tree stump. He held the ax hesitantly with one hand. With the other, he grasped the monkey's elbows in an awkward imitation of Peng. The monkey, not quite an adult, looked even smaller next to Arun's height.

"The Khmer Rouge can kill humans," Arun said. "Why can't I kill just one monkey?"

He raised the ax, closed his eyes, and hit—rather, tapped—the monkey on the back of the head. The monkey cried out and turned around to see where the blow had come from. It looked more curious than hurt, trying to see behind Arun's back where he hid the ax.

Arun tried once more. It was like watching a monk try to kill a monkey. He hit it again with a gentle thud. The monkey turned to Arun and made a face, as monkeys do when they mock you from the trees.

I thought then about making up a story of how the monkey had escaped, but Peng would never believe it—a tiny monkey with its arms tied behind its back, evading two grown men.

I would have to do it.

I took the monkey from Arun, held down its head, aimed, and swung the ax—hard, but not in the right place. Later I learned the precise spot to kill quickly, so that the monkey wouldn't suffer long. One hit and it's finished, like breaking a coconut shell. You hear when you do it right. And then the body is still. But not that first time. The monkey was shaking and kicking and covered with blood. I had to hold on to it tightly so it wouldn't slip from my hands. I put its head down again and struck two, three, four more times, until I lost count and its body finally stopped twitching.

I was shaking by then, my own hands slick with blood, feeling sick from the smell, remembering the night my cousin had died in my arms. Arun looked as if he had seen a ghost. We didn't speak or look at each other as we carried the monkey back to the compound.

At first they called us the "monkey group." Later, just "monkey people." Of the three of us—Arun, Darith, and me—I became the expert. The others tried to avoid it.

No one wanted the job of killing monkeys. We were all Buddhist, old and new people alike. Even though the Khmer Rouge had forbidden Buddhism, killed or disrobed the monks, destroyed the temples and turned them into killing places, still in their hearts the people were Buddhist. They still believed in karma, in the consequences of actions. They believed in the Buddhist precepts, that you do not kill.

No one wanted to do it.

But I did it.

All my anger at the Khmer Rouge I aimed at those gray monkeys who taunted me from the trees and pissed on my head. I hated this job, to kill every day. Five, six, seven. Sometimes more. But I did it. I had to do it.

And then I could not stop.

Later, I came to know soldiers who told me how once you have killed, it never leaves you. I could see it in their eyes—a certain intensity, like light pushing through water from the bottom of a well. The way they spoke to me, as if to a comrade, made me uneasy. Some took pleasure in the killing, felt lost when they returned home, and were drawn back to the battlefield, in body or in dreams. Others chose to disappear altogether, taking their own lives, or fleeing into solitude, away from the human world, like *ta asay*, the hermit on the mountain, like my great-grandfather, who disappeared before I was born. My father told me he was a great commander with a long white beard. He came home half crazy, sick of war. In the end he left his family. He crossed the Thai border alone and no one in Cambodia ever saw him again.

I did not want to kill the monkey king, not at first. I did not even notice him until later in the season, when we camped at a large pond that served as headquarters for our small teams hunting and fishing in the forest around the lake. He arrived each sunset with his troops to forage in the meadow on the other side of the pond. He sat on a tree stump in the middle of the clearing. The other monkeys chased each other around his throne, fighting over every scrap of food. The king himself hardly ate, just sat with his arms folded. He swiveled his head from side to side, keeping watch.

Sometimes he dropped to the ground and walked slowly among his troops, towering over the others, before he ascended again to his stump. He moved regally, taking his time, which is how I imagined Prince Sihanouk would walk, although I had never seen the prince and should not have compared him to such an animal. That monkey had a commanding presence. If the group spread out too far, he signaled—a short followed by long whistle—and those who had strayed came scurrying back. When it grew dark, he made a different call, and they immediately retreated. Not one monkey stayed behind. They all followed him, gliding into the trees, disappearing into the canopy of forest.

In the beginning, I went after those that were easier to catch. The old people taught me how to trap. I learned how to make a circular cage with a single door that slides up and down. The door, weighted with a heavy piece of wood on the top, has sharp sticks like teeth at the bottom. It is pulled up by a vine threaded through the top of the cage like a pulley and attached to a stick pinned to the ground. This trigger is set where the monkey must pass it to reach the food. If the monkey touches the vine or stick, even lightly, the trap is sprung and the door falls.

To get the monkey out of the trap, you drag it by the tail so it can't bite you. Once you've gotten hold of it, you tie its arms at the elbows behind its back, take it out, and hit it with an ax. Then you carry the dead monkey back to clean.

You hang the body by a liana vine from a tree branch. First, you cut away the skin from around the neck, then cut off the hands, feet, tail. You slit open the chest and peel the skin down, as if stripping off a shirt. Without its skin, the monkey's body looks like a human's, its muscles formed like ours. It smells strange, fishy. The oily flesh glistens. You slice open the stomach, remove the guts, and bury them in the ground so they will not smell. Finally, you cut off the head.

We smoked the bodies whole, like fish, leaving the meat on the bones for soup. At first the people in the forest refused to eat it. I tried it once but couldn't swallow. I looked at Arun's stricken expression as he tried to chew. "Not delicious," he said, and spit it out. After that, as long as we remained in the forest, we never ate monkey again.

But out in the villages where they were starving—where we, too, could be soon—they were glad to eat anything. They cooked the monkey meat in a sour soup with morning glory leaves. They said that in the stew, you couldn't tell what it was.

I killed hundreds of them. But I could not catch the monkey king. The old people told me, "You'll never get that one. He has a spirit that protects him." It was true, he evaded every trap I set, although I managed to catch some of his troops and many more from other groups—so many I lost count. Sometimes I had to kill the baby and mother together, because if you killed only the mother, the baby would starve, so I killed them all.

It was a terrible, terrible thing. But I had to do it. I did it so the Khmer Rouge would trust me, so that I could continue our activities in the forest, the beginnings of our quiet resistance. I had started to talk with Arun and Darith, at first in tentative whispers, while we worked away from the Khmer Rouge. Later, we became more organized, expanding the circle of those we could trust. We developed a system of lookouts, messaging, and food caches. We debated where the Khmer

Rouge kept weapons and whether we should try to acquire them. Arun traded secretly for a radio from a village outside. We hid it in the underbrush and listened at night, Darith doing his best to translate French broadcasts and the English static of Voice of America and the BBC. We hoped to hear some mention of Cambodia, but there was nothing at all, as if Cambodia no longer existed in the world.

In our isolation, we did not know what was happening beyond the jungle. Only the forest seemed real, and the deepening ties of our friendship. But I knew if the Khmer Rouge didn't trust you, you wouldn't stay in the forest for long—the soldiers would take you away "to cut bamboo." So I earned the respect of the Khmer Rouge and the old people by working hard. When we drained the ponds, I designed a bigger, heavier bucket that only two of us were strong enough to use, in order to empty the water faster. They could not fault me. If I had to kill monkeys to stay in the forest, I would kill monkeys.

It was a job I decided to do well. I felt neither pleasure nor horror. Only when I saw their skinned bodies did I think, *They are almost human.*

Each time, I felt a shock of recognition, to see how much they looked like us. And I told myself, I must harden myself against this. I still have to do what I must do. I sacrifice the monkeys for our safety. A trade. Their lives for ours.

I made a mistake once. I had five monkeys lined up. I struck them one at a time. Bang, throw aside. Bang, throw aside. When I looked at the pile of dead monkeys, I saw one rise and run away, weaving like a drunken man.

I called to Arun, "Quick, get the bastard enemy! Don't let him escape!"

We chased it down. Arun caught and held it as I began to interrogate. "You bastard enemy, why do you want to escape?"

Arun looked at me as if I were crazy. Then he added, "Why do you want to spy?"

He laughed. He knew what I was doing. I took a stick and continued, "Why do you want to attack the revolution? You think you can hide from us? The revolution is strong. We will cut off your roots, never let you grow to defeat us." I slapped the stick in my palm as I paced back and forth. "So tell me, how did you get here? Where do you come from? You think you can hide here in the forest? Where is your headquarters? Who is your leader?"

I pointed the stick at the monkey's face. The monkey was mute, just like the people. It didn't matter what you said or didn't say, you were still the enemy.

"Why don't you say anything?" I asked.

The poor monkey sat there.

"Shit, this bastard doesn't talk," I said to Arun. "Take him away."

"Take it easy," said Arun.

The monkey wriggled in his hand.

"You see, the enemy still wants to struggle against the revolution."

"Let this one go," said Arun.

"No, we can't."

"Take it easy."

"We can't," I said again. "It will die now anyway."

I took the monkey from Arun and held down its head. Before I struck, I said out loud what I usually said silently: "I'm sorry. Sooner or later we all have to die. Maybe in your next life, you will be a king instead of a monkey. Maybe you will be born in England or America."

That is what I prayed for them each time.

After a while, those gray monkeys became too easy to catch. All I needed to do was put food and water in the trap and scatter grains of rice to lead them into the cage. They could not resist. Even though they must have seen how many of their companions disappeared, the method worked every time. Only later the day came when we saw no more monkeys in an area, so we moved and I made new traps. As we followed them, they became harder to find and the forest quieter than before.

Not even the old people could believe how many monkeys I caught. They came to respect me as an expert trapper. But as they watched the oxcarts loaded with carcasses leave the forest, they warned me again, "Don't try to catch that monkey king. You'll never get him. Never. He's lived a long time. He will die by himself, alone."

But I was going to get that monkey. I studied where he came and went. I learned the language of his signals. Even when I couldn't see him, I knew when he was calling back his troops, when he was reprimanding them, when he was commanding them to leave. I learned his preferred places and patterns of travel. As I followed his troops, I kept quiet, careful not to show myself. By then Arun and Darith had given up catching the monkeys, leaving it to me, while they worked draining the ponds. One morning I told them I'd be back by sunset, and I went after the monkey king alone.

I went to one of his favorite clearings and made a trap—a strong, beautiful trap. I had improved the design, creating a better door, a more sensitive trigger mechanism. That day I made three cages—one very large one for the monkey king and two smaller ones. I put a lot of rice and water in the traps. I climbed into a tree and made a blind, surrounded by thick branches. I waited inside the enclosure, sweating and swatting mosquitoes through the morning.

The monkeys arrived at noon. The little ones fanned out into the meadow, but the monkey king stayed at the edge. His white halo of hair flared against the forest. He moved slowly, climbed up onto the high end of a fallen log, and scanned the clearing with the somber expression of an old man. As he looked from side to side, his long white beard swayed across his gray chest.

He stayed on the log a long time. Only his troops came out into the open, playing and eating and bickering as usual. I'd not only put food in the traps but also scattered it in thick trails leading into the cages.

Two juveniles scampered into the smallest trap. They were so busy eating they didn't notice the door fall. Only after the food ran out would they realize they couldn't escape. I calculated how long the rice would last before they'd start to panic and alert the others. Ten minutes, maybe.

Finally, the monkey king dropped to the ground and walked slowly into the clearing. He stopped and picked up a few grains of rice to eat. Then he looked at the large trap I had made for him. Several monkeys had gone in and out already, too light to trigger the door, just as I had planned. I didn't want to catch the small ones and miss him. Right now three of them squatted inside the large cage, eating.

The monkey king approached carefully, ignoring the rice trail at his feet. He took a step, looked to the left and right, took another step. When he reached the cage, instead of entering, he examined it from the outside. He backed up and began to walk all around the perimeter.

I thought, *Grandfather, hurry up. Don't think so much.*

The pile of rice was dwindling in the small cage. It would run out at any moment. I waited, sweating in the heat of the blind and the suffocating moisture of the leaves.

Come on, grandfather, go in.

At last he approached the door. Two monkeys ran out of the cage past him, but the third stayed inside, crunching the rice. The king grunted and the last one darted out. He stood at the opening and sniffed.

Still, he didn't enter. He stepped halfway in and hesitated, his head and one arm past the door.

I thought, *I've got you now.*

I leaned forward in the blind, willing him to step inside. The forest was quiet.

Just as he shifted forward, about to take that final step, a large black bird shrieked overhead—shrill, imperative, in a long horrible scream. Startled, I nearly fell out of the tree, grabbing a branch as one foot crashed through the bottom of the blind.

The monkey king leaped back. As he jumped, his tail whipped around and hit the vine. He was out of the cage by the time the door fell, bang, its teeth locked into the ground.

He signaled to leave—a loud urgent whistle—and bounded out of the clearing. The other monkeys followed. Their fleeing sounded like rain, hundreds of hands and feet passing through the leaves. Only the two captives remained, leaping frantically in the small cage.

I knew even then that the monkey king was gone for good. It was as the old people said, nobody could catch him. I'd never get near him again, although I would continue to try.

I dropped to the ground and entered the clearing. The bird had settled into the branches of a nearby tree, watching me. I wanted to kill that bird, sitting as if it had done nothing. Why did it have to scream at just that moment? Why had it warned the monkey king? Or was it warning me?

I rarely saw those birds in the forest. My father had told me those black birds are the companions of the dead. They come to guide spirits of the dead into their next lives.

But I wasn't dead.

I took a stick and aimed, hurling it as hard as I could. The bird flew off—passing so near my head I could see the ragged tips of its feathers and hear its black beating wings. It landed in a tree on the other side of me and began to groom its breast and pick between its ugly toes. I wanted to wring its neck.

"Go now. Get out of here!" I threw another stick. "Why did you come here? Who are you waiting for? *Who died?*"

Why was it so quiet now?

Whose spirit had it come to guide?

I thought of Arun and Darith waiting at the camp, the others hidden in the forest. Had the Khmer Rouge found them out? Fear seized my stomach. My pulse pounded in my head. My hands felt numb.

The two juveniles still leaped crazily in the cage, panicking and pissing on themselves. They stunk so badly I didn't want to go near them. I pulled up on the door, yanking hard to release it from the soil. They were young, with very little flesh on them.

"Go, get out of here!" I shook the top of the cage. Confused, they couldn't find the exit at first. Then they shot out across the clearing.

I didn't know then, couldn't know, what would happen to us. How our small resistance would grow and eventually become careless. How I would be selected to escape to the border, on a mission to find others to join us. How just days before the fall of the Khmer Rouge, many of my friends would be massacred in my absence. How I would find Darith stumbling on a road, stunned, as he told me how each of them, including Arun, had died.

I couldn't know. All I knew then was that the monkey king was gone and I'd never get near him again.

I looked up at that damn bird still perched in the tree, preening its wings. Its feathers gleamed blue and black. I looked for something else to throw at it.

"You, too! Go now!"

I fired a rock, and missed. It turned to gaze at me, opening and closing the hard sliver of its beak.

"Go!" I yelled again. I grabbed another stone the size of my fist, but before I could release it, the bird lifted off without a sound, rising into the sky. I flung the rock anyway, aiming at the space it had left on the branch. Then I picked up another, and another, hurling stones into the empty air.

JACOB RUBIN

University of Mississippi

LITTLE STONES, LITTLE PISTOLS, LITTLE CLASH

It's gotten better around the neighborhood since I cut my hair. Hipsters and random Australians playing acoustics on stoops have stopped yelling at me as I come up Bedford. A month ago, when I was hanging out by the East River in one of those almost parks between the warehouses, a Hasid tapped me on the shoulder and called me "music devil." A bunch of his bearded colleagues were creeping toward me and I had to do running-back shit just to get away. That same week a homeless dude charged me with a wrench outside Popeye's Pickle. But that's all in the past now. The crew cut helps.

Glen's got a new project, too. It's called Kiss Me If You're Asian. He wants me on board. I can't, I told him. These days I prefer strumming chords alone in my room on my small gurgly amp. Sometimes I sing, but usually I hum or just breathe with passion. What kind of animal blood does Glen have pumping through him? Tell me that. Where did he learn to crave disaster? He—he more than anyone—

should know that all you're ever building, all the Egyptians and the guys before them, the guys with the ziggurats, all they were ever building was the big pile of noise that falls on top of you when it all crashes down.

It all started when Larry Goldsmith, our lawyer, scheduled a meeting with Randy Kowalski from a company called Roaming Licensing Pro. A windy-ass March afternoon and I arrived a little early to the address Larry had given me on Sutton Place. The doorman took my name, rattled me up to the sixth floor in the old elevator, and there stood Randy in his doorway—a short pink person in ironed khakis and an immaculate dress shirt.

"Come on in," he said.

It was a sleek one-bedroom with wall-to-wall carpeting, and vertical blinds against the far wall, keeping all the light out and making the room feel very secretive. I wasn't sure why we were here rather than an office. A stereo hidden somewhere was echoing in Gregorian chants. It sounded like the sound track to a beheading. A slipcover curtained a piano-shaped thing by the blinds.

"A piano, huh?" I asked. "You play?"

He looked at me and then looked at the piano-shaped thing. "That's not a piano," he said. Then he smiled hatefully, like a game-show host. My eyes wandered to the lone photo on his glass-topped dresser. "My ex-wife." He loped over to it, loped back, and handed me the framed image of a smiling fifty-year-old woman on a beach. She wore sunglasses decorated with plastic mermaids.

"Cool," I said.

"No, it's not. Amstel?"

"Okay."

I took a seat on the couch. When Randy returned from the kitchen he had my bottle in one hand and a briefcase in the other.

He handed me the Amstel and said, "Scooch over," then sat next to me. "You must be just absolutely thrilled," he said. "What, working with one of the *Voice's* Five Bands to Watch."

As he talked he rubbed his hands on his thighs and I wondered if he were a kind of very polite sexual predator. You read about that sort of thing all the time.

"Yeah," I said. "They misquoted us, though. Glen didn't say, 'I'm going to fuck as many girls as God did.' He said, 'In my wildest dreams I screw like Jesus.'"

Without smiling he said, "That's great."

I sipped the Amstel.

Randy said, "Ian, nothing would waste both our time more than my sitting here pretending to care about your band or its garbage music. That is," he said, motioning, "a piano and on it I play the compositions of Chopin, Rachmaninoff, and other geniuses you've never heard of. Listening to your breed of rock music, for me, is like putting my ear on a grenade. I have no interest in it. What I *am* interested in lies in this briefcase here."

I was kind of stunned and said, "Okay, Mr. Randy."

He lifted the briefcase onto his lap and took his time entering the combination. There was a tantalizing click, and the top yawned open. He set it down between us on the couch. Inside there was a lot of Bubble Wrap, which Randy balled up with care and leaned over and placed beside the couch. I saw now that underneath the Bubble Wrap lay a single piece of paper. It had the word *sliche* typed on its top left corner and was otherwise blank.

Randy winked at me, and I knew now for sure he was a pedophile, and I was about to bolt for the door when Randy cleared his throat and in his calmest voice said, "*Sliche.* The word is *sliche.*"

I smiled.

"*Sliche.*"

I smiled again. It was joyous. A tickling under my knees and at the back of my neck. It felt like a million fairies were tending to my sensitive locations.

He said it a few more times until I was so tickled I had to cross my arms and rub my elbows against each other, with what I'm sure was a queer smile on my face.

"That's quite a word," I managed to say.

Randy smiled, this time with pleasure.

He explained it all to me in his living room but kept peppering the explanation with *sliche,* so it was hard to listen to it and not giggle and, say, think of daisies. His history in advertising. Slogan work. His search for a "crosslinguistic brand name." Words that work like music. Affects the brain, he said. Neurochemistry. A lot of it sounded like, "*sliche sliche* the Restoration *sliche sliche* money." He wanted us to put the word in a song and split the profits. "Guaranteed hit," he said. "Guaranteed."

He produced from the same briefcase a slim contract.

"I'll have to talk about it with the guys," I said, smiling like a baby in front of a mobile.

"Sure, sure."

He wasn't at all pushy.

I was feeling music. The word was music itself. He produced a sleek ballpoint from his pocket. I had to shake it a few times to get the ink to the nib of the pen before signing.

Time must've coughed at Randy's because it was blue night outside when I left. Rehearsal started at six. I ran to the A train. In those days we practiced at Cataclysmo Studios on Twenty-eighth. Glen didn't countenance lateness, and I kept mumbling *sliche* on the packed screeching train just to straighten my nerves. But it didn't work as well when you said it yourself, and I was convinced the magic had worn off. That I'd dreamed up poor, lonely Randy. Entered a kind of space-time break populated by savvy sexual predators. I once saw a *Star Trek* like that.

"You're out" is how Glen greeted me when I panted into Studio H. Egg crates and frayed black foam were tacked onto the walls. It stunk of ash. Phil lay on the floor, fiddling very seriously with his crotch. Through the wall you could hear the desirous and amateur sounds of bands cooking up their dreams. "Tale as old as time," he added. "A-hole shows up late to rehearsal. A-hole gets kicked out of band. Band makes millions. Fucks nations. A-hole cries in corner." Then to clarify, he said: "You're that a-hole."

"I can explain."

"A-hole explains. No one cries."

"I was at a meeting."

"Meeting," Phil mumbled and giggled and dug further into his crotch.

"Dude," Glen said, "this be a problem. If you can't juggle managing this band and playing guitar in this band Week Two. Then what about Week Four. Or for that matter, Year Ten when we're saving Africa. That's what happened to Rex. The fucker burned out."

"It was a big meeting. Really big."

Glen whisked his hair around like a dog coming out of a pool. "The only thing that's big in here is your bullshit attitude. Now I don't like repeating shit—"

I closed my eyes. "He wants us to write a song with *sliche* in it."

"Why didn't you say so? *Sliche*. Yeah. Kind of like microfiche."

He was smiling. It was like a photo where you catch someone at the absolute peak of a smile, and might've been unsettling if *sliche*, that simple angel, weren't in the air, gracing us.

"I like it," he said. "Like it a lot."

"Sliche," Phil agreed.

I smiled.

"Retard fucker, why didn't you say so?" Glen said and slapped me.

I smiled more.

We debuted it at Satchemo's Razor. "This is a little something called 'Unleash the *Sliche* (Por Favor),'" Glen said. Then we snarled into it.

Oh, boy, we taught 'em something. We were like priests of rock delivering a lecture to schoolboy heathens who had heard of God and his lifestyle but couldn't see what the big deal was until now. They howled and used their fingers to whistle or just stood there, stiff with passion. We were like cowboys who traveled through time to an era when they had Corvettes, then went back in time (with the Corvettes) and rode them through the Wild West until all our corrupt enemies and all the sweet corseted prostitutes went more or less ape-nuts because they'd never seen a Corvette before—and therefore had never seen a group of men rock a Corvette with such skill and such conviction. Oh, man, this is what it was all about. I did the Keith Richards. I did the Chuck Berry. My hips were animal. Do what you want, I said to them. Make a strawberry shake.

You could hear girl-hearts whimpering.

"Sliche is you / *Sliche* is me," Glen sang, and the fireball word blazed out of the speakers, over the enthralled crowd, and against the walls. We were melting the place. When we finished, the crowd was hooting and hollering and many were smiling ear-to-ear. They cheered so much we played it again. Then one more time. No one complained. I even saw Galt Heldrin, the Norwegian leader of Retard Riot, the scariest band on the Lower East Side—I saw him bobbing his head. Man, Galt spooked me. He made Glen look like Nelson Mandela. People said he knifed dudes all the time and once, when he was horny, forced his mom to give him a hand job. Usu-

ally when you heard stories of Galt he was breaking a chair over a sleeping person or taking a dump on a parked car, but he looked pleased hearing "Unleash," or at least sedate, like a dog awoken between naps.

After the show, backstage Glen bear-hugged me then noogied me and said, "You fucking prick! Fucker!" then slapped my face pretty hard, which was him at his most affectionate. Phil hugged me, too, and said *sliche* a few times in my ear. Phil was always retreating into himself. He had that gentle, stilted nature common to drug people. "What's that?" he said, pointing to something in the corner, then twisted my nipples when I looked. The three of us hugged. Backstage and sweaty! A bewildered crowd through the graffitied walls, and us hugging! How many times had I dreamed of it. Music is a mood. It's a sugar in the air and we were inhaling it!

We entered the electric dark of the front barroom at Satchemo's Razor like knights. She approached me like a sex-fiend goddess out of a dream of white lilies. I was standing at the bar when I heard a voice say, "You're fucking hot," and I turned and there she was.

"I know you are but what am I?" I asked her. Then I said, *"Sliche."* It was all just coming to me.

She purred. "Let's say you and me find a closet and mouth."

We did. She attacked me like a cougar from Mumbai. We wrestled against the mop bucket and brooms. We whispered *sliche* to each other and though we got raw and mean it all felt G-rated because of that clean word, I think, its purity. We nibbled and ducked like little children discovering their adult places.

"I go to a lot of shows, man. And nothing like that," she said to me after we found our way outside. Her name was Michelle. My feisty, pink-haired Michelle. Our cheeks were as red as Santa's hat in the spring night. I lit her cigarette. I wanted to protect her. "You guys have giant balls."

"Thank you."

"You need to be signed, man. I used to intern for Simese. You let me know when you're playing next, and I'll get some people down here."

"Oh, I'll get some down here!"

"What?" she said.

"Sliche."

"Cool. Gotcha." She smoked her cigarette. "Oh, shit. Here comes Heldrin," she said. "I heard he rapes his friends."

It was him all right, clinking toward us in a leather straitjacket and alligator boots. He looked like that actor Klaus Kinski, whom I once saw slap a horse in a movie, and the way he stared at us now with his jaded and hateful blue eyes, I was sure he was going to slap us both, or, say, mutilate us. He stared and stared. It was like he was trying to see through us in order to discern the shape and attitude of our skulls. He bared his teeth, growled at us, then strutted down the block toward Houston.

My heart.

"Wow," Michelle said. "Galt growled."

My heart was thudding. "Is that good?"

"Oh, yeah," she said. "That means he respects you. It's like some ancient code."

We recorded the single at Sound Haven Studios on Clinton Street. From the shabby glass-paned exterior you'd never have guessed how fancy and immaculate the studio inside was. Randy organized the whole thing. Called me with the place, said we had three hours of studio time, all paid for. The man knew what he was doing. Ever since I'd signed that contract it was like we had a fairy godmother fluttering over us. Larry Goldsmith wanted to know how it was exactly that Saturn and PlayStation were inquiring about licensing a song that hadn't been recorded yet. Word of mouth, I told him.

Best not to mention Randy. We had to forget that detail and move on. The future was reaching out its arms—we only had to grab on and get pulled forward. We were shuttling through the darkness on a train for glory. I was a part of the team. Glen no longer pantomimed retching when I entered the room and Phil in his coy way had signaled real intimacy. Walking out of Cataclysmo one night he and I saw a dead squashed pigeon behind a parked RV. "That makes me sad," he said. "Because it's dead." I nodded. He sighed and said, "Now I gotta find a doobie and smoke it."

When I absolutely had to, I referred to Randy as "That Guy." Like, "That Guy set up some recording time for us at Sound Haven," or "That Guy got us a gig at Plato's Orgy." Glen and Phil nodded as if I were referring to Fate himself. *Sliche*—it was easy to believe we'd grown that magic word ourselves.

And there we were at Sound Haven Studios, the kind of place you dream of, equipped with a green-ass pool table and a fridge full of oddly shaped beers with foreign-ass names. Dumbfounded fish milled about the epic tank. Surfboards had been mounted on the tan wainscoting just as decoration. And who of all people is manning the board but good ole Howie Churchill?

"What the fuck, my man," he said.

"What the fuck is right!"

We hugged.

Howie and I worked as engineers together at Toblerone Studios back when I was still playing with Bear Trap Accident.

"Look at you," he said. "The fucking Restoration. I heard that new single's kick ass."

"I heard your mom's dick is pretty cool, too," Glen said, then slapped him on the back and started laughing.

Howie looked at him, then realized he was supposed to laugh, and said, "Yeah. Cool."

We recorded the song in under an hour. How many times I had witnessed a session from exactly where Howie sat, how many times helped some freckled indie rocker lay down his mopey version of pop, and always knew, as I fiddled with the panel and tested the Shure SM58s, that it was *me* who burned, *me* who slept and ate with songs inside his limbs? And to stand below those tiered ceilings now, to slip the Sennheisers over my head and hear Glen growl *sliche* into the fist of my brain—oh, the delight. I preached through my Fender and felt my lonely soul fly somewhere far from this place.

After we finished I found Howie in the sound booth blasting "Unleash the *Sliche* (Por Favor)" on the Yamaha NS-10Ms. Nothing ever comes out as raw and wanting as it does on 10Ms. The sound just devoured the room. It was a beautiful gnashing machine of music and Howie and I were small inside it.

"God, that's a song," Howie said when it was over. He faced the Studor.

"We like it," I said.

Howie swiveled around in his chair and there was wetness in his eyes. He had an awed, almost converted look about him, as if he'd stared right at beauty and beauty had blinded him.

"You all right, man?"

"It's like everything we always talked about," he said. "The Resto-fucking-ration. You're doing it, man! You're fucking doing it! You're sitting right there fucking doing it!"

I should've known right then that some things are too good to be true. That sometimes music dupes you into thinking the world is more shimmering and electric than it is, and that you are more deserving of golden life than you really are.

"Howie," I said.

"What?"

But *"sliche"* was all I could say.

"Damn right," he said.

He played the song five more times on full volume.

I was a block from Señora Boing Boing's when I heard a voice say, "Your band's the shit."

This was Orchard Street, and when I turned I was expecting some frail hipster in a bowling shirt. Hipsters. They infested the area, making the world worse by adding to the clever people in it. I know because I used to be one. That life is being eager for bands, for tips and coolness. It's the disease of not being anyone in particular.

This guy was older, though. A graying ponytail drooped from his otherwise balding head. He wore a sports jacket over a Mickey Mouse T-shirt and those retro-futuristic black sunglasses people wear after eye surgery.

"Glen, right?"

"Ian."

"I know." He smiled, looked blind. "Want to get a soda pop?"

"I'm meeting friends."

"Archibald Vine." He extended his arm. "Call me Archie."

"I really gotta go."

He took off his glasses and changed his face. He looked like an actor playing a dirty cop on a TV show. He smelled like orange rinds.

"Quick quesh," he said, then, looking from side to side as if he were about to offer me drugs, asked, "How much is Randy Kowalski paying you for *sliche?*"

"Cynthia's a free soul in a free body. I give her free love. Everyone gets paid," he said. Then he lit the top of the hookah and dragged on the nozzle. "Randy's got OCD like a rat. Don't know if he told you that. Probably not."

We were lounging at Marrakech Village on Spring. Silk curtains veiled the many nooks, and a conspiracy, a midday darkness was going on. A few businessmen had a table to themselves, a few lazing hipsters, too. All of us were easing into the air of privacy as into a deep, deep couch. Sitar music tickled the room, and sleek waitresses sauntered about the tables. It was like a classy crack den. "Slim honey," Archibald said, as one waitress passed, "we're gonna need more of this apple cinnamon. It's pretty much changing my sphere."

"Sure thing, boss," the waitress said. She had a dot on her forehead.

"Cynthia, Randy's ex-wife?"

"Yeah. We're in love." He took another huge hit from the hookah. His face swelled up, then exhaled theatrically. "She rocks my world."

"And you used to work for Randy?"

He laughed. "Not *for*, kid. *With*. Prepositions."

"Well, that doesn't seem right," I said. I was thinking of how clean Randy's apartment was.

He laughed again. "I like your style, guy. Like your sound, too. Little Stones, little Pistols, little Clash. Could make better use of the high hat, though. Need that hat. Can't fear the most sacred of hats."

"Listen, Archie, *sliche* has done us good," I said. "I'm not trying to jeopardize anything." That word *jeopardize* seemed important.

"Hey, you want to live in a one-syllable universe. That's cool," he said. "Can't even say 'universe' in Kowalski's universe. Me, though, personally. I think it's all a bit"—he checked over his shoulder, then whispered—"*fandelfilly*."

Something in my eyes flinched.

"*Fandelfilly*," he said again and my throat hardened. My lips quivered. The bar around us shrunk and a sweet loneliness descended. It couldn't have been more obvious that all the huddled figures around their towering hookahs were just visiting—as we were all visitors—on a long trolley ride into death. All headed to darkness and gray nowhere.

"Fandelfilly," he said once more and I was weeping. I had to escort my naked and humiliated face to the bathroom and splash water on it. I stared at my hardened red eyes. After a few minutes, I'd worked it down to a frown and returned to the table.

"Where do you come up with this stuff?" I asked.

He pointed at his temple. "This beautiful machine."

We smoked for a half hour. I knew what he was going to offer before he did, and I felt bad about it, of course, but not as bad as I expected myself to. There was a truth in *fandelfilly* that I was tapping into. It was like being entrusted with a precious jewel. It seemed so right at the time. It seemed like the very seed of music was being planted in our palms.

"Why us?" I asked after many minutes.

"Honestly." He hit the hookah. "Demographics."

We spent a lot of time crying together. It brought us closer. The three of us formed a ring in our studio at Cataclysmo and took turns saying *fandelfilly*. When I said it, a tear eked out of Glen's eye and he jumped up and pranced around and started kicking at the bass drum with his cowboy boot, saying, "Goddamnit!" Phil rubbed his shins and rocked back and forth. It got to be too much. We were *inventing* sadness. But then somehow someone would say *sliche*, and we'd take turns repeating it and everyone would smile with tears in their eyes and it felt like we'd been through a war or a long disastrous cruise together.

After we debuted *"Fandelfilly, Fandelfilly"* at Agent Orange, Michelle said she loved me. She said, "I love you, Ian, and your hero's balls."

"Fandelfilly," I said and wept and we held each other with a great sincerity. *"Sliche,"* I added, and she barked like a terrier. We were young children, don't you see? We were fresh and dewed and didn't have to

know who we were. We found an old dusty bar and humped behind it. We kissed with time-ending passion and said our good-byes.

"A word, please" is how Randy greeted me from the chauffeured Mercedes. It was 1:30 by the time I left Agent Orange, so he must've been waiting outside a while.

"No prob," I said. I think I whistled. "No prob at all."

"I gave you *sliche*. Do you remember that?" he said, once I'd made the mistake of joining him in the backseat. It was a special edition Mercedes with facing seats. A partition separated us from the driver. "I *gave* it to you."

"Of course," I said, tightening my face so as not to seem cheery despite that impish word. The cab of the Mercedes jostled us not at all. Stone solemnity. It was like a room floating above the lonely public avenues.

"I gave you *sliche*."

"Randy," I started, then stopped. I wanted to say something but could barely bring myself to look at him. He must've suffered some attack. His forehead was a red and pimpled nightmare. Rashes had abused him. He looked like the "before" face in an acne medicine commercial. "Oh, man."

He scratched his temple.

We drove in silence.

"Do you know how I feel about Archie Vine?" he asked. He scratched more. It sounded like a mouse burrowing through a wall.

"You don't like him."

He started giggling to himself, looking around at the corners of the cab like he was bursting with amusement. "Oh, boy," he said. "You *are* bright!"

"Randy."

"Do you know that Archie Vine—did, did you know he's *fucking* my ex-wife?"

"Oh, no, Randy."

"Oh, no, Randy. Of course not," he said in my voice.

The door might've been locked from the outside. Randy had a way of seeming crazy, and I was hoping he'd say *sliche* again just to lighten the mood.

"No, you had no idea," he said.

Not only had I known, but I'd met Cynthia that night. Archie brought her to the show. Any fool could see why Randy longed for her. A woman's looks aren't about age, they're about energy, and Cynthia, by god, possessed life. She was giggling and winking at every little amusement and kept saying what cultivated heinies we all had. I wasn't sure whether Randy had seen her leave Agent Orange. Whether this was some kind of test.

The driver was winding us through the veiny streets of Chinatown.

"Do you know what it's like to lose your wife?" he asked me.

"Randy," I said.

"And to find out she's making woodpile with a ponytailed fucker like Vine?"

"It must suck."

"Suck! Fff!" He kneaded his small hands. "Suck!"

"Listen."

"*Fandelfilly*—ugh. So cumbersome. So Vine."

I was weeping now. "Randy," I said.

"I'm gonna bury you."

"We just want to rock."

"I'm gonna bury you deep into the ground."

"Randy."

"Buried."

"Please, Randy," I said, "don't bury us."

That's how the conversation ended: me saying, "Please, Randy, don't bury us," and him shaking his head, then laughing, then shaking his head again. Eventually he kicked me out of the car, which was a relief since I was sure he was luring me to a dungeon somewhere, the kind of place that's all lobster tanks and bantering deviants.

I watched him speed off. No question, it was sad. What can you say about a man with horrid acne driving around Chinatown talking to himself? The long neon McDonald's sign declared its light over dismal Canal. What did he mean, bury us? What could he do? I wandered around that shuttered world hoping to run into someone, so I could ask them to say *fandelfilly* and have that purifying sadness wash over me, but there was no one except the silhouettes of bums. I walked and walked and my phone buzzed in my jeans. "Ass queen," Glen said when I picked up. "Loft party on Grand."

It was only a few blocks away. Amazing how these gigantic lofts are tucked inside the most barren stretches downtown. Just a few blocks away from where I'd motored around with Randy, this place. I was like Alice, stepping through a mirror and tumbling into this world. A hip young artist named Damien Damien lived there, apparently. I was introduced to him—a foppish blond—but he might've been someone else. Tufts of human hair had been plastered to neon canvases. The ceilings could accommodate giraffes. Half-finished handles of Grey Goose, Ketel One, and Johnnie Blue had been scattered on mantels and counters. The women cleared the hair from their eyes as if they'd practiced many times in front of friends; everyone so beautiful, or so assured of their beauty that the reality of their looks didn't matter. I'd stepped through the mirror and ended up in this world that existed only in magazines and songs.

"Get over here," Glen said to me. He and a pack of confident, chittering girls were huddled by something on the windowsill. It was a radio, I discovered as I got closer, carrying in a frayed tin-can version of *"Fandelfilly, Fandelfilly."* It warbled into us like a communiqué from outer space. We all stood around the simple machine, sunk into our private melancholies. After it was done, many clapped. One Latina eyed me and Glen like we'd built a pyramid.

"I'm gonna get so many blow jobs in my life," Glen reflected.

"Where's Phil?"

"Retard," he said pensively and shrugged.

I wandered all over the party before finding him. He was lying on the kitchen floor, his head next to the fridge, absorbed in the world of his headphones. Some drunk dude could've opened the Sub-Zero door and accidentally bashed his head, but he was lost in his Stantons and didn't care. He noticed me after a few minutes and returned his face to this world. He smiled and proffered them. "Check it out," he said.

I slipped the headphones over my ears. There was a pause, then I heard it. It sounded like one of those tapes high school teachers use in Spanish class, the ones where a man with a deep but enthusiastic voice repeats *María va a la playa,* over and over, except this time it was Phil's voice and all he was saying was *sliche,* and then, after a pause, *fandelfilly.* I knew something was wrong with it, but it was soothing and cathartic and I had to ply the headphones off me.

"Cool," I told him.

"I know it," he said. "The world's really simple when you know what you like."

It was the most philosophical I'd ever seen him.

Who can say when things went south. What were the signs?

Our show at Apocalypse Day Care, when the bikers raised lighters as a joke and called Glen a succubus? The video shoot for *"Fandelfilly, Fandelfilly,"* when the director, some goateed hotshot Archie knew, asked us if the song were in English or what, and Glen saying, Your mom's mouth speaks English, and the director saying, Why don't you say that to my face, and Glen saying, Is this white thing your face, and me saying, We all have faces, guys, we can agree on that, and Phil, meanwhile, passed out from god knows what in the parking lot? Was it the cauldron of grumbles after "Unleash"? The boos after *"Fandelfilly"*? Larry Goldsmith calling me a "pubic situation" because he got us a gig at The Weeping Camel but heard we'd become laughingstocks on the street? Me feeling like a stupid prisoner in a stupid prison with a rotting secret?

There was, too, the falling-out between Michelle and me. Our body adventures gone clumsy. After another roller coaster of lust and redemption we'd find ourselves at different corners of a bathtub or grocery store trying to think of anything we could possibly say. I wanted to run away from her after we were through and I knew she felt the same, but didn't want her to, and so said *sliche* again and again, in hopes of old magic, but the word was just used-up air.

"That means nothing," she'd say. Then, "Hit me."

She wanted me to say *sliche* to her while lightly punching the back of her head.

I had done it once. In the basement. After our show at Apocalypse.

"Again," she said and waited, bent over, the back of pink bobbed hair facing me. "Give me hot love."

"Sliche," I said and punched the back of her head—okay, I did it twice.

"Oh, yes," she said. "And again, kind sir."

It was like she was waiting for the bus, albeit a bus she really wanted to come.

I wound up, I pulled my fist back. "I'm sorry," I said.

"Do it."

"I can't."

"Oh, c'mon, man." When she saw I wouldn't, she said, "I knew it."

"Knew what?"

"Don't play dumb, crone. You tricked me."

My stomach. "Tricked you?"

"I thought you were rock 'n' roll. You're not rock 'n' roll!"

"What am I?"

"Exactly!" she said, and stomped off.

I spent the time watching her pull up her Levi's and straighten her hair trying to think of what to say. Then she left.

None of it would have mattered if *dreffdreff,* Archie's latest brain-child, hadn't quailed. He promised it would make *fandelfilly* look like kiddie porn, that it would reduce our fans to a state of weeping mon-keydom. It didn't. Crowds stared at us like parents when we played it. Michelle said it made her feel like she was late for something. I knew what she meant. When Glen sang *dreffdreff,* I had to suppress the urge to bite my nails.

In a cab on my way home is when I heard the real problem, the real sign, howling through the radio. Sounded like a firecracker had been stuffed into the kick. Then the voice: a drugged-out cat rid-ing a scud missile—Galt, the Riot. "The Restoration is *framped, framped, framped.* The Restoration is *framped, framped, framped.*"

Who the fuck does the Restoration think they are, I was thinking, before I realized it was us.

"The Restoration is *framped, framped, framped.*"

"Restoration is a gay! Restoration makes it angry," my driver an-nounced before slamming us into a parked Volvo. He was still curs-ing and punching the horn when I stumbled out the door and down the block. *"Framped!"* he yelled, causing a pack of pizza delivery guys on the corner to turn and scream, "Eat it, shove it, fuck it!" then ride their bikes, like kamikaze planes, into the crumpled shell of the taxi. I wasn't bleeding but I was red in my mind. My pulse thumped in my knuckles, and I had to walk all the way up, forty blocks, to Columbus Circle to feel human. There by the edge of the park I found a pay phone and called Archie.

"Yup?" he said.

"Have you heard the new Retard single? It's Kowalski. *Framped.*"

He said, "Don't ever fucking say that to me again."

"You got us in to this. You said *dreffdreff* would work. *Fandelfilly*—nobody likes it anymore."

He said, "Neurochem 101. The buzz dies, my friend. The boys in research love *dreffdreff* and so do I. Hang in there with it."

"*Framped,* though. That's Kowalski. It's his revenge."

"Don't fucking say that!" Then I heard the dial tone.

While we were parking the van by the side door of The Weeping Camel, we noticed the police barricade across the street with the protestors behind it. It was mostly fifteen-year-old kids waving posters that said THE RESTORATION BE SO FRAMPED, or I PUKE. It was like a cult of rage.

"That's awesome," Glen said, sipping his Dasani.

A stubby figure ran along the front line, exhorting the protestors like a ballerina sergeant. Randy, I thought. Had to be—but I scurried into the cold backstage before I could identify him. I saw him everywhere these days—on the A train, at movie theater urinals—and it was never him. A few nights before I had a dream he laid me down on a pool table and read words that made my teeth hurt while Galt ground coffee in the background.

"Axl Rose hath been here," Glen kept saying in the greenroom. A large cooler of beer stood like a pagoda in the middle of the room. "Axl Rose hath in this room been," he said again.

The crowd through the wall sounded like a furious seashell.

I paced and paced. I guzzled beer but each one made me more sober.

I should've said it all! That's when I had my chance! Galt, *framped, sliche,* Archie, woodpile. The words were dancing on my tongue. I was waiting for the right moment to explain it to them, explain everything, but then Phil, who'd been drumming his sticks on his thighs, looked at us both like brothers and said, "Here we are, guys. Strike me dead, we made it."

I chugged my beer and couldn't say a thing. Phil, with his orange hair and orange freckles, Phil, who never looked the part—who seemed like he should be milking cows somewhere or being religious with virgins—Phil was so *happy.*

"Fuck, yeah," Glen said.

I smiled, too. I managed that. After all, had we not written songs that free people, free to listen to any song they wanted, chose to listen to? Were we not a band? Could some berserker Norwegian with a special word squash all our mojo?

By the time we exposed our three thin bodies to the searching lights and packed floor and mezzanine of The Weeping Camel, the crowd, four hundred strong, was whistling and clapping, hungry for us. Some stood there like cattle, antsy for the lightning to come and strike them. A lot of preening eager female faces, I saw, and beyond the sea of heads, a few guys in open button-down shirts leaning their elbows on the back bar. The reps Larry had sent, they'd come! The Weeping Camel! Here we were! The stage still sticky from decades of beer and merciless rocking. Glen and Phil and I all looked at each other just to believe it for a second, then beasted into "Unleash."

The sound system was a colossus. We shelled them with noise. Glen barked and caterwauled at the hopping, hair-wielding ladies, and me, well, I showed them what the fuck a guitar is. Got experimental. I did the Han Solo. Did the Dalí. It was over before we'd started. Phil smashed the high hat and the crowd was parched and throating, so we went right into "So Long to the *Dreffdreff,*" which opens with a Queen-esque fuzzed-out emancipation proclamation, a speech of love and destruction my fingers delivered to the sound-beaten walls. Then Phil dropped out and Glen started barking and the crowd joined in, too, a whole section of them pumping their fists chanting, *"Dreffdreff! Dreff-dreff!"* I did the Blind Man Crossing the Highway. I did the Marty McFly.

We destroyed the last note.

"Framped! Framped! Framped! Framped! Framped!"

It felt like someone had slammed a hammer on my toes.

"Framped! Framped!"

Stomping their feet. Pumping their fists. Like a Nazi rally. All of them.

Feedback screeched out of Glen's mike.

"Framped! Framped!"

He covered his ears. "What the fuck is going on?" he said.

"Fuck you, too," I said.

Two linemen in Anthrax T-shirts clambered onto the right side of the stage and leaped headfirst into the drum kit. A pack of *framped*-chanting businessmen and emaciated hipsters noticed this and started climbing onto the stage. Sneers and white rage were the faces.

"This way," Glen said, grabbing my elbow and rushing me through the wing, the dark hallways backstage, and out the service entrance into the balmy night. We heard the drum kit getting crushed and the echoing chants of *framped, framped, framped.*

Outside, the police barricade had been knocked over and the protestors were rushing through The Weeping Camel's double doors. The red letters in the marquee flickered on and off. We found Archibald and Cynthia at the corner of the street.

"This is craziness," I said to Archie.

"Hold that thought," he said and started walking toward the middle of the street where the barricade had been knocked over. A stubby figure was loping toward him: Randy. Oh, god, it *was* him.

Cynthia rubbed her hands together. "I love it when they get like this!"

"Right here, right now," we heard Archibald say.

"So be it," Randy answered.

It took place in the middle of the street with the rioting all around them.

They shoved each other a few times, then the words. Those possessed words going back and forth and thank god I can't remember them. One made you feel like an electron spoon had been tapped against your temple. Another made your lungs shiver. At one point someone said, *"plurm."* It went on like that until the squadron of cop cars arrived, and one cop shined his brights on them and got out of his car and split them up by force. They were taking full swings at each other now that they'd been parted, then Randy screamed something and disappeared into the night.

Archie pulled his lapels many times and retreated toward us. "Showed him," he muttered. Cynthia hugged him and made some ironic *oooi*ng sounds.

By then a stable of sirens was flashing and hooting over the scene. There must've been ten cop cars encircling the action, all those blue uniforms sprinting into and around The Weeping Camel. We watched in a kind of ecstatic daze as they handcuffed pairs of rioters and shoved them in a giant police truck. Cynthia kept patting her hands together like a child anticipating a gift, and I don't know how long we stood there, but at a certain point I noticed Glen was gone.

"Glen! Glen!" I tried. I wandered back to the service entrance, where I found him staring into space, that thing in his hand.

"I've got some bad news," Glen said. He was smoking a cigarette and looked dazed. Usually he only smoked after having intercourse.

"What's that?" I asked, pointing at the weird flannel thing in his hand.

"That's kind of what this is about."

"What *is* that?"

He looked down the street as if the words he was trying to find were down there somewhere. "Phil's elbow," he said.

It was like a bomb shelter in the waiting room, us huddled together under the bald fluorescent lights, just waiting to be hit. Out in the hall you could hear groaning and the beeping of important machines, but from where we sat there squeaked only the nurses' sneakers. After about a half hour the doctor entered, shrugged, and said, "Yeah, so, he's dead."

Phil's mom was crying so much the doctor told her to quiet down.

"Okay, okay, we get the point," he said.

She looked at him like he was a god. "My son is dead!" she wailed.

"Sons die every day, ma'am. Simmer down."

"WHAT?!!" she wailed more.

"You heard me."

She looked at him beyond astonishment.

He was fed up with us. "You people," he muttered, then stormed out of the waiting room.

"Fuck you!" Glen called after him, rubbing Phil's mom's back. She was rocking back and forth and squeezing the big brown purse that lay in her lap. You could see her knuckles turning white, she was squeezing it so hard. "Fuck you!" Glen screamed again. I wanted to say something reassuring but had no idea what that would be.

Archie and Cynthia seemed cowed, too, sitting in the orange plastic chairs with their heads down. Posters on the tiled walls showed people smiling in hospital beds, looking thankful. Archie chewed his gum at a remorseful pace. The fluorescent lights brightened every part of all of us and no one looked good. I was thinking about how when you thought of Phil now, it would have to be in the past tense, and I thought I might throw up because I had secretly tailored this entire situation and I was choking on all the silent words I'd never said. We all hung around there, alive and useless. Cynthia started singing this technoish cover of "Kumbaya" that was actually very tasteful when we heard a crumpling noise, and there stood Randy in the doorway with a bouquet of blue roses. He looked like an apologetic Martian, his face a horror of acne.

Without looking in the direction of Cynthia and Archie, he hobbled his way over to Phil's mom, knelt in front of her, and presented the bouquet. "My sincerest apologies," he said. "I knew your son only through business. He was a talented drummer, and I can only imagine what else. A small token of condolence."

Phil's mom gazed at Randy. Eyelashes stranded around her eyes. "Thank you," she said.

Glen looked appreciative, too, if a little suspicious since he'd never met Randy, who now turned to leave, sending a glare in Archie's direction. I followed him into the hall.

"Psst, Randy," I said.

"What."

"What are we gonna do?" I was whispering.

"We? Do?" He had a tic going in his eyes.

I made sure none of the nurses in the hall could hear me, when I said this: "*Framped.* That's yours. That's your word. You did this."

"That's a—that's a hefty allegation. Especially with no proof."

"I've got evidence."

"The contract." He smirked. "Have you read it?"

"Of course." Then I said, "Okay. What's it say?"

"Nothing incriminating. Nothing that mentions the word *sliche* or the niceties of the agreement."

He said the word now but it had no effect. I wanted it to—I wanted it to buoy me.

"Goddamnit, Randy! Phil's dead! Worse than dead!" This wasn't an exaggeration. They'd found pieces of him all over the stage. They found tooth marks on his ankle.

"That's rock and roll, Ian," he said.

"No, it's not!"

He stared at me like a complete fool and moved in so close to my face I could smell his forehead. "You really think this is the first time I've seen a dead someone?"

His eyes were wild. He paused with them that way to let his stare prove, I think, that I knew nothing about the real workings of the world, then he turned and limped down the hall, past the oval nurses' station toward the bank of elevators.

"Let him go," Cynthia said behind me, laying her hand on my shoulder. "He's won this round."

"What?!"

"There, there," she said. "To the victor go the spoils."

The zooming noises of the highway forced the rabbi to raise his already old voice. Whatever had surrounded the burial ground a long time ago, it was now a between place. Just beyond the fence of the cemetery, there was the highway, and on the other side of that, a minimall with a Wendy's and a grimy liquor store. It was gray and the grass smelled like bad wine.

Galt had stopped throwing rocks at birds to howl a little. He stood by the giant oak about ten yards from the grave. Even Rabbi Liebensthal seem to recognize his behavior as a legitimate, if obscure, ritual of mourning. It was like something from the Far East. He picked up pebbles and threw them at whatever birds roosted on the branches above, then howled to the sky in his leather getup. He was a wolf coming to join our mourning and no one begrudged him. I wasn't too hollow to be scared of him.

We all helped shovel dirt on top of the tomb. Each load made an uneventful sound. Poor dead Phil. Nobody knew what he really was, what he really wanted, and now he was dead. I don't think even he knew. You have to live much longer to know who you are, and now he was buried in pieces, another incomplete mound of bones and organs deep in the soil. It was all my doing. Dead rotting Phil was my fault. The police had interviewed us and written up the whole thing as some teenage riot. I managed to lie to them. Didn't even lie, really, because the truth seemed so absurd. They asked me questions and I said yes to every one.

When we'd finished with the burying, Phil's mom stood up to read aloud from his wish journal. I didn't even know he kept one. She was trembling in her black gown and veil. The marbled composition book shook in her hands.

"I wish to play the solo to 'Moby Dick' exactly the way John Bonham does it. I wish to have people say about me, 'He really rocked.' Maybe even, 'He was the best. Okay, or one of the top five.' I wish to know more about cheese and about physics, too, like the way the universe began—" she sniffled but kept on. Rabbi Liebensthal rubbed her back and made a sympathetic and encouraging face. "Note, I would like there to be world peace and no hunger, but I'm trying to be realistic. Otherwise there's no point to a wish journal." She turned the page. Tears welled up in my eyes and I must've been making sad noises because Glen patted my back. He was standing next to me in his red suit. "Be strong," he whispered. "We gotta be strong for Phil." But what did he know? What did he know about the sick cost of our stupid dreams?

Phil's mom continued: "I wish sex was as good as it is in movies and TV. I feel like that's kind of a big lie the corporations have made up so we all think—we all think"—she broke down and had to take a deep breath—"we all think if we spend enough money we'll have awesome relations with really hot and sexual ladies. I don't know. Maybe I haven't banged the right people." She was weeping full on, and I heard some whimpering within the procession like leaves being stepped on. "But the way I see it," she continued, "sex really isn't that different from asking your waitress for more coffee and trying not to sound like an a-hole when you do it."

The grief struck her down back into her chair and she hid her face in the shoulder of the man next to her. She was finished. They were sitting in plastic fold-up chairs around the area of earth where her son was buried. The highway hosted its loud auto noises. Glen was whimpering a little now, too, and I rubbed his shoulder and let him cry. I was crying, too. "It's all right," I said. "We're okay."

The rabbi then stood over the grave and intoned some things in Hebrew that none of us understood, though a fool could tell, just from the sounds, that they were ancient and meaningful. He chanted prayers in that muttered but moving way that rabbis do, and the sounds of that old punished language—it was beautiful. It felt like some wisdom was happening. And throughout the ceremony, Galt howled by his tree. We were all glad he was there. As strange as he was, we were glad. Making those noises, he sounded like a part of nature.

I would like to go back to school, though. There are subjects I want to learn more about. Cavemen, for instance. *Homo afarensis.* Neanderthal. All that stuff. I want to learn about their cultures. Because the way you always see them presented in the Natural History Museum, they're only wax figures with clubs—you get the feeling they had no customs at all, no rules. Was it really just that the strongest man got the most reproductive girl and the tastiest meat? What about the first guy to make fire? To rub two sticks together and watch that new orange thing take to life. That must've counted for something. Or the guy who had words for things? Who first walked out of the cave on a clear winter night and came back in to tell everyone that the stars looked incredible. Who said, Guys, you gotta come see this. The sky, well, yeah—so basically it's a miracle.

MEHDI TAVANA OKASI

Purdue University

SALVATION ARMY

The Field—May 1986

Here, these boys are kings. They rule this field where tufts of grass cling in straw yellow resiliency. The soil that once was dark and soft has become sickly, coating their pants and drying out their throats. Some blame this on the war.

The boys still gather each afternoon to play soccer. The teams—Esteqlal and Perspolis—are often reshuffled when mothers hold up their sons with housework. The captains—Ali (thirteen years, seven months) for Perspolis, and Sina (twelve years, eleven months) for Esteqlal—are always the same because they are the oldest. They do their best to divide the teams equally.

On this particular Sunday, only eleven boys come to play in the first game of five for the championship. Their schoolbooks are strewn along the sidelines like hastily removed clothing. Perspolis takes the field with five players while Esteqlal has six. Sina is allowed to play only if his seven-year-old brother, Erfand, is included. So Sina assigns Erfand to the position of goalie, where he will be out of the way, but not before hyping the position's importance. Erfand spends the time that they *do* play in a steadfast stance—legs set wide apart, arms extended in front of him, hands motioning everyone to stop.

With the game under way, the boys no longer notice the faded hues and torn edges of their T-shirts. They've learned to play in sandals, maneuvering quickly to slip one back on when it falls off. They live in their imaginations. The field is so green that it looks almost artificial. Their names are emblazoned on team jerseys. Each boy has his favorite number. They can imagine the roar of the crowd cheering for them. Here, in the space of a few afternoon hours, they forget their fathers' broken cars, the crack in the house's foundation, the scarcity of meat and how its absence at the table is measured by the shame in their mothers' eyes.

But on this day, neither team will claim victory. On this day they will not return for dinner, and when a sibling is sent to call them home, the field will be empty. When news of the boys' disappearance reaches the parents, mothers will flood the field, followed closely by fathers. They will see the abandoned soccer ball and the schoolbooks along the sidelines. The parents will know, instantly, that the image before them will blaze forever in their memories.

The Bedroom—March 1994

Heideh decides on this Sunday morning that the spring cleaning will begin in her bedroom. She woke feeling expectant, a sort of fluttering in her chest. The Persian New Year, the first day of spring, is two weeks away. There is much to be done, Heideh thinks, remembering her mother's cleaning strategy every Eid. She always staged a planned attack against the filth that accumulated throughout the house from the simple exertion of living. The cleaning lasted for two weeks, moving from the living room—the least lived-in space, its furniture reserved only for guests—to the kitchen. They dusted the ceilings, washed the walls, and had the rugs professionally cleaned.

In Malden, Massachusetts, Heideh's own living room on the first floor of a three-story house is very much lived in. Their two-bedroom apartment has molding that accents the living room ceiling, and tarnished yellow wallpaper inside the closets that depicts what Reza calls "Minutemen" in various postures of firing. If not for section eight housing, Heideh couldn't afford this apartment on her waitress's tips. She works at Mirage, an Iranian restaurant in Watertown. On a good night she makes eighty dollars. Her means are modest, but she cleans with ardor, as if her mother were standing at her back, running her finger over a surface to check for dust. It will begin here, with her bedroom closet, and finish in the kitchen. Anything she no longer uses will be discarded or donated to the Salvation Army.

She can hear her sons, Reza and Noah, watching television in the living room. She goes in to check on them and finds them still in their pajamas with bowls of cereal in their laps.

"Not on the couch," Heideh says. "Are you two going to pay to remove the stains?" Without looking at her, they both slide off the couch, sitting on the floor and placing their bowls on the coffee table. Their eyes don't leave the television as their spoons seek out the rainbow-colored cereal that crackles in the bowls.

Walking the short hallway that connects her sons' bedroom to her own, Heideh stops in Reza and Noah's bedroom to survey the cleaning that must be done. The landlord called this the master bedroom, although Heideh doesn't understand his logic: It is only slightly larger than the room she occupies. Despite her constant reminders, her sons' beds are unmade, their clothes tossed on the floor, books and toys piled in heaps. Heideh almost trips over Reza's backpack left in the middle of the room. It's a blue L. L. Bean backpack with his initials stitched in white lettering: R. T. He wanted it because everyone at school had one. It came with a lifetime warranty, which Heideh saw as evidence of Reza's commitment to education. The bag is unzipped, and when she picks it up by the strap, notebooks fall to the floor. Somehow the sight gives her a vague feeling of nostalgia. Reza, now twelve, is the same age as the students she once taught in Iran. But that was six years ago, in a life that she abandoned. *Abandoned* is exactly the word she employs when she thinks about her departure from Iran, never allowing herself to forget the ones she left to an undeserved fate.

Exactly six months before Heideh fled, her husband, Hassan Tehrani, a man twenty years her senior, was appointed Minister of Zoning. They moved into a mansion on the grounds of the Ministries' offices and Hassan Tehrani hired a domestic staff. He demanded that Heideh quit teaching because it compromised his integrity. They had appearances to uphold. But Heideh continued teaching geography to children in Karaj, a suburb thirty minutes north of Tehran where electricity and running water were luxuries. When Hassan Tehrani found her out, he warned her—"only once more will I say this, then, finished!"—but Heideh didn't listen. Then the boys went missing.

As she picks up the notebooks and replaces them inside the backpack, she sees a green piece of paper. It's folded awkwardly from being jammed between other weightier books: Reza's report card. She unfolds it and is stunned to see Cs in English and history. She slaps the side of her face in disbelief. Reza has never received Cs. She has been adamant about his grades. Heideh is not the kind of mother to ignore her son's education. Every evening she asks him about school. But standing with Reza's report card in hand, Heideh recalls that his answers have grown shorter these past several months. "What do you want me to say?" is usually how he responds when Heideh presses him about his classes. "You wouldn't understand anyway." The first time Reza spoke to her like that Heideh masked the injury by getting angry. But Reza retorted, "What do you want me to do, go over the entire lesson with you?" It was his tone that set her off, the under-current of frustration and annoyance directed at her. At first it baffled Heideh, but then she excused it because of his age, the changes he was going through. But here again before her eyes is evidence of his carelessness.

Reza and Noah laugh in the living room as the volume of the tele-vision swells. Did he intend to hide this from her, and if so, how might he justify it? He's had this in his backpack since Friday after-noon and now it's Sunday morning. She starts to the living room but hesitates. No, she will let Reza come to her. For today, she will give him the benefit of the doubt. She will let him finish his breakfast, and when they clean his room, she will give him an opportunity to confess. This will allow her to know her son, know what kind of man he is becoming. She places the report card back inside Reza's back-pack and returns to her room.

Looking inside her closet, which is neither deep nor wide, she pushes aside the blouses and pants she wears to wait tables at Mirage to get at the dresses in the back that she brought with her to the United States. For six years these dresses have sat in this closet in Malden. Since she began working at the restaurant soon after her ar-rival, she hasn't had occasion to wear them. Often Heideh works the lunch shift, then drives home to prepare dinner for Reza and Noah before driving back to work the dinner shift. When she gets home at night, Reza and Noah are already asleep.

She can't understand why she has saved the dresses. There was never any occasion, and now the dresses no longer fit. She has grown too large. She thinks about marching Reza into her bedroom and making him face these dresses, trying to make him understand everything she gave up to provide him with a decent life. But he would not understand. He would sense her anger and shut himself in, like a house readied for a hurricane.

She takes the dresses off their hangers and lays them on the bed, recalling Tehran, how the sequined silver dress was in fashion when she wore it to her cousin's wedding in 1976. A tan pantsuit, purchased on holiday in Vienna, still smells faintly of fried cilantro. Inside one of the pockets Heideh finds a folded piece of paper. It bears a child's handwriting. The words *What the Flag Means to Me by Ali Mohamadee* are centered at the top of the lined paper. Heideh sits on the bed; the surprise of this paper makes her fingertips tingle.

When she looks up from the page, the room distorts. The bottles of perfumes, lotions, creams, and lipsticks arranged atop her oak dresser seem like the skyline of a vast city. She looks out the only window in her bedroom to a small patch of grass no more than fifteen feet wide that separates her building from the next. The essay was written for a schoolwide contest about the newly designed Iranian flag. The principal had ordered the assignment to make the boys patriotic in the midst of a war that sent thousands of young men to their graves. A war that Khomeini could have ceased in 1982 when Saddam's forces withdrew. But for Khomeini it was about the conquest of Karbala. Theirs, he told the Iranian people, was the just cause. She chose Ali's essay to represent her class in the competition, not because it was sentimental, but because when read carefully, it called into question in a child's language the nature of the Revolution.

The flag is a symbol of our country. It stands for everything that has been sacrificed to make Iran. But our flag has changed; the symbol is no longer the same. My father says that is like erasing history, forgetting all those Iranians that came before us, those who fought for this country before we were born. Now, more men are dying for this new flag. I wonder, how will they feel if in another twenty years the flag is changed? Will they approve, or will something of our history be lost?

At the time Heideh read the essay she was disillusioned with the Revolution herself. Ali's essay didn't win the school contest, of course. The winning essay was written by a boy whose father was killed in the war.

Heideh refolds the paper and places it inside her dresser drawer. She does not know why she keeps it; neither can she justify throwing it away. Is his death a certainty? Perhaps not. Perhaps he lived. Perhaps he is alive in another part of this world, making a life, just as she is doing here in Malden, Massachusetts. How old would he be now? Twenty-one? Still, these thoughts do not completely banish the guilt that has swelled up in Heideh upon reading that essay, seeing his name across it, in his own handwriting. She cannot forget her responsibility in his kidnapping. Ten other boys went missing. All of them taken from Karaj. And all these years have not lessened Heideh's guilt.

But there is a task before her now and she will see it out. Today she will go through her house and set aside everything that is not used, or, rather, everything that can be spared. She will keep only the essentials. She will finish with her bedroom before moving to the rest of the apartment: Reza and Noah's bedroom, the living room, and the kitchen. But it is here, in her bedroom, where the forfeit begins.

The Vans

Chasing the ball down center field in a dust cloud, sweat streaking the sides of their faces and running into their ears, the boys do not hear the vans over their own shouts. When they do notice, it is too late to run. Both vans have pulled up onto the field, one in front of the goal where Erfand stands with his eyes closed, anticipating Ali's kick, and the other behind the boys. Before the boys can slow their fierce run to an amble, soldiers in faded green fatigues slide open the van doors and jump out, quickly blocking escape routes. Ten soldiers, five from each van. Each soldier quickly grabs a boy, except for one who, having tucked one boy under his right arm, walks around the van and grabs Erfand by the back of his neck. Teams Esteqlal and Perspolis are mixed as boys are pushed inside the vans. The dust that the vans first disturbed when they pulled onto the field has not yet resettled before they take off again, throwing up more earth in their wake.

They leave behind a field that within days falls into desolation and is called first The Lot, and later, when no bodies are returned, The Cemetery. Bereaved families visit on Fridays en masse to picnic on that faded earth, eating sweets and reading verses from the Koran. Inevitably there are tears, and since there are no gravestones to wash, they use the rose water on their own tear-streaked faces.

Inside the van, the boys are jostled about. It seems as if their legs are of no more use, the way they tremble. Three soldiers sit on the van's floor with the boys in the back. The other two, one driving, the other navigating, are up front. At first no one speaks. Some of the younger boys whimper. A few, including Ali, are silent. Then Erfand, who had been keeping goal for team Esteqlal and anticipating Ali's kick, turns to one of the soldiers and says angrily and with conviction, surprising the rest of the boys in the van, *You ruined our game! This was the championship, for god's sake!*

The Living Room

By the time Heideh has finished with her bedroom, she has filled two large Filene's Basement shopping bags with clothes, the dresses from Iran among them. She sets these by the front door before going into the living room.

"Boland sho," she says standing in front of the TV. "It's already ten thirty." On the television, cartoon robots transform into big machines that begin firing weapons at one another. Reza and Noah are curled up on opposite ends of the couch. Their cereal bowls sit on the coffee table, holding shallow pools of pinkish-colored milk.

"Mah-mahn, we're watching this," Reza whines. "It's Sunday." He doesn't lift his head from the armrest of the couch. Noah rests his head on the other armrest; their feet meet in the middle. Heideh tries desperately not to lose control. She will deal with the report card in time. Reza will account for himself.

"We have only two weeks left before Eid. There is too much to do and I need help. I have only two hands."

"So? We don't have to do all this cleaning every year. You're the one who makes us. I mean, who cleans the ceiling anyway?"

"Look." Heideh almost shrieks pointing up at the ceiling. "Spiders are building palaces and you're questioning me? You want to start the New Year in filth? Is that what you want?" Lately, it seems that Heideh is always raising her voice, asking twice, maybe three times, before anything gets done.

"I don't care," Reza mutters.

"What?"

"Nothing," Reza says quickly. "Wha-do-you-want us to do, anyway?"

"Go through your room and put aside the clothes that are too small. Gather up your toys. We're taking everything we don't need to the Salvation Army."

"But I need all my stuff," Reza says, returning his gaze to the television. "I still use everything."

"Reza, your closet is filled with shirts I haven't seen you wear in years. And all those toys! You should be ashamed. You're almost thirteen and still playing with little action figures!"

"Those aren't mine. They're Noah's."

"Don't put this on Noah. He's not dancing little plastic men around the room by himself." Reza is still not looking at her. Heideh thinks about snatching the remote from his hand and smacking him over the head with it. Instead, she says his name with a tone at once cautionary and threatening.

"Fine. Just let us finish this show. There's only twenty minutes left," Reza says. Then, with what Heideh perceives as a truly American tone, he adds, "Come on, Mom." Noah quickly echoes, "Yeah, come on, Mom."

"Twenty minutes," Heideh concedes. "And I don't want to hear any complaining when you help."

She stands a moment looking at the living room. This is her life, what she has made of it. When they first moved into this apartment they had little furniture and the near-empty rooms stood as a measure of the loneliness Heideh felt in her heart. But over weekends Heideh began to frequent yard sales in Boston's wealthier suburbs, and from other people's lives she bargained items to salvage her own. Crystal table lamps, silk throws, accent pillows, paintings of ocean towns, artificial flower arrangements, Ceylon brass candleholders, glass figurines postured in dance, artistic picture frames. Every item she purchased reaffirmed her faith in a future for her sons. The beauty of these objects comforted Heideh, as if, like a cocoon, the decor would protect her sons against the squalor of their neighborhood, inspiring them to grow into respectable, affluent men.

Heideh notices a framed picture of Noah's birthday party on an end table. People crowd around the dining room table on which Heideh has laid out three different stews, two kinds of rice, dolma, salad Shirazi, a roasted chicken made golden with saffron. Standing at the head of the table, Heideh has one arm around either son. Noah leans into her, his birthday cap jammed into her breast, but Reza's gaze, she notices, is turned away, like he is trying to break from that posture. Heideh notices how her own smile tapers off at the corners of her mouth in fatigue.

Framed school pictures of Reza and Noah sit atop the entertainment unit. They smile like children who have never known war, who, in fact, have no memory of lives other than their own. Standing at the edge of the living room, Heideh notices how easy it is for Reza to betray her, how unburdened he seems watching his television show. What does he know of duty? It was foolish, Heideh thinks, surveying the living room, to place her hopes on furnishings.

The Drive

At one point, the vans pulled over, and the boys are now consolidated into a single van. The boys have lost track of time, but when the doors were opened, Ali noticed that it was getting dark. The soldiers in the second van didn't board the first. Now there are eleven boys and five soldiers. There are no windows in the van, so they cannot tell where they are. Ali realizes, looking into the faces of his friends, that he's never seen them really frightened before. Ali's parents had warned him about boys being grabbed and made to fight in the war. He hadn't thought that it could happen to him. He took the warnings to stay close to home for overblown caution. But here he is huddled in a speeding van, cornered by older men who smell of ripe onions and moldy bread. Men whose experiences Ali recognizes in three-day stubble, in legs splayed wide apart to accommodate bulges they constantly readjust, in the way their eyes perceive the boys' fears with the same curiosity that a cat shows toward a languishing mouse.

Sina, the second oldest, has become protective of his younger brother, Erfand, whispering reassuring statements into his ear. Erfand curls up and lays his head on his brother's lap to sleep. The other boys hug their knees tightly to their chests and Ali notices how this makes them look smaller. Ali thinks about his mother and how she'll be in the kitchen now, steaming the rice, stewing potatoes in a tomato and onion broth, and wondering what has kept her son out so late. Soon she will become frantic, and Ali worries how that will affect her blood pressure.

"Don't look so afraid," one of the soldiers speaks up. He's taken off his green cap, revealing a buzzed head. "You're about to have an adventure." He laughs at his own joke, but he is the only one.

Being confined induces the need to know the time. As the van speeds on, the boys can hear the blare of horns. They wonder where they are. Mostly, they feel the vibrations of the van floor as it trembles beneath them. Huddled together away from the door, the boys can hear each other breathe. How quickly they were usurped.

The soldiers sit by the doors of the van, their legs outstretched, talking about their hometowns and when they'll be back, what they miss most. They rest their rifles between their legs.

"I don't know about you two, but when I get back to Hamadan I've got prospects," the first soldier says. He's got bright green eyes that stand out against his olive skin.

"What kind of prospects?" the second soldier asks, adjusting his belt over his large belly.

"You think I'm simpleminded like a Turk? I'm not telling you," green eyes replies.

"Ha," the fat one laughs. "You guys from Hamadan are all the same, thinking you're better than everyone else. Probably you don't even have a prospect. You're just showing off."

"I do indeed have a prospect and don't think you can trick me with your Turk ways. I know your kind. If a donkey stood stock-still in the middle of the street, you'd heat its ass with your own breath to get it moving."

"Cut it out," the third soldier speaks up. He's wiry and wears a pair of crooked glasses. "Can't you just agree that he's got prospects," he says to the fat one before turning to green eyes, "and can't you just accept that the Turks are craftier?"

"Oh! So the guy from Esfahan thinks he has all the answers," the fat one says.

"Your kind," green eyes points to the wiry one with the crooked glasses, "is the worst of all. You'd have us beat each other senseless and then steal both our prospects."

From the look of them, Ali thinks, they aren't too old. But he has only a vague sense of their age, knowing that these soldiers are much younger than his father, but older than any of his friends. They look dangerous holding their rifles. Green eyes notices Ali watching him and asks, "Your father a Turk?"

"No," Ali says.

"Where's he from then?"

"Abadan." Green eyes starts to laugh and the other two join in. Ali doesn't know what he's said that's funny.

"Were you born there?"

"Yes."

"How long have you been living in Karaj?"

"We moved when I was ten."

"How old are you now?"

"Thirteen years and seven months."

"Have you been back since?" Green eyes is smiling now, and Ali believes that he's pleased.

"No."

"What's your name?"

"Ali."

"Well, Ali, welcome home."

The Kitchen

Heideh takes out chicken thighs from the freezer and places them in the sink to thaw. She scoops three cups of basmati rice into a bowl and fills it with water. She gently runs her fingers through the rice; the starch washes from the grains. She empties the water, cupping her hand against the side of the bowl to prevent the rice from falling out, but some grains are always lost. She refills the bowl and repeats so that with each wash the water becomes less murky, until, finally, she fills the bowl one last time and sets it aside to soak for dinner.

She stands in the middle of the kitchen. The sound of the television in the living room infringes upon the silence. When life seems most hopeless, Heideh retreats to this room. Here the days seem manageable, uncertainty giving way to the practicality of cooking.

Vegetables are chopped, ingredients are mixed, and from disparate parts a single dish is made. Sometimes Heideh asks herself why she labors to cultivate in her sons love for a culture they do not understand. It would be easier to assimilate completely. To place frozen dinners in the oven, let them befriend other children whom she is never to meet, and speak only in English instead of perpetually reminding them to address her in Farsi. Yes, it would be easier to step back and watch. But that isn't the way Heideh was raised. She cannot shake the thought that one day her sons will be men and want to know where they came from. Even if they do not recognize it now, the day will come when an American will turn to them and ask, "Where are you from?" And that question will invert everything her sons understand about their identity. Because no matter how fiercely they claim this country, it will never claim them back. And God forbid that Heideh is buried by the time her sons finally realize this, because there will be no one to guide them back to themselves.

Heideh turns to the cabinets. She takes down a set of twelve dinner plates decorated with purple irises. The irises have faded; two of the plates in the set are chinked. She takes out a stack of newspaper from the recycle bin and begins wrapping them. She will buy new plates for the New Year. A week after they moved into this apartment, Heideh realized she had a space of her own, rooms that she could adorn as she pleased. Hassan Tehrani, her husband, wouldn't ever be able to find them. In leaving him, Heideh abandoned a life of maids and drivers, but it was also a tense life, one in which she feared Hassan Tehrani's easily provoked anger. Now, six years later, wrapping dinner plates in newspapers that blacken her hands, Heideh thinks about Hassan Tehrani's warning. It was before the boys went missing. Before she knew his part in it.

"You will not make a fool of me," Hassan Tehrani said. "Tomorrow our driver will take you to the school and wait while you hand them your resignation." He stood in their bedroom. The children were asleep. His blue silk pajamas seemed to fill the room. "Enough is enough. As my wife, you have an image to uphold."

"What does my teaching have to do with you?"

"It is below us. People think you work to get away from this house. It is an embarrassment to me. You are the wife of the Minister of Zoning! How do you think it looks to have you teaching geography to village children!"

"I don't teach for the sake of appearances. Your concern is meaningless to me." Heideh was accustomed to their arguments and had perfected a tone for these instances, calm but not placid, firm but not hysterical.

"On this issue," Hassan Tehrani said turning away, "there will be no more discussion." If only Heideh had listened. If only she had subdued her pride, relented to his will, then perhaps those boys would have met some other fate. But she didn't listen to him. Instead, she learned to conceal her whereabouts three mornings a week with the help of her driver and nanny. She continued to teach geography, until Hassan Tehrani discovered her lie. Had Heideh known exactly what he was capable of, she would never have taken such risks.

The boys were abducted on Sunday, after morning classes. The next day when Heideh went to school, she noticed that several of her students were missing. That Ali wasn't in class alarmed her. After the bell sounded, Heideh asked her driver to stop in front of Ali's house. The moment she got out of the car, she knew something was wrong. The courtyard gate was open and she could hear wailing. Ali's younger sister was kneeling at the threshold of the courtyard, drawing on the ground with chalk. She looked up at Heideh and said with the cheerful innocence of a four-year-old, *"Ali rapht."* Ali, gone, as if he were off on an adventure.

At the dinner table that night, between spoonfuls of stew-soaked rice, Hassan Tehrani asked, "How was your day, my darling?" Immediately, Heideh knew that he was involved. His tone, the smile of perceived victory on his face, the words *my darling,* delivered like a knife. Heideh learned, from his own lips, that he had hired someone to follow her. The hired man had identified her students and given their names to him. He had learned that after school, the boys went to the field to play soccer. He needed only to make the call to his friends in the Revolutionary Guards.

The night Heideh fled, Reza was six and Noah was four. Their driver, Agha Akbar, a kind and decent man, had been the one to introduce Heideh to the man they called Tomas. Tomas arranged their escape for an exorbitant price, money that Heideh got by selling her jewelry. The night Heideh fled, Hassan Tehrani was hosting a party with some three hundred guests. Agha Akbar removed Reza and Noah from their beds and took them down the back stairs and placed them in the car. They slept through the first part of their journey, but at the border to Turkey, Heideh woke them. Tomas had a truck waiting. They hid inside among cartons of pomegranates. Once they crossed the border, they dismounted the truck and got into a car waiting to take them to Istanbul. Tomas met them there, where they pled political asylum.

By the time Hassan Tehrani discovered that his wife and children were missing, Heideh and her sons had crossed the border. He was too proud to call the police. Heideh had left him a note. Later, from the safety of America, Heideh learned through her mother that Hassan Tehrani made no attempt to track them down. Instead, he claimed that his wife and children went missing on a trip to the Caspian. He held a funeral. That was the kind of man he was. Two years later, he remarried.

Heideh finishes wrapping the last of the dishes and places them into plastic bags. She begins going through the drawers. They seem too cluttered. She works with haste, her heart quickening as she empties the contents of entire drawers into plastic bags. If only she had avenged those boys instead of fleeing. If only she had gone to their parents and told them her husband was the man responsible and left Hassan Tehrani to their angry hands. Heideh's fear for her own sons had stopped her. It would not have been below Hassan Tehrani to divorce her and claim sole custody, preventing her from ever seeing them again. Heideh turned her back on justice and her duty to those boys and their parents and left. No, abandoned. And even though it burned a hole in her stomach, Heideh endured. Being a mother, she soon understood, was about knowing what to forfeit.

When she woke Reza and Noah at the border into Turkey, she told them that there had been an attack during the night. Bombs destroyed their house and killed their father. They were lucky to have escaped. Now they would be going to America. To her surprise, Reza and Noah just looked at her blankly, no trace of emotion in their sleepy faces. *Do you understand?* she asked them. They nodded. Then, when Reza opened his mouth and said *I'm hungry,* Heideh realized that she was all her sons understood. They didn't ask about their father until years later, on a Saturday night, Heideh remembers, when they were watching a movie in their Malden apartment. The father on screen was becoming exceedingly frustrated with the family dog, but because of his children's love for the animal, he relented. Noah turned to her and in the most casual of tones asked, *Do we have a father?* It angered Heideh that she had to martyr Hassan Tehrani again.

"Yes, you had a father. But he died saving us from Iraq's bombs. He got us out of the house in time, but he couldn't save himself."

"So he is like a hero?" Noah looked at the television where a giant Saint Bernard was wreaking havoc on the kitchen.

"Yes," Heideh answered her son flatly. "He is like a hero."

The Gymnasium

Here, the boys are at the edge of everything they know. The town is Abadan and it borders Iraq. Some twenty miles to the west is enemy territory; the Persian Gulf is to the south. When the van stops and the boys disembark, what they see is not a town. Ghosts must live here, Ali thinks, looking at the crumbled buildings and empty streets, overturned and half-burnt palm trees. This is not the Abadan of his childhood. The soldiers take them into what looks like a school. They enter a gymnasium where hundreds of cots are laid out. Inside, to the boys' surprise, are hundreds of other boys, grouped in clusters or lying in bed.

"It looks like a camp," Sina whispers to Ali. "Why are we here?"

"This is where we get ready to fight," Ali says, realizing the meaning of those words as he speaks them. The room smells heavily of stale undershirts and boiled meat. Teams Esteqlal and Perspolis are told to line up in front of a table, where several soldiers take down their names and ages, then hand each of them a pillow, blanket, and a metal bowl and spoon. They are told to look for an empty bed. The boys manage to find beds near each other. Erfand, Sina's seven-year-old brother, is not at all scared. As soon as he sets his new possessions onto a bed, he wanders off to join a group of boys in one corner of the gym who are kicking a soccer ball around.

"You are children of what village?" Ali looks up at a boy sitting on his cot. His bed is made and his spoon and metal bowl sit next to him. "I'm a child of Bandar Abbas. My name is Zoha. I'm thirteen, but I'll be fourteen in two months." His skin is dark. He almost looks Indian. And he speaks with the regional accent of southern Iran, high pitched syllables that run together so that it's difficult to understand where one word ends and another begins.

"I'm Ali. We are all from Karaj," he signals to the rest of the boys. "How long have you been here?"

"We came yesterday."

"Did they grab you, too?" Ali looks around to see whether any soldiers can hear.

"No. I signed my name to a list."

"What list?"

"The list the soldiers brought to our school. They came and talked to us about the war. They said that if we do not fight, the enemy will invade and kill our mothers and sisters," Zoha says placidly. "So I signed my name. Most of the boys from my school did, too. Didn't the soldiers come to your school?"

Ali hesitates only a moment before speaking. "Yes, they came to our school, too." When Sina looks at Ali quizzically, Ali tells him under his breath that it is too late to escape. Here, the boys are among those who are ready to die. In the face of such zeal, there can be no compromise. Now they must fight.

"My older brother has been martyred," Zoha says. "When his body came home, the neighborhood cried for him for three days. Everyone stayed up late at night and people kept coming to our house with food. They placed a large picture of my brother on our street and decorated it with flowers and lights. Everyone knew his name. I want to be like him." Zoha's speech is too calm, Ali thinks. His hair has been buzzed short and his yellow T-shirt hangs from his body. He holds a rosary in his hands, moving the beads while he speaks to Ali. "Do you have a brother in the war?" Zoha asks.

"I only have three sisters and they are younger."

Zoha nods knowingly. "Do not be afraid, Ali. You are going to become a martyr and everyone knows martyrs go straight to heaven." Zoha looks at Ali fiercely, as if suspecting his allegiance.

"I'm not afraid," Ali says. Zoha hesitates a moment before smiling. Ali wants to ask him whether there is any way to contact his family, but he doesn't; to express a desire for his family now would make these soldiers think less of him. "How long will we be here?" he asks instead.

"I do not know," Zoha says. "When the colonel decides, we will go to the border." Neither boy says anything, and just as Ali is about to move away, Zoha asks, "Have you seen Ayatollah Khomeini?"

"No," Ali says. Zoha looks disappointed. "Have you?"

"Not in person. But I have seen his face in the moon, just like everyone said I would." When Ali looks at him with disbelief, Zoha's voice gets stern. "You have to believe and look hard, but he's there. I saw him. Believe me." His zeal frightens Ali.

"I believe you," he says.

From across the gymnasium, a soldier with a thick beard yells for the boys to line up for dinner. Zoha picks up his metal bowl and spoon and stands up to go. Ali watches as the boys, some as old as sixteen, some as young as eight, pick up their bowls and move to get in line.

"What do we do now?" Sina asks, eyeing his brother, Erfand, who is vying for the soccer ball among a group of older boys. Ali turns to Sina and can see that he is doing his best to hold back his tears.

He wants to reassure his friend, but lacking the words with which to do so, Ali says flatly, "Do not cry," before picking up his metal bowl and spoon to get in line. When they reach the front, a soldier empties a stew of potatoes and some sort of meat in tomato broth into their bowls. They are each handed a piece of bread.

Reza and Noah's Bedroom

The room that Reza and Noah share has twin beds at opposite ends, a single desk, and nightstands that hold matching lamps. There is one window that looks out onto the neighboring brown house.

When Heideh calls Reza and Noah to clean, Reza picks up his backpack from the middle of the room and places it next to his desk before sitting on his bed. He says nothing. Heideh opens the closet. Inside hang her sons' clothes, one half of the closet allotted to Noah, the other to Reza. Their toys, action figures and colorful plastic pieces that Heideh cannot identify, sit in a yellow bucket. The entire closet is far too cluttered. She begins removing clothes and throwing them in the center of the room. Heideh does not feel like herself. All these years, she thinks, have been reduced to this house, to these things. What does it mean? Noah picks up a G.I. Joe action figure and runs him across the floor, pretending the clothes that Heideh tosses in the center of the room are bombs. He makes explosion noises as each item of clothing lands before him. Heideh pauses in her work and looks at Reza. She can't believe he hasn't confessed.

"Do you have any news from school? Anything to tell me?"

"No," Reza says without looking at her. So this is how my son lies, she thinks. His voice does not even quaver. Heideh cannot play this game. She marches over to the desk and grabs Reza's backpack, pulling the report card from inside.

"What is this?" she asks.

"Oh. I forgot to show you. It's my report card," Reza speaks more softly now. She can see him feigning forgetfulness.

"Forgot? You forgot or you were never going to show me?" Heideh is standing in front of him now. Reza still sits on his bed, leaning back and away from her. Noah stops his play and kneels to watch his mother.

"No, Mah-mahn, I swear I forgot." His voice betrays his fear.

"Two Cs, Reza? You got two Cs? Why would you do this to me? You know how important this is. Why?"

"It's not that big a deal, Mah-mahn. C is average. Lots of kids in my class get Cs."

"No big deal? No deal?" Heideh can feel herself losing control, her tongue refusing to cooperate with the torrent of sentiments she wants to communicate. "It is a big deal. It is everything!" She wants to say more, but she can't, because if she opens her mouth the past that she's kept hidden will escape. Instead, she turns from Reza and goes to the closet, pulling out more toys and clothes, speaking more to herself than to Reza. "How can you not understand? How can it matter so little after everything that I have done?"

"Mom, what are you doing? That's my stuff!" Reza protests suddenly, realizing that the clothes in the quickly growing pile on the floor belong to him.

"Not one word," Heideh screams from inside the closet. "This is too much. My own son is breaking my heart." As she pulls Reza's belongings from inside the closet, she thinks about Ali. How beautifully his essay alluded to duty, to tradition, to the importance of remembering those who came before. Both of Ali's parents were illiterate, and when Ali stayed after school for more instruction, he confided in her his dream of lifting his family from poverty. He wanted to become a doctor. But duty is not a concept her Reza understands. He does not realize that being in America is not a right, but a privilege earned through sacrifice.

"Mom, this is crazy." Reza is standing behind her now, looking with disbelief at the pile of clothes and toys in the middle of the room. Heideh ignores him. Noah, who is kneeling before the quickly growing pile, turns to Reza and says, "Don't worry, you can share my toys."

"I don't want your stupid toys."

Heideh is too upset to hear their exchange. The first day Ali came into her classroom she handed him a geography book and asked him to read about North America. He looked up at her, his eyes a sea of expression, and said, *Excuse me my ignorance, Ghanoom Tehrani, but I cannot read. I am a servant to your instruction.* He did not wince or avert his gaze when the rest of the class burst out laughing. Heideh glances at the floor. Look at these toys!

"Mom!" Reza shouts again. "You can't just give all my stuff away."

"Reza, do not raise your voice at me." Heideh empties the entire contents of the yellow bucket into a plastic bag.

"Why are you doing this? This is so unfair." Reza's whining rings in Heideh's ears.

"Is it fair to me that you get Cs and think everything is okay? I didn't bring you to America to get Cs! You must be the best because your being here means that another boy isn't!"

"What other boy? What are you talking about?" When Heideh doesn't answer, Reza says, "You're being crazy." He grabs the bag full of toys and moves to his bed. "I won't let you take these from me. They're mine."

Then, before Reza can drop the bag to shield his face, Heideh comes at him. She descends with both hands, beating him so hard that she surprises even herself. In the thirteen years that she has raised Reza, she has never seen anything ugly in his face. But now, in this instant, in this room, here, he is grotesque. Eyes that always inspired motherly love in Heideh look, in this moment, both beady and ominous, like those of a cornered rat. Even when he falls to the floor, his hands attempting to cover his face, Heideh does not stop her attack. She pulls him up and presses his arms down to his sides. He is crying. But these are not genuine tears. They are selfish, self-serving. Heideh cannot stop herself. She slaps him again. One. Two. Three.

Then she stops. Words are coming. She feels them in her throat. *Nothing is yours! You hear me? Nothing!* Then Reza's eyes reemerge in Heideh's vision. They are colored an almond brown. His eyelashes are long and tears cling to them like dew beading on leaves. She releases him and he stands there shaking.

"Get a trash bag and put everything I give you into it. Everything here is going to the Salvation Army. There is nothing more to discuss. You hear me? Nothing."

The Colonel and His Golden Keys

You are soldiers now, men of Iran. Here, you stand for your country. Here, you defend the blood of your fathers and our glorious Revolution. In your hearts you must find courage. You must face the enemy without fear. For fear in time of war is like poison in your veins. Fear on the battlefield will kill you. You must not let it overcome you. Think of your mothers and sisters at home. From their plight you must gather strength. Iran needs you and you must be willing to lay down your life for her. Now some of you are younger than others. But on the battlefield years do not matter. What matters now is that you fight and fight hard. Know this: Even the smallest among you can find the strength to change the course of history.

The enemy is treacherous. The enemy will not show you mercy because you are young. You must not for one moment hesitate. In this war, there will be no retreating. But know this, soldiers: Allah is on our side. Allah will watch over you because you fight his battle here on this earth.

Find comfort in this fact: Life does not end here. Should your body be broken, and your blood spilled, it will only water the ground for generations that flower after you. Your soul will fly. It will return from where it first came. Should you fall, you will have martyred yourself for Iran, for Islam. There is no greater accomplishment in this world. Nothing greater. To lay down his life for Islam is the noblest thing a man can do. Yes, soldiers, there is nothing more worthy than being a martyr for Islam.

Here, in my hand, I hold a golden key. Each of you will be given one of these on a chain to wear around your neck. Do not lose these keys. Do not give them to anyone. For should you fall on that battlefield, these keys will unlock the gates of heaven. With these keys you will enter paradise, where life will roll before your eyes unlike anything that you have ever seen. The shell of your body will fall and gravity will not touch you. You will float in a paradise of green lush hills. Beautiful virgins will surround you and see to your every desire because they will know that you are a martyr. Your place in heaven will be one of distinction. There is no love like the love of Allah, so fear not, soldiers. Do not let doubt enter your hearts. Fiery is our will. Devout is our faith. Let your hearts burst with love for your countrymen, for love of Iran, and for love of Allah.

The Car

In silence, they drive the seven miles to the Salvation Army next to the Johnnie's Foodmaster. Their red Hyundai is packed with possessions to be given away. Reza does not meet Heideh's eyes. He sits in the backseat instead of in the front, which is his way of swearing at her. She will let him be angry. Noah plays with the radio dial and settles on a song by the Beastie Boys.

"Reza," he says turning in his chair, "this is the song you like. 'Sabotage!'" Reza ignores his brother, staring intently out the window. Noah turns back around to face forward. He rocks his head to the music, stumbling over the words. Heideh reaches over and runs a hand through his hair.

Later tonight, when the kitchen fills with the smell of sautéed onions and frying chicken, once the wet heat of steaming rice fills the empty corners of their apartment, she will call Reza to her. She will look into his face and try to explain. That there was a boy. That he was poor. That when she taught him geography, pulling down maps of the world where countries appeared in vibrant colors, she knew, in the bottom of her heart, that he would never see any of those places. That he would never leave Iran. Then she will tell her son how one day that boy was taken away.

The Border

They are brought to the front lines in truckloads. When the trucks stop, the boys dismount and look onto a terrain that is the land between borders. Here, evidence of humanity is scarce, as if the boundaries between nations are adverse to the living.

The earth underfoot is hard and dry. Tight clumps resemble rocks, but crumble easily. They are some twelve miles west of Abadan. Standing here, Ali feels as if he is at the end of the earth. To the south the Persian Gulf opens its watery mouth.

They stand around for what seems like hours as more trucks transport soldiers to this camp. Tents are set up and weapons are unloaded. Soldiers wear green army fatigues and carry Kalashnikov 47s. But the boys are not given uniforms or weapons. They wear the same clothes they were wearing on the soccer field. That was two days ago. Around their necks, from chains, hang the keys. With his fingernail, Ali scratches at his key and the gold paint flakes.

Everyone is strangely quiet. Sitting on a box of ammunition, a soldier is reading from the Koran. He sings the words as they are meant to be sung, in long mournful wails. His voice makes Ali feel that something terrible is about to happen. The sky seems almost motherly in its serene watchfulness. No clouds veil its face.

The enemy is there, on the other side, the colonel finally says, pointing in the distance. The boys begin to line up, shoulder to shoulder. The shorter boys stand in front, the older soldiers in the back, as if they are about to have their portrait taken. Ali stands in the second row. The colonel tells the younger boys in front only to run. Do not look back; do not stop; charge across the field, running as fast as you can. The soldiers with the guns will come up behind you. The field is a jungle and you are the machetes that cut down the paths.

Allah-hu Akbar!

They are off. Ali can hear only his own breathing heavy in his ears. He is still wearing the sandals he had on on the soccer field in Karaj. They slow him down, so when his left sandal falls off, he does not stop to retrieve it, but lets the right sandal fall away as well. Rocks jab his feet. But he is used to running barefoot. The soles of his feet have adapted. The golden key slaps against his collarbone. He tries holding it tightly as he runs, but this slows him down. He positions the key around his neck so that it falls against his back. On the periphery, he sees that he is passing most of the other boys, but they are quickly spreading out across the field. Sina is holding Erfand's hand and they are both running. With his free hand, Erfand is trying to hold his pants up. The sight of them, two brothers hand in hand, running at the enemy unarmed, forms a hard ball in the back of Ali's throat.

He does not see the enemy yet, but he is certain they must be there, camouflaged by the landscape. Is that the enemy? No, it is only a rock. Sweat burns his eyes. He does not know what he will do once he comes face-to-face with the enemy, given that he has no weapon. But as his mother always says, *Allah is great and he will find a way.*

His mother, who is in the hospital now from missing him. His father, who beats his head with both hands to endure the weight Allah has asked him to bear. His sisters, his dear little sisters, sitting on the rug and crying.

Then Ali hears a roar to his left. It is loud enough to feel in his stomach. He looks over to see a great fountain of earth spit up into the air, ballooning like a mushroom. Then it is the earth beneath his feet that spits up. Now, Ali is in the air with pieces of earth falling around him, watching as the golden key slips from his neck and is hurled away into the dusty immeasurable distance.

The Salvation Army

Heideh pulls up to the curb in front of the Salvation Army and has Reza go inside for a cart so they can more easily transport the contents of their car. Noah waits on the pavement while she parks.

Inside, two older ladies stand behind the counter. They wear blue-buttoned sweaters pinned with the red Salvation Army logo. One of them wears bright red lipstick; the other has tied her hair in a bun with chopsticks. They smile, and Heideh feels that it's genuine.

"May we help you?" the lady with the bun asks.

"We are here for donations," Heideh says.

"I'm sorry, but everything here has a price. Nothing too expensive, though. Is there anything in particular that you are looking for?" Heideh understands the confusion.

"No. I mean I am here to give donations." She signals to Reza who pushes the cart behind her.

"Oh. How nice. Please come over." Heideh turns to Reza. He lets go of the cart and stands aside. Heideh wheels the cart over to the ladies behind the counter. Noah stays close to his mother, alarmed by the look of the place, the eclectic mixture of furniture, housewares, and clothes. As the ladies unload the cart, they comment on the beauty of the items.

"Are you moving?" the one with bright red lipstick asks.

"No," Heideh says. When she perceives the lady waiting for clarification, she contemplates how to explain what she has done. To somehow communicate that by filling her apartment with these secondhand luxuries, she had hoped to make her life whole. But now she understands that in this country of endless promises, she can never be whole. Sometimes, the only way to know yourself, Heideh thinks, is by what you are willing to forfeit. "Just doing some spring cleaning," she finally says.

Heideh turns to look for Reza. He momentarily vanishes among limp clothes clinging to hangers, kitchen appliances whose surfaces have yellowed from the years, chairs with armrests disgorging stuffing from their seams, olive lampshades of the sort found in funeral homes. When Reza reemerges from behind a rack, Heideh stares at him. Her gaze is vast, until it seems as if his whole life has stretched before her, from the moment she bore him and cradled him to her breast to the unknowable future that, like a boundless field, disappears into the horizon. She cannot let him go without knowing that he is ready, that one day he will champion his duty to the world, aware of the sacrifices that were made for him. All of this is on the tip of Heideh's tongue. But inside the Salvation Army she can only call Reza to her with the look in her eyes. *Come back to me.*

Reza stands his ground, defiant. He shakes his head, having locked eyes with his mother, and turns from Heideh, disappearing down an aisle. Noah sees Reza move off and runs after his brother. In their wake, Heideh takes a sharp breath, and turns to face the two ladies of the Salvation Army as they carefully remove from the cart everything she has forfeited.

LARRY N. MAYER

New York State Summer Writers Institute

LOVE FOR MISS DOTTIE

When she first arrived, dreaming of gold-dust castles, speaking her King's English, Ruby Williams was entirely mixed-up, confused, foolish—but not crazy. Steel will and all, if we had knew about the crazy, we might could've stopped her. Instead, she end up denigrating her own name. 'Cause that night on the evening news with Mr. Walter Cronkite, from out the backseat the squad-car window, you see her purple-feather bonnet blowing off her audacious head, feather bits whirling to the pavement. Ruby—waving handcuffed arms like mortal coils—claim she the heir to some great fortune. She keep screaming at the camera that she the wife of the Reverend Dr. Martin Luther King Jr. and that she the rightful owner of the late Miss Dorothy Parker ashes. Imagine that. If only. Beside, whatever respect we mined for ourselves since 1955 scatter like silver sand in the wind.

We might could had told her some sense. Drop it we'd say. Move on. Miss Dottie gray ashes ain't worth nothing to you. Toss 'em down the incinerator chute, like the rest of her rubbish. Like you been taking it for the last two years, while you dropping your boy, Roosevelt, at the neighbors, on your way to Miss Dottie residence, what you call, "being her personal custodian." And still no green card. Beside, who you think you are? You ain't nothing but a coconut. Brown on the outside. *Think about it.* Your papa, a cardiac physician down in the West Indies? Witch doctor, maybe. Don't steal what you ain't never earned. The burnt remains of a white lady? Shrouded in a old fur coat? Take one of Miss Dottie hotel ashtrays, instead. Rim your finger 'round they curves. Smoke her butts. Then see what color your fingers be. They ain't no pink-velvet poppies. Just remember, you ain't all fragrant and sweet.

But Ruby insist, like she cognizant of some juicy inside secret. Like the inside lining of Miss Dottie gray fur be tore wide open and you could see her plum loving-heart beating inside. *Like if Ruby jump the line, nobody ain't gonna notice.* Like we couldn't smell them mothballs in the hallway every time she come home late from work. But this time she really wrong. Like she the Queen of Sheba, she grab on to the King name, Coretta Scott and all, like a badge, and smack it hard against her big protruding chest, which hidden under Miss Dottie mangy fur. Ruby buy herself a map of Westchester, an off-peak ticket on the Harlem River Line, and decide to get a holt of Miss Dottie ashes for herself. Riding first class, no less, Ruby think she the second coming of Miss Rosa Parks. Unfortunately, the rest of prime-time America know she ain't nothing but a fraud.

That all she knew at first, back in 1965, when Ruby Neal Williams, with her girdled ass and Dorothy Dandridge titties, got all them foreign notions in her head about her own self getting famous—a Hollywood starlet in New York! After she and her boy, Roosevelt, had moved from somewhere, some Barbados-Bermuda-Bahama-you-ain't-*my*-mama island. First, to the East Harlem Project, and then to Broadway, "The Marble Hill Homes"—you'd'nt dare call them project houses—in the Bronx. "The West Side," she said. Because if you go high enough, the west side become the east side and the east side become the Wild West. West side, east side, sunrise, sunset—it all the same. Ruby act like she ain't never heard the sun don't *really* move.

When every morning, sure as death, Ruby ride the subway to Pennsylvania Station, stroll willfully cross town—down past Macy, right on by Gimbel's, damn near genuflecting as she stride on by Altman, Bloomingdale, Best, Abraham, Lord, Taylor, and Strauss, and then back up Fifth Avenue, thirty-four blocks, rain or shine—holding her cloche hat (the one with the purple peacock feather, the one Miss Dottie bestow on her) against a steady north wind, progressing—the swirling fog of early risers, hot-dog vendors fiddling with they umbrellas, polishing steam tables—hauling her own self forward and upward like a pushcart, then stopping and comparing, always comparing, at the jaded flapper mannequin on the corner of East 49. Stone-still hips. Heartless eyes.

Like that disapproving plastic bitch going to tell Ruby right from wrong. Show her how colored costume fashion jewels is replacing rhinestone and crystal. Like Mr. and Mrs. Saks Fifth Avenue, and they kin, got the secret to life. Nobody—not even the Lord, if he all he allegedly be—can't tell nobody how long to wear they skirt.

She preen for the longest minute at her store-window reflection. Setting her hat just so, lining up her face with that pasty-faced mannequin, bearing its affront—like that pink doll have any dream—seeing her own translucent outline becoming one with the doll. Before smearing that silly red lipstick on her own far-reaching lips, like she blind. Puckering like the sultry flower of the flaming heart. Ruby, that poor little thing, no taller than a shrub, putting on makeup like airs. No tropical plant could never survive in this place. Not even in a purple-peacock bonnet and mock-fur coat, not even in the middle of spring. You had to worry. That poor girl out on the street, and she still waiting on that green card.

The token booth clerk talk to her one morning: "Take the crosstown shuttle. That's too far for a lady to walk." But Miss Ruby hardheaded. Walking all forty blocks, stubborn like a mule.

"I ain't shuttling for no one," she said. "Never will, never did."

Until Ruby Williams at last find herself ascending into the heaven of the great park, then the boat pond up ahead, where she finally see the gold-fretted marquee that, in fool-fire words, say VOLNEY HOTEL. The whirling April blooms drive her forward, the scent recall the place from where she running. Driving her. Pushing. But them fancy toy boats and golden schooners won't glow till warm afternoon, when all the nice girls and boys, running from they school, majestic sailboats in hand, encircle the shimmering pool. Uptown, her own boy, Roosevelt, be getting home from his school, too. No worry: Fix him yucca stew in the morning, plenty of meat in it. Study hard, she tell him, be a doctor. Heal all them sick white folk in America. Miss Dottie—Miss Dorothy Parker—say she'll pay for it, too. The old lady ain't got much no more, but she throwing it all away. At the pond later in the afternoon, Miss Dottie give Ruby a storybook for her son. About a little white mouse who against all odds sails across the pond, in a thunderstorm no less, in a toy white schooner, and wins.

But it still early, a typical day, and Ruby Williams got time at the East Seventy-fourth Chock full o'Nuts—where all the other respectable Negro women work except Ruby, of course, because she spend her day cleaning rooms in that dusty old hotel—for coffee heavy on the sugar, and a slice of cream cheese on raisin-nut bread, for a dime. Swearing one day her green card gonna come like a railroad ticket to the New Jerusalem. Excepting on Tuesdays, Wednesdays, and Thursdays when, like some fancy madam, she hire herself out, the personal custodian caretaker of one hotel resident, none other than Miss Dorothy Parker.

The two of them, laughing together. Forgetful fools, tossing peanut shells and smoking some noxious fumes, flicking they own ashes on Miss Dottie rug, like neither got a care in the world. And at the end, who you think pick it all up?

And it's mighty sad. They no less than fifty old white ladies living up in that smoke-filled fire trap and maybe even more yapping dogs. All of 'em suffering from arthritis, heart disease, and much, much prune juice. *The damn dogs, too.* Though Miss Dottie stick mostly to the pills and the sauce. *Walk Momma's Bonzo. A number one and number two for Little Minkie. Hold my hand, please. Oh, how terribly frightening!* Dogs and dust everywhere, and the more Ruby scrub and sweep and clean, the more moldy and ashen those damned hotel carpets seem to grow. But Ruby know one thing: It's just around the corner from the new Whitey Museum of American Art, which she later find out, it really called the Whitney.

When she first come to New York City back in 1965, she call roaches "brown moth larvae." After one year, Ruby tell us her dream. She screaming out a burning window, hollering for her boy, Roosevelt. The building up in flames. Broken glass raining down the pavement. White moths fluttering in, every which way. Ruby finally come to confess—the two-room apartment she stay at with her boy, on Fifth Avenue and 125th, ain't even got no window. That woman don't hardly own wool socks for that child. But she got time to write postcards. *I live on Fifth Avenue,* she tell her people back home, *the famous Fifth Avenue.* What so famous about that? Uptown Fifth Avenue ain't the same as Miss Dottie Fifth. People been telling her all along. Ain't no Whitey or Whitney up there.

So she pick up what little she have, her precious boy, Roosevelt, and move up to the Bronx. That when we first seen her. She couldn't wait no more. 'Cause you know the only thing she love more than Miss Dottie is herself. And the only thing she love more than herself is that boy, Roosevelt. She say she doing it all for the boy. The extra commute downtown, the way she mind her hair. I say, first of all, Ruby Williams, get that child a pair of socks!

But Miss Dorothy Parker treat Ruby like a favorite niece, never letting no tardiness, or nothing like that get in the way of their "relationship." If Ruby say she don't want no extra for doing this or doing that, Miss Dottie don't pay her no mind. Throw her a bonus, and tell her, "Money can't buy health, but I'd settle for a diamond-studded wheelchair. In fact, Ruby, if I had any decency, you know I'd be dead."

And then, as if premonition weren't no more than a weather report to white folk, Miss Dottie begin secretly forecasting her own demise. "When I go," she declare, "it's going be one terribly loathsome day. Overcast, dreary, maybe even worse. And to all those poor folks watching and standing in the storm, all I beg, dear Ruby, is to *please excuse my ashes.*"

Excuse her ashes? Ruby don't understand 'cause she don't want to. *The glass ashtray look clean.* She offer Miss Dottie a bite of her nut-raisin sandwich. But Miss Dottie ain't even hungry. Instead, she wipe some cream cheese off Ruby chin and tell her to save them crumbs for the pigeons.

In February 1967, the Reverend Dr. Martin Luther King Jr. deliver a speech about the casualty of the Vietnam War. At first, Ruby too busy perverting her waist and hips in the mirror, delighting in her own image, in a outdated fur-collar wrap-over coat Miss Dottie give her. And that just the *first* one. Then Ruby get crazy worried about Roosevelt. *Like Uncle Sam going to take away a six-year-old illegal immigrant Negro boy and send him to fight some white-man war.* Ruby start working for Miss Dottie five days a week, six days, saving her money for Roosevelt education, bringing home trinkets and old clothes, and picking up the newspaper every morning on her way downtown.

"Am I dead yet?" Miss Dottie ask her one night as Ruby about to leave for home. "Please, Ruby, be a doll, check the paper."

But thank goodness she alive. "You alive," Ruby tell her. "That's what people say. Look here, it don't say nothing about you being dead."

"I don't care what anybody says about me as long as it isn't true."

It was then that she give Ruby that rumpled old fur coat, stinking like them mothballs in the old-lady closet and looking like it had the mange.

'Cause Miss Dottie know she 'bout to die real soon, and she know it going to be a nasty day. But no matter how baleful the sky become, no matter how much it rain, no matter how many barbs of lightning split the blue gray heaven, the old lady still find herself inhaling and exhaling, underneath her bedcovers, disappointed, blinking, alive. Even her dogs is waiting, curled up tight every night, riding her suspirations, like some woven living shroud. First time she seen it, Ruby surprised by all them scruffy, mangy Pomeranians. But Miss Dottie love them strays. Like them dogs was her next of kin. Matter of fact, at any given Miss Dottie have three or four in her two-room apartment. Once, late at night, Miss Dottie even salvage a three-legged mongrel off Sixth Avenue, the so-called Avenue of the Americas. She take the dog home, clean up the damn pooch, and present it to Miss

Eleanor Roosevelt who live two buildings down, in her own luxury brownstone. Tell her it a special breed.

Ruby love that fur coat and Miss Dottie let her wear it all spring. One morning she spread it like a picnic blanket and help Miss Dottie onto the tattered couch. The two of them laughing and crying like some midget lovers. And while she read the weather report and the obits to Miss Dottie, she drop her nut-raisin crumbs onto the collar. Miss Dottie give Ruby a big old hug and ask her to come here. "Let's share a gentleman," she say. 'Cause Miss Dottie call her long fancy cigarettes *gentlemen*. She keep them under her skirt, so they dampish and hard to spark.

But Ruby fetch a gold lighter from the marble table.

They pass the smoke between they lips. Pass it back and forth, one gentleman between the two. They talk about ex-husbands, carelessly flicking they ashes onto the floor. Homosexuals and cheats. "Philanderers," Miss Dottie tell her. "Rogues." The room begin to smell foul. So Ruby dutifully open the window. From deep inside Miss Dottie closet, she take an old gray blanket and lay it on Miss Dottie lap to keep her legs warm. The blanket smell like mothballs and smoke. *"Peeyu,"* Miss Dottie exclaim. "If I've got any luck left in my account, I'll suffocate on the smell." Even the dogs is cowering by the door now. Trying to get out.

If Miss Dottie die, Ruby have to get a new job. Harder to find than a runaway dog. *But what she care?* She busy pondering if Miss Dottie 'bout to set her a inheritance. Like Miss Dottie owe her something. If she do, it 'cause Miss Dottie ain't quite right.

Too nervous to sit, Ruby dust off the coffee table maybe ten times, making small circles, and watch the sky outside, talking about her son, Roosevelt, and how someday he going to a college for medical physicians. She take the crumbs from the collar and spill them onto the outside sill. She pour Miss Dottie a drink, a strong one how she like it. They call they drinks *ladies*. They light another smoke. "Ladies and gentlemen," Miss Dottie announce. They laugh. They clink they delicate ladies together. The dogs whine. And they words swirl like vapor out into the deaf city.

Even now Miss Dottie try to be cheerful. But inside, the woman dying. Always smiling, but her eyes look miles away, making some joke like, "I can't do *anything* anymore. I used to bite my nails, at least . . . and now . . . and now . . . what to do, with all those dusty old coats, Ruby?"

Ruby Williams just suck her lipstick-stained teeth. Ruby pour her another one of them ladies Miss Dottie so love, and tell her to hush her pink mouth quick. Ruby turns to open another window, check the forecast. 'Cause whatever they drinking reek like the foul-smelling preservative Ruby use to buff the marble tile of the hotel lobby. Miss Dottie damn near kilt herself three times in the last two years, and Ruby concerned that Miss Dottie trying to take her, too. Ruby stand on tiptoe, reach across tangled houseplants, and unhinge another window. Miss Dottie pretty little pink nostrils dilate, eyes scrunch, and she inhale the smell like holy smoke, remembering some old dream she once have. Smiling, she tuck her chin under and fall asleep in the middle of a breath. Miss Dottie ain't barely five feet, and inside that wheelchair she look like a tiny girl withering from consumption. Miss Dottie the only grown woman in New York City shorter than Ruby and just a smidgen. A warm breeze touch the top of both they heads.

"Please excuse me, Miss Dottie," Ruby say, all proper like. 'Cause she fearful Miss Dottie passed. 'Cause even them dogs sniffing around her little feet now. "You ain't put nothing funny in your drink this time? We can't afford to lose you just yet, ma'am." She shake Miss Dottie by the shoulder. Miss Dottie slap her hand.

"For Heaven's sakes, child," Miss Dottie remark, holding up her glass as if to raise a toast. "Please, look at me. Do I look like some ditzy Hollywood pinup who's lost it all?"

To be honest, Ruby ain't really sure what a Hollywood pinup look like. Don't know what ditzy mean. And ain't even sure what they is to lose. But nonetheless Miss Dottie look real sad.

"Miss Dottie, why Ruby don't wheel you and the dogs across the park today?"

"Rats," shouts Miss Dorothy Parker, looking out the window. "Not another nice one. What's an old girl to do these days? No more, no more. No more ladies, no more gentlemen, please." She toss her drink to the carpet and let out a sigh. Either her heart give up on her, or she 'bout to give up on her heart. She a dying flower, and with them pills and liquor and smoke, Lord knows what gonna come first. Them little dogs sniff and vie for position, but Ruby right there to scatter them, shush them away.

Underneath the hotel canopy, she puff up Miss Dottie silk scarf, and the ship of the misguided—wheelchair, dogs, and all—set forth. A crazy wind come by. And like a hungry city pigeon, Ruby purple-feather bonnet soar upward before it fall hard, into a yawning barrel of trash. Panting hard, them dogs labor to the garbage. Sign say, LITTER A FIFTY DOLLARS FINE. But dogs could piss free. It's a hoot every damn minute.

At the corner, they nearly trampled by a honking bus. "I should be so lucky," Miss Dottie remark. "Every spring comes back, with nasty little birds, yapping their fool heads off. How can a lady get her beauty sleep?

"Let's go," Miss Dottie say. "There's a quiet doggie park by the river." Them three or four mutts of hers bark like they understand loyalty. Then the one Miss Dottie call Minkie pee right on Ruby blue-white-and-red leather pump. With pointed toe, Ruby unhinge the wheelchair lock.

"Take me to the other side already. I'm done being famous."

At Columbus, well on the west side now, Ruby in a big old hurry again. Holding her hat with one hand, steering Miss Dottie with the other, by Amsterdam she out of breath. Even them dogs is panting as they about to pass under a awning: in familiar fool-gold letters, FAMOUS DAIRY RESTAURANT. Ruby hitch the break and swing old Miss Dottie around. The leashes and dogs all twisted. And shading her own reflection, Ruby push her own brown nose to the dirty window. Miss Dottie don't seem to care one smidgen.

"It's a famous place?" Ruby say. "It don't look so great from out here, Miss Dottie."

"It's just an Old Testament haunt, Ruby. Nothing fancy. They don't eat meat with milk. They shun pork. Yet they call the place famous and people line up around the corner, like the war's still on."

Ruby hardly listening to a thing Miss Dottie telling her, too busy smearing on that oxblood lipstick again, squinting inside the window, wondering if she can bring home some special treat for Roosevelt. To give that girl her proper respect, when she want, she don't never give up. And to be fair, she love that boy Roosevelt more than anything in this passing world. When she drop him at a neighbor you could see the hurt in her eye.

"No offense, Miss Dottie, but if it's for the Jewish only..."

Miss Dottie mutts search the old lady eyes, bobbing they heads and tongues, like the fool creatures they is. She give them some fancy strips of ham she keep in her purse, and then tie all three or four of them to a post. "Come on, goddamn it, let's eat."

———

It's three o'clock by now, no more crowd. A black-fedora man, in a crumple-black suit, smelling like some stale peanuts, cut in front of them. Ruby swear he helt the door and smelled like macadamia.

"Why everyone so pale in here?"

"Must be the buttermilk and the inbreeding," Miss Dottie tell her. "Centuries of eating the same lousy food."

Ruby face turn near chalk pink, then moldy ashen gray, when the cashier girl escort them through the narrow aisle to a vinyl red booth across from a rumbling air conditioner, tucked away in some tumble-down backroom. *Why we going there?* she think.

Ruby park Miss Dottie chair by the table and hear somebody mumbling strange prayers to his self. In the next booth, the man look like a near bald-headed albino turtle. Miss Dottie whisper to Ruby, "Under the air conditioner, right there . . . there's the famous Jewish writer . . ."

The writer twist his neck. "Miss McCarthy," he say. "Miss Mary McCarthy." He dig deep into his gum with a toothpick. "What brings a *shikse* like you to my little restaurant?"

"My father's name was Rothschild."

"I don't care if your name was Lovechild, Rothschild, or Rockefeller. I don't pay for nobody, Miss McCarthy, and I don't want nobody to pay for me. My heart simply won't allow it." The toothpick falls to the floor.

"Who asked you?"

"The vegetarian chopped liver and the soup of the day. I eat the same every day, and nobody pays for me." He start plundering the pickle jar.

"You know," he say, "it smells terrible, but in this juice, pickles are never getting *farschimmelt*." He hold one up, dripping. Miss Dottie look sick. Ruby confused.

"You know, my boy got a Jewish name, too," Ruby say. "We named him Roosevelt after that old president. My husband..."

"You poor dear, the less we mention husbands the better." She pat Ruby on the thigh. "The only reason I married the old fop was to change my name from Rothschild to Parker, and to get a couple of fancy bras."

The Jewish writer pay them no mind, cutting his pickle into neat little cubes, arranging them like tiles on his plate.

"Besides, the only men I care for are these here gentlemen." She pat herself on the lap, feeling for her smokes. "Should we just...?"

Ruby concur. She stand up.

Miss Dottie grab a glass ashtray from the Jewish man table and slip it into Ruby soft pocket.

Without eating, without saying good-bye, the two womens is up and out.

"He didn't even recognize me. Didn't even know my name— nobody does," Miss Dottie insist.

Ruby quiet now. Her mind working fast. Buttoning up Miss Dottie coat.

"A gentleman, please, Ruby, it's time for a gentleman."

Ruby light Miss Dottie cigarette. She unchain the dogs.

"Oh, if only, if only the rains would come."

Miss Dottie seen it in the Sunday papers. Sometime in early June. Ruby seen it later, on the television set. Breaking up Roosevelt cartoons, interrupting his shows. Umbrellas turned inside out, water rushing the streets. Flood warnings in effect—an unrelenting week of whirling rain and ancient winds.

Miss Dottie shout victoriously into the mouth of the phone, that evening. "Ruby, dearest, I think we've finally made it to the promised land. By tomorrow morning the myth of Dorothy Parker shall be no more than a myth."

That night Ruby seen her son to bed. "Never." She cover him in a quilt of black, gold, and red. "Never will you go fight no one else's battle." He ask her to light a candle. A small room, a candle, a quilt, a stewpot from back home, a leaky faucet, some frozen sausage links, and strange city birds cooing under the eaves. In the wavering gold light, on her knees, on top Miss Dottie old wraparound coat, which she lay onto the bare floor, Miss Ruby pray for recompense. Then she tuck herself into a old cot at the other end of they one-room place. Roosevelt tune his small AM radio, put it under his pillow, and lay his head back down.

Back at the Volney, Miss Dorothy Parker also restless. First, she lock her dogs in her tiny bedroom and force open all the windows so later it be wet, but at least it don't smell. Second, she empty her cupboards, and scatter crumbs of cookies and bread all about her living room carpet. "It's all for the birds," she laugh. Then she unroll the slats of the blinds and unhinge all them living room windows, too. A balmy air hover and sweep through the apartment, followed by a crazy howl from the trembling Minkie, who inside the coat closet. The rest hiding beneath Miss Dottie bed. Vinyl slats and rattling windows tear against theyself while Miss Dottie light a candle at her forgotten maple desk.

The rising and falling shadow on the far wall show her writing furiously like she haven't wrote in years. Lawyer or no lawyer, she want all them greedy gold-digging rich friends of hers who ain't called in years to get nothing. And finally she write, "In appreciation of my dear companion, Ruby Neal Williams, for her support and loyalty, I hereby bequest $5,000 to her young boy, Roosevelt."

Two in the morning. Miss Dottie head roll to the desk, her pen drop to the floor, and the misguided lady fall into a deep sleep, which at first she mistake for death. The dogs now sleeping. And there a flash of final quiet, before a ascension of charcoal pigeons flapping and spilling through the windows. She confused. For even in slumber she know that only the living could dream. In the morning, she open her eyes slow, and curse the yellow precious light that now poking through the slam-shut windows. But for the muffled cooing of dozens of the fat pigeons on the floor when she turn her head, she might still think she dead. The place smell like bad bourbon. The dogs, too, be crying again, and scratching they paws against the door.

When Ruby call the phone ring twelve times before Miss Dottie answer.

"What, for Heaven's sakes? What's a lady to do these days?"

"A mistake," Ruby tell her. "The storm pushed out to sea and we getting more beautiful weather."

Ruby hear Miss Dottie trying to light a damp cigarette.

"I sicken of the calm."

When Miss Dottie Parker suddenly pass from a coronary in her apartment at age seventy-three, on Thursday, June 8, 1967, Ruby dream continue. It was Ruby who found the lady corpse in bed, curled up with her four dogs. It was Ruby who open all the windows so it don't stink. It was Ruby who light one last gentleman for her, push it between her blue flesh lips. Ruby who watch it fall to the floor. Ruby the first to call the police, and Ruby whose face appear on the front page of the *New York Times*. A snapshot of Ruby in a silk-satin dress, her face paler than flesh, hugging them poor dogs, three or four of them licking her tearful cheeks. No one care who Ruby was. There weren't no foul play. It was a photo about Miss Dottie dogs.

But Ruby got plenty of time to pick through Miss Dottie wardrobe before the police come. Clicking and clanking those hangers, like champagne glasses, like she born to the manor. Eyes rimmed red, she shifting a burning cigarette between her own lips, the wardrobe light up as she touch the fabric of each gown. Brocade. Organdie. Crepe. Linen. Velvet. Like the wings of a moth. The lady. The delicate lady. Corpse-cold Dottie.

And then the blue black satin gown, she find it, shining like a lady dreams. She outfit herself quick. Swallow her cigarette butt to leave no sign. Slide it over her head and arms like holy water, her chest, her sex, her legs tingling, the dress draped like a fine cloak. In her tiny little bare feet, standing tiptoe, she pucker at the mirror like Black Cinderella. She fit herself into Miss Dottie high-heel shoes, rising up she feel like the Second Coming.

When she find the news article on Friday morning, Ruby Williams start experiencing lofty visions, a cockamamie scheme to get a holt of what she believe rightfully hers. The *New York Times* said that Mrs. Dorothy Parker of 23 East Seventy-fourth Street was to be cremated on Friday, June 9, at Ferncliff Crematory in Hartsdale, New York. It say something about Miss Dottie estate. Ruby imagine a estate as best she know: an eighteenth-century mansion, huge white columns, a formal garden surrounded by massive stone walls, pedigree hunting dogs chained to a noble and ancient magnolia, and a smokehouse in the back. Ruby don't even know what a smokehouse is. But more important, Ruby never imagine what she conjure in her mind ain't nothing more than a fancy funeral parlor up in Westchester, New York. You give Ruby some flight of fancy and she liable to weave her own shroud.

She move her lips real slow to the words. "The celebrated queen of the Algonquin Round Table, Mrs. Dorothy R. Parker, has left her entire estate to the great civil rights leader, the Reverend Dr. Martin Luther King Jr."

White people crazy. Yes, something again about a unnamed Negro boy who getting $5,000 for college. And poor Ruby? Nothing. *What that Dr. King have to do with Miss Dottie anyhow? These people got a lot of explaining to do.* She flick on her television set. And there, sure enough, on national news, Dr. King in Memphis, his wife by his side, slightly irritated, but sincere: "Dorothy who?" And that's all she need to hear.

Because if Ruby Williams stashing the devil like lipstick in her purse, or hiding it like bad hair under a purple hat, she ain't about to give up just yet. With or without approval, she got to risk. Wait too long already.

In the morning she so worked up, she forget to feed her son, she forget to check her mail slot, she even forget that for the first time in two years she don't even have a job. While her son going to his last day of school on a glass of warm milk and wrinkled pants. She give him a big hug at the door. He nearly slip on her tears.

Instead, she fooling with pots and pans in the kitchenette, measuring her own reflection in a favorite copper stewpot. While the marvelous sunlight of the week fade, she getting a true vision without no gloss. A photo on a cloudy day. She never seen ashes before — her momma and poppa buried in simple wood caskets. But she suppose a woman of Miss Dottie stature need a five-gallon receptacle, in the least. People is a lot of stuff in there. And copper do look an awful lot like gold.

She put on her hat. Take it off, then put it back. Well, you know how every tongue got to confess. Ruby Neal Williams ain't no different. She swear she love Miss Dottie like her own name. She swear the only will and testament come from above, and finally she swear that all she want is rightful possession of Miss Dorothy Rothschild Parker ashes.

And that's why she so tore up. She gonna pretend she Ruby Rothschild, a lost cousin from the Old Testament side of Miss Dottie family. She obsessing now. *How I'm going to appear like a Rothschild and make a rightful claim to them ashes? The Jewish—they just a special kind of white folk.* So she put on Miss Dottie satin gown and high-heel shoes. But now her butt stick out too wide like a crosstown block. And the skin? No one gonna believe that. A Rothschild? Come on. Most of them people either pasty pink or ashy-looking with long, sad faces. What kind of face she gonna wear?

She get her big pot from off the stove—the only thing she ever credit her momma, beside her big titties—and bring it to the so-called living room. Piled on the floor some dusty old records from Miss Dottie, what she never listen to. Nina Simone. Billie Holiday. Al Jolson. *What she know about American music?* That ain't on no citizenship exam. She sit on the cold linoleum, sweep her palms across the vinyl, whisking from both floor and records a coat of dirt-white powder. She look at her face in the heirloom. *She don't look Jewish.* Then she laugh or cry like a insane pigeon and forge the dust flecks onto her skin. You'd swear it either love for Miss Dottie or some crazy pain.

Footsteps in the hallway. Getting louder. They coming to take her away. Then again. Ruby convinced. Clunk. With Ruby Williams, why everything got to be drama? Hold it together, girl. She wondering if Miss Dottie mad about the satin dress. The coat? The ghost of Miss Dottie? A thump she hear against the door. A note from immigration? Her green card? She clutch the copper pot to her chest. She thinking she might be crazy. *Do you love me, Dorothy Parker? Do you love me?* A buzz at the door and she shaking. It's just the super trying to eke a honest living.

She fool with her makeup for another forty-five minutes, puckering and unpuckering, mouthing the words to Dr. King famous dream speech, opening and closing that fur coat, like she gonna be on the evening news herself. She finally learned something. After all, passing as Mrs. Coretta Scott King a lot more sensible than saying she a Rothschild.

And who do you think everybody that night see on *The CBS Evening News with Walter Cronkite*? You see that woman holding tight to her copper pot heirloom while they putting the cuffs to her, right outside her home. Her head rolling, white eyes shooting up to the sky like some crazy Roman candle.

By the time we heard them sirens right by the building, by the minute we seen her in cuffs, we all pressed together into one window to ask: Did she steal them ashes? Did she break in or did she just pretend? Had she gotten the money, too? And how you gonna wear a coat like that in the middle of June?

You can't steal no one ashes and expect to be free, Ruby. Not in this country. And it a damn shame, 'cause you know her green card finally arrive that morning. Her boy one day from finishing the first grade. Who 'bout to look after Roosevelt now? Her white eyes staring out the television set, some claptrap drivel about how she still have a dream. Nobody can't take it away, she say. Nobody. Her purple-feather bonnet falling to the pavement. And though it break my heart to say, she still clutching tight to that copper pot when we all look away.

ERIN BROWN

University of Virginia

MULES

So here are two people. Three, if you count the nun. One, maybe two hundred altogether if you count the thick-booted soldiers, the children selling dirty oranges or slick brochettes piled on plates, the barefoot women, the men with flour sacks on their heads veiling them in shade, and, on either side of the two long, cinder-block barricades that rein these people together in a dusty plaza, the money changers who sit in plastic lawn chairs under the scalding sun and wave dark fistfuls of paper in greeting at the travelers coming toward this place from Accra in the west or Lomé in the east. The two roads meeting here, at this sprawling, seething pen (no place to sit! no fountain to drink from!), and who can tell whether this is where they begin or end?

This is not a question for the one, maybe two hundred who mill about in the plaza. Some move more briskly than others. Some seem to know exactly where to go, maneuvering expertly between the two barricades. The women carry pots on their heads: industrial-sized tin bowls filled with rice, corn, yams, knotted rags. They walk quickly, with long, straight necks. As the two people watch from where they are rooted in the dirt near the first barricade (or the second, depending on your destination), the man has the impression that they are standing in the midst of a flock of beautiful peacocks. He nudges his wife.

"Don't they look like peacocks?" He is immediately ashamed. He knows how it sounds.

His wife doesn't glance at him. She is concentrating on the nun (a rotund African woman with an open face and gray habit) as she shows their papers to a ridiculously young soldier who swings his gun by his side like a stick. His wife doesn't turn toward him, and he thinks she has not heard and is relieved, but then she says, "Walt. Focus."

He blushes.

He is an older man, and white, and he clutches the handles of his duffel bag so tightly in his right hand that his fingers sting. Walt wears light-colored clothing like his wife, Marie, and like Marie he has a thin khaki purse slung over his neck and tucked into his shirt. He has some money hidden there, but he has taken his passport out and given it to the nun. He did this much earlier, before the initial checkpoint at the first barricade (just a glance at their documents and then they were in, Sister Nathalie smiling as if to say *nothing doing*, or *it's a breeze*, but then this plaza, these soldiers, this smell he can't quite place, and he knows they're not through yet, not even close). Walt now wonders if anyone was watching as he reached inside his shirt to pull out the purse. He looks behind himself once, quickly, then stares ahead and slides his left hand into the pocket of his pants, making a fist.

They have been lucky in life.

The nun—Sister Nathalie—is still talking to the soldier, her voice pleasant and rolling like her body and her laugh. They met Sister Nathalie only a few hours ago, but already Walt can't remember what it was like to be claimed by her outside of the Accra airport. Whether she had called their names or held a placard or just walked up to the two of them and introduced herself in thick, broken English. Walt did not anticipate this, that he would begin to forget the important details, the *how* and *when* and *how* again.

How. Patrick in San Francisco as he placed the bottles of medicine in a plastic Safeway bag: *The Sisters will take care of you. Let them do the talking.* Marie at her computer, drinking tea and studying the Walgreens pharmacy logo, fiddling with the graphic design program and printing out sheet after sheet of prescription stickers. Laughing. Giddy. Curling into him one night as he was approaching sleep and placing one hand flat against his chest, wrapping the other around the back of his head, whispering, *This is our Everest.* Their son, John, calling from Los Gatos. John the consultant who thinks big, applies little, has never been anywhere but Cabo. John who believes only in number crunching and fiscal years, and who would not understand their aim, even if they told him. The unyielding tenor of his voice. *Who goes to Africa for one week?*

(But he was right, of course. They extended their stay to twelve days, and planned on visiting the slave forts along the coast on the way back. Marie is hoping to do some watercolors.)

Walt thinks he might not even remember the *what:* the pills that huddle in his duffel with names that sound to him like cartoon superheroes. Combivir, Videx, Retrovir, Crixivan. Robots with hearts of gold. Stowed away in two jumbo-sized aspirin bottles and twelve prescription containers with Marie's confected pharmacy labels. The duffel that Walt has let no one else carry—not the porters at the airport, not Sister Nathalie, especially not his loose-limbed Marie. The duffel that he clutches tightly now, as he surveys the border that is not what he expected, not at all, though already he can feel the scene that he had imagined while still in California slip away, quiet and deferential as an overlooked guest. (He had pictured an orderly line and all manner of wide-brimmed hats for purchase, he remembers that much.) Walt shifts his weight from foot to foot, waiting for Sister Nathalie to explain their situation so that he can begin to pocket it in bits and pieces.

This much Walt knows: He will forget the *how,* he will forget the *what,* he will only remember the *why. We have been lucky,* he thinks. *We are lucky people.*

The young soldier has picked up his gun with both arms and has started to walk toward the middle of the plaza, where two wooden shacks obstruct the ceaseless flow of travelers. There is a line of people in front of the first shack. The second one appears to be empty. Sister Nathalie turns to Walt and Marie.

"It is nothing," she says. "But he is young and will not pass you through without the smallest inspection of papers." Her hands are deep polished mahogany as she unwraps a corner of the brightly patterned *pagne* from around her waist and folds a few bills back into the fabric. She makes a knot out of the cloth and tucks it back around her. "Perhaps we should have tried one who has seen more and whose needs are greater," she says, smiling and shaking her head.

"Perhaps?" says Walt. He takes a deep breath. Looks only at the first tin-roofed shack, where the young soldier is now standing impatiently next to the line. He knows he should be grateful that Sister Nathalie speaks any English at all (Patrick said that the Sisters of Banwaré spoke only French and Éwè), but does she have to be so cavalier? Does she have to be so goddamned cavalier?

"It's fine," says Marie, next to him. "Walt? It's fine. Let's just." She nods toward the shack.

"I thought you did this all the time," he says to Sister Nathalie as they walk toward the shack, Nathalie carrying their two small suitcases on her head.

"With what friends? We have not been so lucky," she says. "Only the doctor has come to us. Your Patrique."

"Patrick came over a year ago." A personal mission, then, only a few bottles and a giant bag of throat lozenges. Now it's a group effort, as he explained to Walt. *I've got doctors all over the Bay scraping out their supply closets for this clinic,* he told him. *And willing friends,* he added, *like you.*

Sister Nathalie pivots the upper half of her body so that she is looking at Walt, keeping her neck straight and unmoving under the weight of the luggage. She beams. "Patrique! So generous! A heart for the world!" She smiles so broadly that her eyes squeeze shut, and it is as if she is peering at Walt. "How he loved the babies and the soy cheese."

"I can imagine," says Walt, though he can't imagine it, doesn't know what soy cheese is, doesn't recall Patrick talking about babies as he gave Walt their instructions. Doesn't even know how Patrick found the Sisters, whether this was ever mentioned. All he remembers are the statistics that Patrick rattled off like multiplication tables: *Six percent of those who have been tested, but only 2 percent have been tested. Actual numbers estimated at 13 to 17 percent and rising. Could reach a quarter of the population by the end of the decade.* Patrick trying to talk them out of their choice of airline. They had insisted on an American carrier. *Why bother with Accra? Just fly Air France into Lomé. Sit tight during the stopover in Lagos while they unload the Chinese businessmen.* When Walt refused, said he had heard about the husks of burnt airplanes that line the runway in Lagos, Patrick had laughed. *Whatever you do, don't get off the plane. Just sit tight.* He didn't say anything about babies. Walt hears cheerful accusation in Sister Nathalie's voice.

Marie pushes her gray hair back from her face. She looks wan. Overbaked. "Are there babies at the convent?" she asks Sister Nathalie.

"Babies everywhere!" cries Sister Nathalie. "Everywhere!" She rests a hand on Marie's arm and Marie grasps it, laughing lightly.

When did they become confidantes, the wife and the nun? Walt has the feeling, familiar to him by now, that he is superfluous, merely following in Marie's wake as she successfully navigates these rocky peninsulas of awkwardness and discomfort. She is a valued member of search committees, maintains college friendships. She calls John weekly, and though she hears nothing of boyfriends or blind dates, at least she can report that their son is healthy, that he buys a new pair of running shoes every eight months and has painted his kitchen chocolate, with cream moldings.

They join the line in front of the shack, about twenty people long. It appears to be moving, though slowly, and the dark faces turn and stare, eyes hard and bright. Walt meets the steady gaze of a man who is carrying a pygmy goat across his shoulders, the beast's legs tethered together like a Thanksgiving turkey's. Walt looks at the man intently, shakes his head twice. The man adjusts the weight of the goat and says something to the others in a curt, brittle language.

"Yovo," he says, and laughs. Then he looks back at Walt. "Hello, Swiss?" he says. "Texas! You, Texas!"

Walt studies the sky. It is also hard, bright, and flat, and Walt wonders if Africa isn't one-dimensional after all, if he can't just step off this blanched backdrop and into some other, more inviting setting. Though he has been away from America for only twenty hours, he feels nauseated by his sudden need for it. He wants to watch the fog roll in.

Marie and Sister Nathalie are talking animatedly as the line shuffles forward. Marie is smiling, but Walt can see the way she glances toward the shack every time they move, can hear how her voice wavers on the vowels, and he knows that she is nervous, too.

"What other activities do the Sisters sponsor in Banwaré?" she asks. "I mean, besides the clinic."

"So many!" Sister Nathalie windmills her arms around as if she is scooping up achievements to present to Walt and Marie. "The nutrition, the schooling, the small business for the women . . . Soy cheese as well, and such lovely batiks and wooden crafts!" She nods at Walt. "You will buy some, and bring them back for your children's children. *Here is a piece of Afrique*," she intones, *"where Grand-mère and Grand-père did such good works."*

Walt glances at Marie. "We'll take a look," he says.

"Take a look! You will buy!" Sister Nathalie laughs loudly. And then, as if she has noticed Walt's thin smile, she adds, "For you are our guests!" She clasps Marie's hand and swings it gently between them. "So old and so rich—you must have twelve, fifteen grandchildren, *non?* Such a big family for such prosperity!"

Marie looks at the ground, smiling softly. "No grandchildren," she says. "We have a son."

"A son who is not married?"

Marie shakes her head.

"You must find him a woman! Perhaps here. An African jewel for your son!" Sister Nathalie puts a hand to her side and laughs. "His own African diamond!"

Walt shifts uncomfortably. He can hear Marie's quiet "perhaps," Sister Nathalie's boisterous rejoinder, the ticking patter of conversation as his wife skillfully turns it to another subject. He clenches his jaw. The nun's obstinate joviality is wearing thin. How to tell her that their son has no interest in Africa, in batiks, in women light or dark? John has accused them of earnestness each time they've brought him trinkets from their vacations over the past few years. *And you probably paid too much,* he said once, holding up the hammock that they'd carried from Costa Rica. *What did you think you were buying with this? Some kid's education?* He took Walt by the shoulders and shook him lightly, smiling. *You're not responsible,* he said. *It's a country, not a cause.*

There was a time years ago, Walt remembers now, when he shied away from giving his son much of anything, for fear of what they would do with it all when John got sick. It's silly now—so outdated!—but back then he thought it inevitable that his son would eventually become HIV-positive. He never told Marie. How could he admit such treachery? When John came home from UCLA each Christmas (it must have been the early nineties, though how could that be, it feels like yesterday), Walt couldn't look at him—his healthy figure, his well-cropped hair—without wondering which of his clothes, his embroidered shirts, his jean jacket, would be cut up and sewn together for his square of the quilt. That burgundy tie— would Marie use it for the border? They didn't talk much during those years. They still don't talk, probably never will. And Walt knew back then that John felt the silence as judgment and punishment both, but he couldn't bring himself to name for his son the thing that crowded his days with a faint and steady hiss. When he read, finally, that the AIDS quilt would be put away and stored in a warehouse in Atlanta, that it had been packed carefully, the squares resting evenly atop one another as if in irrevocable sleep, Walt had laid down his newspaper and wept with relief. Then he had called Patrick and offered to go. *We have been lucky,* he explained, and they had.

They are next in line. Walt bends first one knee, then the other. His palms are sweating, and he realizes that he has kept his left fist in his pocket this whole time. The building has a thin porch jutting out from under the tin roof with a few steps leading up, and they wait at the foot of these steps, not speaking. Sister Nathalie keeps Walt's and Marie's passports for them, along with her own *carte d'identité,* tucked into the front of her skirt. As they move up the stairs, she bends a little and takes the suitcases off her head, holding them with both hands.

Inside, flies buzz lazily around a patch of sunlight near the doorway. Two soldiers sit on one side of a long metal table with a folding chair opposite, and benches line the walls. There is no one else. The soldiers wear fatigues, dun-colored berets perched aslant on their heads. One of them wears a necklace of ammo, and Walt decides he must be a general. Walt, Marie, and Sister Nathalie stand in front of the table.

Marie looks around. Her face is flushed. She leans back and steadies herself with one hand on the chair.

"Nom, prénom," says the general.

Walt runs a hand through his hair. He and Marie spent the bulk of the flights, first from Oakland to New York, then from JFK into Accra, quizzing one another on their French. *Ne melangez-pas. Prenez avec repas.* Walt can list all the hours of the day, discuss eating schedules and side effects, but now he can't remember the most basic words.

"Walt," says Marie. "What did he say?"

The general points at Marie. "Madam Walt. *Prénom.*"

"No," says Walt. "Not her. Me." He points to Sister Nathalie. "You tell them. Tell them."

Sister Nathalie steps forward, fanning their passports out in front of her like a card dealer. She speaks quickly in Éwè, clipping along over their names and her own. She doesn't make eye contact with the soldiers, but stares instead at a corner of the table where Walt can see that some child has drawn a circle in the dust. The general takes their passports, and slowly, methodically, copies their information into a large rectangular book. Walt sees that, in place of their address, he writes *Seattle,* where their passports were issued.

"*Vous-allez où?*" he says, and again Sister Nathalie replies, this time naming the convent in Banwaré.

"Ah," says the second soldier to Walt. "You will enjoy the mountains."

"What?" says Walt. He looks at Sister Nathalie. "Does everyone here speak English?"

Sister Nathalie says nothing. The second soldier begins to clean his shoe, rubbing a strip of dirty *pagne* over the toe.

The general has been looking back and forth from Walt to Marie. He yawns, puts down his pen, gathers up their passports, and stands. He barks at Sister Nathalie. She laughs and adjusts her habit. She reaches out her hand for the papers and says something that sounds like a joke or a question, Walt isn't sure, but the general has already turned and appears to be ignoring her. Sister Nathalie's shoulders slump forward for a moment. She turns to Walt.

"He would like to examine your bags. He says it is customary. He would like for you to follow him."

"Wait," says Marie. "Wait!" Her voice rises sharply, and Walt sees that her arms are tight against her sides. He moves closer to her and whispers.

"Honey," he says. "Not so loud. They're only playing at French."

"That's the least of it," she says. Her eyes are wide and white. Walt doesn't know what she means by this, but he feels as if it is directed at him, his culpability, as if he himself has called her onstage for the last, unmanageable act of a disconcerting play. As if he has asked her to wear ram's horns and speak in limericks.

They follow the general out of the building and down the stairs. The sun surprises Walt again with its unremitting heat, a relentlessly pointing finger. The general leads them toward the second shack, which rises starkly from the neutral earth. He stops once to shout at a young boy with a plate of beignets on his head who is trailing after the group, singing a low song under his breath. "Yovo, yovo, *bonsoir*," the boy intones, landing his high-pitched voice heavily on each syllable. "*Ça va bien? Mer-ci!*" The general raises his hand in a flat salute and brings it down as if to cuff the boy, who darts away, laughing.

The second shack is exactly like the first, though there is no one inside, save a mangy dog asleep on her side under one of the benches, teats lying slack against the floorboards like a discarded glove. She raises her brown head when they enter, and then, hearing or smelling nothing of promise, returns to sleep, thumping her tail once in weak greeting. Marie has taken hold of Walt's hand, and she rubs her thumb against his palm distractedly. They sit on the bench nearest the door.

The general stands in the doorway and calls out to someone. Presently, a younger man in ill-fitting fatigues comes in wearing a businesslike frown. The two men speak to one another at the same time, their words crashing together like speeding cars, and then the general walks out and the other soldier sits heavily on the opposite bench with his gun in his lap.

"What now?" Walt jerks his head at Sister Nathalie. "Will you please explain exactly what is going on here?"

Patrick had said this wouldn't happen, that the border was a formality, nothing more. *Bring some money, that's all,* he had said. *If they stop you, play dumb. Whatever you do, don't call the consulate. Our laws are stricter than theirs. You'll never see your way out of a holding cell at JFK.* But there hadn't been a problem at JFK. Walt had his doctor's note, stating that he had back pain, he needed the Demerol, the aspirin. Why would anyone look in the bottles? He and Marie look like tourists of the blandest kind. The note wasn't even asked for. But this now, this feels like more than a formality. Walt closes his eyes briefly and imagines a dark room, dirt floor, loud noise, a tin plate, no trial. His skin goes cold, and he rubs his arms. Sister Nathalie is talking.

"He goes to get his customs official." She glances at the soldier on his bench, who appears not to be listening. "I would not worry at this moment. No, I would not worry. Later, though..." Her voice trails off and her expression becomes smooth obsidian before opening into a smile.

Marie is already reaching into her shirt and pulling out her purse. Her voice shakes as she says, "How much?"

"Marie!" Walt grabs the hand that is clutching the purse. "Not yet. Wait a bit. We don't even know. Okay?" He releases her hand. "Can you just sit tight?"

She pulls the purse over her head and shoves it at him. Her mouth is small as she says, "You do it, then."

He takes the purse, hangs it around his neck alongside the other one. It is suddenly so hot in the shack that Walt's throat constricts. Small beads of light dance across his eyes and his voice feels smothered as he looks at the soldier and says, "Can I go outside?" The soldier stares. Walt nods at Sister Nathalie, coughs. "Does he hear me? Can you ask him?"

Sister Nathalie turns toward the soldier, but before she says anything, he points his gun at Walt. He points his gun at Walt, and then points it at the door, but in that moment before the gun swivels away from his chest, Walt feels a sickening heaviness in his stomach, hears Marie's quick "Oh!" and knows, finally, how fast it could happen, a place like this. He is off the bench in a moment, measuring his steps and trying to keep from running out the door and onto the small porch. He places both hands on the railing and waits for his breath to return. Not for the first time today, he admits to himself that he is indeed too old for this, and the thought reassures him with its flat factuality. There is a broken flip-flop lying in front of the shack, the plastic thong detached from the sole, and he lets his eyes rest on it before looking around. There seem to be more people in the plaza than earlier. People moving hurriedly in both directions. A woman, not moving at all, standing still in the middle of the chaos, a basket balanced perfectly on her head but seeming, Walt thinks, like it could topple at any moment. The woman peers in front of her, craning her neck without tilting her head. Turns and looks behind her as if she can't remember her point of departure.

A conversation with Patrick, only a few days ago. *Why won't they get tested?* They'd done their homework. Knew that, even in cities where the test was available, no one was willing. *Togolese are the happiest poor people you will ever meet,* said Patrick. *No vegetables, stomachs out to here, but by god, enough corn to go around.* Walt had been confused. *What does that have to do with the test?* Patrick had smiled, launched into a story about a man he met on the road, in a city, on a bus, Walt can't remember. *He said to me, "We all know we are going to die. Why should I know when, and how? Why should my living be darkened by my death?"*

Walt watches the woman unload the basket from her head. She squats low to the ground, raises both arms, lifts the basket inches above her head, pulls her neck back like an inquisitive bird, sets the basket on the ground. She takes the items out brusquely, impatient as a postal clerk. Places them, hard, on the ground: an iron pot. Two tin bowls. Ladle. Scarf coiled like a rope. Slingshot. She rummages in the bottom of the basket and pulls out a small handful of peanuts, which she begins to crack and eat, dropping the shells in the dirt.

And this is her life, thinks Walt. Corrects himself. *And what would I pull out?* He looks over his shoulder at the doorway, through which he can make out Marie's silhouette. What would their life look like, coming out of a basket? A vegetable peeler with a sure rubber grip.

Blueprints and fiber supplements. Backrests, eye pillows, potted ferns, cocktail onions. Their son.

They won't admit it to one another, but he knows Marie feels the same way. *Our son. Our son.* Knows also that she blames him for this, for the guilt and the relief that propelled them here, for the son who won't know what they're doing and wouldn't care if he did, for the years of silence and prosperity: their debt to the world a leaning gun, a crouching lion, a calm and waiting thing.

Walt watches the general return from the eastern side of the border. He is walking with another man. Not a soldier, but an imposing man nonetheless, in a pressed gray suit and (he thinks he can see them in the dirt) brown loafers. As they approach, Walt notes that this man has a face like a badger, hungry and mean. He is talking to the general, but he is looking at Walt, and Walt turns and enters the shed, sits next to Marie, and rubs her shoulder. "I'll talk," he says.

The two men enter together, and the badger sits behind the desk. The soldier who has been keeping watch stands immediately, throwing his shoulders back and cradling his gun. The badger doesn't look at Walt and Marie, but instead stares hard at Sister Nathalie. The general hands him the passports, and he glances down, flips through them, spending time on the stamped pages. Walt wonders what he thinks of their stamps from Mexico, France, Britain, Costa Rica. If he recognizes the names of the countries.

The badger looks up again at Sister Nathalie and says, in perfect English, "You will open your bags."

Sister Nathalie stands. So does Walt. "Let me," he says to her. He is too gruff, he knows, and Sister Nathalie looks at the ground and sits again, her hands in her lap.

Walt props open the two small suitcases on the table. The badger rifles through each one, his hands wandering over Walt's shirts and extra shoes, Marie's sundress and underwear. For a moment, Walt thinks about leaving the duffel wedged between his feet on the floor, but he knows they've seen it, and he bends and lifts it to the table. "Just my carry-on," he says, clearing his throat. He's afraid that despite his age, his voice will break.

The badger unzips the bag. He takes out Walt's mystery novel. He takes out the energy bars. He takes out the small packets of anti-malarials, the Imodium, the fourteen bottles of pills. He sets the bottles up on one corner of the table, largest to smallest. He looks at Walt, smiling. "You are ill?"

"Yes." Walt takes the letter from his doctor, written on hospital stationery, the same hospital that donated their surplus medication. His hand shakes as he hands it over, and he grits his teeth.

The badger takes the letter. He reads it very slowly, mouthing the words. Walt can see that he is struggling.

"Demerol," he says, "and aspirin. For my back." He reaches around, mimes massaging his lower back.

The badger acts as if he hasn't heard him. He continues to read, though faster now, and then he very carefully folds the letter and places it on top of Walt's and Marie's passports. "Very well," he says finally, and opens one of the aspirin bottles.

Walt turns and looks at Marie, who has wrapped her arms around herself and is staring at the space just above the badger's head. She opens her mouth and then closes it again.

The badger stirs his middle finger inside the bottle. Reaches his thumb and forefinger in and pulls out a large pill, reads the small black print, turns the pill over and runs his finger around the blue band that encircles it. "Retrovir," he says, pronouncing it flawlessly. "What is this please?" He looks up at Walt. "You will explain yourself, please."

Marie's voice, quick and urgent from behind him. "It's generic," she says. "It's the same thing. But generic. It's not . . . Sir," she says, and stops.

Walt loves his wife, secretly plans on dying within minutes of her while holding her small, white, wrinkled hand, but he has the sudden urge to twist her arm until she cries out. Marie is a terrible liar.

The badger has opened all of the bottles now, and spilled a few of the pills from each one onto the table. The other aspirin bottle holds the same blue-banded pills. The rest of the containers have different pills, some large, some small. The badger mixes them together on the table, cutting the pile with the side of one hand, dividing it and then mixing it back together. He says something to Sister Nathalie in Éwè. He scoops the spilt tablets back into one bottle, caps all fourteen, and barks at the soldier on the bench. Then he looks at Walt. "You will sit, please," he says.

Walt sits between Marie and Sister Nathalie and waits, the thin plank digging into his thighs, the wall rough against his back. Marie runs a handkerchief across her face, dabbing at her eyes. The sleeping dog raises her head and snaps at a fly, stands and turns in a tight circle, and then lies back down in the same position. Walt feels acutely the uselessness of his hands. He can think of nothing worth saying other than *ne mangez pas.*

The badger makes notations in a small notebook that he took from his suit jacket. He writes for a long time. Finally, he flips the cover closed and places the notebook back in his jacket. He stands, pulls the jacket tight across his shoulders, and paces back and forth in front of Walt and Marie before stopping and extending a hand to Walt. When he speaks, it is as if he is digging up and dusting off each word.

"You will excuse me, please," he says. "How was your voyage?"

Marie grips her knees.

"Fine, thank you," says Walt, shaking the offered hand.

"And your family? All in good health?"

"Yes."

"I am pleased." He begins pacing again, his hands clasped loosely behind his back. Walt can see a long wrinkle in his left pant leg rising up over his knee like an escarpment. "I apologize for the confusion," he continues. "It is a confusion, is it not? Surely you do not mean to sell the drugs?" He stops, turns, waves his hand toward the table, and tilts his head at Walt. "For that is very illegal," he says, "and cannot be tolerated."

Walt stares at the badger's shoes, scuffed and bulging at the toes. Tries to remember any part of what Patrick told him to say. "No," he says. "It's a gift. *Cadeau.*"

In the corner, the soldier shifts the gun in his hands, rocks back on his heels.

"A gift." The badger looks over at Sister Nathalie. "And how do you know this woman?"

Walt doesn't answer.

"Or perhaps," continues the badger, "she is a friend? A friend to whom you bring these gifts? A friend with a clinic somewhere, sick children in need of aid, men and women slowly dying for want of these . . . *médicaments*?" The badger's voice has grown disdainful. His tiny eyes are narrowed as he glances toward Sister Nathalie. "And you think she will give away these *medicaments* like so many bonbons? To what sick? She will sell them in Lomé. She will sell them in the Marché du Nord for money, and then she will return to her home, to her *soeurs,* saying, *Look what I have done, look how God has provided.*" His voice rises, balloons suddenly. He rubs two fingers together. "I know this woman. I have seen her. She has no need for your drugs. Only money." He turns to Sister Nathalie and bellows at her in Éwè. She continues to look down at her lap.

Walt stands up. He feels Marie tug on his pant leg, reining him back, but he steps forward and faces Sister Nathalie. "Who is lying here?" he says. "Can I ask? Can I just ask that? Can I just—?" He stops, because the badger has held up one hand and the soldier has raised his gun and lowered it again, and Marie has laid a firm hand on the small of his back. "That's all I ask," he says, and sits down.

"You see she has no answer for you." The badger's expression is sympathetic. "We are all powerless under God's watchful eye."

The zipper on Marie's purse is stuck. He can't remember what he's supposed to say.

"But of course there is still the question of your wrongdoing. Oh, you are not wrong people, of course not. We are in a gray area, can we agree? What might one do?"

Walt jimmies the zipper back and forth. What are the words? What are the words? Drops the purse with a slap against his chest and pulls his own purse free.

"There are options, I believe. I wonder if you can help me. You, a learned man, what do you suggest?"

Walt rips the money from his purse and holds it in front of him. Their house key slips from between the notes and falls to the floor with a heavy rattle. Marie plucks it up like a hen and jams it in her pocket. She is shaking.

"*Cadeau,*" says Walt breathlessly.

The badger plants his feet and stands in front of Walt for a long moment. He raises his eyebrows and turns up one corner of his mouth. He reaches out, very slowly, and allows his palm to hover next to Walt's outstretched hand. Walt lays the money carefully on the badger's palm, and watches as he wraps his fingers gently around the cash and slides the whole thing, fist and money, into the front of his suit jacket. When he pulls his hand out again, it is empty. The badger stretches it in front of him once more and grasps Walt's own sweaty palm.

"I am so very sorry you have been inconvenienced." He nods toward Sister Nathalie, whose head is turned to face the opposite wall. He barks an order at the soldier, who immediately stands, slings his gun over his shoulder, and begins collecting the bottles of pills, placing some in his pockets, hugging the larger containers to his chest like an infant. "We shall take these *médicaments* so that they do not trouble you any longer." His smile is a wink and a nod. "Please enjoy our mountains, our beautiful country. Please try the coffee. I am sure that your visit will be enjoyable. You have much luck, a beautiful wife. You will find friends in every town, I believe." The badger directs a few more unintelligible words at Sister Nathalie, sweeps his hand toward the soldier, and the two men walk out of the shack. The sound of their feet on the steps as foreboding, Walt thinks, as gunshots.

"Oh, God," says Marie. "Oh, Christ."

The shack is silent for a long moment. The dog sleeps, Marie breathes unevenly but quietly. Walt stares down at his hand, wipes it along his pant leg, looks at it again. He knows the rage to come, feels it cresting like a wave behind his eyes, and he stands, walks over to the nun, shakes her shoulder before he knows he's doing it, shakes it hard like a sieve.

"I can't believe," he says. And then, "Of all the bullshit."

The nun looks up at him with deep, deep eyes. There is something there—is it exhaustion? Fear? Despondency? He can't tell, and this enrages him further. She starts to say something, but her voice comes to him as if from the back of a large auditorium. *Good works,* he hears. *Schooling, nutrition, good living. Sorry,* he hears, and *worthy.*

But he keeps shaking her. Shakes her like he would shake his son. He watches himself jag the nun's torso back and forth, and he feels as if he is watching the scene from a distance of a few feet and many years. *Health and happiness,* he wants to shout. *That's all we want for you!* More, too, he knows, so much more. What would his son do if he could see Walt and Marie in this situation? Would he laugh? Rail against the injustice? When has John ever railed? When has he ever acknowledged his burden?

The dog stretches languidly in her corner and stands. She trots to the doorway and rests in the patch of blinding sunlight before cocking an ear and setting off after some apparition. Walt lets his hand fall from the nun's shoulder. He looks around the voiceless room, where dust has already begun to settle over their footprints. Only three fresh sets now to make: the nun, the woman, the man. Three pairs of feet leaving, never to return, and shouldn't he be grateful for this, after all? Shouldn't he feel as if he has earned it, the air-conditioned room to come, with a bed and white pillows supporting his back? Cold beer and maybe a steak, why not a steak, the relief that now, having done their part, having tried and failed but having tried nonetheless, now, finally, they can go home.

SUZANNE RIVECCA

Stanford University

LOOK MA, I'M BREATHING

After it was over, it seemed silly to say she'd been in danger. The man hadn't hurt her nor had he threatened to. A professional writer, Isabel made a living out of transforming such molehills into mountains. And after it was over, after her friends had stopped calling to make sure she was all right, after she'd stopped reading the courthouse papers, she sat in her living room and stared at her name on the spine of her recently published memoir and wondered if she had the right to feel traumatized at all, or if she, like any "wunderkind" facing a sophomore slump, was merely courting a sequel.

It was true: She had wanted the apartment, had tried hard to look legitimate and solvent. When she wrote "Writer/Teacher" as her occupation on her rental application, she noted in parentheses the name of the famous school where she taught, the school she never would have gotten into as a student and whose campus she still sometimes got lost on after working six months as an assistant professor of

English, as she wandered across identical quad upon quad, stepping briskly as a fired groundskeeper. She wrote down her faculty Web page in case the landlord thought she looked too young to hold such a position. And under "personal references," she cited the best known of her colleagues: a political theorist who made forays into satirical fiction. People recognized his name as noteworthy even if they couldn't remember why. She made sure to capitalize the proper letters in "Ph.D."

The landlord hadn't seemed impressed. There was something off about him: His stoicism bordered on blankness. He appeared to be gazing determinedly through a blind spot. But now and then he seemed to catch a glimpse of whatever lay beyond it, and a sudden flash of feeling would kindle in his eyes, as if he were being shown some internal reel of images that did not quite cohere. He was a lanky man in his early fifties. His hair was still dark and plentiful. He wore a tool belt around his waist.

"There's three nice big closets," he said. "One's probably big enough to be a small study, if you don't mind not having any windows while you work."

"Well," Isabel said, smiling, "I can write anywhere."

He was holding a hammer. He put it down on the kitchen counter and showed her around—the newly tiled kitchen with its dishwasher, the bricked patio surrounded by cedar fencing, the washer and dryer hidden in a cunning little storage shed, the redone bathroom. He narrated the tour with an account of all the repairs he'd made, how he practically had to gut the place, redo the wiring, renovate down to the studs. He wanted to preserve its historical integrity. Pointed out his choice of octagonal black-and-white tiles for the bathroom: "Authentic," he said, "just like the nineteenth century." Described how he scraped dingy paint from the scalloped wainscoting, inch by inch. He told her all this in an almost perfunctory way, but with a slight air of irritation, as if there were something combustible, propulsive, underneath. She would come to recognize this as typical. He spoke as if he expected every topic to erupt into an angry debate for which he was amply armed.

"My great-aunt—my wife's aunt, actually—owns this place, the whole building," he said. "She lives in the flat upstairs. This downstairs apartment has been vacant for years. I retired last year and started really working on sprucing up these family properties."

"Well," Isabel said, "you've done a beautiful job with the renovation. Everything looks just spectacular."

"Thank you," he said. He smiled for the first time. The smile was a surprise: It transformed the cragginess of his face, making him look boyishly grateful.

Encouraged, Isabel talked too much—and rapidly. She displayed a girlish enthusiasm that fit her poorly, even though it was genuine. She *did* love the place, she wanted to live there, but she always felt insincere when she gushed, even over something that truly excited her.

The landlord seemed to appreciate the effort that went into her litany of embellishments, a wish list of domestic accoutrements worthy of *Queen for a Day:* how great it would be to have a washer/dryer, no longer to have to lug her laundry through the filthy streets of her sketchy neighborhood; how she'd been longing for a nice, big clawfoot bathtub instead of her tiny three-cornered shower with its trickly water pressure; and the patio!—how wonderful to have an outdoor space where she could finally grow herbs, annuals, and perennials, all the graceful California flora flourishing in twisty-limbed profusion, so different from the austere and sooty foliage of the Midwest. It was Little Match Girl territory: the stuff of her memoir.

"I'll tell you what," the landlord said. "There was a woman to see the place earlier this morning, had a baby with her, and she might be coming back with her husband any minute. So I don't know. What you gotta understand," and he loomed close, Isabel forcing herself to meet his dark eyes, because she didn't want to seem shifty, "is that the decision is my aunt's, not mine. Since she owns the place. But you're welcome to step out on the deck and finish the application, and I'll see what I can do."

Isabel let him lead her outside. She sat down on a patio chair and finished her application, rooting in her book bag for her credit score and her current landlord's number. She wrote carefully in a penmanship that did not come naturally to her: exaggeratedly rounded, almost childish, each letter unmistakable as the oversized examples in an alphabet primer. It took her about ten minutes. She lingered a moment to look around the yard, with its twining nasturtiums and rosebushes. Then she opened the French doors of the patio and stepped inside to find that the previously empty kitchen was now full of strangers.

The landlord stood there with a young couple: a pretty woman whose saucer-eyed infant dabbled his fingers in her broom-colored ponytail, and her husband, a hipsterish and artfully tousled young professional. The man and the woman oozed the kind of sheepish magnanimity that comes from securing the exact outcome they had strived to get. Next to them sat an elderly woman on a kitchen stool. She was gazing at the baby.

Isabel stood in the middle of the kitchen with her application. The landlord saw her there and his face tightened with one of its brief, pained spasms of feeling.

"Isabel," he jumped in, gesturing toward the old woman, "this is my great-aunt, Marjorie. She's ninety-two years old."

The old woman whinnied out a shocked laugh. "Now, why on earth did you tell her that?"

The young mother piped in, "It's because you look so much younger!" She grinned at the landlord for support. He just kept looking at his aunt. Then he hustled Isabel into the living room as the couple fussed over their checkbook and the lease agreement.

"Look," he said, lowering his voice, "if my aunt hadn't happened to show up when those people came back in, you would've gotten the place. But she likes the idea of renting to a family."

"Oh, I understand," Isabel said. She briefly shimmered with hatred for the family in the next room—their shameless kowtowing, dangling that baby in the old woman's face.

The landlord was still talking. "I would've let you have it for one simple reason," he said. He spoke low and flat and close to her ear, but without looking at her, as if they were Secret Service agents. "You're smarter than them. And I'd rather rent to smart people. They're easier to reason with, in my experience."

"Oh," Isabel said.

Later she wondered why this comment hadn't raised a red flag. But at the time, as she and the landlord stood together in this oddly conspiratorial posture, all she could think about was how badly she wanted the place. Wanted the bucolic mystique of this neighborhood with its bald hill, its water tower, its hidden, snaking staircases and communal gardens, its tumbledown beachy cottages. Wanted to begin some hazy, pastel phase of living: not a life so much as a restive afterlife, compared to what had passed earlier.

Then the landlord said, "Listen here. Tell me how this sounds to you."

He explained that he had another family-owned property, less than three blocks away, in the same neighborhood. A turn-of-the-century little white dormered house with a picket fence, backyard with an avocado tree and rosebushes and fuchsia, big country kitchen, wainscoting and pocket doors and wood floors and window seats and stained glass.

"Meet me there tomorrow morning," he said, "and I'll show you around. I haven't listed the place yet, but I'm renting it more than 60 percent under market value, as long as I can get a tenant in there I trust. I go on instinct. I go on gut. And I have a good feeling about you."

When she saw the house the next morning, her first thought was, *This isn't fair.*

Nothing about it was fair. Not the white clapboard siding, dilapidated and weathered in all the right places, not the overgrown rosebushes, high on the crest of a hill. Not the gabled windows. Not the front door's heart-shaped keyhole. Isabel waved and smiled when the landlord appeared, emerging from a basement entrance holding a rusty toolbox.

"This is beautiful," she burst out.

The landlord gave one of his rare, satisfied smiles, and said, "Thought you'd like it."

He seemed excited, less inhibited than the day before. He kept up a running commentary as he led her through the house.

They entered a rustic slate-tiled kitchen.

"Check this out," he said, indicating the cabinetry. "After the '89 earthquake, I went down and salvaged these drawers from what was left of the old court building. See, they still have case names on them."

Indeed, the drawers were affixed with tiny metal frames encasing old, laminated file names in sepia ink: *Needham v. Connor. The State of California v. Charles A. Grissom, Esq.*

"That is awesome," Isabel said. "A little piece of history."

"Yeah," the landlord said.

He had tons of examples like that. He'd taken the metal roof off an old shed and used it for the walls of a partly enclosed deck off the master bedroom: lopsided and crude, strangely silvery and futuristic, with a view of green hills. He'd built a makeshift closet in the smaller bedroom with a homemade rack, plywood shelving, and a shower curtain. He pointed out the skylight in the master bath— "found that in a junk shop for five dollars, installed it the next day"—and the octagonal tiles he'd scavenged from a condemned house downtown.

"You're very resourceful," Isabel said.

She felt a little ridiculous. She was beginning to realize that she was not herself around this man but instead became a chirping affirmer. *So strong, so smart, so good at everything!* She didn't know why she was acting like this. This man was her father's age.

A fluffy little Pomeranian—the current tenant's—suddenly bounded down the back stairs and flounced around the landlord's feet, panting with happiness. Then its mood changed and it began growling, nipping at the cuffs of his pants.

"You know how I feel about you," he said to the dog.

Isabel laughed. She crouched down and petted the dog. "Do you have a split personality?" she asked.

The landlord gazed down at them impassively, as though waiting out a storm. Isabel got up. The dog scampered away.

"You're gonna love this," he said. "Let me show you the setup in the basement."

She followed the landlord outside and down a short flight of stairs to the lower entrance. He switched on the light. "Well," he said, the corner of his mouth quirked up, "what do you think of *that*?"

Isabel looked around. The place smelled dank and earthy. It had been converted into an underground bachelor pad, complete with kitchenette, bed, desk, computer, a tiny bathroom cordoned off with rickety Plexiglas borders.

"Wow," she said. She couldn't think of anything else to say.

"And check this out," the landlord said, motioning her over to an elevated area next to the galley kitchen. His voice was full of shy pride. Isabel peeked around the corner and saw an enormous octagonal bathtub on a redwood platform, buffed so the porcelain gleamed. It was easily the cleanest thing in the entire basement.

"That's so cool," Isabel said. She felt exhausted.

"When I'm working on the apartment, I stay down here and just walk on over to my aunt's in the morning," the landlord said. "I figure I might as well be comfortable. My son, he's eighteen, stays down here with me sometimes when he's helping me with projects. Cassie—that's the gal who lives in the house right now—can't even tell we're here, that's what she says. We're just in and out, don't cause her any bother."

Isabel smiled.

"Look at this," he said, turning and snatching something from the window ledge. He showed her an old sallow photograph.

"This was taken when I was about your age, when I first moved to the city," the landlord said. "I was studying violin then, living in an SRO. It was the real artist's life, you know? The real bohemian experience. I imagine that's the stage you're at right now."

Isabel felt, as she took the photograph in her hands, that he had brought her to the basement so he could show her this.

She peered at the picture. A younger version of the landlord—heavily bearded, slimmer, but with the same blank, dull eyes, and a plaid shirt buttoned to his neck—lolled on a bare mattress, his head propped against the wall. He looked stoned, and much less angry.

"How old are you here?" Isabel asked him.

"Oh, about nineteen. Twenty, maybe."

"I'm twenty-eight," she said. She meant it to come out as casual, insignificant, but she got it all wrong. She saw his face darken. "I know I look young," she hastened to add.

He shrugged. "Huh. Yeah, you do look young. I was just guessing."

She flushed. She decided that it would be a mistake to explain further, to tell him she'd only pointed out her age so he'd know she was a responsible adult and not some collegiate party girl. She kept her mouth shut and inhaled the stale damp air.

"My wife grew up in this house," the landlord suddenly announced. "She shared that big downstairs room—the one that's used as a living room now—with her three sisters. And she has four brothers besides." His face briefly lost its harshness and became almost tender.

"Catholic?" Isabel blurted out. Then inwardly she swore at herself: What compelled her to ask this question every time someone mentioned having a big family, as if she herself hadn't been raised Catholic—traditionalist, Vatican II–rejecting Catholic, at that? As if her own parents, an almost-priest and an almost-nun who believed their union had been divinely engineered by Saint Brigid, hadn't practiced birth control. She remembered putting away the laundry one day and finding condoms in her dad's sock drawer. Had she put that in the book? She hadn't.

"I was raised Catholic, that's why I asked," she said.

He shot her a dark sideways look. "Do you go to Mass here?"

"Uh, no," she said. "I don't practice."

Afterward, she couldn't remember how they maneuvered past this awkwardness and emerged into the sunlight, if one of them jump-started the action with a throat-clearing or a grunt, or if they just ascended the stairs like chastened parishioners. Somehow, they were outside again. She thanked him. And then as she turned to leave the landlord did an odd thing.

"Isabel!" he said, in what seemed unabashed joy and triumph.

He whisked his hand from behind his back and brandished an avocado, one he must have surreptitiously plucked from the backyard tree and squirreled away somewhere on his person. He had conducted the rest of the tour with the green fruit nestled in his pocket like a charm.

"Take it," he said. He was beaming. Isabel smiled back, embarrassed for him.

"Thank you," she said. The fruit was warm and slightly mushy.

She went and sat in a nearby park, a big flat plateau of green overlooking the city. The park was full of women with baby carriages. When she got up to go, she left the avocado in the grass.

He said he'd call. But after a week passed with no word, Isabel began to worry.

It was May. She had twelve weeks of leisure before she had to teach again, and she was fretful, sleepless, pacing around the ugly apartment that reminded her of every rented house she'd grown up in with its putty-colored walls, curling linoleum, synthetic-fiber carpet that stuck straight up like a cheap doll's hair.

Outside was no better. She saw a man taking a shit on the street—well, technically, taking a shit in a shallow cardboard box, which he then carried ahead of him like a lunchroom tray: an act that disturbed her more than the occasional gunshots heard at night.

Isabel was supposed to be working on her next book. But she didn't want to write it. She didn't know what more she had to say. She told herself that if she could just get settled someplace decent, she'd be able to concentrate. She left a message on the landlord's voice mail, sitting at her desk in a bathrobe, trying to sound crisp and busy: "Hi, Glenn, this is Isabel, the girl you showed the house to last week. I really loved the place and, um, I was just calling to check in and see how the process is coming along." She thanked him and re-cited her number into the receiver.

After days passed and he didn't call, she began to imagine para-noid scenarios.

"I know what happened," she told her friend Andy, over coffee. "He looked me up, went and read my book, and was horrified."

"By your life?" Andy said.

"No," said Isabel, "by my eagerness to disclose it graphically."

Andy paused and stirred his coffee. "It's not graphic."

"Yeah, well, it doesn't matter, because I know this type of guy. This kind of old-school, stoic guy who believes you don't air your dirty laundry in public, that it's a weakness and it means you're unstable. Plus I think he's Catholic. So he's got to hate me."

Andy said, "You think the pope sent out an alert to all parishes? With your face on it? Like in the post office?"

Isabel said, "That pope's a Nazi."

"Hey. *Ex*-Nazi, if you don't mind."

Andy was a lapsed Catholic, too, although his defection had more to do with indifference than antagonism. He was a round blond man, endearingly bearish, who unself-consciously danced with his wife in public and treated Isabel like a pesky and beloved little sister, although they were the same age. They had met when he profiled Is-abel for the local arts magazine where he worked as a features editor. He was her only male friend.

"Well," Isabel said, "it's driving me crazy. This place is my dream house. If my nine-year-old self saw this house, she'd lose her shit."

"Didn't you say the landlord lives in the basement?" Andy said. "Isn't that kind of creepy?"

"He doesn't live there," Isabel snapped. "He just stays there when he's doing repairs on the other place. Besides, I'd rather have some guy in the basement than drunks pissing all over the street and passing out."

"Really?" Andy said. He seemed genuinely surprised. "You'd rather have a guy in the basement?"

Isabel walked home, annoyed at Andy for his cynicism. He and Beth lived in a beautiful rent-controlled flat near the waterfront with huge windows and built-in bookcases and a garden. Plus, they had each other. She decided not to call Andy for a few days.

An old man ambled toward her on the sidewalk. He was dressed like a weekend golfer in khaki shorts and athletic socks and a bright polo shirt, his hair white and groomed. He stopped to address her. She thought he needed directions.

"You're a human piece of shit," the old man said. He looked her straight in the eye, his face a scrubbed pink dumpling, his blue eyes watery and clear. "Nothing but a human piece of shit."

Isabel walked away from him. Her hands shook as she unlocked her front door, even as she told herself it was dumb to feel personally offended by someone who was out of his mind.

She made chamomile tea and tried to relax. She checked her voice mail: nothing. She checked her e-mail and that's where she found it, buried in her in-box with the junk mail and announcements of readings and multiple notes from her editor with the subject line "checking in": a message from the landlord.

Isabel stared at the boldfaced subject line—"House"—and put her cup down. Her stomach felt like a whirlpool. She couldn't remember giving the landlord her e-mail, but she must have put it on the application. She clicked on it.

Hi Isabel. Glenn here. Thanks for your interest in the house as well as the apartment that you saw earlier. Coming from a creative artist such as yourself, I consider it a compliment. My initial impressions of you were that you were practical yet funky. And as such would like the house with all of its special touches. But after reading your application, doing an online search, and taking a look at your published work, I became aware that you are as well an intense artist who perhaps would require a more vital environment than this neighborhood would provide. Upon discussion, my wife agreed with me. My wife is friendly with a young engaged couple looking for a prenuptial nest, and we decided that they would be a better fit.

As an artist, violinist, who dropped out of college and moved to San Francisco because I needed stimulation for my art, may I suggest you try the theatre district? Don't laugh. With some self-defense spray and your intense awareness you'd be ok.

May your creative energies stay focused. Don't forget all great artists have one thing in common. Inner resources, and you've got those in spades.

Isabel read the message twice. Twenty minutes passed before she was able to compose a terse note in response, thanking the landlord for his time and consideration. Then she called Andy.

"I was right," she said. "He 'researched' me and got scared off. Am I so off-putting? Is my memoir that scary?"

Andy said, "He's the one that sounds a little scary. 'Nuptial nest'? And all that shit about researching you? I think you dodged a bullet."

"I don't even know," Isabel said. To her dismay, her throat felt hot and thick. "I'm starting to think it's me, that I'm a person who freaks people out."

Andy told her she was being ridiculous and that she'd find a better place.

After hanging up, Isabel crawled into bed and lay on her back, looking up at the ceiling. Her stomach was queasy. She thought of her junior year in high school, how she used to throw up from nerves and misery almost every day after lunch. The school counselor found out and told her parents. "I'm puking because this school's misogyny makes me *physically sick*," she remembered screaming at her mom.

But no. It wasn't just outrage. She hadn't puked her way through high school in proud servitude to some abstract feminist ideal. Isabel got up and opened the bottom drawer of the filing cabinet where she kept extra copies of her memoir. How had she portrayed the puking episode?

She flipped through and found the section. She'd devoted five pages to it. "Day after day," she had written, "I unwittingly enacted what I refused to accept: the belief that bodies are capable of ideological fidelity. That a corpse can smell of lilies. That a woman can recline in a vat of boiling oil, serene as a mermaid. That the flesh is a reflection of the soul."

Isabel closed the book. There was nothing about the anxiety of those days or their loneliness. Had she been so soldierly, so numb? She knew she hadn't. She had thrown up because she was a nervous wreck from studying like a maniac and working twenty hours a week to pay for AP tests so she could escape from her hometown and get into a good school, a school with a *name,* and never have to come back. The pressure was self-inflicted. Her parents believed that sincerity of effort and purity of intention far outweighed grade point average. Isabel hated that their expectations for her were so modest and homespun and banal and at the same time so completely out of her reach. She was convinced they wanted to keep her there, keep her hidebound and ignorant and normal, married to a churchgoing man with a job in computers, chatelaine of a sensible bungalow, and it terrified her. She believed that personal autonomy was attainable only through extraordinary achievement and the inevitable detachment that accompanied it. At first she found the isolation that came from her hard work to be a boon. But lately she thought of it more as an unhappy consequence: necessary, and outweighed by the beneficial aspects, but something to be endured.

Isabel put the book back in the filing cabinet and shut it. She knew she should start looking at apartments again. But the process seemed so daunting—talking to people, providing credentials, waiting on credit reports and background checks—and she was suddenly furious that she didn't have someone to do it with her. She was furious at all the people in her life who'd gotten married, had kids, moved across country, told her she was admired but not loved, failed to read her mind, left her here to do this by herself. But it was the kind of fury a mother feels when her kid runs across the street and just misses getting hit by a car: boneless, surging, and fanged with love. At that moment, if she could have gathered them all in a large room—she pictured the basement conference room at Saint Stephen's where her youth group had met—she would have reached for them, grasping. She would have said, *I'm not fine. I'm not fine. I'm not fine without you.*

A couple of days later, the landlord left a phone message while she was out. His voice was leaden and rough. He said, "Isabel, Glenn here. I don't know if you've come to your senses yet or if you're still interested in the house, but I managed to convince my wife you'd be a far better tenant than the engaged couple. She saw my reasoning. So it's yours if you want it, for certain this time."

There was something smug and deadened in his voice—*I managed to convince my wife*—and Isabel knew she didn't want to see the man again. Still, she was tempted by visions of that house.

"Do yourself a favor," Andy said when she told him, "and do not respond to this guy. He's too much of a whack job, and he lives in the basement. Please."

And Isabel, though tempted by the offer, had bitched so much to Andy about the landlord's inappropriate e-mail that she would lose face if she took the place now, and she didn't want Andy to think she'd been complaining just for the sake of complaining. "Yeah, I know," she said. "I won't. It's just...the house. You know? But I'm over it."

Two weeks passed. Isabel read a lot, played solitaire on the computer, ended up sleeping most of the day and night. She got into the habit of drinking in the wee hours—not much, just a nightly scotch and soda. It was after one of these nights—midday with the sunlight streaming through the picture window and her head tender and pulsing with hangover—that she received another e-mail from the landlord. Its subject line was "Communication as Consummation."

Isabel clicked on it and saw that it was several paragraphs long. She read straight through without stopping.

Isabel,

Your instincts are correct, but your intuition is inchoate. My intentions were honorable, however. If you will excuse one last breech into familiarity so as to set the record straight and attempt to remedy any further injury that only imagined injustices can inflict.

There is always the potential when a man and woman meet for a life-altering event to take place. Where one party is left overwhelmed and unable to continue on as before. Such occurred on April 19, when a naive young woman, seemingly unaware of her own enchantment and power, innocently befriended a man whose life had long since steered into one of banal existence. She showed him what might have been, but when it was over, he was left with the reality of what will always be.

But what of her? Did he damage her as well? Did he usurp her self-confidence going forward? Does she have now another red flag to further smother her spontaneity? He hopes not. That would be a crime. She was so young, so beautiful, so trusting. Like Johanna in *Sweeney Todd*. It's not her fault that a man could be attracted to first her intelligence and beauty, then her youth and laughter. That this ethereal attraction was so profound that the baser attractions were nonexistent confounded him. That imagined reciprocity wasn't her fault either. When he showed her a picture of himself when he was 20, she did ask him how old he thought she was. "28? Maybe she's telling me she's not too young for me," the deranged individual thought. When he mentioned he had a wife, he thought he saw out of the corner of his eye a slight jerk of her head as if in disappointment. Or so he delusioned.

Yes he wanted her, yet he loved her. He knew that he was not the perfect man for her, yet he wanted her around. He wanted her near. Like a third-grade boy wanting to sit next to the prettiest girl in class, he wanted to be close to her. How close? How close is close? In his ultimate fantasy, he imagined lying with her fully clothed and embracing. No tastes, no scents, no ravenous hunger. Just the compression of two separate entities until their cells collide and there is an interchange of all past pain and longing. But he didn't expect that nor would he ever have initiated it. Just to have her in the same house, and see her on occasion, would have delighted him. But that was not to be, and a few weeks later she responded to his attempt at familiarity with a terse businesslike note, totally at odds with her prior congeniality. And he knew she was wisely severing the relationship. He made one last feeble attempt, but was so distraught that she most likely sensed his need and was repulsed.

But he did love her. His most lasting memory of her will be the first. As he was telling her about the closet in the rental property, he noticed her flinch with her eyes. This is a very fragile girl, he thought, and immediately a feeling of sympathy and protectiveness came over him. He will always be protective of her, not like a father, but more like a grandfather, with adoration and worship. She was the closest thing to Jane Eyre that he will ever encounter. It concerns him that someone of her genius has to suffer. He would have done anything within his means to protect her. In his ultimate fantasy he saw her as the lyricist for his imagined musical based on The Damnation of Faust. He saw her accompanying him on his semiannual solo sojourns to NYC to see the Broadway musicals that always bring tears to his eyes.

Since you only know how much you love something when you tell it good-bye, it is a rare luxury to be prescient at the final moment of any relationship. Had I known on that Sunday when you left the house. That final touch, that final glimpse, that final sound of your voice. They would have been embedded in my consciousness forever. But now they are lost, and this is all that remains. Good-bye.

She laughed.

How could she not? The melodrama. *The Damnation of Faust.* How he referred to himself in the third person. It was so over-the-top that for several seconds she just sat in front of the computer, open-mouthed, on the verge of giddiness, murmuring *What the fuck?* As if someone were there with her. And her first impulse was to find a witness. It was how she'd felt after her book had been accepted for publication—the feeling of having received a bizarrely random tribute, one that was predicated on someone's false perception of her.

Andy was at work. Isabel's other friends in the city were colleagues at the college; they didn't know her very well. But she wanted to be among other people, away from the computer.

She stepped outside. The sun was bright and the street smelled of stale piss. The usual group of day laborers played cards on the corner. She walked several blocks to a coffee shop, slipping in and out of crowds of uniformed children, squalling drunks, ragged men and women pushing shopping carts, baby-faced hipsters in 1940s vintage. She felt an irrational need to collar someone, anyone, even the drunks and the children, and blurt out what had happened. Preface it with *Tell me what I'm supposed to think of this.* But instead she ordered black tea and sat on a bench outside the café. She watched the people.

After a few minutes, her eyes filled with tears. She tried to stanch them, but they overflowed and ran down her face. She reacted as she would have to a bout of public incontinence: pulled her coat tightly around her and walked home as quickly as possible.

Isabel lived in quasi denial about her memoir being a memoir. She hated to see it shelved alongside dreary accounts of addiction and disease and familial disgrace. Her favorite author, a dead man, a writer's writer, called these books the "Look Ma, I'm Breathing" genre: disclosure for the sake of disclosure.

But she never would have written her story as fiction. It *was* disclosure for the sake of disclosure. She *wanted* people to know these things had happened to her. She wanted people to look her in the eye and talk to her while knowing full well she'd been taught to idolize martyrs, had worked and lived as ascetically as a monk, and had recorded it all with such brittle and sphinxlike restraint that no one, not even the most cynical, could accuse her of exaggerating. She wanted people to squirm under the weight of it, knowing they couldn't bring up her past in any but a literary context, knowing that, eternally, she had the last word. A last word with a large print run.

The book ended with a description of the last time she went to Mass, when, on a whim, she walked into a Catholic Church in the city she was living in. She was nineteen. It was the only non-Latin, nontraditionalist Mass she'd ever attended. There were only a few people in the pews. The priest faced the congregation. As he presided over the Sacrament of transubstantiation, his rote competence struck her as banal as a vacuum salesman's pitch. He seemed like a nice man. She sat through the whole Mass unmoved, only a little startled by the parts she wasn't used to: the folksy hymns, the shaking of hands, the Communion dispensed by ushers and laypeople. She walked out of the building into the sunlight with a condensed impression, finally, of everything her parents hated about the new Church. And her only emotional response was surprise that the enemy was so tepid and meek, after all.

She wrote, "And I felt a tender exasperation toward my parents, as if they were children afraid of the bogeyman."

That wasn't true.

What she'd really thought was, *I forgive them*. And then realized there was no need to. Her parents, the Church, her teachers, the high school oafs—she had already forgiven all of them. It was easy to forgive the people left behind. The people she couldn't forgive were those who had left *her* behind. Almost everyone she had slept with. The friends who'd moved away. None had victimized her. None had been committed enough to victimize her.

Perhaps this was why, as the landlord continued to e-mail, she did not feel angry. Not even threatened. Not at first. Just abuzz with a disturbing, nauseating curiosity, as though turning over a boulder to see the mess of grubs and worms. No, she wasn't exactly angry. He had not been stoic, after all; he had been moved. He had brazenly shone a light on her vulnerability: *This is a very fragile girl.* Then, instead of recoiling, he drew closer.

She didn't want him to come closer. But she did not feel entitled to push him away.

The next e-mail came three days after the last.

Isabel,

No I won't just go softly into the night. Not when there is a greater need afloat. I was at the DMV today, and saw all the ugliness and ignorance and thought of you and how the fine should look out for each other. I want to be your bodyguard, but first you must trust me, so I want to establish my pedigree with you.

Isabel rubbed her eyes. It was four in the morning; her sleep patterns had been disrupted by too much daytime napping. The e-mail had been sent a mere twenty minutes earlier. She shivered. She imagined the landlord in the basement of the rental house, fortified by the nobility of his mission, typing away as the tenant and tiny dog slept upstairs. She wondered if he had some way of telling how quickly his e-mails were read.

The landlord followed his opening declaration with a long litany of vital statistics: birth date, parents' occupations, high school years, SAT scores, significant relationships.

He described his career trajectory, from playing violin in a quartet to getting a "temporary" job at the phone company that lasted for thirty years. He wrote about how his mother had died of a heart attack a month earlier and how he'd attempted mouth-to-mouth resuscitation.

I realized later that Mom was the greatest love of my life. She was a brilliant woman. I could tell she never cared for my wife too much, but yet she never said a bad thing about her.

By the way we are 90 degrees apart on the Zodiac. You and me. Talk about incompatible. You're fixed fire and I'm fixed earth. As opposed to active or mutable. Probably one reason I thought I understood you so quickly. You're definitely a strong person with a sense of purpose. Like me.

I have an enormous ability to stay on task and concentrate for extended periods. I worked 24 hours straight through the night before that couple with the baby moved into the flat.

And my new project, Isabel, is you: your well-being, your happiness. You are just too fine a commodity to allow to be ravaged by the baser forces at play in this town. I'm honestly not asking for anything in return. Why can't an older guy with all the time in the world and everything he needs help out someone like you, an artist who needs time for her work? Of all the things I liked about you, I think it's your joy that I remember the most. You walking down the sidewalk that morning, your green shirt on, and the smile on your face when you saw me. You looked 15.

A week later came the e-mail that ended it. She was almost relieved as she read it. He'd snapped at last. It was like a fever breaking. There was no salutation.

Your silence has given me the opportunity to reflect. I'm starting to hate you. And to think I compared you to Jane Eyre.

I had an insight today. I think you're a chameleon. You take on whatever colors will gain you the most in any situation. I wonder if you really have your own artistic vision, or are just giving others what you think they want.

I first noticed it today, when I listened to your phone message of a month ago. You sounded hot. You definitely were working me. Oozing charm in every inflection and intonation. You wanted this house. I remember when I first heard it. You sounded like a whore, the ultimate opportunist. Not the precious fragile girl I had met the day before.

Before I go, I'm going to share a little of my life philosophy with you, since I know you're smart enough to maybe see a glimmer of truth in it, if not now, maybe some time in the future. Use it in another book, if you ever get beyond gazing at your own navel.

All women are animals. And they will only go for a man who can bring out the animus in them, even though intellectually they despise that part of themselves. The lipstick dykes, of which you may be one for all I know, have convinced themselves that they can live without a man, but never say never. We're animals for a reason. I'm not the man to do it, but I can see the potential fire in you, and though you may deny it or neglect it, I hope someday it will be aroused and you will learn.

Strong butch women have made this country unsafe for the rest of the women. How? They were the suffragettes. Once women got the vote, due to their innate emotionalism, they liberalized the criminal laws. Now all women live in fear. If only white men could still vote, the streets would be a lot safer. Only weak men allow their women to live in fear. Now they're afraid of doing what's right for fear of going to jail.

When their innate vulnerability is stifled and denied by the politically correct, that is when women start to idealize being hurt. Being punished. Like you. Although I have to say: Most of them don't start as young as you did. But I guess you always were precocious. You wrote you could make yourself climax by the age of five, simply by thinking about being beaten. Because of Catholicism? Expiation? I don't think so. I think it goes deeper than that. I think you picked the easy answer. What you wanted was to be protected. What you needed was for your fragility to be affirmed. It wasn't. Simple as that.

I'm not too worried about you though. Beneath that fine-arts exterior, despite that weakness for humiliation, you're a scrapper, a dirty fighter, you'll do what you need to do. I can see you as a white slave in a Chinese whorehouse. Convincing each master he's the best. Whatever it takes to survive.

Isabel shut off her computer. She went to the bathroom and threw up. When there was nothing left she kept dry heaving until something stirred in her, like a small foot put down gently.

She got up from the floor and brushed her teeth. She turned the computer back on and printed out each e-mail from the landlord, one by one, and looked up the county clerk's Web site. She dressed in her severest and most asexual clothing: black pants, gray button-down that accentuated the flatness of her chest, clunky boots. Then she walked outside, stepped over blocks of passed-out bodies, and took the bus downtown to the courthouse.

The building's exterior was white and tiered as a wedding cake, but the inside looked sterile and joyless. Isabel had to fill out five separate forms. It felt as if she were writing the same information over and over again.

The clerk, a young Hispanic woman with long nails and wavy, copper-highlighted hair, told her what to do. There were other women in the room, too, filling out Requests for Orders to Stop

Harassment; Isabel was the most dressed up and looked younger than all of them. At first this made her nervous, but as she stepped forward and committed herself to the process an old self-preserving reflex took over: a restrained bravado that made her look the clerk in the eye, refuse to apologize for not being worse off or battered or poor. She filled out the exhaustive forms with lucid encapsulations and in impeccable penmanship. She filled out the civil harassment report. Then filled out the request. Then applied for the fee waiver and the petition to have the sheriff serve the papers. *I would like the court to serve him,* she wrote. *I do not want to ask any family member or friend to have contact with this man; he's clearly volatile and unpredictable.*

Months later she would reread the papers, struck by the desperate pomposity of her language, and cringe.

The clerk took the papers and said, "So the next step is to come back in three hours after they've been filed and endorsed by the Superior Court. And then you'll receive your date for the hearing."

"Is he going to be at the hearing?" Isabel said.

The clerk said, "He has the option to be."

"Will he be able to talk to me?"

"No," the clerk said, shaking her head. "He isn't allowed to address you directly. You'll sit in separate sections of the courtroom. There's a bailiff present. Everything's very controlled."

The clerk's dark eyes were wide and kind.

"I want to minimize contact with him as much as possible."

"He probably won't even show up," the clerk said. "A lot of times they don't."

When everything was filed and endorsed, Isabel didn't want to go home. She thought of her computer, its ON button glowing neon green in the corner of the living room. She couldn't think of where to go.

When she finally showed up at Andy and Beth's front door, she immediately launched into a defense of her presence before Beth could even say hello.

"I'm sorry for dropping in on you," Isabel said. "It's just that I don't feel comfortable going home right now. This man's been stalking me, and I just filed a restraining order, and he knows where I live, and I just need to be somewhere other than there. If you can just let me sit in your living room and read or something for a while. I won't get in your way."

Beth's eyes widened. She opened the door. "Isabel, *what*? What? Get in here."

Their house was quiet and warm and orderly. There was a cat and a fireplace. Tacked to the fridge was a handwritten schedule of whose turn it was to cook, and which recipe from *The Moosewood Cookbook* would be used. The walls, a warm brick red, felt safely enclosing. Beth brought her a cup of tea.

"Andy's still at work," she said. She looked tired, with grooves under her eyes and her straw-colored hair loose.

Isabel had always felt intimidated by Beth, who was tall and willowy and had been raised by missionaries in Uganda and spoke three languages. Isabel explained what was happening in her most moderate tone, not wanting to sound like an overreacting writer, worried that Beth wouldn't believe her, that Beth suspected her of trying to seduce Andy, even though Beth made sympathetic noises and touched Isabel's knee during the creepiest parts, as if they were watching a horror movie together.

"Something kind of like that happened to me once," Beth said when Isabel finished.

"Really? What?"

"Well," Beth said, adjusting her skirt and scooting closer to Isabel on the floor, "this was when Andy and I were dating. It was this wacko who lived in the Catholic Charities shelter across the court-yard from my building. The guy would jerk off sitting in his win-dowsill, hissing to get my attention. Then he tried to break in one night when I was sleeping. I called Andy and he drove me to his house. And after that I never really lived there again. I had to break my lease, move in with Andy, and the freak loitered around the front of the building the whole time I was moving. I seriously thought Andy was going to kill the guy."

Isabel looked at her. "Jesus Christ," she said. "Well, now I feel comparatively lucky."

Beth shook her head. "I don't know. The person you're dealing with has access to your personal information. And he's much more articulate and self-possessed."

Isabel felt a sudden urge to be close to Beth. She wanted to scoot into the curve of her lean, strong arm, put her head on her shoulder, ask her if she was sure, positive, that Isabel was a good person, a person who didn't deserve this, a person not at fault.

She wondered if Beth had ever read her book.

"This makes me want to go back and change the book," she blurted out. "Change everything in it."

"Your book?" Beth said. "Why?"

"Because," Isabel said, "I keep picturing him reading it. It makes me seem so cold and hard. And I was never like that. I don't want people thinking they can hurt me and I won't feel it. They read that, they think I'm immune to everything. And I'm such a fucking mess. I want to write a book called *I'm a Fucking Mess, Now Leave Me Alone*. You know?"

Beth laughed. And so it all came off as gallows humor, Isabel mak-ing a self-deprecating joke to diffuse the intensity, and she could tell Beth was relieved; Beth had been worried she would break down.

"I need to work on my lesson plan for tomorrow, honey," Beth said, "but you can totally stay here, okay? As long as you need." She squeezed Isabel's shoulder.

When Andy came home, they all had dinner. They discussed the upcoming hearing.

Andy said, "You're going to verbally eviscerate him in front of that judge. He'll be sorry he was ever born."

Beth added, "He's fucking with the wrong girl."

"He has no idea what he's in for," Andy said. He chuckled. "It's going to be awesome."

Isabel looked down at her salad. Then she looked up and smiled. "Yeah," she said.

The night before the hearing, she wrote down everything she wanted to say. She ironed her outfit: a button-down pink shirt and gray pants, the ensemble of a postcollegiate interviewee. Her strategy was to look as young as possible while sounding as old as possible.

Andy and Beth drove her to the courthouse. They both took the morning off work. Isabel was touched at how they stuck by her, flanking her on either side like parents, their faces wary and more serious than she had ever seen them. They kept scanning the crowds.

Isabel spotted the landlord as she waited in line to give the clerk her case number and sign in. There were at least twenty other civil harassment cases being heard in the same courtroom, and offenders and accusers lingered uneasily in the same line, not speaking. It was easy to tell which was which. The accusers were mostly female and had someone, if only a court-appointed advocate, with them. The offenders were all male and unaccompanied, with haunted, defensive eyes. They did not look prepared.

Neither did the landlord. She was surprised to find him much slighter than she remembered, without his tool belt and jeans. And his air of gruff authority was completely deflated. He looked shell-shocked. His face was unshaven and sallow, his hair mussed, and he wore all white: a stained white T-shirt and white sweatpants. He stood six people ahead of Isabel in line. She pointed him out to Andy and Beth.

Andy craned his neck. "What does he think he is, a Hare Krishna?" he said.

"My god," Beth whispered, "what a creep. He looks deranged."

Isabel kept her head down as they filed into the courtroom. It was completely full. The defendants sat on one side and the plaintiffs on the other. In front of the judge's bench was a long table with two chairs and a microphone on each end. The bailiff told everyone to stand, and the judge entered the room. She swam in her black gown, a small middle-aged woman with short curly hair like Isabel's mother's.

"Good," Beth whispered. "It's a woman."

There were eight cases before Isabel's. The first to testify was a young black woman who kept one elbow on the table with her keys loosely in her fist and gestured, jangling, while she talked. The defendant wasn't there.

"Obviously he can't understand that 'restraining order' means 'stay away.' This got renewed once already, and he still keeps coming around, to where I work, to the house, while I'm alone with the kids, and I'm thinking he is never going to leave me alone." Underneath the fear and strain in the woman's voice was a pragmatic, frustrated intelligence breaking through like cracks of light.

Isabel looked down at her notes, feeling sick. What was she doing here, wasting taxpayer money, a bourgeois lightweight spooked by objectionable e-mails? She licked her lips and read, *I was disturbed, not only because this man is my father's age with grown children and is a virtual stranger to me, but because he is so estranged from reality as to construct a narrative of intimacy and attachment based on absolutely nothing.*

It seemed so impossibly formal. She stole a glance at the landlord's yellowish, vacant-eyed face across the aisle. He was watching the woman speak, watching her walk away from the table and talk to the bailiff after getting her order renewed for another three years. He sat through the next six cases with the same lack of expression. And when Isabel's name was called, his was called with it, and Andy patted her shoulder and hissed, "Kill him," and she knew, with weary inevitability, that she would.

Isabel and the landlord sat down at opposite ends of the table. It was like a game show without buzzers. They didn't look at each other as the judge leaned forward and said, "Ms. Hyde, would you make a statement explaining why you filed this request?"

Isabel bent her head toward the microphone and began to speak. She felt the landlord staring at her. She kept looking up at the judge, watching the woman's face change as she unspooled her long memorized sentences, hands folded in front of her, voice high and flat and sweet. She relished the jolt on the judge's face. She thought of how she must look next to this haggard, jowly, unkempt man: tiny and neat as a bandbox figure, chillingly youthful. *You looked 15.*

She talked and talked. She was conscious of using the phrase "estranged from reality" several times; she switched to "lacking in rational judgment." She ended with, "I filed this order not because I felt my life was in danger, but because I wanted to prevent his behavior from escalating further, to nip this in the bud before it grew completely out of control."

Then it was the landlord's turn to respond. He sighed. He shuffled the papers in front of him, slumped in his seat, and cleared his throat with a phlegmy croak.

"I had hoped," he said, looking down, "that the e-mails would provide a dialogue between us. I never expressed a sexual desire for her. I offered to help her and hoped for a friendship. Only my final e-mail would have alarmed a normal person, and even in that one I was trying to serve a legitimate purpose. She told me she was a Catholic. I assumed she understood guilt." He coughed. "Her book—she wrote a book, it's widely available, out there for public consumption"—the contempt in his voice brought a reflexive, close-lipped smirk to her face—"and it makes a point about masochism, especially among females. I provided a theoretical and biological sociological explanation for why certain girls and young women have this problem, to start a dialogue."

He raised his voice. "Your Honor, it's excerpts like these that invite communication about these issues. *The nuns and brothers were not sadists.*" He kept going, his voice becoming more forceful, measured, staccato, like a filibustering senator quoting the Constitution. With a horrible start, Isabel realized he was reading from her memoir.

"They did not enjoy paddling children, and it was their obvious reluctance and distaste that snapped me out of my repeat-offender stupor quicker than a real beating ever could. I would have preferred the worst physical pain to this grudging, put-upon delivery, this intimation that they and not I were suffering the real punishment."

He had a copy of her book in his hands. The judge looked at Isabel, almost involuntarily. The little girl on the cover, indolent and dark-haired, dressed for her first Holy Communion, also looked in Isabel's direction.

"Now," the landlord continued, slapping it shut, "this is a girl who masturbated from the age of five to fantasies of physical harm. This is all in the book. It seemed notable to me that there's a connection between this denial of her own vulnerability and the masochism she displays at school. She didn't tie them together in the book. All I was trying to do was bring it to her attention, as a reporter might do while interviewing."

"Sir," the judge began. "Sir, you've said—"

"I wasn't threatening," the landlord said. His voice wavered. "I never threatened her, that's the last thing I'm going to say, I'm sorry, Your Honor."

There was a pause. Then the judge said, "Ms. Hyde, do you want to respond?"

Isabel looked up at her helplessly: her black robe like a cleric's, her rimless glasses and the eyes behind them. For a moment she was so overcome with shame she wanted to run out of the room. Then she thought of Andy, behind her. How he probably wished he could storm the bench and do this for her. Isabel found her anger where it always was. She sat up straight and stiff.

"I think," she said, "his defense of his actions as stemming from some attempt to initiate 'dialogue' with me is baseless. I never mentioned my writing to him, never invited his feedback or response. My being the author of a book doesn't justify these intrusive and unwanted personal attentions and it doesn't mean I invited them. What he wrote was of a personal nature. It was not a book review. He called me a Chinese whore."

That just popped out. Then she remembered, aghast, that he had called her a *white* whore in a Chinese whorehouse. She half-expected him to correct her. She pointed her eyes down to signify she was done.

The judge cleared her throat and said, "All right. The restraining order is granted for three years. Under this order the accused cannot come within fifty feet of the complainant, cannot call, e-mail, write, or otherwise initiate contact with her, without facing imprisonment. Mr. Elkin, you are free to go; Ms. Hyde, please wait a moment for your paperwork."

The landlord got up and shuffled out. She saw the bailiff, a large black man, stop him at the door and confer with him in a curt, revolted way, using choppy hand gestures. She couldn't look anymore. He had left her book on the table.

Andy and Beth took her out to lunch to celebrate.

"You were great," Beth said. "You handled yourself so well."

"He threw me," Isabel said. "With the book thing."

"Well, he shot himself in the foot," Andy said, overenthusiastically dumping fruit salad on his and Beth's plates, "because that just proved he was nuts. It's like some psycho waving around a Britney Spears album and claiming her lyrics were speaking to him."

"Except Britney Spears doesn't sing about being a masturbating masochistic toddler. Unless there's a subtext I'm not getting."

They didn't laugh. Isabel hadn't expected them to. She kept eating her salad.

"It doesn't matter what the book said," Andy told her. "He had no right."

They ate for a while in silence. Isabel looked at Andy. She knew he'd read the book, and she assumed Beth had, but neither had ever discussed it with her. It was embarrassment, she knew, and respect. They liked her; they didn't want to think of bad things happening to her, or of her thinking bad things about herself. Now she saw they were also ashamed for her. And she knew the landlord had given the most emotionally charged and forthcoming response the book would ever receive—peerless in its fierce claim on her attention, its reckless disregard of her reserve, peerless and unforgivable.

Isabel looked down at her plate.

"Well," she said, "my next book is going to be a treatise on the mating habits of the dung beetle. Fuck this shit."

They laughed harder than they needed to.

———

Isabel found a new apartment on the opposite side of town, an affordable place with a coin-op laundry in the basement and an elderly landlady who called her Imogene. Andy and Beth helped her move. Fall semester began and she put on her professional clothes and tied her hair back and taught her classes, the students peering at her with curiosity and deference, having read the book, knowing the details of her horrible life. She felt relatively normal.

Her editor kept calling about the new book. First she asked for a hundred pages. Then she asked for fifty.

"Anything you can give me," she said. "We can't extend the deadline much longer, Isabel."

Isabel didn't know how to answer. A dreamy inertia settled over her whenever she thought about the new book.

"I've got ideas," she said slowly. "I've got ideas."

And she did, vaguely. She thought of doing a biography of her namesake, Saint Isabel of Portugal, who had lived a tranquil and nonbloody life, as far as saints' lives went. But deep down she knew she couldn't write the life story of anyone other than herself. Then she tried to get all fired up about some global injustice, so she could write a passionate screed about it. But the news—war, genocide, rape, species nearing extinction—just made her feel helpless and stupid.

She taught her classes and took a lot of walks. She got in the habit of tackling the new book very late at night, after grading papers, with a glass of scotch in one hand, leaning against the headboard with the computer in her lap and waiting to have something to say. But her mind always wandered back to the hearing. The landlord all in white. Her silky pink shirt with its itchy tag. Most of all she thought of herself at the very moment she started to speak, before he had brought out the book and shamed her. How she opened her mouth and things came out, elegant and lucid things, and she was like the nightingale placed in front of the king in the fairy tale, watching respect and recognition dawn on the judge's face—this doll-like girl, she speaks so well!—watching the stenographer look up at her for an instant and grimace sympathetically, that subtle empathy women convey like a shoulder squeeze, and, surrounded by the blank walls of her new apartment, she held the scotch in one hand and knew it was useless, knew that nothing would ever come out of her more purely or clearly than things like this: these distilled episodes, these illuminated lamentations, sculpted in all the right places, these testimonies of harm.

KEVIN A. GONZÁLEZ

University of Iowa

STATEHOOD

It's your thirteenth birthday and you're halfway through your fifth O'Doul's. You're keeping score for 501, kneeling on the stool beside the blackboard, ready to dodge any dart that bounces off the wire. At Duffy's, the bar is also the front desk. Your father sits there, telling stories. He's the only local in a crowd of expats, and they all listen to him. "Washington," he says. "Supreme Court. World Series of Lawyers. I kicked ass." "Cassius Clay," he says. "Kayoed Coopman in five. I was there. Ringside." "Raúl Juliá," he says. "We sang at the Chicken Inn. The two of us. Calypso. Before he was famous. And then, he died." He always bows his head after Raúl Juliá. He stretches his thumb and index and cups his forehead. His hand shields his face like a visor. He points at a soggy *San Juan Star* headline. Any headline. "This," he says, "is why Puerto Rico should be a state." He's got winner on the dartboard, but if no one tells him he's up, he'll keep talking all night. You know he'll keep talking all night.

You imitate the dart shooters when the bar is empty. You know everybody's style. Warren Z. holds the dart up to his forehead like he's a sailor on the lookout post. He's got a wooden leg that nobody knew about until a dart bounced off the bull's-eye rim and stuck to him through his jeans. He just kept walking, dart in leg, feeling no pain. Pete Gibbons touches the dart to his cheek and opens his mouth when he shoots. From a side angle, he looks like a video-game ninja who throws up darts. His wife, June, never hits the dartboard. Instead, she hits the wall. The Camel poster. The scorekeeper's stool. Once she punctured the red part of the neon Budweiser sign and made it bleed. You don't keep score when she plays. No one does: It's too dangerous. Jimmy Joe Baker stands on one leg and trembles. Dirty Dave clacks his tongue three times before each shot, and his bad breath sprays out. Oscar Beefeater holds his gin and tonic in one hand for balance. Norm, the bartender, lets the darts explode out of his wrist. "Wrist," he said, trying to teach you. "Wrist, wrist, wrist." He grabbed your wrist in his hands and moved it back and forth like a fulcrum. "Wrist!" he said. "See? Wrist." He's one of the worst shooters. Your father brings the dart back over his shoulder like he's throwing a football. He owns Hammer Heads. You own Hammer Heads. Everyone owns Hammer Heads. Warren Z. sells them. He's also a bookie and the Darts League president and a real-estate agent. He looks like a weasel.

After the game, Jimmy Joe buys you an O'Doul's for keeping score. Pretty Pat, one of your father's girls, gives you a twenty for your birthday. She says you have to bet it on the illegal video slot machine. If you win, you keep half. If you lose, you lose nothing.

Your father has four girlfriends. You keep their names straight and never let on that you know what you know. "So discreet," your father tells your godfather. "This kid, he'll juggle six skirts someday." In English class, the nun asked everyone to describe themselves using one adjective. "Cute," Nicole said. "Fast," Javi said. "Smart," Bondy said. "Discreet," you said. "Discreet?" the nun said. You winked. "You know," you said, "discreet." She sent a letter home to your mother, and that's when you forged your first signature. Your mother keeps busy bending and rebending clothes hangers, trying to record the perfect answering machine greeting, flicking all the light switches on and off exactly twenty-two times before putting her mama's-boy new husband to bed.

Pretty Pat tells you which buttons to push, and how many times. You hit all-fruits. You hit three triple bars across the middle and play the bonus round. You keep trying to hit the cherries, the ones that pay the best. You play till after the croupiers file in from the casinos, which close at four. You lose everything. Duffy's never closes.

On the way to Pretty Pat's, she stops to pee in the Banco Popular parking lot. There's a foldout couch at her place. You've slept on it before. Your father tosses you a pillow. "No sweat, Tito," he says. "You'll pop those cherries someday." He steps into the bedroom and shuts the door. Laughter leaks through the frame. The next morning, your father asks if you saw Pretty Pat peeing by the bank. If you *saw* her. "The glowing relief," he says. "The almost pleasure." You nod. "How her eyebrows," your father says, "unraveled." You keep nodding.

You're spending July with your father while your mother's on her honeymoon. You hadn't seen him since the divorce. Nineteen months, and he shows up in a Bronco with a glove box full of country, a cassette case full of Willies. Boxcar Willie. Moonshine Willie. Willie Nelson. He sings their songs out loud, badly. His building is on Isla Verde Avenue, beside Andy's Café, where they sell dope instead of coffee. It's across the street from Duffy's and Burger King and the Travelodge. He's got a caved-in double bed: no sheets, no visitors. Many sirens pour through the windows at night, compliments of Andy's. On the weekends, you visit your grandfather in his mansion. Your father brings him chocolates from Domenico's and you play Monopoly until they fight. You go to Duffy's every day. Although it's right across the street, your father takes the Bronco, because after midnight the Burger King's just drive-through. Duffy's has an early bird breakfast at six, and the late-shift hotel workers come in for it. Sometimes you're still there. Sometimes your father rear-ends Mitsubishis at the drive-through. "Whiskey River," Willie sings. "Take my mind."

Happy hour is from four to six, both A.M. and P.M. Matilde, the owner, won't give you your O'Doul's at two-for-one because they're nonalcoholic. She busts your father for legal advice and gives him drinks as consultation fees. She refuses to give refunds for the pinball machine. A full rack only has eight ribs on Tuesday, Rib Night. On Wednesday, two mixed drinks get you a half-priced appetizer. On Thursday, the San Juan oldies station broadcasts live from the dart room. They have a twenty-song lineup and Duffy's is always tuned in. At any time of day, there's a 10 percent chance they're playing "My Girl" by the Temptations or Del Shannon's "Runaway." You hate Thursdays. Monday is Darts League Night, new to Duffy's. Your father was a Reef Crabber until your mother had him arrested at the Reef Bar & Grill for refusing to pay child support, and he was too embarrassed ever to go back there. He was a Dunbar's Viking until Phil Hunt pointed at you and said, "Who's this little prick, and what's he doing here on league night?" and your father hit him with a barstool and got eighty-sixed from Dunbar's. Norm, the bartender, started the Duffy's Devils, and he keeps telling all his teammates that the secret's in the wrist. They're in last place. The other teams call them the Wristies. "Tito!" your father jokes. "Wrist! Wrist!" He makes a masturbating motion with his hand. He's a devil.

Frankie bartends on weekday afternoons and league nights. She's got fake tits. "Go," your father tells you. "Give her a hug. Feel them." She's another of his girlfriends, but she's not like the others. She's your friend. She knows what's going on, and she doesn't seem to care. She lives in one of Duffy's guest rooms with Linda, who's a waitress. Sometimes you take naps on her bed. Sometimes she looks after you while your father's out with Cheryl, girlfriend number three. Cheryl is married to Counterfeit Bill. Counterfeit Bill says he was asked personally by Reagan to run for governor of California, but that he was too busy inventing a kind of packaging foam. In her room, Frankie teaches you Five-Card Draw. Seven-Card Stud. Six Back to Five. Pregnant Threes. She teaches you Free Enterprise. Take it or Leave it. Guts. Murder. She hands you a bottle of strawberry Boone's Farm. "Don't tell," she says. "I always wanted a kid." There are two beds and HBO and a stained hair dryer screwed into the wall. "Ante in," you say. It's your pinball allowance against her tips. You never take anything if you win. "Ask me anything you want," she says. "Anything."

You're the official Devils scorekeeper because your math is better than everyone else's. You solve arguments before things get out of hand. "Tito!" they say. "Two triple eighteens and a twenty?" "One twenty-eight," you say. "Tito!" they call again. "Five seventeens and a bull's-eye?" "Wrist!" you say, and they all laugh. "One ten," you say. "One ten."

After the Devils get skunked, you shoot by yourself while your father fucks Frankie in her guest room. Sometimes they fall asleep after they're done, so you wait a few hours before knocking. Late into the night, you walk back and forth, from line to board, shooting, retrieving. If halogen lights could tan, you'd be blistered. Your Hammer Head flights flash by like hubcaps. You begin to develop your own style. It's not all about the wrist. It's elbow. Stance. Finger place-ment. Follow-through. It's practice. It's vision.

Your mother's mama's-boy husband's son is obsessed with Super Nintendo. He's in tenth grade and you're in eighth, but you go to dif-ferent schools. After fall semester starts, he comes over every week-end. "Be nice to him," your mother tells you. "*His* mother is a lesbian." They put bunk beds in your room. You have to eat pork chops every Friday because they're the kid's favorite. You're watching the Cubs on WGN Chicago: tied game, bottom of the ninth, Sandberg at the plate. "There's a drive!" Harry Caray yells. "It might be! It could be! It—" Your mother's mama's-boy husband's son turns on *Street Fighter.* You scream. He screams. You hit him. He hits you back. You pull out *Street Fighter* and toss it down the balcony, fifteen flights. Everyone agrees it's a good idea you start spending weekends with your father.

On Saturday mornings, you play football on the beach. Your fa-ther has a good arm, but no depth perception. He lost an eye in prep school. The glass from his glasses splashed into the pool of his retina. It was a drinking accident, a brawl. "The background is always flat," he says. "I don't know what a sunset looks like." In the afternoons, you watch college football and eat french fries at Duffy's. Norm lets you control the remote. At night, you shoot with the shooters. No one calls you "that little prick."

At four A.M., you tell your father you're tired and he tells you that you have a brother. He's a day older than you. His name is Pepito. He's half-Japanese. He has a black belt in karate. Also, he's a better dart shooter than you. Also, he can throw the football farther. Also, he's invisible. "Invisible?" you say. "Or imaginary?" "How dare you?" your father says. "How dare you say that about your brother when he's sitting right there?" He gestures toward an empty stool. He waves at the empty stool. Then, he speaks to it. "Don't worry, Pepito," he says. "Tito doesn't mean it." "Tell him," you say, "that I say he's an asshole." Your father turns toward the empty stool. He puts his hand to his ear like he's listening to someone. He waits five seconds. He starts laughing. "Oh, Pepito," he says. "Pepito, I can't tell Tito you just said that about him. He's my son, too, remember? And yes, you may be right, but I can't repeat what you just said. It's just too hurtful." Your father turns back to you, grinning. "Tell him," you say, "to go fuck his father."

In school, you get all As. This is never a problem. "Your English," the nun from English class says, "is remarkable." During class, you practice your dart grip with a pencil and she thinks you've raised your hand. She happily calls on you. You tell her it's all one big mistake. "What's the mistake?" she says. "Everything, Sister," you say. "Everything's a mistake." Some girls suddenly have breasts and older boyfriends. You start buying condoms in Duffy's men's room for a dollar and selling them at school for two. Everybody wants one, especially the older boyfriends. You make friends with the ninth-grade class. You make the basketball team. You forge everybody's parents' signatures when they get in trouble. Your mother quizzes you the day before the tests. She throws the notebook at you if you don't know the answers. There are many sponges in her sink. One for spoons. One for forks. One for knives. One for pans. One for plates. One for the other sponges. They are color coded. "Goddamn you," she says, "if you mix them up."

At Duffy's, you gamble the condom profit against Frankie. She serves you Boone's Farm with ice when she's working, and you're discreet about it, like it's Hawaiian Punch. Frankie doesn't live at Duffy's anymore. Her roommate, Linda, left Puerto Rico. Everyone wa-wa-

wa-wa-wonders why she went away, but you know why it was. You were at your father's the day he got the call. No one knew Linda was pregnant: not your father, not even Frankie. She needed someone who spoke Spanish to hook up the adoption. Your father rushed her to emergency, Johnny Cash on the deck. "I fell in," he sang, "to a burning ring of fire." You were there when the nurse brought the baby by mistake and Linda put her hands over her eyes. "Take it away," she cried. "I don't want to fucking see it!" A local celebrity couple with connections got the baby. "Blond, blue-eyed," the doctor told your father, smiling. "You sure you don't want it? Those are very, very hard to come by."

Frankie now lives on her boyfriend's sailboat at San Juan Marina. His name is Troy, and they've been together for twelve years. She tells everyone they have an open relationship. You don't know if there's such a thing as a closed one. Your father sits with Troy at the bar, telling stories. "The eye," your father says, "I lost in Nam." Troy asks him where he was stationed. "I," your father sips his drink, "don't like to talk about that."

Frankie gives you another Boone's Farm on the rocks. You finger your Hammer Heads' points inside their case, in your pocket. It's the playoffs, and you can't shoot till the league game ends. You can't be in the league till you're eighteen: There was a motion to make an exception. You had the team captains on your side. Your father convinced the bar owners, all but the Reef and Dunbar's, and now they let you play the weekend tournaments. Warren Z.—bookie/darts salesman/real-estate agent/league president—made the case against you. "No exception for Tito," he said. "Then we'd have to let in every underage kid who wants to play." He said it as if there actually were other underage kids who wanted to play. Your father started calling him Weasel, and it's caught on. "Hey, Weasel," Jimmy Joe says. "You got this week's lines?" You pull your darts out of the case.

Frankie is serving Weasel a vodka tonic. She shoots you a wink. You wink back. Weasel is wearing beige Dockers over his wooden leg. You can't remember which leg it was. Eenie, meeney, miney, moe: You think this will be funny. You shoot a Hammer Head at his left leg. Before it lands, you shoot another. He screams. He screams again. Everyone looks at you and you can see yourself, reflected off a rusted mirror that has a beer bottle drawn inside it, and you know exactly what everyone is thinking. *Who the fuck do you think you are, laughing at jokes you don't get? Who the fuck do you think you are, you little prick?*

Matilde has removed the dartboard and put a bumper-pool table in the space. Everyone refuses to play bumper pool. Troy, Frankie's boyfriend, was killed by a drunk driver in front of Duffy's. The drunk driver was a rich eighteen-year-old girl with a father in the Senate. She got off scot-free. The *San Juan Star* writers can't let it go. THE FIRST MURDER, a Viewpoint headline reads, IS ON THE HOUSE. Your father holds up the paper. "This," he says, "is why Puerto Rico should be a state." Frankie takes a leave and sits on the customer side of the bar, saying nothing. Your father is helping with the civil suit. In the old dart room, the scorekeeping blackboard now says RULES FOR BUMPER POOL at the top. Matilde filled the whole thing out in laborious cursive. It took her an entire afternoon. One night, you erased everything but the title. Beneath RULES FOR BUMPER POOL, you wrote: "Bump. Bump. Bump. Bumpetty Bump. Then, Bump again." Matilde is still searching for the culprit. She can't find a good bartender from two A.M. till ten. Outside, there's a drought, and it's the hottest autumn anyone remembers. The ceiling fans do lazy laps. Matilde is a sweaty trigger.

Your father's foot slips on the gas and his Bronco kills another Mitsubishi at the drive-through. He signs a check for some teenager, happy to trade a taillight for a hundred. There are no questions asked, no numbers exchanged. The Burger King workers call this "the Bronco lottery." Drawings are at least once a month. Afterward, you and your father sit on the caved-in bed, munching Whoppers. "Why," you say, "do these gringos come here? Why Puerto Rico? What do they want?" Your father finishes chewing and swallows. "Nothing," he says. "And that's why." He says Norm was a big shot at Microsoft until his son OD'd. He says Linda got pregnant from a married man in Texas and couldn't bring herself to abort. He says Pretty Pat's husband left her for a Prettier Pat. He takes another bite. "Who *are* these people?" you want to know. Your father shrugs his shoulders. "What about Frankie?" you ask. "That," your father says, a bite of Whopper tumbling in his mouth, "I don't know." He swallows and sips his Pepsi. "But there's always something."

In three months, you've won $500 in dart tournaments. Your father says Pepito has won over $10,000, but that he competes internationally, in a whole different league all together. The trophies all say your name, the date, the bar, and the sponsor, usually a beer brand. You're a better shooter than your father, but you can't beat him one-on-one. Your father says Pepito always kicks his ass. You bring home a new trophy almost every other Sunday. Your mother arranges them by date. By height. By beer sponsor. Domestic and imported. Before she goes to bed, she opens and closes all the cabinets, cupboards, closets. "What are you looking for?" you ask. "Nothing," she says. "Go to bed."

You don't like Captain Liz, girlfriend number four. When your father goes home with her, you ask to stay with Frankie. After her shift, you walk to San Juan Marina holding hands. You sit on Troy's sailboat's deck, drinking Boone's Farm. You start playing with the helm. "Your father," Frankie says. "I thought he might have been someone for a second." You push the depth-finder's button on the console. It lights up: nine feet. "*¡Mira!*" she says. "I'll be right back." She climbs down into the cabin. *Mira* is the only Spanish word she knows. The tone in which she says it sounds like scolding. She returns with a small jewelry box. She pulls out a joint. She lights it. You take a swig from the bottle. "Here," she says. "It's the best shit they got at Andy's." You take a drag. This is the one thing your father told you not to do.

"I feel," Frankie says, "like I could tell you anything." You look up at the sky. You cough. There are never any stars in San Juan. "Do you think I'm pretty?" Frankie asks. "Yes," you say. "I used to be," she says. "Why," you say, "are you here?" You hand her the joint. She takes a long, slow drag. "I don't think," she says, "you want to know." She gives the joint back to you. The bottom of the sea is nine feet below you, but you're much more than nine feet above it. She tells you she was raped in the Everglades. She tells you Troy tracked down the guy. She tells you they dumped the body somewhere between Fort Lauderdale and Bimini. You don't say anything. Her eyes blaze, dry, through the smoke. She says she's happy she got that off her chest. Then, she asks if you'd like to see it. "What?" you say. "See what?" "Oh," she says, "my chest."

After the U.S. Navy accident in Vieques, you become a nationalist. You start reading political philosophy. Your mother arranges the volumes alphabetically. Bastiat. Berríos. Bolívar. Burke. You wear T-shirts with portraits of patriots and poets on the front. Albizu Campos. Martí. Betances. Corretjer. You start using the phrase "Yankee imperialists." "What have I done," your father says, "to deserve this?" You don't let each other finish sentences. You are both unyielding and blind. "Why," your father says, "can't you be more like Pepito?" "You mean you don't want me to exist?" "Well," he says. "If that's what it takes to get you to stop wearing Che Guevara on your chest, then yes, I don't want you to exist." Then he says, "But don't think for a second that Pepito isn't real."

By November, your father has moved in with Captain Liz. There are two bedrooms and one is sometimes yours. Your rich grandfather isn't dead yet, and your father is running out of cash. He gives consultations for free drinks. His specialty, once civil rights, becomes DUI law. Captain Liz's husband is on the lam, somewhere in the States. Together, they smuggled dope from South America in a twenty-four-foot Pierson, but she was never charged. The dope paid for the apartment. She wants everyone to know she really is a licensed captain.

You still get As in school, but your mother lets you study by yourself. You start dating a girl a year older than you. You skip a few dart tournaments to take her to dances. Movies. Minigolf. Sometimes, on the weekends, you stay with Frankie at the marina and get high and mess around. Sometimes you don't think anything is real, that there's a camera in every corner of your room, filming every move. Your mother skips around the house without stepping on the cracks between the tiles. She no longer cooks pork chops every Friday: The husband has moved back in with his mama.

On a Sunday morning, Norm calls your father at Captain Liz's and says it's an emergency. You drive to the police station, Merle Haggard on the deck. Matilde is under arrest for having an illegal video slot machine at Duffy's. She grips the bars of the holding cell. "A smoke," she says. "I need a smoke." There are lines running through her face and bags under her eyes. "So," your father says. "You want a cigarette?" He pulls a pack of Marlboros from his shirt. "How bad do you want it?" He slides a cigarette out of the pack and holds it up. "What do you want from me?" she says. He clutches the cigarette between his thumb and index finger and dangles it just outside her reach. "I want you," he says, "to get rid of bumper pool."

You've won eight straight cricket games against your father when Counterfeit Bill, your father's girlfriend's husband, walks in. "Is Matilde here?" he says, sneaky, and she's not. He asks your father if he can have a moment. They sit at the bar, Bo Diddley blasting from the oldies station. "I need some legal advice," Bill says. Your father lights a cigarette, orders a fresh drink. "I love the fried shrimp here," Bill says. "You ever try it?" Your father shakes his head. "Last night," Bill says, "I asked Matilde if she would give me some of that batter, the kind she uses for her shrimp, so I can make it at home for me and Cheryl, and she said yeah, to just ask the bartender for it when I left. And then, when I left, around three, I asked the bartender for my batter, and the asshole told me to go fuck myself. So I told *him* to go fuck *him*self. Then, he kicked me out, pushed me out the door. This was all in front of people, you know. All those guys from the casinos were here. My wife was here. It was fucking humiliating." He looks as if he's just about to cry. "Bill," your father says. "The bartender's new. He probably had no idea what you were talking about. Matilde probably just forgot to tell him, that's all." "I don't care," Bill says. "I want to sue. I want you on my case." Your father looks at you and rolls his eyes. "Sue on what grounds, Bill? Tell me, what's your case?" Bill's hands snake through the air. "I was humiliated," he says. "I want punitive damages. Don't you think I deserve something? I mean, what do you think?" Norm looks at you from behind the bar and shrugs his shoulders. Your father sips his drink. "I think you batter grin," he says, "and bear it." Norm bursts out laughing. Bill stands up and kicks his stool. He calls your father an ambulance-chasing asshole. A shameless motherfucker. Your father says nothing. You can hear the Bo Diddley lines falling from the ceiling between Bill's

curses. *Got a tombstone head and a graveyard mind* / "Dirty cocksuck-
ing spic." / *Lived long enough and I ain't scared of dying* / "Son of a
spic whore." Your father doesn't move, arms perched on the bar like
surrendered weapons. Bill kicks his stool again and it falls apart.
Then he leaves, sobbing.

The next day, when you walk into Duffy's, Matilde is pacing back
and forth, talking to the cops. There is a pool of blood on the men's
room floor. The steel towel rack has been ripped off the wall, and it
is bent and bloodstained, jutting from the trash can. The two A.M.
bartender is nowhere to be found. A cop soaks up a blood sample.
"Counterfeit Bill?" you say. "Maybe," Matilde says. "Norm said he
made some scene the other night." She hires someone to clean the
mess, and calls the *San Juan Star* to place another ad for bartender/
receptionist. "I," she says, "have just about had it with this shit."

The week before fall finals, your team makes it to the semis of the
McDonald's Invitational. You're down by two with three seconds on
the clock. Your father and your girlfriend are there. You introduced
them before the game. The starting forward has fouled out, so you're
in. Somehow the ball ends up in your hands and you miss at the
buzzer. "Pepito," your father says, "would've hit that shot. The team
would've won." You look away. "Well," you say, "it's a shame he's not
real." Later that night, you ask your father what he thought of your
girl. "Carolina?" he says. "You know, you're wasting your time. Pepito
already fucked her." On your next date, you threaten to leave her if
she won't have sex with you. When she bleeds, Pepito dies. You try to
forget her name, but it's also the name of your town. Even after
you've left her, it's a name that follows you everywhere.

During Christmas, your mother and the mama's-boy husband try
to work things out. He takes her to Punta Cana for the holidays. For
you, this means winter break at Captain Liz's.

When you walk into Duffy's, Matilde is singing along to "Jingle Bells." She's tending bar, and gives you and your father drinks on the house. There are no bags under her eyes and no lines running through her face. "What," your father says, "are you so fucking happy about?"

"I sold it," she says. "I sold this shithole to the Travelodge." Your father looks as lost as a child. You look around. On the walls are rusted mirrors with the names of beers written inside them. There is a dartboard whose black numbers have turned white, and a pinball machine that tilts if you look at it, and always a 15 percent chance of the Temptations or Bo Diddley or Del Shannon singing in the background, and sixteen rooms with HBO and stained hair dryers screwed into the wall. There are coasters that look like giant hosts, chipped and stacked by the lemon bowl. WELCOME TO PARADISE, says a sign behind the bar. NO BULLSHIT, says another. UNATTENDED CHILDREN, says the last, WILL BE SOLD. You look at your father. You smile. You're trying to remember how long it's been since you were a child.

THEODORE WHEELER

Wesleyan Writers Conference

WELCOME HOME

One of the first things Jim Scott did when he got back to Nebraska from Iraq was check on his dog, Sasha. Jim had had Sasha, a German shepherd, since he was ten. He was twenty-two now. He came home to find the dog lying on an old beach towel in the garage, slapping her tail against the cement next to a motorcycle he had ridden only a handful of times. Sasha's drool was brown and black, spilling onto the concrete floor from the side of her mouth. Jim crouched down next to the dog, rubbing hard between her ears. Andrea watched as she leaned on the doorframe, her face beaming as it had been since she'd picked him up from the airfield. A red leather purse hung over her shoulder; car keys were clutched in her hand. Jim served sixteen months in Iraq—he had been gone a long time.

"She used to run with me when I rode my bicycle," Jim explained to his wife. He was having a little trouble understanding how Sasha had gotten so old. His hand filled with her dull fur as he ran it over the stringy muscles of her legs. Jim could feel lumps all over her body, especially on her ribs, where muscle and fatty tissue had turned into benign tumors. The dog set her head down hard and breathed heavy snorts out of her nose. It jarred Jim to see her like that. He didn't want to believe his dog was dying.

It was cold outside in Nebraska and the garage was just marginally warmer. Jim and Andrea could see their breath when they spoke. An ice storm had passed over just days earlier, followed by light snow, the cold now having settled into the soil. Jim knew it would take time to readjust to the low midwestern temperatures after living in the desert.

"Let's go inside," Andrea said, stepping behind her husband to put her hand on his shoulder. "She'll still be here later."

The house where Jim and Andrea lived was a two-story log cabin recessed from a gravel road, near a small forest east of Lincoln. Their property was bounded by farms on all sides, but there was pasture-land cleared behind the house, sloping hundreds of yards to the east into the fallow ground of a neighboring farm. A screen of white pines protected them from the north wind. The house had been con-structed with discarded telephone poles held together by cement in-stead of logs and mortar. Inside the timber exterior was a frame house with two-by-fours, insulation, and drywall. They'd gotten a good deal on it from a guy Jim knew from his ROTC days. They used Jim's en-listment bonus for the down payment.

Near the front door was a termite-eaten stump, about ten feet high and five feet thick, half-glistening from the ice that enveloped it. The tree was decomposing—chunks of it had fallen to the ground. Mud and decaying sawdust congealed like wet coffee grounds at its base. Jim tore a piece off with his bare hands as he walked past. It was paper-thin in places, where the termites had bored holes. Jim hated the stump. He'd planned to uproot it once they moved in, but hadn't had the time to remove it before deployment.

"We're going to have a party for you." Andrea's voice shook with happiness as she unpacked Jim's rucksack, piling his fatigues onto the closet floor. She had rewashed his civilian clothes the night before, restless for his return. "My mom is going to make potato salad. I ordered a cake from the bakery."

Jim stepped from the window and picked his wife up by the hips, swinging her to the bed. She was a small woman but had full hips and thighs. She straightened her black hair. Jim found her form fascinating and enjoyed staring at her. Her face was rounder than one normally saw in Nebraska, her jaw less prominent than in the common handsome women of the plains. Jim kissed her eyes happily, letting his lips drag across her nose because it made her giggle, before lying back on the bed with his arms behind his head. Andrea lay against his chest, touching his ears. It was strange to be back, surreal that he had finally arrived home, but he was enjoying this physical play, however tenuous it was. If he could get through the first couple of days things would be okay.

"Your scalp is sunburned," Andrea noted as she rubbed his head, surprised by the flaky skin under his short hair. "Did you wear your helmet?"

"It was heavy."

"You should have worn it."

"I did. I wore it when we were on patrol."

"Why not all the time?"

Jim grabbed Andrea by the armpits and rolled her over with him on top. He slid his legs under and between hers, twisting their bodies so she couldn't move.

"You don't wear a helmet swimming," he said. "I burn easy anyway. I was red the whole time over there."

"I'm glad you're back."

"You got the pictures I sent? Me swimming in Saddam's pool?"

"I have them downstairs."

This kind of talk annoyed Jim. He wanted to feel her body against his, to press his face into her stomach. Andrea slid on the bedspread so that he fell to the side of her with their legs locked, their bodies bending into an embrace.

"You're hurting me a little," she said.

Jim was more muscular now than he had been when he left. Andrea first noticed when she picked him up from the airfield: His shirt fit tighter around the biceps and in the shoulders. His face was the most different. With his hair cut short, his ears were like later additions to the rest of his head. And his nose had never looked bulbous before, but it did now. He was red in the face, too—and not just in a skin-peeling, sunburned way. His whole face was inflamed and swollen, like he had been a heavy drinker for a long time. The kind of habit that made capillaries burst under the surface of his skin. Andrea touched his nose, examining its new texture.

"I'm going to have to do something about Sasha," Jim said, the somber tone of responsibility moving his voice into a lower register. He released Andrea from his embrace and rolled to his back, folding his hands together on his stomach.

"What do you mean?"

"She's really suffering out there. Haven't you been watching her? She looks like shit. Like she has the mange."

"I did what you said to. I fed her twice a day and let her run the pasture in the evening when she wanted to."

"When she wanted to? You have to keep her moving."

Andrea sat up at the edge of the bed, staring at the wall. It hurt her that he would accuse her now, tarnishing their reunion. He's grumpy from travel, she thought. It's only natural. The good things were still to come in their lives. She reminded herself of romantic dinners and the home improvements they could work on together. They shouldn't fight.

"Andrea, a good dog is like a car. If you take care of it, it will appreciate in value." Jim stood up as he said this, moving into her line of vision so that he could talk down to her.

"Give me a break."

Andrea tried to look away, but he tapped her chin back with his fingertips so that she couldn't avoid his stare. He didn't want to fight, but it felt instinctual to make her understand exactly where he was coming from. Even though he knew it was the wrong way to act, Jim couldn't help himself.

"You just got back," she said. She stood up from the bed. "Let's have some fun. Okay?"

"We're going to have to move that stump if there's going to be a party. I'm tired of it already. What's your dad doing today?"

"The family's coming over for dinner tonight," Andrea said, referring to her parents. Each had been an only child growing up, but Jim's parents lived across the country and wouldn't see him for a few weeks. Andrea walked to the dresser and opened a drawer, pulling out red see-through lingerie. "But they won't be here until later."

"Is your dad bringing the truck?"

"Probably not."

"Maybe your car has enough power to pull it," Jim said. He was standing at the window again, sizing up the stump. It looked fragile from his vantage, but he knew the wood inside was petrified. It wouldn't be an easy job at all, knocking the stump over with Andrea's sedan.

"Are you sure this is a good idea? Let's just get Dad's truck. I can call him later, tell him to bring it. And some chains."

"I got the chains."

"Let's do it later this weekend then. We can relax tonight. We can have some fun."

Andrea slipped out of her shirt. She wasn't wearing a bra. Her jeans fell to the floor, revealing red lace underwear that matched the lingerie she was holding.

"I'm going to the little girl's room. You going to be here when I get back, tough guy?"

"I don't think so," Jim said, his hands gripping the windowsill. Out of the corner of his eye, he saw Andrea flinch, bringing her hand up to her face as she stood in the bathroom doorway. "I'll check on the dog first."

He didn't mean to fight with her, to hurt her feelings in such a stupid way, but he couldn't help it. It made him sick to think about that stump, to have to consider the condition his dog, Sasha, was in. He wanted to be close to his wife, to kiss gently under her chin, but it wasn't going to happen while he felt like this.

A week before Jim returned home, an army psychologist came to prepare Andrea for the problems she might encounter. Jim's unit had already left Iraq by then and was hanging out in Kuwait for a few weeks to detoxify in sandy tents. The army tried to ease them back into civilization, from combat to Kuwait, to massive military airfields, to crowded airports in Chicago or Atlanta, and, finally, to the regional airfield at home. It was an easy thing to say *I'm coming home*, but it took weeks to carry off.

The army psychologist had a briefcase full of pamphlets when he visited Andrea. This was the unreal part of Jim coming home, a stranger telling her to not be surprised if her husband acted like a different person. The man told her to watch out for psychotic episodes and to make sure that Jim didn't drink too much. He gave her a handful of little cards, each one listing the symptoms for a different mental disorder and who to call if the case merited it. She was told that Jim would be prone to alcoholism and recurring periods when he'd feel the need for violence, but to call only if it was an extreme case.

"If you think we're trying to scare you," the man said, "you're right."

The psychologist was a small man with a dark crew cut. He was pudgy, soft and feminine in the way that middle-aged men get when their hips spread out.

"If he wakes you up in the middle of the night with a knife to your throat, call us. If he points a steak knife at you, or pushes you, try to think if it's normal behavior for him or not. You don't have to call for everything. Flashbacks are common. It's a normal thing that just seems worse than it really is. If you're not sure, in a nonemergency situation, feel free to e-mail us."

Andrea wondered if the psychologist had pulled himself out of civilian practice for another term at this assignment. The man was very enthusiastic about his job, but he didn't look like a soldier. It appeared that he enjoyed scaring her, that he got off on freaking out army wives. Jim had never done any of the things the man was describing. Anything like that would be abnormal. They were still newlyweds, as far as Andrea was concerned, so it seemed like a joke to her, the things this man was claiming. A perverse army joke that wasn't really funny.

The psychologist told her that Jim had had trouble in combat. He wouldn't shoot his rifle. Jim wasn't a coward—he stood strong in the line of fire—but he didn't pull the trigger. He underwent counseling to alleviate the disorder, but it didn't work. There was no explanation for it. Even after he insisted on going back to his unit, Jim wouldn't fire his rifle in combat.

After the psychologist left, Andrea called her mother and cried. She was feeling down about an e-mail Jim had sent her and what the army psychologist told her hadn't helped matters. In the e-mail, Jim confessed to her that he'd had nightmares after he learned that he was coming home. He dreamed about being stuffed into the back of a sheriff's car when he returned to Nebraska. He was shackled around the wrists and ankles. Al-Jazeera was there with cameras. The local press asked him questions in short, rapid-fire English, but he had no excuses. There was only one thing he could answer. *When I woke up, I was armed.*

For weeks while he detoxified in Kuwait, Jim had the same nightmare, often multiple times in one night. He couldn't lie down without facing the short dreams that ended with the same response coming from his lips. It happened so often that it seemed like a presentiment to him, like a reliable vision of things to come.

Andrea had been excited for her husband's return. She had plans for their house, a list of projects that the two of them could ably complete once he got home. The basement was to be finished and the driveway repaved. It angered her, the turn things had taken. She had lived alone in that house for sixteen months and deserved to have things work out well.

"He hasn't done anything wrong," Andrea said to her mother over the phone. "Why is he having nightmares? Why is that man saying things about him? He isn't guilty of anything!"

It took almost an hour for Barb to revive her daughter's spirits. Her husband was coming back alive, Barb reminded, she shouldn't let some little army spook scare her. Jim could finish his degree then get a good job. Even better, he could find work in construction immediately if he felt like it. Something he could work hard at and that would make some money. Something that would help clear his head and put bread on the table. "People around here still want to help a hero," she said. As a real-estate agent, Barb knew the opportunities available for an able young man with connections. This wasn't like Vietnam, Barb told her. People would help him. Most of the people they knew supported the war—felt like it was their duty to aid returning soldiers—so Andrea shouldn't worry herself sick.

"Still, with all the facts we have, you might want to prepare yourself for the possibility that this might not work." Barb certainly didn't like hearing about the potential for violence either, but it was something they should take seriously. "If Jim is changed—if he's violent—you don't have to stick around."

"He's my husband, Mom. If he is hurt in some way, I'll stay by him."

"Of course. I'm not saying take your responsibilities lightly. You love each other. But someone has to play the devil's advocate."

"Jim would never try to hurt me. He would sooner die. He can step away if he needs to. But he won't need to."

They would throw a big party when Jim got back. It was only a few weeks away. Andrea couldn't believe it. Why shouldn't they be happy? They'd been waiting so long for this. It was cold but they would barbecue anyway. Who cares? Even if it snows. Everything was working out fine.

Jim emerged from the garage with a maul in midafternoon. Andrea had been finalizing that evening's plans on the telephone. Leaving the maul outside the door, Jim stopped into the kitchen to fetch a beer and kissed Andrea on the top of her head.

"I'm sorry about earlier," Jim said. "We'll have fun later."

"I'm sorry, too."

"There's just some things that I have to do now."

"You'd just come home."

"We're both sorry. We'll make it up to each other later."

Jim picked up the maul as he stepped outside, loosely holding on to the end of the shaft. It pleased him to let the weighted metal of the ten-pound head swing past his leg.

He worked around the edges of the stump at first, plowing through the rotted wood with ease. Because the wood offered so little resistance, the maul nearly flew from his grasp the first time he swung it. He collected the pieces he broke off in a bucket, carried them a few dozen yards into the forest, and dumped them there to rot. It was satisfying work, picking off the soft spots and shoveling them into a bucket. It felt good to work this way again, watching his breath freeze in the cold. The cool smell of mud revitalized his lungs in ways impossible in the desert.

The closer to the center of the stump Jim got, the harder he had to hit. The blade wouldn't cut. He hadn't taken the time to sharpen it before starting. But still he worked at the stump, smashing the decaying fibers with the weight of his maul, which bounced off the petrified wood with a dull noise, not cutting at all. It was like pounding on rubber. The harder Jim swung, the faster the maul bounced back at him. It would have made more sense to wait for his father-in-law's truck, but the work was invigorating, so he didn't stop. Jim swung the maul with a roundhouse motion, putting his back into the work, but it didn't matter. The petrified wood wasn't going to break.

Andrea opened the front door to see what the commotion was. She had heard Jim grunting and was concerned. Jim told her that he was just working up a sweat. With Andrea watching, he swung the maul as hard as he could. He lifted the maul above his head and let it fall into the stump, breaking off a piece of softer wood near the top.

"See," he told her, "it's coming along."

Jim worked at the softer wood while Andrea watched him to show that he was making progress. He wanted to demonstrate what he could do. He was stronger now than before and enjoyed using this new muscle. It felt good to work in front of his wife. Andrea grabbed a coat from inside and settled into a deck chair.

"You're really making some progress here," Andrea told him. "It's really looking good."

The exhibitionist thrill of performance made Jim feel stronger. Determined to make headway with the petrified wood, Jim swung as hard as he could—too hard to control the head of the maul. The wedge struck the core of the tree sideways, putting the shaft in a bind. The handle shattered from the strain, leaving just the end of the shaft in Jim's hand.

Jim looked comical, staggering on one foot in the soft bed of broken timber, swinging the splintered handle. Andrea didn't know whether to laugh or cry. She stood on the porch, asking Jim if he was okay.

"It's no big deal," he told her, regaining his balance. He stared down at the broken maul, disappointed in himself for putting the handle in a bind. "I was just messing around. It will take the truck to finish the job. It would have needed the truck anyway."

"But you're okay?"

"You can laugh about it," Jim said, trying to chuckle. He smacked his legs to knock the snow and mud off. "Lucky the damn thing didn't fly through the window."

Jim opened the side door of the garage and sat down next to Sasha. The big dog dragged her head to his thigh and nestled into the fabric of his jeans. He sat with his legs together, his body in a stiff L. He draped a hand over Sasha, his thick fingers moving gently in the dog's fur. Jim loved to sit with his dog like this. He modulated his breathing to match the slow inhalations Sasha managed as she slid to her side, easing her back into his leg. This was the easy intimacy of his loveless youth that Jim missed. The indulgence of sitting on a dirty concrete slab with his dog. It was warm enough, with the two of them letting their weight coalesce together. It was simple just to sit there and breathe, allowing his mind to recycle.

Jim didn't have many friends from high school or college. There wasn't anyone that he could call up on the phone when he was lonely. When he was young his parents worked double shifts to keep their heads above water. They were gone a lot, straining futilely to pay off credit card debt and the mortgage on their small house in North Lincoln. There weren't many kids Jim's age to play with on the block they lived on. It was an old neighborhood with small houses and cramped lots, and there were just elderly women around during the day and college kids drinking on porches in the evening. As a little kid, Jim stayed at home after school and played in the backyard by himself. He fungoed Wiffle balls and tackled himself in imaginary football games.

On Jim's tenth birthday, his father came home from the second shift he worked with a present for his only child. Jim was asleep on the couch where his mother had kissed him good-bye when she left for her second shift hours earlier. *M*A*S*H* played quietly in the unlit room. Jim's father woke him, pulling the blanket off his head. He turned on the lamp. His father set a burlap sack in his lap as he sat up. When Jim grabbed the edge of the sack he giggled, lifting the seamed edge until the sack opened. A German shepherd puppy sleepily poked its nose out into the open, licking the air with its sticky tongue. It was a surprising gift. A man Jim's father worked with had sold it to him. "This is your dog," Jim's father had said. "You name it. You play with it. You take care of it. If you take care of it, it will be a good dog."

Andrea's parents came over to the house late in the afternoon with potato salad and a sheet cake from the bakery. It was a child's cake with toy machine gunners stuck on top and *Welcome Home Jim!* spelled out in icing. Jim was setting up a propane heater on the back deck. There was a vinyl shelter tied to the porch to block the wind. With the heater on, it would be warm enough to eat outside. The ice on the deck was melting.

"You're home," Barb exclaimed, the bowl cradled at her hip. "I can hardly believe my eyes." She latched onto Jim with her free arm. Stan, Andrea's father, walked behind her with the cake in his hands. "It's good to see you, Jim. Very good to have you back."

Jim thanked them for coming, staring down at the green plastic toy gunners on the cake. After Barb released him, he turned to the grill and lifted the hood to check on the dripping brisket. He picked up a meat fork, laughing about the machine gunners on the cake as Stan set it on the table. Jim had played with the same kind of plastic army men when he was young, but he'd never made the connection between them and himself as a soldier before. It was an odd gesture, he thought, to put those things on a cake.

Andrea came out to the deck and grinned at Jim with her parents, happily sharing in their exuberance. They circled around Jim and patted him on the shoulder, congratulating him on his safe return and the fulfillment of his duty.

Barb and Stan had taken to Jim from the first time they met him, having no reservations about the quick marriage and Jim's impending departure to the war. They had wanted more children of their own but, due to complications with Andrea's birth, weren't able to have any. Jim was a welcome addition to their family. Stan talked to his coworkers about him lovingly, as if he were the son he never had. It was hardly a secret that Stan wanted Jim to start at his insurance agency as soon as he finished his degree.

"Why don't you leave the brisket to me, honey," Andrea said, taking the meat fork from Jim's hand. She pulled two beers from her apron pocket and handed one to her father and the other to Jim. "Dad wants to show you something."

Stan took Jim's arm, pulling him toward the side of the house. "We have a surprise for you. It's a little welcome-home gift that we all worked on this summer."

Jim stepped off the deck toward the forest forty yards from their log home. The snow was thicker near the trees, where it hadn't been trampled, but the native grass near the forest still pushed through. There was a hollow twenty feet into the trees, a streambed that had been dry for years. A slight embankment led through the brush to an area that had been cleared.

"What's this?" Jim asked, taken aback, as they inched down railroad-tie steps into the streambed, holding on to a railing to keep from slipping on the ice. Aspen and oak formed a bare-branch canopy above the hollow; fallen limbs were stacked near a fire pit. Stan had cleared the debris and laid cedar mulch to form a path with tiki torches lining the outside ring. The area had been considerably refined since Jim had seen it last. Benches made from split timber had been arranged around the pit, forming a semicircle. There was a wood box behind the benches filled with starter pieces—short ends of lumber left over from a construction project.

"This is great."

"Don't mention it," Stan said, smiling at his son-in-law as they stood together next to the pit. Stan was shorter than Jim, soft around the middle with long arms and big hands. He wore a plaid flannel shirt buttoned at the sleeves and collar. He stood with a slight slouch, his hands hanging at his sides. His hair was thick and, due to the round shape of his head and full cheeks, the style looked something like a bowl-cut, even though it wasn't. "What do you say? Should we start it up?"

"Later," Jim said, taking a seat on the bench behind him. "We can try it out after dinner. It wouldn't be good to let it burn unattended. Even with the snow."

"Of course," Stan said, sitting across from Jim in the semicircle. Stan moved his head from side to side slowly, appreciating his own work. "You're right. Safety first."

"We won't wait too long," Jim said. He rubbed his hands together. "Just until the sun is about to set." He was freezing, sitting on the ice, and wanted to get back under the heater. He wasn't used to this kind of cold. "It really is great."

They spoke about Jim's trip home, about the detoxification tents and the long, agonizing flights. Stan asked about the weather in the Middle East and difficulties with the operations, but Jim gave what he knew were short, unsatisfying answers.

"What do you think you'll do now? You've thought a lot about it, I bet."

"I want to go on a motorcycle trip," Jim said, leaning forward on the bench. "I bought that bike before I left, but never really got a chance to ride it. It should still run. Maybe I'll go up to Alaska and around there."

"You'll want to settle back in first, of course."

"Sure. I'm glad to be home."

Jim was trying to say the right thing but had no clue where to start. He was having trouble gaining footing. He had some idea of what Stan wanted to hear, but he had never been able to humor people. When the truth was elusive, Jim had never been good at filling in the blanks.

"You'll want to finish school now," Stan suggested. He stood up and motioned that they should go back up to the house, rubbing his hands together. "It will feel good to get back into the program. Andrea said your textbooks are still in the basement."

"I haven't thought a whole lot about it," Jim said. "But I will."

———

When Jim was deployed, he had a lot of optimism about the war. Cars around town were still covered with prowar magnets. The president had just been flown onto an aircraft carrier to declare the mission accomplished. Excited to serve his country, he felt privileged to aid in the cleanup and to establish a new democracy in Iraq. They were tearing down statues and occupying marble palaces when he left Nebraska, but the parades had stopped by the time Jim arrived.

A big part of his job overseas was to provide security for the crews clearing debris, until the insurgents moved in and there were IEDs all over the place. Then he was moved to the highways, where he rode next to fuel tankers. He sat behind a machine gun in an armored Humvee, shouting commands at cars blocking the road. He didn't know Arabic, so it was a tough job, screaming at men with mustaches who cowered in their cars.

Jim had been an ROTC kid when he was at school. His parents didn't have much money and had moved from Nebraska to Idaho at the start of his freshman year, so it was nice to have the extra cash for school that his ROTC scholarship provided. But he also enjoyed the maneuvers, marching on campus, engaging in the daily physical activity, and the queasy anticipation of going to basic training. There was an extra thrill of going to college in a military uniform, a sensation that went beyond the mundane university experience of classes and parties. There was community service to occupy his time and an established group of friends in the same situation as he was. When he left school after four semesters to enlist in the army, it was because he couldn't handle school anymore and was in danger of flunking his classes. ROTC was the only thing he really liked about college. He wasn't bookish. He didn't care about prereqs and reading requirements. But he was great at military. It was a natural move.

In Iraq, Jim and his fellow soldiers knew that things weren't going well—they witnessed the evidence of it every day—but it wasn't something that he thought about much. The daily work was tough. It required all of his concentration to do the job right, to keep himself and his friends alive. And when something did go wrong, like the death of Cory Miller, it wasn't the war or a president that Jim blamed, but the men who had killed him. It was easier to think locally, to concentrate on the jobs that they were doing and the men they sometimes struggled against. To hone in on the everyday security, to keep one's eyes open. For Jim, it wasn't so much about killing the enemy, but noticing them and anticipating what they were going to do before they did it.

When he did have time to think, it was Andrea who occupied his thoughts. They had met in school at an ROTC party the winter before she graduated from the College of Hair Design. They married quickly after her spring graduation, when Jim had decided to go to war. Instead of taking a honeymoon they bought the house, moved their things in, and had a few good weeks together before he was deployed. When Jim left, there were still boxes that hadn't been unpacked. Jim was living an exciting life and he had trouble keeping up with it. There were monumental changes every other week. He needed the security that Andrea provided, along with the promise of the after-war institutions of a wife and home. They did love each other, though, he was certain of it.

Jim had been safe, perhaps overly cautious, his whole time in Iraq. When on patrol, he ached for his wife, deeply in the pit of his stomach, so that he had only one goal: staying alive long enough to see Andrea again. To feel himself pressed against her. Jim wouldn't have made it out of the desert if it wasn't for the promise of touching his wife. He believed that.

He wanted to be home with her, tending the garden and making quick love on weekday mornings before school. He worried that

Andrea would never touch him again, would never put her hands on his in an assured, lovely way. It made him fear death, the prospect of never again being touched by his wife. Despite the fact that he couldn't fire his rifle, the army psychologists had assured him that he wasn't afraid of dying. He knew this already. It was the idea of inviting death nearer to himself, of bringing it into his proximity, that frightened him. He hated the terrorists, the Islamists, and the sectarians because they all worshipped death. Jim wouldn't have minded seeing them dead. It was just that he couldn't take the chance of implicating himself. He couldn't fire his weapon. Even if he were a coward for it, he had made a promise that he would be touched by his wife again. The only way this could happen would be if he were clean—if he were able to step off that plane in Nebraska without death following behind, urging him to kill or be killed.

Andrea and Barb were setting dinner on the patio table when Jim and Stan made it back to the house. Jim ran to the garage to fetch Sasha and carried her out in his arms. He laid her under his chair and they sat to eat. Barb said a short prayer before they began to load their plates, passing around the steaming dishes until all had their fill. As evening approached, the sun setting sooner than they thought it would, they ate quickly and in relative silence. They ate the brisket and garlic bread first, then turned to the potato salad, green-bean casserole, and strawberry Jell-O. Barb was the first to broach the subject of the war.

"I heard that the care package we sent met a grisly end," she said, referring to the box of homemade cookies and back-issue magazines that had been mailed to Jim through her office.

"It's true," Jim replied. "They shot a rocket into our barracks when we were on patrol. We had just changed shifts a few days before, which was lucky."

"Did you get to open it?"

"No. It was still sitting on my bed. I hadn't gotten to it."

Barb was a tall woman with short blond hair. She was strong and physically able in a handsome way, maintaining a sense of confidence through middle age. She was doing local work for the USO during Operation Iraqi Freedom, sending care packages to the troops, and was interested in Jim's opinion of the action he had participated in. Stan prompted Jim to explain how the military was trained to identify enemy combatants in an urban setting. He thought it would be a safe topic, but the conversation inevitably turned to mistakes that had been made by a few isolated marines. In the local papers, there had been quite a bit of attention paid to the military tribunals involving these massacres and rapes.

"I don't really know about that," Jim admitted. "It was mostly pretty boring what we did. Pretty standard patrols, running security and the like. We didn't do raids or anything like that."

"You have seen some of the news, though," Barb said. "The pictures are all over the Internet of our soldiers doing bad things. Have you—"

"Give the boy a break, honey," Stan interrupted laughingly as he took his dishes to the kitchen. "He's only just got back. There's no need of an interrogation."

"We found bodies that had been cut up," Jim said. "Iraqis only." He played with his remaining food, scraping the excess mayonnaise from his potato salad to the edge of the plate. "They were mutilated. There were wounds on their stomachs where organs had been cut out. Some of them were missing their heads. They were burned most of the time."

"That's horrible," Andrea said. She stood up and helped her father clear the table, loading her arms with half-empty serving dishes. "Let's talk about something more hopeful."

"The Iraqis, they said we harvested their dead. Forty bucks for a kidney, twenty-five for an eye." Jim talked unabashedly, in a way that made the others uncomfortable. His pronunciation was aggressive, tinged with anger. "That sort of black-market stuff went on, mostly art and marble, luxury cars. But you never know. Some of us could have been organ farmers. People were making money all sorts of ways."

"It's disappointing," Barb said, her voice shaky. "We all had such high hopes when the operation started." She motioned into the kitchen that Stan should bring the cake outside. "I didn't believe those stories at first. Until that Lynndie England thing happened, who would have thought this stuff was possible?"

"It's possible," Jim said. His dog, Sasha, shifted uneasily at his feet, sighing as she went back to sleep. "I met guys that went ape there, like they had fallen off the map. Either they forgot what we were there for or they never knew. Some of them just didn't care. There weren't many consequences for bad behavior."

"Try not to be bitter, though, Jim," Stan said, coming from the kitchen with the sheet cake. Andrea trailed behind him with a glass pitcher of spiked punch and a bread knife. "Even if things went badly for some, your country still needed you."

"And we do, too," Barb said. Andrea sat down next to Jim, laying the bread knife in the middle of the table beside the cake.

"She's right," Stan said. "And it works both ways. We're here for you, if you need help with anything."

"We know it wasn't easy. We want to help."

"You didn't do anything wrong, Jim. You don't have to feel guilty."

"I want to cut the cake," Andrea said, pulling the dessert closer to herself. She read it again, memorizing what the blue frosting looked like, whipped and piped into a message. *Welcome Home Jim!*

Stan poured a glass of the punch and passed it to his wife. Then he poured again, filling and passing until they all had drinks in front of them.

"I didn't even shoot."

"What's that?" Stan asked.

The two of them, Jim and Andrea, began picking the plastic machine gunner toys off the cake, putting them into a pile on the table next to the bread knife. There was blue frosting stuck to the bases of the green figurines. The frosting was beginning to melt off the gunners onto the table due to the propane heat. This is a real mess, Jim thought.

"I didn't fire my rifle in combat."

"We know it, buddy. It's nothing to worry about."

"That's over," Barb echoed. "What matters to us is what you do now. The things you do for your family. For Andrea and yourself."

Andrea was cutting the cake carefully. She portioned the entire cake, cutting sixteen pieces. It was stupid, she would think later. To ruin the cake like that, with just the four of us to eat it, was just plain simpleminded.

Andrea was in the basement, watching a morning talk show. She folded laundry while the dryer roared from the next room with a second load. Jim dug in the back of the upstairs closet. He opened a cigar box to reveal a single-shot zip gun he'd made. He grabbed it, examining the gun in the dim single-bulb light of the closet. A short length of smooth pipe fitted onto a wooden stock with a firing mechanism. (Jim used a thick rubber band and roofing nail.) Any bullet would work, but ammunition from a .22 rifle was safest. Pushing aside his dress shoes, Jim shook a .22 round out of a box from the back of the closet.

He recalled making the gun, crafting it to pass away the pointless, lonely summer days after he'd graduated high school, as his parents prepared to move out of state. The gun had been surprisingly easy to make. They could be made out of almost anything, but stems from coffee percolators and car antennas were the most common materials. He'd whittled away at a piece of lumber with his hunting knife, watching daytime TV, and this was the fruit of his labor. A new gun. He could take only one shot with it, but that's all he would need. Jim wanted to use this gun instead of his rifle. He'd made the zip gun and it would work. It would be just enough.

In the garage, Jim found Sasha panting in the winter cold, her tongue draped lazily from the side of her mouth. She wanted to jump up on him and lick his face. Jim wanted her to do this, too, but knew that she couldn't. It was sickening to watch her struggle. He picked her up, snaking an arm under her chest and rump, weak legs hanging down under her body. The zip gun stuck out of his back pocket. She brought her head up to look at him, her tongue laboring toward his face, before dropping it onto his flexed bicep.

"It's okay, girl."

The sky began to spit semifrozen drops again. Another ice storm. It was a bright day despite the light rain, an intense sun filtered through scattered clouds. He carried Sasha down into the hollow by the fire pit and laid her on the snowy ground. There were footprints in the snow from the day before, when Stan had shown Jim the fire pit. The dog licked at the air, staring dumbly into the canopy of the forest. Cold rain dripped from the bare branches above. Jim pulled out his zip gun and loaded it, putting it to the back of Sasha's emaciated neck, where he could see the spinal cord enter the skull. He kneeled down to kiss her under the eye.

When Jim released the rubber band the metal tube bent just slightly from the force of the exploding charge, sending the bullet off course, lodging itself sideways in Sasha's skull. She jumped when the bullet hit her, yelping from the top of her throat. The muscles in her legs flexed. Her paws arched as if she were trying to extend her claws, scratching at Jim's jeans. She tried to shit, or her body did involuntarily, but it got stuck halfway out, stringy and dry. Desperate, Jim reached for his pocketknife, and wildly stabbed the old girl in the neck and then again in the ear to put her out of her misery. She managed another half-yelp, but then it was over. She had quit moving. Her heart had stopped beating.

Sasha was laid out like a gory museum piece—teeth displayed below her shriveled jowls, blood running out of her. The dog's body trembled in shock, her dead mouth gasping for air. Even when the heart stopped, her brain still sent electrical impulses telling the lungs to draw another breath. The body died in stages. Just because the heart had given up, it didn't mean everything else did simultaneously.

Jim fell back onto his seat, dropping the stained knife to the ground. He rubbed his face hard, stunned at how it had happened. A contaminated finger traced blood onto his cheeks. He remembered the day he watched Cory Miller die, after a roadside explosion. Miller had been blown out of the gunner's hatch. They found him some thirty feet away from his Humvee. Jim lay on the ground with Miller, holding him, trying to keep him from shaking. Jim thought that Miller was telling him something—his mouth was moving, but Jim couldn't hear what he was trying to say. Helicopters were roaring overhead, waiting for a second shot. If the insurgents fired again, the helicopters would track them down and destroy them.

When the medic arrived to put an air tube down Miller's throat he said that the man was already dead. Jim berated the medic for giving up. He shouted into the medic's ear over the whooping of the helicopters. Jim told the medic that he had seen his friend's mouth moving, that he wasn't dead. As they stood there watching, Miller's body was still shaking. "It's just his lungs," the medic said. "He's lost too much blood. Trust me. The man's heart is kaput."

When they got back from patrols later that day and Cory Miller's girlfriend called, Jim was the one who answered the phone. Under procedure, all the phones and computers in the barracks should have been rounded up until Miller's family had been told about his death, but they had just gotten back, so no one had taken them away yet.

Jim wanted to call Andrea before they disconnected the phones, but when he picked up the receiver there was no dial tone. He said hello, but there was no answer. There were a lot of dead connections over there. There weren't many landlines, so they were at the mercy of a satellite. A loud ring, but no one on the other side.

He could hear breathing on the line, background noise from the other end. "Is there anybody there?" he asked. It was just a coincidence. Someone calling in at the exact moment he picked up the phone to call out.

Carly spoke slowly, her voice broken as if she already knew what had happened, "Is Cory around?" When Jim heard Carly's voice, he hung up the phone. She was a good girl, Miller's girl. Jim liked her. She'd sent candy for the whole unit once. Jim had spoken to her a few times before, holding the line while Miller got out of the shower. But he couldn't talk to her then. He couldn't talk to Carly and he couldn't call Andrea anymore, even though he was desperate to talk to her. He didn't have the words to explain to either of them what had happened.

Jim buried Sasha under the stump, falling to his knees at the base of the tree, letting the cold mud stain his hands. He lay there with his legs tucked under, his torso bent over to touch the earth. It was so bitter, he thought. This is all bitterness.

He walked to the garage and pushed the door open with his muddy hands. He tore the dusty tarp off his motorcycle, picked up a fuel can, then unscrewed the cap from the tank to pour in the pink gas, hoping it wasn't stale. He didn't remember when he'd last filled the fuel can and didn't know whether Stan had thought to do it while he was gone. Jim was sloppy in pouring the gas and spilled it over the tank and onto the floor. He just wanted to splash it in, to get enough in the tank for a short drive. Just to the city. Or, better yet, farther out into the country, staying on the gravel roads.

If the motorcycle didn't run, he didn't know what he could do to fix it.

As Jim walked his bike into the driveway, Andrea came out of the house, looking at him from the porch with the portable phone in her hand. She walked to the edge of the porch and leaned against a support column in her gray sweat suit and tube socks. Jim hadn't told her he was going to put his dog down.

"What's wrong?"

Jim had blood on his clothes and hands. He was covered in it from his knees to his neck. The broken zip gun was in his back pocket.

"What happened to you?"

"I'm going for a ride. Just to the city."

They looked at each other from across the yard. The sleet came down harder, pelting the already iced ground with freezing rain. They stared at each other, the two of them, standing frozen in the cold.

NAM LE

Fine Arts Work Center in Provincetown

LOVE AND HONOR AND PITY AND PRIDE AND COMPASSION AND SACRIFICE

My father arrived on a rainy morning. I was dreaming about a poem, the dull *thluck thluck* of a typewriter's keys punching out the letters. It was a good poem—perhaps the best I'd ever written. When I opened my eyes, he was standing outside my bedroom door, smiling ambiguously. He wore black trousers and a wet, wrinkled parachute jacket that looked like it had just been pulled out of a washing machine. Framed by the bedroom doorway, he appeared even smaller, gaunter, than I remembered. Still groggy with dream, I lifted my face toward the alarm clock.

"What time is it?"

"Hello, son," he said in Vietnamese. "I knocked for a long time. Then the door just opened."

The fields are glass, I thought. Then tum-ti-ti, a dactyl, end line, then the words *excuse* and *alloy* in the line after. *Come on,* I thought.

"It's raining heavily," he said.

I frowned. The clock read 11:44. "I thought you weren't coming until this afternoon." It felt strange, after all this time, to be speaking Vietnamese again.

"They changed my flight in Los Angeles."

"Why didn't you call?"

"I tried," he said equably. "No answer."

I twisted over the side of the bed and cracked open the window. The sound of rain filled the room—rain fell on the streets, on the roofs, on the tin shed across the parking lot like the distant detonations of firecrackers. Everything smelled of wet leaves.

"I turn the ringer off when I sleep," I said. "Sorry."

He continued smiling at me, significantly, as if waiting for an announcement.

"I was dreaming."

He used to wake me, when I was young, by standing over me and smacking my cheeks lightly. I hated it—the wetness, the sourness of his hands.

"Come on," he said, picking up a large Adidas duffel and a rolled bundle that looked like a sleeping bag. "A day lived, a sea of knowledge earned." He had a habit of speaking in Vietnamese proverbs. I had long since learned to ignore it.

I threw on a T-shirt and stretched my neck in front of the lone window. Through the rain, the sky was gray and striated as graphite. *The fields are glass.* Like a shape in smoke, the poem blurred, then dissolved into this new, cold, strange reality: a windblown, rain-strafed parking lot; a dark room almost entirely taken up by my bed; the small body of my father dripping water onto hardwood floors.

I went to him, my legs goose-pimpled underneath my pajamas. He watched with pleasant indifference as my hand reached for his, shook it, then relieved his other hand of the bags. "You must be exhausted," I said.

He had flown from Sydney, Australia. Thirty-three hours all up—transiting in Auckland, Los Angeles, and Denver—before touching down in Iowa. I hadn't seen him in three years.

"You'll sleep in my room."

"Very fancy," he said as he led me through my own apartment. "You even have a piano." He gave me an almost rueful smile. "I knew you'd never really quit." Something moved behind his face and I found myself back on a heightened stool with my fingers chasing the metronome, ahead and behind, trying to shut out the tutor's repeated sighing, his heavy brass ruler. I realized I was massaging my knuckles. My father patted the futon in my living room. "I'll sleep here."

"You'll sleep in my room, Ba." I watched him warily as he surveyed the apartment, messy with books, papers, dirty plates, teacups, clothes: I'd intended to tidy up later, before going to the airport. "I work in this room anyway, and I work at night." As he moved into the kitchen, I grabbed the three-quarters-full bottle of Johnnie Walker from the second shelf of my bookcase and stashed it under the desk. I looked around. The desktop was gritty with cigarette ash. I threw some magazines over the roughest spots, then flipped one of them over because its cover bore a picture of Chairman Mao. I quickly gathered up the cigarette packs and sleeping pills and incense burners and dumped them all on a high shelf, behind my Kafka Vintage Classics.

At the door swing, I remembered the photo of Linda beside the printer. Her glamour shot, I called it: hair windswept and eyes squinting, smiling at something out of frame. One of her ex-boyfriends had taken it at Lake MacBride. She looked happy. I snatched it and turned it facedown, covering it with scrap paper.

As I walked into the kitchen I thought, for a moment, that I'd left the fire escape open. I could hear rainwater gushing along gutters, down through the pipes. Then I saw my father at the sink, sleeves rolled up, sponge in hand, washing the month-old crusted mound of dishes. The smell was awful. "Ba," I frowned, "you don't need to do that."

His hands, hard and leathery, moved deftly in the sink.

"Ba," I said, halfheartedly.

"I'm almost finished." He looked up and smiled. "Have you eaten? Do you want me to make some lunch?"

"Hoi," I said, suddenly irritated. "You're exhausted. I'll go out and get us something."

I went back through the living room into my bedroom, picking up clothes and rubbish along the way.

"You don't have to worry about me," he called out. "You just do what you always do."

The truth was, he'd come at the worst possible time. I was in my last year at the Iowa Writers' Workshop; it was late November, and my final story for the semester was due in three days. I had a backlog of papers to grade and a heap of fellowship and job applications to draft and submit. It was no wonder I was drinking so much.

I'd told Linda only the previous night that he was coming. We were at her place. Her body was slippery with sweat and hard to hold. She turned me over, my face kissing the bedsheets, and then she was chopping my back with the edges of her hands. *Higher. Out a bit more.* She had trouble keeping a steady rhythm. "Softer," I told her. Moments later, I started laughing.

"What?"

The sheets were damp beneath my pressed face.

"What?"

"Softer," I said, "not *slower."*

She slapped my back with the meat of her palms, hard—once, twice. I couldn't stop laughing. I squirmed over and caught her by the wrists. Hunched forward, she was blushing and beautiful. Her hair fell over her face; beneath its ash blond hem all I could see were her open lips. She pressed down, into me. "Stop it!" her lips said. She wrested her hands free. Her fingers beneath my waistband, violent, the scratch of her nails down my thighs, knees, ankles. I pointed my foot like a ballet dancer.

Afterward, I told her my father didn't know about her. She said nothing. "We just don't talk about that kind of stuff," I explained. She looked like an actress who looked like my girlfriend. Staring at her face made me tired. I'd begun to feel this way more often around her. "He's only here for three days." Somewhere out of sight, a group of college boys hooted and yelled.

"I thought you didn't talk to him at all."

"He's my father."

"What's he want?"

I rolled toward her, onto my elbow. I tried to remember how much I'd told her about him. We were lying on the bed, the wind loud in the room—I remember that—and we were both tipsy. Ours could have been any two voices in the darkness. "It's only three days," I said.

The look on her face was strange, shut down. She considered me a long time. Then she got up and pulled on her clothes. "Just make sure you get your story done," she said.

I drank before I came here, too. I drank when I was a student at university, and then when I was a lawyer—in my previous life, as they say. There was a subterranean bar in a hotel next to my office, and every night I would wander down and slump on a barstool and pretend I didn't want the bartender to make small talk with me. He was only a bit older than me, and I came to envy his ease, his confidence that any given situation was merely temporary. I left exorbitant tips.

After a while I was treated to battered shrimp and shepherd's pies on the house. My parents had already split by then, my father moving to Sydney, my mother into a government flat.

That's all I've ever done, traffic in words. Sometimes I still think about word counts the way a general must think about casualties. I'd been in Iowa more than a year—days passed in weeks, then months, more than a year of days—and I'd written only three and a half stories. About seventeen thousand words. When I was working at the law firm, I would have written that many words in a couple of weeks. And they would have been useful to someone.

Deadlines came, exhausting, and I forced myself to meet them. Then, in the spans of time between, I fell back to my vacant screen and my slowly sludging mind. I tried everything—writing in longhand, writing in my bed, in my bathtub. As this last deadline approached, I remembered a friend claiming he'd broken his writer's block by switching to a typewriter. You're free to write, he told me, once you know you can't delete what you've written. I bought an electric Smith-Corona at an antique shop. It buzzed like an aquarium when I plugged it in. It looked good on my desk. For inspiration, I read absurdly formal Victorian poetry and drank scotch neat. How hard could it be? Things happened in this world all the time. All I had to do was record them. In the sky, two swarms of swallows converged, pulled apart, interwove again like veils drifting at crosscurrents. In line at the supermarket, a black woman leaned forward and kissed the handle of her shopping cart, her skin dark and glossy like the polished wood of a piano.

The week prior to my father's arrival, a friend chastised me for my persistent defeatism.

"Writer's block?" Under the streetlights, vapors of bourbon puffed out of his mouth. "How can you have writer's block? Just write a story about Vietnam."

We had come from a party following a reading by the workshop's most recent success, a Chinese woman trying to immigrate to America who had written a book of short stories about Chinese characters in stages of immigration to America. The stories were subtle and good. The gossip was that she'd been offered a substantial six-figure advance for a two-book deal. It was meant to be an unspoken rule that such things were left unspoken. Of course, it was all anyone talked about.

"It's hot," a writing instructor told me at a bar. "Ethnic literature's hot. And important, too."

A couple of visiting literary agents took a similar view: "There's a lot of polished writing around," one of them said. "You have to ask yourself, what makes me stand out?" She tag-teamed to her colleague, who answered slowly as though intoning a mantra, "Your *background* and *life experience.*"

Other friends were more forthright: "I'm sick of ethnic lit," one said. "It's full of descriptions of exotic food." Or: "You can't tell if the language is spare because the author intended it that way, or because he didn't have the vocab."

I was told about a friend of a friend, a Harvard graduate from Washington, D.C., who had posed in traditional Nigerian garb for his book-jacket photo. I pictured myself standing in a rice paddy, wearing a straw conical hat. Then I pictured my father in the same field, wearing threadbare fatigues, young and hard-eyed.

"It's a license to bore," my friend said. We were drunk and walking our bikes home because both of us, separately, had punctured our tires on the way to the party.

"The characters are always flat, generic. As long as a Chinese writer writes about *Chinese* people, or a Peruvian writer about *Peruvians,* or a Russian writer about *Russians...*" he said, as though reciting children's doggerel, then stopped, losing his train of thought. His mouth turned up into a doubtful grin. I could tell he was angry about something.

"Look," I said, pointing at a floodlit porch ahead of us. "Those guys have guns."

"As long as there's an interesting image or metaphor once in every *this* much text"—he held out his thumb and forefinger to indicate half a page, his bike wobbling all over the sidewalk. I nodded to him, and then I nodded to one of the guys on the porch, who nodded back. The other guy waved us through with his faux-wood air rifle. A car with its headlights on was idling in the driveway, and girls' voices emerged from inside, squealing, "Don't shoot! Don't shoot!"

"Faulkner, you know," my friend said over the squeals, "he said we should write about the old verities. Love and honor and pity and pride and compassion and sacrifice." A sudden sharp crack, like the striking of a giant typewriter hammer, and then some muffled shrieks. "I know I'm a bad person for saying this," my friend said, "but that's why I don't mind your work, Nam. Because you could just write about Vietnamese boat people all the time. Like in your third story."

He must have thought my head was bowed in modesty, but in fact I was figuring out whether I'd just been shot in the back of the thigh. I'd felt a distinct sting. The pellet might have ricocheted off something.

"You could totally exploit the Vietnamese thing. But instead, you choose to write about lesbian vampires and Colombian assassins, and Hiroshima orphans—and New York painters with hemorrhoids."

For a dreamlike moment I was taken aback. Cataloged like that, under the bourbon stink of his breath, my stories sank into unflattering relief. My leg was still stinging. I imagined sticking my hand down the back of my jeans, bringing it to my face under a streetlight, and finding it gory, blood-covered. I imagined turning around, advancing wordlessly up the porch steps, and drop-kicking the two kids. I would tell my story into a microphone from a hospital bed. I would compose my story in a county jail cell. I would kill one of them, maybe accidentally, and never talk about it, ever, to anyone. There was no hole in my jeans.

"I'm probably a bad person," my friend said, stumbling beside his bike a few steps in front of me.

That afternoon, as I was leaving the apartment for Linda's, my father called out my name from the bedroom.

I stopped outside the closed door. He was meant to be napping.

"Where are you going?" his voice said.

"For a walk," I replied.

"I'll walk with you."

It always struck me how everything seemed larger in scale on Summit Street: the double-storied houses, their smooth lawns sloping down to the sidewalks like golf greens; elm trees with high, thick branches—the sort of branches from which I imagined fathers suspending long-roped swings for daughters in white dresses. The leaves, once golden and red, were turning brown, dark orange. The rain had stopped. I don't know why, but we walked in the middle of the road, dark asphalt gleaming beneath the slick, pasted leaves like the back of a whale.

I asked him, "What do you want to do while you're here?"

His face was pale and fixed in a smile. "Don't worry about me," he said. "I can just meditate. Or read."

"There's a coffee shop downtown," I said. "And a Japanese restaurant." It sounded pathetic. It occurred to me that I knew nothing about what my father did all day.

He kept smiling, looking at the ground moving in front of his feet.

"I have to write," I said.

"You write."

And I could no longer read his smile. He had perfected it during our separation. It was a setting of the lips, sly, almost imperceptible, which I probably would have taken for a sign of senility but for the keenness of his eyes.

"There's an art museum across the river," I said.

"Ah, take me there."

"The museum?"

"No," he said, looking sideways at me. "The river."

We turned back to Burlington Street and walked down the hill to the river. He stopped halfway across the bridge. The water below looked cold and black, slowing in sections as it succumbed to the temperature. Behind us six lanes of cars skidded back and forth across the wet grit of the road, the sound like the shredding of wind.

"Have you heard from your mother?" He stood upright before the railing, his head strangely small above the puffy down jacket I had lent him.

"Every now and then."

He lapsed into formal Vietnamese: "How is the mother of Nam?"

"She is good," I said—too loudly—trying to make myself heard over the groans and clanks of a passing truck.

He was nodding. Behind him, the east bank of the river glowed wanly in the afternoon light. "Come on," I said. We crossed the bridge and walked to a nearby Dairy Queen. When I came out, two coffees in my hands, my father had gone down to the river's edge. Next to him, a bundled-up, bearded figure stooped over a burning gasoline drum. Never had I seen anything like it in Iowa City.

"This is my son," my father said, once I had scrambled down the wet bank. "The writer." I glanced quickly at him but his face gave nothing away. He lifted a hot paper cup out of my hand. "Would you like some coffee?"

"Thank you, no." The man stood still, watching his knotted hands, palms glowing orange above the rim of the drum. His voice was soft, his clothes heavy with his life. I smelled animals on him, and fuel, and rain.

"I read his story," my father went on in his lilting English, "about Vietnamese boat people." He gazed at the man, straight into his blank, rheumy eyes, then said, as though delivering a punch line, "*We* are Vietnamese boat people."

We stood there for a long time, the three of us, watching the flames. When I lifted my eyes it was dark.

"Do you have any money on you?" my father asked me in Vietnamese.

"Welcome to America," the man said through his beard. He didn't look up as I closed his fist around the damp bills.

My father was drawn to weakness, even as he tolerated none in me. He was a soldier, he said once, as if that explained everything. With me, he was all proverbs and regulations. No personal phone calls. No female friends. No extracurricular reading. When I was in primary school, he made me draw up a daily ten-hour study timetable for the summer holidays, and punished me when I deviated from it. He knew how to cane me twenty times and leave only one black red welt, like a brand mark across my buttocks. Afterward, as he rubbed Tiger Balm on the wound, I would cry in anger at myself for crying. Once, when my mother let slip that durian fruit made me vomit, he forced me to eat it in front of guests. *Doi an muoi cung ngon.* Hunger finds no fault with food. I learned to hate him with a straight face.

When I was fourteen, I discovered that he had been involved in a massacre. Later, I would come across photos and transcripts and books; but that night, at a family friend's party in suburban Melbourne, it was just another story shared by a circle of drunken men. They sat cross-legged on newspapers around a large blue tarpaulin, getting smashed on cheap beer. It was that time of night when things started to break up against other things. Red faces, raised voices, spilled drinks. We arrived late and the men shuffled around, making room for my father.

"Thanh! Fuck your mother! What took you so long—scared, no? Sit down, sit down—"

"Give him five bottles." The speaker swung around ferociously. "We're letting you off easy, everyone here's had eight, nine already."

For the first time, my father let me stay. I sat outside the circle's perimeter, watching in fascination. A thicket of Vietnamese voices: cursing, toasting, braying about their children, making fun of one man who kept stuttering, "It has the power of f-f-five hundred horses!" Through it all my father laughed good-naturedly, his face so red with drink he looked sunburned. Bowl and chopsticks in his hands, he appeared somewhat childish squashed between two men trading war stories. I watched him as he picked sparingly at the enormous spread of dishes in the middle of the circle. The food was known as *do an nho:* alcohol food. Massive fatty oysters dipped in salt-pepper-lemon paste. Boiled sea snails the size of pool balls. Southern-style shredded chicken salad, soaked in vinegar and eaten with spotty brown rice crackers. Someone called out my father's name; he set his chopsticks down and spoke in a low voice.

"Heavens, the gunships came first, rockets and M60s. You remember that sound, no? Like you were deaf. We were hiding in the bunker underneath the temple, my mother and four sisters and Mrs. Tran, the baker, and some other people. You couldn't hear anything. Then the gunfire stopped and Mrs. Tran told my mother we had to go up to the street. If we stayed there, the Americans would think we were Vietcong. 'I'm not going anywhere,' my mother said. 'They have grenades,' Mrs. Tran said. I was scared and excited. I had never seen an American before."

I struggled to reconcile my father with the story he was telling. He caught my eye and held it a moment, as though he were sharing a secret with me. He was drunk.

"So we went up. Everywhere there was dust and smoke, and all you could hear was the sound of helicopters and M16s. Houses on fire. Then through the smoke I saw an American. I almost laughed. He wore his uniform so untidily—it was too big for him—and he had a beaded necklace and a baseball cap. He held an M16 over his shoulder like a spade. Heavens, he looked nothing like the Vietcong, with their shirts buttoned up to their chins—and tucked in—even after crawling through mud tunnels all day."

He picked up his chopsticks and reached for the *tiet canh*—a specialty—mincemeat soaked in fresh congealed duck blood. Some of the other men were listening now, smiling knowingly. I saw his teeth, stained red, as he chewed through the rest of his words.

"They made us walk to the east side of the village. There were about ten of them, about fifty of us. Mrs. Tran was saying, 'No VC no VC.' They didn't hear her, not over the sound of machine guns and the M79 grenade launchers. Remember those? Only I heard her. I saw pieces of animals all over the paddy fields, a water buffalo with its side missing—like it was scooped out by a spoon. Then, through the smoke, I saw Grandpa Long bowing to a GI in the traditional greeting. I wanted to call out to him. His wife and daughter and granddaughters, My and Kim, stood shyly behind him. The GI stepped forward, tapped the top of his head with the rifle butt, and then twirled the gun around and slid the bayonet into his throat. No one said anything. My mother tried to cover my eyes, but I saw him switch the fire selector on his gun from automatic to single shot before he shot Grandma Long. Then he and a friend pulled the daughter into a shack, the two little girls dragged along, clinging to her legs.

"They stopped us at the drainage ditch, near the bridge. There were bodies on the road, a baby with only the bottom half of its head, a monk, his robe turning pink. I saw two bodies with the ace of spades carved into the chests. I didn't understand it. My sisters didn't even cry. People were now shouting, 'No VC no VC,' but the Americans just frowned and spat and laughed. One of them said something, then some of them started pushing us into the ditch. It was half full of muddy water. My mother jumped in and lifted my sisters down, one by one. I remember looking up and seeing helicopters everywhere, some bigger than others, some higher up. They made us kneel in the water. They set up their guns on tripods. They made us stand up again. One of the Americans, a boy with a fat face, was crying and moaning softly as he reloaded his magazine. No VC no VC. They didn't look at us. They made us turn back around. They made us kneel back down in the water again. When they started shooting I felt my mother's body jumping on top of mine; it kept jumping for a long time, and then everywhere was the sound of helicopters, louder and louder, like they were all coming down to land, and everything was dark and wet and warm and sweet."

The circle had gone quiet. My mother came out from the kitchen, squatted behind my father, and looped her arms around his neck. This was a minor breach of the rules. "Heavens," she said, "don't you men have anything better to talk about?"

After a short silence, someone snorted, saying loudly, "You win, Thanh. You really *did* have it bad!" and then everyone, including my father, burst out laughing. I joined in unsurely. They clinked glasses and made toasts using words I didn't understand.

Maybe he didn't tell it exactly that way. Maybe I'm filling in the gaps. But you're not under oath when writing a eulogy, and this is close enough. My father grew up in the province of Quang Ngai, in the village of Son My, in the hamlet of Tu Cung, later known to the Americans as My Lai. He was fourteen years old.

Late that night, I plugged in the Smith-Corona. It hummed with promise. I grabbed the bottle of scotch from under the desk and poured myself a double. *Fuck it,* I thought. I had two and a half days left. I would write the ethnic story of my Vietnamese father. It was a good story. It was a fucking *great* story.

I fed in a sheet of blank paper. At the top of the page, I typed "ETHNIC STORY." I pushed the carriage return and scrolled down to the next line. The sound of helicopters in a dark sky. The keys hammered the page.

I woke up late the next day. At the coffee shop, I sat with my typed pages and watched people come and go. They laughed and sat and sipped and talked and, listening to them, I was reminded again that I was in a small town in a foreign country.

I thought of my father in my dusky bedroom. He had kept the door closed as I left. I thought of how he had looked when I checked on him before going to bed: his body engulfed by blankets and his head so small among my pillows. He'd aged in the last three years. His skin glassy in the blue glow of dawn. He was here, now, with me, and already making the rest of my life seem unreal.

I read over what I had typed, thinking of him at that age, still a boy, and who he would become. At a nearby table, a guy held out one of his iPod earbuds and beckoned his date to come sit beside him. The door opened and a cold wind blew in. I tried to concentrate.

"Hey." It was Linda, wearing a large orange hiking jacket and bringing with her the crisp, bracing scent of all the places she had been. Her face was unmaking a smile. "What are you doing here?"

"Working on my story."

"Is your dad here?"

"No."

Her friends were waiting by the counter. She nodded to them, holding up one finger, then came behind me, resting her hands on my shoulders. "Is this it?" She leaned over me, her hair grazing my face, cold and silken against my cheek. She picked up a couple of pages and read them soundlessly. "I don't get it," she said, returning them to the table. "What are you doing?"

"What do you mean?"

"You never told me any of this."

I shrugged.

"Did he tell you this? Now he's talking to you?"

"Not really," I said.

"Not really?"

I turned around to face her. Her eyes reflected no light.

"You know what I think?" She looked back down at the pages. "I think you're making excuses for him."

"Excuses?"

"You're romanticizing his past," she went on quietly, "to make sense of the things you said he did to you."

"It's a story," I said. "What things did I say?"

"You said he abused you."

It was too much, these words, and what connected to them. I looked at her serious, beautifully lined face, her light-trapping eyes, and already I felt them taxing me. "I never said that."

She took a half step back. "Just tell me this," she said, her voice flattening. "You've never introduced him to any of your girlfriends, right?" The question was tight on her face.

I didn't say anything, and after a while she nodded, biting one corner of her upper lip. I knew that gesture. I knew, even then, that I was supposed to stand up, pull her orange-jacketed body toward mine, speak words into her ear; but all I could do was think about my father and his excuses. Those tattered bodies on top of him. The ten hours he'd waited, mud filling his lungs, until nightfall. I felt myself lapsing into old habits.

She stepped forward and kissed the top of my head. It was one of her rules not to walk away from an argument without some sign of affection. I didn't look at her. My mother liked to tell the story of how, when our family first arrived in Australia, we lived in a hostel on an outer-suburb street where the locals—whenever they met or parted—hugged and kissed each other warmly. How my father—baffled, charmed—had named it "the street of lovers."

I turned to the window: It was dark now, the evening settling thick and deep. A man and woman sat across from each other at a high table. The woman leaned in, smiling, her breasts squat on the wood, elbows forward, her hands mere inches away from the man's shirtfront. Her teeth glinted as she spoke. Behind them, a mother sat with her son. "I'm not playing," she murmured, flipping through her magazine.

"L," said the boy.

"I said I'm not playing."

Here is what I believe: We forgive any sacrifice by our parents, so long as it is not made in our name. To my father there was no other name—only mine, and he had named me after the homeland he had given up. His sacrifice was complete and compelled him to everything that happened. To all that, I was inadequate.

At sixteen I left home. There was a girl involved, and crystal meth, and the possibility of greater loss than I had imagined possible. She embodied everything prohibited by my father and plainly worthwhile. Of course he was right about her. She taught me hurt—but promise, too. We were two animals in the dark, hacking at each other, and never since have I felt that way—that sense of consecration. When my father found out my mother was supporting me, he gave her an ultimatum. She moved into a family friend's textile factory and learned to use an overlock machine and continued sending me money.

"Of course I want to live with him," she told me when I visited her, months later. "But I want you to come home, too."

"Ba doesn't want that."

"You're his son," she said simply. "He wants you with him."

I laundered my school uniform and asked a friend to cut my hair and waited for school hours to finish before catching the train home. My father excused himself upon seeing me. When he returned to the living room he had changed his shirt and there was water in his hair. I felt sick and fully awake—as if all the previous months had been a single sleep and now my face was wet again, burning cold. The room smelled of peppermint. He asked me if I was well, and I told him I was, and then he asked me if my female friend was well, and at that moment I realized he was speaking to me not as a father—not as he would to his only son—but as he would speak to a friend, to anyone, and it undid me. I had learned what it was to attenuate my blood but that was nothing compared to this. I knew what it meant to grow apart, but nothing had prepared me for this. I forced myself to look at him and I asked him to bring Ma back home.

"And Child?"

"Child will not take any more money from Ma."

"Come home," he said, finally. His voice was strangled, half swallowed.

Even then, my emotions operated like a system of levers and pulleys; just seeing him had set them irreversibly into motion. "No," I said. The word shot out of me.

"Come home, and Ma will come home, and Ba promises Child to never speak of any of this again." He looked away, smiling heavily, and took out a handkerchief. His forehead was moist with sweat. He had been buried alive in the warm, wet clinch of his family, crushed by their lives. I wanted to know how he climbed out of that pit. I wanted to know how there could ever be any correspondence between us. I wanted to know all this, but an internal momentum moved me further and further from him as time went on.

"The world is hard," he said. For a moment I was uncertain whether he was reciting a proverb. He looked at me, his face a gleaming mask. "Just say yes, and we can forget everything. That's all. Just say it: Yes."

But I didn't say it. Not that day, nor the next, nor any day for almost a year. When I did, though, rehabilitated and fixed in new privacies, he was true to his word and never spoke of the matter. In fact, after I came home he never spoke of anything much at all, and it was under this learned silence that the three of us—my father, my mother, and I—living again under a single roof, were conducted irreparably into our separate lives.

My apartment smelled of fried garlic and sesame oil when I returned. My father was sitting on the living room floor, on the special mattress he had brought with him. It was made of white foam. He told me it was for his back. "There's some stir-fry in the kitchen."

"Thanks."

"I read your story this morning," he said, "while you were still sleeping." Something in my stomach folded over. I hadn't thought to hide the pages. "There are mistakes in it."

"You read it?"

"There were mistakes in your last story, too."

My last story. I remembered my mother's phone call at the time: My father, unemployed and living alone in Sydney, had started sending long e-mails to friends from his past—friends from thirty, forty years ago. I should talk to him more often, she'd said. I'd sent him my refugee story. He hadn't responded. Now, as I came out of the kitchen with a heaped plate of stir-fry, I tried to recall those sections where I'd been sloppy with research. Maybe the scene in Rach Gia— before they reached the boat. I scooped up a forkful of marinated tofu, cashews, and chickpeas. He'd gone shopping. "They're *stories,*" I said, chewing casually. "Fiction."

He paused for a moment, then said, "Okay, son."

For so long my diet had consisted of chips and noodles and pizzas that I'd forgotten how much I missed home cooking. As I ate, he stretched on his white mat.

"How's your back?"

"I had a CAT scan," he said. "There's nerve fluid leaking between my vertebrae." He smiled his long-suffering smile, right leg twisted across his left hip. "I brought the scans to show you."

"Does it hurt, Ba?"

"It hurts." He chuckled briefly, as though the whole matter were a joke. "But what can I do? I can only accept it."

"Can't they operate?"

I felt myself losing interest. I was a bad son. He'd separated from my mother when I started law school and ever since then he'd brought up his back pains so often—always couched in Buddhist tenets of suffering and acceptance—that the cold, hard part of me suspected he was exaggerating, to solicit and then gently rebuke my concern. He did this. He'd forced me to take karate lessons until I was sixteen; then, during one of our final arguments, he came at me and I found myself in fighting stance. He had smiled at my horror.

"That's right," he'd said. We were locked in all the intricate ways of guilt. It took all the time we had to realize that everything we faced, we faced for each other as well.

"I want to talk to you," I said.

"You grow old, your body breaks down," he said.

"No, I mean for the story."

"Talk?"

"Yes."

"About what?" He seemed amused.

"About my mistakes," I said.

If you ask me why I came to Iowa, I would say that I was a lawyer and I was no lawyer. Every twenty-four hours I woke up at the smoggiest time of morning and commuted—bus, tram, elevator, usually without saying a single word, wearing clothes that chafed against me, and carrying a flat white in a white cup—to my windowless office in the tallest, most glass-covered building in Melbourne. Time was broken down into six-minute units, friends allotted eight-unit lunch breaks. I hated what I was doing and I hated that I was good at it. Mostly, I hated knowing it was my job that made my father proud of me. When I told him I was quitting and going to Iowa to be a writer, he said, *Trau buoc ghet trau an.* The captive buffalo hates the free buffalo. But by that time, he had no control over my life. I was twenty-five years old.

The thing is not to write what no one else could have written, but to write what only you could have written. I recently found this fragment in one of my old notebooks. The person who wrote that couldn't have known what could happen: how time can hold itself against you, how a voice hollows, how words you once loved can wither on the page.

"Why do you want to write this story?" my father asked me.

"It's a good story."

"But there are so many things you could write about."

"This is important, Ba. It's important that people know."

"You want their pity."

I didn't know whether it was a question. I was offended. "I want them to remember," I said.

He was silent for a long time. Then he said, "Only you'll remember. I'll remember. They will read and clap their hands and forget." For once, he was not smiling. "Sometimes it's better to forget, no?"

"I'll write it anyway," I said. It came back to me—how I'd felt at the typewriter the previous night. A thought leaped into my mind. "If I write a true story," I told my father, "I'll have a better chance of selling it."

He looked at me a while, searchingly, seeing something in my face as though for the first time. Finally he said, in a measured voice, "I'll tell you." For a moment he receded into thought. "But believe me, it's not something you'll be able to write."

"I'll write it anyway," I repeated.

Then he did something unexpected. His face opened up and he began to laugh, without self-pity or slyness, in full-bodied breaths. I was shocked. I hadn't heard him laugh like this for as long as I could remember. Without knowing why, I started laughing, too. His throat was humming in Vietnamese, "Yes...yes...yes," his eyes shining, smiling. "All right. All right. But tomorrow."

"But—"

"I need to think," he said. He shook his head, then said under his breath, "My son a writer. *Co thuc moi vuc duoc dao.*" Fine words will butter no parsnips.

"Mot nguoi lam quan, ca ho duoc nho," I retorted. A scholar is a blessing for all his relatives. He looked at me in surprise before

laughing again and nodding vigorously. I'd been saving that one up for years.

Afternoon. We sat across from each other at the dining room table: I asked questions and took notes on a yellow legal pad; he talked. He talked about his childhood, his family. He talked about My Lai. At this point, he stopped.

"You won't offer your father some of that?"

"What?"

"Heavens, you think you can hide liquor of that quality?"

The afternoon light came through the window and held his body in a silver square, slowly sinking toward his feet, dimming, as he talked. I refilled our glasses. He talked above the peak-hour traffic on the streets, its rinse of noise; he talked deep into evening. When the phone rang the second time I unplugged it from the jack. He told me how he'd been conscripted into the South Vietnamese army.

"After what the Americans did? How could you fight on their side?"

"I had nothing but hate in me," he said, "but I had enough for everyone." He paused on the word *hate* like a father saying it before his infant child for the first time, trying the child's knowledge, testing what was inherent in the word and what learned.

He told me about the war. He told me about meeting my mother. The wedding. Then the fall of Saigon. 1975. He told me about his imprisonment in reeducation camp, the forced confessions, the indoctrinations, the starvations. The daily labor that ruined his back. The casual killings. He told me about the tiger-cage cells and connex boxes, the different names for different forms of torture: the honda, the airplane, the auto. "They tie you by your thumbs, one arm over the shoulder, the other pulled around the front of the body. Or they stretch out your legs and tie your middle fingers to your big toes—"

He showed me. A skinny old man in Tantric poses, he looked faintly preposterous. During the auto he flinched, then, a smile springing to his face, asked me to help him to his foam mattress. I waited impatiently for him to stretch it out. He asked me again to help. *Here, push here. A little harder.* Then he went on talking, sometimes in a low voice, sometimes grinning. Other times he would blink—furiously, perplexedly. In spite of his Buddhist protestations, I imagined him locked in rage, turned around and forced every day to rewitness these atrocities of his past, helpless to act. But that was only my imagination. I had nothing to prove that he was not empty of all that now.

He told me how, upon his release after three years' incarceration, he organized our family's escape from Vietnam. That was 1979. He was twenty-five years old then, and my father.

When finally he fell asleep, his face warm from the scotch, I watched him from the bedroom doorway. I was drunk. For a moment, watching him, I felt like I had drifted into dream, too. For a moment I became my father, watching his sleeping son, reminded of what—for his son's sake—he had tried, unceasingly, to forget. A past larger than complaint, more perilous than memory. I shook myself conscious and went to my desk. I read my notes through once, carefully, all forty-five pages. I reread the draft of my story from two nights earlier. Then I put them both aside and started typing, never looking at them again.

Dawn came so gradually I didn't notice—until the beeping of a garbage truck—that outside the air was metallic blue and the ground was white. The top of the tin shed was white. The first snow had fallen.

He wasn't in the apartment when I woke up. There was a note on the coffee table: *I am going for a walk. I have taken your story to read.* I sat outside, on the fire escape, with a tumbler of scotch, waiting for him. Against the cold, I drank my whiskey, letting it flow like a warm current through the filament of my body. I had slept for only three hours and was too tired to feel anything but peace. The red geraniums on the landing of the opposite building were frosted over. I spied through my neighbors' windows and saw exactly nothing.

He would read it, with his book-learned English, and he would recognize himself in a new way. He would recognize me. He would see how powerful was his experience, how valuable his suffering—how I had made it speak for more than itself. He would be pleased with me.

I finished the scotch. It was eleven thirty and the sky was dark and gray-smeared. My story was due at noon. I put my gloves on, treaded carefully down the fire escape, and untangled my bike from the rack. He would be pleased with me. I rode around the block, up and down Summit Street, looking for a sign of my puffy jacket. The streets were empty. Most of the snow had melted, but an icy film covered the roads and I rode slowly. Eyes stinging and breath fogging in front of my mouth, I coasted toward downtown, across the College Green, the grass frozen so stiff it snapped beneath my bicycle wheels. Lights glowed dimly from behind the curtained windows of houses. On Washington Street, a sudden gust of wind ravaged the elm branches and unfastened their leaves, floating them down thick and slow and soundless.

I was halfway across the bridge when I saw him. I stopped. He was on the riverbank. I couldn't make out the face but it was he, short and small-headed in my bloated jacket. He stood with the tramp, both of them staring into the blazing gasoline drum. The smoke was thick, particulate. For a second I stopped breathing. I knew with sick certainty what he had done. The ashes, given body by the wind, floated away from me down the river. He patted the man on the shoulder, reached into his back pocket, and slipped some money into those large, newly mittened hands. He started up the bank then, and saw me. I was so full of wanting I thought it would flood my heart. His hands were empty.

If I had known then what I knew later, I wouldn't have said the things I did. I wouldn't have told him he didn't understand—for clearly, he did. I wouldn't have told him that what he had done was unforgivable. That I wished he had never come, or that he was no father to me. But I hadn't known, and, as I waited, feeling the wind change, all I saw was a man coming toward me in a ridiculously over-sized jacket, rubbing his black-sooted hands, stepping through the smoke with its flecks and flame-tinged eddies, who had destroyed himself, yet again, in my name. The river was behind him. The wind was full of acid. In the slow float of light I looked away, down at the river. On the brink of freezing, it gleamed in large, bulging blisters. The water, where it still moved, was black and braided. And it occurred to me then how it took hours, sometimes days, for the surface of a river to freeze over—to hold in its skin the perfect and crystalline world—and how that world could be shattered by a small stone dropped like a single syllable.

OTIS HASCHEMEYER

University of Tennessee, Knoxville

THE *FANTÔME* OF FATMA

A bell made from one piece of hammered steel hung outside the chief's door. Inside, they sat on pillows with a silver tea tray in front of them. The chief wore an embroidered white tunic and black head scarf, had clear eyes and a trimmed gray beard. Miles thought him beautiful, but then felt guilty that he'd objectified the chief in a way that he wouldn't objectify a white person. But then again, so many of the Malians seemed beautiful. They drank tea together. Miles glanced at Wolfy as she brought the teacup to her lips, wondered what she felt, if she were as happy as he was being here in the intimacy of the chief's hut. Beyond Wolfy, Deon sat with folded legs under a loose skirt and fidgeted with its hem. The chief glanced at her often, speaking in a French made more exotic by his sonorous and clipped pronunciation. Miles heard the words *escarpment* and *attention*.

Karl, leaning over his folded knees, gestured with one hand. "He says if we want to climb on the rock, we have to be respectful of the spirits that live there, and respect the ancestors of the people who lived there from before, in villages in the cliffs, and that we should not damage or take anything we find." Karl turned back to the chief. "Also, he says to have good experiences."

"Ask him where we can put up a new route," Rodney said.

"I don't think he knows about the climbing," Karl said.

"Ask him anyway," Rodney said, flexing his wrist back and forth, stretching his forearm muscles.

Karl asked, and the chief responded. Karl said, "He says it is all new."

Quietly and away, Rodney said, "Well, we know that's not true."

It had been Miles's dream to come to Mali, and he'd done the research. He knew that the fingers of Fatma had been climbed before, before Europeans, before Dogons, before people who came from elsewhere, before history and names. The people used sticks braced in the cracks to negotiate difficult sections, had villages and sacred places on the peaks to worship and follow the stars, to remain safe from their predators. At that time, the flora and fauna had been more dense. The Harmattan had not yet come and more water fell. But Rodney was concerned with recent history, with climbers bagging first ascents and naming their routes.

They drank more tea. Karl talked with the chief, and Miles tried to understand. Rodney and Wolfy talked about getting on the rock, what grades they might want to start with. Wolfy was the best climber among them and a large reason Rodney wanted Miles and Wolfy along. Then the chief addressed Deon. She smiled and then laughed, jutting her chin out. "What does he want?" she asked.

Karl said, "He asks why you are here."

"Why is he asking me?" she said, laughing again. "Don't I look like a rock climber?" Karl didn't say anything, only extended his hand toward her. She said, "Tell him, I'm just here to see."

The chief spoke to Karl, and Karl asked Deon, "Are your people from Mali?"

The chief smiled.

"God, no," she said. "They're from Oakland."

When they'd finished their tea, the chief stood at the door and looked only at Deon. Miles caught the word *fantôme*. After addressing her, Karl interpreted, "He says there is a ghost who frequents the rock."

Driving in a *bachee* to the camp, they commented on the quaint and superstitious chief of the village.

Their first night in the Spaniard's camp, Miles scanned the crags with Rodney's image-stabilizing binoculars. Le Main de Fatma turned out into the desert like four fingers and a thumb, the buttress as the open palm. The Hombori Mountains, the rising escarpment, and the spires of Le Main de Fatma pulled what little moisture there was from the air, and the villagers in Hombori pumped up the ancient waters that had leached into the aquifer. But at the Spaniard's camp there was no water, and they had to bring their own.

Not many climbers came to the Sahel, so they were alone in the Mali desert at the end of the season. Soon the Harmattan winds would blow day and night, bearing the Sahel and the distant Sahara: sands and bones and desiccated flesh. In the center of their enclosure was a platform and thatched hut, and Miles and Wolfy sat on a rock wall, one of a maze of stone walls set against the persistent evening wind. Miles laid the binoculars down. As the sun set off to their left along the orange desert floor, he whispered, "You excited?"

"Totally," she said. They stared into the Sahel and the hand rising from the sand and scrub brush. Echoing faintly in the wind was the song of the *muezzin*, the call to prayer, and on the road, some distance away, a bus stopped, allowing passengers to exit and pray under the gaze of Le Main de Fatma. After talking to the Spaniard, Rodney returned to tell them that he didn't think the Spaniard would help them find a new route. "He wants them for himself," Rodney said. "That's what I think."

"Sounds paranoid," Miles said.

"We're nobodies. That's the thing."

Miles put a hand around Wolfy's knees. "Maybe we can't just come in here and colonize the place," Miles said, and looked off at the two-thousand-foot quartzite towers, red and pink with iron oxide. "Personally, I just want to climb."

"That's the way things are done," Rodney said. "The way life marches on. This into that. Colonizing. It's pretty basic."

"Yeah," Deon said, rising from her suitcase on the platform. "Just like fucking."

"I heard that," Wolfy said, imitating Deon's black English, which Deon herself imitated. They smiled at each other. Deon took a step closer and they hooked each other's little fingers and pulled them apart.

For a divinity student, Deon swore a lot, and when Karl mentioned it, she said, "What? I can't believe in God and say, 'Fuck?'" Karl was flirting with her, but Deon didn't notice. She was interested in Rodney. Miles rubbed Wolfy's knee, thinking first that it was nice not to worry about such things, then thinking just of Wolfy's warmth, then of their circle of light and the desert, of Rodney, of the difficulty of doing anything, sand and ancient people and time and of a colossal stone head lying in the middle of nowhere. The face with blunt features had eyes without lids. Once he recognized he was thinking of "Ozymandias," he struggled to recall the words of the poem but couldn't.

The next night around the fire, Deon told them that when hiking earlier that day, she'd come to a pass between two boulders when she'd heard a call that she couldn't identify. When she looked around, she didn't see anything or anyone. She put her hand on one of the boulders to step through and then heard the cry again and small rocks scattered about in front of her. This time when she looked up she saw an African boy leaning out from a crevasse. She stopped and then the boy came down. Deon said she hadn't been frightened, mainly, she thought, because of the way the boy moved down from the rock and seemed to come toward her. She described his movements as loose. From a distance, he urged her to go around the boulders by another way, gesticulating with hands and the movements of his arms.

Rodney and Karl said they'd seen an African boy climbing on the cliffs, too. Rodney said, "All free solo. No rope. We trailed him, and then he disappeared. I mean, I saw some of the things he was climbing."

Rather than scout lines, Miles and Wolfy climbed on the western edge of the formation and hadn't seen anything except desert, sun, giant birds hovering in the thermals, and bats cooing aggressively in the cracks where Miles and Wolfy had to wedge their hands to climb. Miles drank wine from his purple-stained plastic cup. Wolfy leaned her head against Miles's shoulder. He stretched out his stiff legs.

Karl said, "I've seen free solos."

"Would you do it?" Rodney interrupted, taping a cloth around a stick and taping a carabiner to that to make a tool he'd use to push bats farther in the cracks.

Karl continued, "He was climbing only in leather shoes."

Later, sharing Tasty Bites, vegan Indian food in plastic pouches, with their hosts, they asked about the boy they'd seen. The Spaniard's wife, a Peul woman, had cataracts in her left eye that occasionally flashed opal white in the glare of the fire. With a hood over her head, she spoke in a mix of Fulfulde Massina and Spanish, and her husband translated in his lilting English. She said the boy appeared several years ago on the cliffs, that he lived in the old caves, hid at night. Some villagers left food for him tied to a post where the dogs would not get it, or at the base of the rock. Mostly, she said, he survived like the ancient people, pulling bats from the cracks or birds' eggs, taking water from the cisterns in the rock. She said the village people tried to get him out once, but they couldn't, and they saw his presence as the will of God. "Now," the Spaniard said, translating, "he steals in the village and is treated with reverence. It is the rumor his sister is sold in slavery."

Rodney said, "There isn't slavery anymore."

The Spaniard in brightly colored parachute pants crossed his legs. "It is here. It is in your country. Sex slavery. Agricultural slavery. People promise dreams," he said. "If that."

Miles was the first one awake and out of his tent the next morning to see the *fantôme* of Fatma crouching on their wall, overlooking their camp. He was folded upon himself, noticeably lean and squat, about the size of Wolfy. His arms were long and embraced his knees, and he wore shorts and a dirty red T-shirt. His toenails poked from the holes worn at the tips of his shoes.

Miles said, "Hello. *Bonjour.*"

The *fantôme* didn't say anything. Miles noted his elastic ease, his dark skin chalky with dust, his thick, cracked hands and strong forearms. Miles approached and held out his hand. The boy unfolded one arm and placed his hand into Miles's hand. The boy did not grip with his hand at all, but only let it lie there. Miles felt the dry, calloused skin.

Miles could not discern the boy's motives for crouching there and left it at that. "Okay," he said. Strange things happen, Miles thought. He pumped the fuel canister to start the stove for tea. As the others emerged from their tents, Miles remained quiet and nodded in the direction of the wall and the boy. Miles then fixed a bowl of granola and soy milk and brought it over to the *fantôme*. The boy did not take it, and Miles put it down on the stone wall next to his feet.

The boy remained motionless, taking them in, until Deon emerged. Then, just discernibly, his eyes followed her. "I think he likes you," Karl said.

"At least someone does," Deon said, and laughed. "He probably just wants a glass of water," she said. She poured water into a used plastic cup and rubbed the inside with her finger, tossed the purple liquid out onto the sand. Then she filled the cup with fresh water and handed it to the boy. He took it, watched her, then drank. When he was done, Deon filled the cup again and gave it to him. His eyes showed no emotion, but the corners of his mouth turned very slightly upward.

"You've made a friend," Wolfy said. She approached the boy and then hoisted herself up onto the wall to sit next to him. She ate her granola and then motioned for him to eat his. After she placed it into his hands, he did begin to eat, pushing the oats into this mouth with his fingers.

Karl tried speaking to the boy in French and then Spanish. The boy didn't respond. Rodney said someone should get the Spaniard's wife. "Maybe she can talk to him."

Miles ran to the Spaniard's hut. The Peul woman and her husband were already up and Miles motioned for them to come quickly, used the word *fantôme*. Neither the Spaniard nor his wife seemed interested, but they came along. Back at their site, near their platform and hut, the Peul woman tried speaking to the *fantôme* in Fulfulde. The boy turned his head at a few words. Then she spoke to her husband.

The Spaniard said, "A great many languages are spoken in the

Sahel. He doesn't speak her language, she doesn't think so. Maybe he may not speak." Then pointing at scar tissue on the boy's shoulder, he said, "He has come from a war. Straight, deep. A machete."

"He called to me yesterday," Deon said, and she told her story of the boulders. The Spaniard asked a question or two and then said a mamba snake had a territory between those rocks.

"A black mamba?" Deon said.

"I brought antivenin," Rodney said. "I'll leave it here if we don't use it."

"A lot of good that would do me," Deon said. "Out in the middle of fucking nowhere. Anyway, I'd prefer not to get bit by a fucking black mamba."

"But there is no reason to go over there," the Spaniard said.

Deon tilted her head. "Well, I was lost then. Wasn't I? I suppose that's my fault."

When they hefted their gear and headed for the col between the two spires, Suri Tondo and Wamderdou, they were surprised that the *fantôme* got up, too, and came with them, sometimes following and sometimes leading as the group worked its way around Wamderdou. Miles trailed, marveling at what was occurring. The boy wanted to be with them, but Miles wasn't sure why. Finally, they ascended a scree field and arrived at the east face of Wamderdou.

The *fantôme* stopped at the base of the rock where a chute led to a chimney and then out to a ledge. He motioned with his hands. Then he began to climb.

"Hold on," Rodney said, but it did no good. The boy slunk up and around the quartzite crack, quartz sand and silica fused under tectonic compression, fine-grained and smooth. He wedged in his feet and ascended, more graceful than even Wolfy, and he did it without a rope. Rodney backed up from the cliff and scanned with his binoculars. "Is this an unknown line?" he asked. Karl looked over his French climbing book.

"I don't see anything," he said.

Rodney looked up. "It's beautiful. A natural." And then he said, "But look at that roof." He passed the binoculars to Karl, and then Miles and Wolfy had a look. Toward the top of the climb a thick slab of rock edged out horizontally from the cliff face. For the climber it would be like a roof edge, and from the base, to Miles's eyes, the roof looked substantial, jutting out maybe fifteen feet.

"What do you think of that?" Miles said.

Wolfy said, "Let's do it."

Miles and Wolfy unpacked their gear and stepped into their harnesses, and Wolfy clipped gear to her loops.

"So that's it?" Deon said. She took out her Emerson and found a place to sit in the shade.

"You knew we'd be climbing," Miles said.

"But who could imagine it would be nothing else?" Deon said.

"Maybe tomorrow, after we bag this," Rodney said, "we'll take a trip. Maybe the next day."

The two pairs followed the *fantôme* past a crack and through a bulge. Wolfy led the pitch as Miles belayed. Every now and again, she'd scream as her hand brushed a bat, but she pushed on and finally stopped screaming. Wolfy built her anchor on a ledge some 150 feet off the ground and tied into it. Miles followed, yanking the placed gear from the cracks as Wolfy belayed from above. Miles could follow this route but the climbing was at the outside of his physical and technical limit. He marveled again at the boy's grace and his ease at climbing without a rope.

Miles's pitch moved through a deep red-colored stone. The climbing was less strenuous, hand-sized cracks, larger holds. He moved onto a face with several small roofs, edged between them, and made a solid placement, compressing a cam and letting its wedged teeth expand in the crack. He then moved along and built an anchor with placements of nuts and cams in a flake and a crack. Finally, he rested on a double hump covered in bird and bat shit. When Rodney arrived at Miles's belay station, Rodney took over the lead. Miles cautioned him to shorten up the pitch when he found a good place to set an anchor. "Three pieces in different features."

"I've probably logged more face time than you," Rodney said. That was probably true. Though Miles had been climbing for many years and had introduced Rodney to climbing only five years ago, Rodney had a trust fund and could climb whenever he wanted.

Rodney's pitch and then Karl's were easier still, passing over a black slab midafternoon. Above was their first major roof, some six hundred feet above the desert, under which the *fantôme* traversed left, following a ledge that moved away from the roof and around. To see him up so high off the desert floor, climbing without a rope, made Miles shiver. But Miles understood that the *fantôme* knew exactly what he could do and what he couldn't, and he did only what he could accomplish—unlike Miles and the rest of them, trying to accomplish something beyond their ability.

Rodney stood out from the rock, laying his weight against his anchor, clipping pro onto his gear loops. "I've been thinking," Rodney said. "He's taking the escape to the right. We'll go straight up and over that roof. That's the natural line, and that will be our first ascent. Straight up the east face of Wamderdou."

Wolfy was game. She took the lead and Miles belayed. He watched her and then looked off into the distance for a moment. The sun had come around, and the heat rippled off the desert. Above, a marabou stork floated in a thermal. A dust devil swirled at the desert floor, rising a hundred feet, well below them. Sweat dripped down Miles's back and pooled at his harness. The stork's shadow rippled across the rock, passed over Miles, a moment's relief from the African sun.

Wolfy found a cam placement above in the crack, clipped the rope in the carabiner, and then made her way up twenty-five feet and approached the first crux of the climb, a blank section without visible handholds in the shade of the roof. Miles leaned out from the rock so he could watch her, clenched the rope in his right hand, pushed down and away from the belay device. He fed rope as Wolfy moved, keeping a little slack in the line. If she didn't have the rope just as she liked it, she would have trouble. The hardest moves required perfect technique but also total body control. If a move was hard enough, Miles knew, Wolfy would search for a way to fail. In those milliseconds, if she found something was not right with Miles's belay, she could blame him rather than rely on herself.

Her muscles in her shoulder and back striated then spread as she mantled off an edge, her fingers curled and turned down and away on the small crimp of rock. She extended her shoulder and arm and stretched her other hand to a smooth bulge of stone, blindly finding it with her fingers as her face pressed the rock. Her fingers walked over the bulge, and Miles was aware that her balance shifted.

She'd woven her blond hair in two pigtails, and they hung down. The crux move was only a question of balance, and Wolfy, if she got her head straight, could do it. Wolfy's fingers hesitated as they tried to gain purchase on the sloping rock. "Watch me," she yelled.

Miles's nerves jumped. She was getting mental. Miles leaned out and shouted into the air, "I am, baby. Stay focused. Eye of the tiger."

Wolfy yelled, "Are you watching?"

Miles saw she needed to get her core muscles involved in the move and try to gain momentum from the right toe, which she'd left dangling. That was the way to handle the move. Miles was also aware that he'd never be able to make the move himself. He would not be able to follow her.

Once she'd edged her fingers over the sloper, she swung her leg below it and found a toehold. She pulled, stuck her hand into a finger-sized crack, and was up. She set two pieces below the great roof that now loomed over her head, but the sun was getting low and the wind began to come up. A few bats had crawled from the cracks, flapped and squeaked in their erratic spirals. She and Rodney decided to leave their anchor placements and try the roof the next day. Miles would have agreed if he'd been consulted. His legs were stiff with the tension of standing out from the rock. Rodney said he would rappel down from the top to look at the great roof tomorrow, see if there was any way they could get over it.

They took the *fantôme*'s escape route right, rappelled one length down the north side of the rock and then down-climbed into the col between Wamderdou and Suri Tondo. They found the *fantôme* sitting with Deon in front of the east face.

"There you fucking are," Deon said. They made apologies, explained their troubles.

"What were you doing?" Wolfy asked her. Miles looked around, saw that the *fantôme* had climbed away.

Deon looked back at them. "He just sat here. I don't know. I read him Emerson."

The next morning the *fantôme* was again on their wall overlooking their tents and hut when Miles got up. When he saw him there, he said hello, poured him a glass of water, and handed it to him. The *fantôme* drank it.

When everyone was awake, Miles said maybe they should go the fifteen kilometers to Hombori. This was for Deon's sake. Rodney looked at Karl. They wouldn't be going to town. Miles didn't think he was testing Wolfy, but perhaps he was.

"But we're going to finish that route," Wolfy said. She looked at Deon and then back to Miles.

"I'd like to see a little of town," Miles said. Wolfy said she would go with Miles. After Rodney had checked with the Spaniard to make sure the east face line was new, he and Karl returned to Wamderdou carrying their fixed lines. Like part of the group, the *fantôme* followed Deon, squeezed into the Spaniard's car next to Miles and Wolfy, and closed the door. He unrolled the window. He'd been in a car before.

The townspeople gathered around them, as interested in the *fantôme* as in the foreigners. They walked through the marketplace, divided between men on one side, roasting meats and smoking cigarettes, and women selling goods laid out on cloth on the other. Wolfy declined meat offered to her on a stick, but Miles ate some. He allowed himself to eat meat if he deemed it culturally appropriate. He passed on roasted bat, but later he had a plate of fish. He threw the scraps on the ground as he'd seen others do, and children ran up to eat from the bones. They knew that, as a tourist, Miles would not have stripped the fish of all its meat.

The sun grew hot. A small boy told them the chief wanted to see them. They met the chief in his compound. He wanted to examine the *fantôme*. The boy stood still as the chief lifted his arm, stroked fingers through his underarm hair. The chief examined the boy's head and around his ears, opened his mouth and looked at his teeth. The chief asked Deon and Wolfy to leave. Then he had the boy drop his pants. Afterward, outside in the chief's courtyard, the chief repeated his name and office, extending his hands to the boy. The chief repeated this many times, and after much coaxing the boy spoke what they believed to be his name.

Miles could read French better than he understood it spoken, so he asked the chief to write down his observations. Then Miles read the chief's remarks for Wolfy and Deon, told them that the chief believed that the boy was a foreigner from a place far away. But the chief also believed he might have come from the ancestors, before the French, the Moors, or the Dogons. The chief said he did not discount the possibility. Maybe his people were formerly here. Maybe they took the camel trains away.

After tea, the chief arranged for a Land Rover and, with a nephew driving, he took them through the town. They passed the shanties built of garbage on the outskirts, the sick and starving, and drove into the desert to Hombori Tondo. They drove through a boulder field toward a pink sandstone village carved high up in the cliffs. Miles's understanding of the chief's French improved as they drove, and he told Wolfy and Deon what the chief said, more or less. The *fantôme* crawled over the backseat and sat in the back of the Land Rover with his knees against his chest.

They climbed ladders and fixed ropes up into the village of conical mud structures, ancient mosques, and the carved caves of the Dogons and Tellem. They passed through narrows and up over boulders, stepping on depressions in the rock worn by hands and feet of earlier times. The chief and the nephew helped Deon. At the end of one of the narrows, at the cliff wall itself, the nephew removed a weathered strip of plywood from a fissure and gave the chief a plastic flashlight from the cloth bag he had slung over his shoulder. The fissure in the rock split down into the cliff and Miles, Wolfy, and Deon had to step over the fissure and into the cave. The chief held Miles's arm. Wolfy didn't need any help. Then Miles encouraged Deon, who finally leaped across and into his arms. Miles was momentarily aroused and just as quickly worried about Wolfy's jealousy. Only when they were safe inside did the *fantôme* follow.

The cave was cool, almost cold after the heat of the sun. Light filtered in from the split in the rock above them. Through the slit in the rock Miles saw sky and knew that at night the stars would be visible. They stepped on what Miles soon realized were human bones. The chief walked with little concern and the bones clacked under his feet. The others did the same, all but the *fantôme*, who walked gingerly and didn't make a sound. The cave smelled of guano and Miles also smelled cool water. The fecund smell and the small sleeping breaths of the bats mixed with the presence of the dead. The chief beamed his flashlight on figures painted on the walls of the cave in a brown the color of dried blood. He shone his light on several symbols, their outlines etched by sharp rocks. He brought the *fantôme* closer and had him look at the markings. Wolfy slid in close to Miles. Deon peered over their shoulders, her hand on Miles's waist. Miles felt as though he were at the origin of time.

Even though the *fantôme* did not seem to recognize the symbols on the cave wall, the chief held a celebration in his honor that evening. After the evening prayer, the chief sent his nephew in the Land Rover to inform the Spaniard and his Peul wife and collect Karl and Rodney. The street was alive with music and dancing. *Griots,* the storytellers, played large beaded gourds; others played guitars and drums. The air and ground vibrated with the stamping of girls in yellow skirts, feet marked with intricate designs in henna; some, the very young, with tight woven braids, smooth brown skin, oval faces and eyes. The chief's wife wore a rich blue robe and head scarf, huge earrings of red and gold, and a golden nose ring.

Wolfy wouldn't eat the food, and neither would Rodney, who feared getting sick, or Karl who had an intestinal condition and restricted his diet. They had boundaries. There were always boundaries. The skin was a boundary. The lens of the eye. Miles hated that, the separateness, and even though it made Wolfy distant, he ate.

Deon picked at a few things, and the *fantôme* ate slowly and seemed to wonder what it was all about. The *fantôme* knew he wasn't a god or an ancestor. But he seemed to know he was being honored. Miles watched an adolescent girl with pleated hair twirl in front of his eyes, and the old women held hands in front of their mouths and trilled—the gourd rasping, all of it an intoxication, the thrill of sound, the whirling of yellow hems and feet. In the midst of the dancing, Miles thought of the cave full of bones, the polished fissure worn smooth by generations of bodies passing through, returning the dead.

Wolfy said to Miles, "You're giving her a lot of attention."

"Who is that?" he asked. He didn't know who she meant, but thought she must mean Deon. He'd talked to her about the food, but that was it. Maybe earlier? The girl dancing? He took Wolfy's hand. She let him hold it, loose and uncommitted. She glanced at him and then away.

Miles's mood turned and he saw that the dancing girl's legs were thin as sticks, and he remembered the shanties they'd passed outside of town, and the children eating his discarded fish bones. Later, when Wolfy still wouldn't speak to him, he said, "I think you're jealous of him." He nodded toward the *fantôme*. "Isn't that what this is about?"

Later, the chief found a place for the *fantôme* to stay, left with him, and then came back to tell them the *fantôme* had returned to the mountains.

In the morning, Miles was sick, and from his tent he heard Rodney insisting Wolfy come back to the great roof. Wolfy poked her head into their tent and told Miles she was going.

"Go," he said.

"I guess it's convenient you and Deon are sick together."

He shook his head. Nausea overwhelmed him for a moment. "Please get out of here."

When the heat was too much, he came out of the tent. Deon emerged from the hut. They wondered together where the *fantôme* was, whether he'd gone with the others. Miles rubbed sunscreen over his face, though not on his forehead, where it would seep down to sting his eyes. He put his hat back on.

Deon said, "I think I'm going to throw up."

Later, sitting on the edge of the tent platform, sipping tea, Miles told Deon he'd go look for the others. He said, "I can't spend too much time with you because Wolfy gets jealous."

"I know," Deon said. She looked at him.

"I don't know what to do about it."

"She and I have been friends for a long time, and just because I'm a total narcissist doesn't mean I don't understand her a little," Deon said. "She tries to keep everything in its place, but it just makes her crazy. Ordering brings chaos. It doesn't take it away. What she's got to do is move in the other direction." She put her hand on his for a moment. Her palm was cool on his knuckles. They swung their legs and looked off toward Le Main de Fatma.

"Unfortunately I love all of her, not just the parts I like," Miles said.

Deon lifted her hand, said, "Well, go get her, you fucking sap."

Walking with only the daypack was the best thing for him. He took off his hat, and the sun warmed his forehead. He breathed in the dry air. In the distance, a haze obscured the horizon line. He rounded Le Main de Fatma. It didn't look much like a hand at first, but as he walked, his perspective changed and he saw the wrist turn and gesture toward the sky. He thought again of "Ozymandias." These fingers twelve hundred and two thousand feet high were all that were left, and someday they would be gone, too.

When he found the climbers, he saw all the work Rodney and Karl had done the previous day. They had fixed ropes up the first two pitches of the climb. High above he saw Wolfy below the roof. Immediately his gut wrenched. He scanned the rock with Rodney's binoculars and saw Karl dangling from a fixed line anchored to the summit above. He held a video camera on a sling. Miles swung the binoculars to the right, found Rodney on the ledge, anchored and belaying Wolfy. Wolfy was twenty feet higher and hung from protection, two equalized pieces, wedged into the dihedral below the roof. Miles arranged some rocks so that he could lie down on his back and view the action. For the rest of the afternoon, Wolfy hung and then attempted the roof and each time she fell, swinging from the rock. Miles saw that the problem was not physical.

Rodney, Karl, and Wolfy came down early, having failed to pass over the roof. When Wolfy descended the last fixed line, Miles got up and found himself, without his knowing it had happened, covered with a layer of desert dust. He greeted her at the base of the rock. She asked, "Where's Deon?"

Through a complex logic, from meat to Deon to Rodney's belay to Miles, Miles knew Wolfy held him responsible for her failure. Maybe he was responsible.

They began in the tent, Wolfy not broaching the subject but Miles knowing what she was thinking. Though their sleeping bags were opened toward each other, their bodies did not touch. She read a book with her headlamp on. They ended out in the desert, under the stars, meteors falling, streaking, and burning up in the atmosphere. Miles knew what Wolfy wanted. She wanted him to convince her he was not attracted to Deon. There was nothing rational about it. Wolfy wasn't jealous of the real Deon. But Wolfy believed that the only thing that would make her feel okay was to have this specter of Deon cast down. And she resented like hell that Miles wouldn't do it for her, answer her questions in the ways she wanted. Miles wouldn't. Not only would Wolfy never believe him, but Miles believed it was wrong to do that to Deon or to anyone.

He gestured. "Look where we are. It's unbelievable."

The desert winds were up and he could hear the wind roaring as it funneled through the spires of Fatma, worn to thick, unmovable sails in the desert. The wind sucked their voices away into the low pressure, the thermal differential, to fly over the sand, the huts, the villages, and into the desert. Miles said, "We're here but we're living in your head."

Though the *fantôme* had not come to the camp the day after the party, he was back the following morning, sitting on the wall and waiting for the group to rise. Why he chose not to come and then to return, no one could answer. Maybe he'd also been sick from the village food. Maybe something else. But Rodney had other concerns. He had the idea that Wolfy should try the roof again fresh, but that Deon should come to the cliff, too. If all else failed, his idea was to have the *fantôme* climb the roof.

"He's not interested in your white route," Deon said. "A straight line up a rock, like there's a straight fucking line anywhere around here."

"Isn't that up to him?"

"It's too dangerous," Wolfy said.

"Anyway, I was planning on doing something else," Deon said, and cocked a hip.

"Please," Rodney said, indulging her.

Karl said, "He'll wear a rope, of course."

They rigged in the morning. When it came time to make the attempt, Wolfy said she needed Miles to belay. This was an apology but also, Miles knew, a necessity. They all jugged up the fixed lines to the crux. Karl hung from the summit with his video camera, Miles belayed, and Wolfy climbed from the crack and over the first crux she'd done two days earlier. She had those moves wired now and they were no problem for her. Miles looked down, saw the tiny figures of Deon and the *fantôme* at the base of the cliff, the red glint of the binoculars in Deon's hands. Then she handed the binoculars to the *fantôme*.

Wolfy reached the crux and pinned her right foot out on the dihedral below the roof. She set her hands, began to move upside down in the crack. Miles leaned out from the rock, pulling the taut sling that held him to his anchor, and looked up at her. Just at the edge of the roof, she reached out, swung her right foot to the right, and held a thin edge with the tips of her fingers, grasping with her right hand above for something, anything. Problems were usually footwork or mental, in that order. But the move could be too hard. Those were ideas to keep away from. Her right foot agitated for more purchase. "Watch me," she yelled. Then she fell.

There was a certain terror to watching her fall, knowing the rope would pull at the biner attached to the protection in the rock, the fear that the cam could pull free, snap Wolfy down to be caught on Miles's anchor. He had three pieces in the rock. But after that, there was nothing. In the end, they depended on these pieces of metal and the rock and the rope. If any of them failed, they'd be dead—nothing on earth could stop them from dying. But gear seldom failed. If accidents happened climbing, it was, ninety-nine times out of a hundred, the climber's error.

Wolfy jerked at the end of her rope. Carabiners and slings clinked, pulled taut from the rock face. At the other end, the rope yanked

Miles's belay device, belay loop, harness, and waist. Threaded in the cracks, the cramming devices and nuts bit into the rock. Everything held.

Before lunch, they descended again. In the heat of midday, Rodney pantomimed what he wanted the *fantôme* to do. Sweat rose on Rodney's forehead as he tried to get his points across. The boy remained chalky and dry. Miles helped the boy put on a harness. On the ground, using a crack at eye level, Rodney and Karl showed the boy how to clip into the protection that Karl had placed above the roof—once the *fantôme* got over the roof, if he did. They demonstrated to him that he'd be safe tying his harness to a cam wedged in the rock. They had the *fantôme* climb up and drop onto the gear. At first the boy didn't want to do it. He had to be eased from the rock by Karl and Rodney to convince him. For Miles, the whole thing seemed like a bad idea.

They ate Tasty Bites from the pouches. Miles gave the boy an extra pair of his climbing shoes to wear. The boy put them on and smiled, looked at his feet. This was the first unreservedly positive expression Miles had seen from the boy. Then Rodney and Karl and Miles ascended up their fixed lines back to their anchors on the third pitch. The *fantôme* followed without tying in, free soloing up the first two pitches. Miles thought the harness was cumbersome for him, and seemed to make the boy self-conscious.

At the anchor, Miles clipped in, seven hundred feet above the desert floor, while Wolfy and Deon watched from below. Miles tied the *fantôme* into the end of the rope. Miles showed the boy how the belay would catch the rope should he fall. Miles wasn't sure what the boy understood. The wind rose. Miles felt his sunscreened skin covered in grit.

The roof loomed above them, casting dark red rock against the sky. The boy began his climb out from the crack. The moves here were likely more difficult than anything the boy had ever done before. He'd never needed to climb anything like this. Deon had said the boy was *loose*. Miles thought the boy was like water. He'd spent years flowing up and over the cracks and crags of Fatma, against gravity. Like water he went where he could, finding routes by merging body and rock, animate and inanimate. The boy would never conceive of doing a climb like the one Rodney had devised. There was no need to go *straight* up Wamderdou.

The boy moved away from the anchor, spent a few seconds clipping into the bombproof piece above the anchor and to the right of Miles. The boy had understood that much, thank god. Then he proceeded to the first crux Wolfy had negotiated the other day. The boy had watched her do it, and he imitated her, grasping the small edge and pushing off to stretch his arms up toward a sloping handhold. The rope seemed to bother him, and then his leg started to shake.

Miles hadn't seen the boy afraid before. His arms were longer than Wolfy's and he grasped the sloping rock and pulled himself up. Sweat popped on his forehead and stained his shirt between his shoulder blades. His knees still shook as he worked his way up under the roof. The boy didn't stop and consider. Miles knew what was driving him. He couldn't retreat. He had to go forward. He moved into the layback off the crack and spread his arms, one hand upward into the crack, then his feet cut loose and swung.

He would never make it. The boy hung on with one hand, stuck a toe on the rock below the roof, and then reached across his chest with his other free hand. He was perpendicular to the ground now. His right hand reached up and over and out of Miles's sight. Then he swung his midsection, got a foot up on a bulge, and slid up and out of Miles's view. He'd done it. Miles felt the rope pull, and he fed slack along with the even tug. He paid out and then more. From his fingers on the rope, Miles knew the boy was pulling rope to clip it into the protection above the roof. Miles's heart was slowing. He was filled with elation for the boy. Rodney was talking in his ear; they'd done it. Miles was listening, not paying attention to the belay.

The boy was well over his last piece of protection. He'd gathered rope to clip the carabiner over the roof but hadn't clipped it. He fell for no good reason. He fell because he'd already done the hardest part. Listing for a moment at the lip of the roof, he toppled backward, gaining speed. In seconds, the rope snapped through the carabiners and pulled the cams and nuts taut in the cracks and yanked Miles from his anchor. The slings pulled. The cams bit into rock. Then the rope took the boy's weight and elongated, sapping his momentum.

Miles's heart beat hard, but he had the boy locked off and safe. Moments passed as the boy dangled at the end of the rope, hanging in space. The boy didn't move. He rotated. He seemed asleep. His arm moved as if pushed by a breeze. One leg twitched. Miles didn't know what to think. He didn't think anything. After moments, the boy crunched up. He opened his eyes and gazed at the rock in front of him. He reached a hand out toward it.

Miles, Rodney, and Karl helped the boy down the face of Wamderdou. When he'd reached the bottom, Deon and Wolfy hugged him, pulled his small body into theirs. With flaccid muscles, he looked like skin over bones as they compressed him.

Wolfy came to Miles. She trembled for a moment, squeezing him. "That scared me."

Miles stayed at the base, appreciating Wolfy's power as she jugged up the fixed lines, her resolve now set like the tectonic pressures that produce rock. She took a belay from Rodney, strung out the lead, wedging into the roof dihedral, jamming one hand deep in the crack, bats be damned. She'd seen the boy do it, and she knew she could do it, too. She swung her feet out, cut loose, and pinned a heel on the edge of the great roof. For a moment, her heel and one hand on the ledge of the roof, she let her arm swing down, shook out her arm for a moment. She had it. The sun was lowering and above her a few bats circled erratically. She pulled herself over, clipped in, and climbed to the next belay ledge, set an anchor. The wind rose, howling through the spires. The boy sat at the base of Wamderdou with his knees folded into his chest. At some point he got up and wandered away.

The next day, they were clear that the boy would not be returning. Karl, in ominous baritone, said, "He'd never died before. That's why."

Rodney and Wolfy linked the climb. They would always have that together, for their lives, into the future. Karl and Miles weren't able to pass the crux and took the escape route to the top. On the summit of Wamderdou, they stood together. Miles looked at Wolfy, harness, black climbing pants, green Windbreaker, her yellow pigtails pleated on her shoulders. The haze of the Harmattan was visible everywhere on the horizon. Ozymandias, time. Glory was fleeting, but it was still glory, and Wolfy's was real. She claimed Wamderdou.

When they reached the base, Miles drew Wolfy away. They walked along, took a wide path, circumnavigating the spires. He turned her to face the fingers of Fatma reaching for the sky. He wanted to show her what he'd seen the day he'd been sick and walked alone, he wanted to share that with her, but their perspective was not yet right. They walked in loose sand, rounding the far side of Kaga Tondo. "Just a little farther," he said. Miles stayed trained on the fingers of Fatma, watching. Then as they walked, the wrist turned, fingers spun, melded, and spread just so, transforming the spires of rock into a gesture rising from the orange desert. Miles knew it was not a hand but only resembled a hand, and that was enough, a metaphor that any person could see and feel, in this spot, a connection of people and earth, an awakening that could be shared by every living human being on earth, drawing from each awe, supplication, and adoration, those divine impulses that drew to this sacred place nomads, travelers, people of every disposition—the Tellem, Dogons, Muslims, and French, those many people of Mali and all wandering pilgrims—to see God in self but also in a gesture of rock against sky.

"Do you see that? Amazing, isn't it?"

Her pale blue eyes, the sun golden on her skin, the last flits of light in her yellow hair faded. "I guess slave traders pass through here," Wolfy said. "That boy's sister was traded."

"I know," Miles said.

They walked around Kaga Pamari and over to their left saw Wangel Debridu. Nearing camp, Miles saw Wolfy crying. He pulled her close.

She wiped her eyes but the tears kept coming. "If you died, I wouldn't want to go on."

"Sure you will," he said. "You will go on," Miles said.

Her tears really started now. He said again, "You will," and wrapped her in his arms. She sobbed, and he felt the power of her, her force and intensity now serving this purpose, weeping for his death, her shoulders pulled up and racked down, the wetness of tears, the remarkable being of her, from her toes to her fingertips.

Back in San Francisco, Wolfy would occasionally see Deon, who'd curse her latest fling, sometimes a boy and sometimes a girl. Miles, getting the news secondhand, knew it would be the rare person, of any gender, who could keep up with Deon. Then both Miles and Wolfy went to Sausalito for Deon's student sermon. She stood at a lectern, her fingers curled over the edge. Her voice rang out as she defined chaos as a place without distinction, a place of tranquillity. Her words took force as her shoulders drew up with breath, speaking over the crowd of parents and well-wishers, speaking above the confusion of her own life. When she was done and they found each other in the crowd, Deon took their hands and said, "Well, how the fuck was that?" They admitted it was really *fucking* good.

Last Miles heard, Rodney was off to China. He called to ask if Miles had seen his binoculars. Miles said he didn't have them. Miles remembered the boy holding them, scanning the crags. If the boy had stolen them, Miles was glad of it. More time passed, and Miles forgot about the *fantôme* and Le Main de Fatma. Then one day, years later, Miles and Wolfy's baby girl toppled backward off the sofa. With the instinct a parent has, Miles caught her, and as he held her in his hand, he remembered the boy falling after the roof of Wamderdou—because he'd already accomplished the impossible, on a climb Rodney forever named *Wamderlust*. The boy dangled there, inert, and then reached a hand out toward the rock. And Miles remembered Karl, dressed in black stovepipe jeans, intoning in his baritone, "He'd never died before." And he remembered their last day: Karl asked Deon if she would like to see the Bandiagara escarpment where many ancient villages were located; Rodney went to town to arrange for a vehicle to take them back to Bamako; and Miles and Wolfy rented a moped and drove to the village they'd visited with the chief. They arrived with only a daypack. They'd never climbed without ropes, but this last day they did, for fun, forgoing ladders and rope and instead scaling the rock, like the ancient people who had made this their home. From the base of Hombori Tondo, they free soloed to the cave of bones.

Miles swiveled his daughter down and placed her feet on the floor. She crumpled to her knees and crawled to her striped tiger with yellow plastic eyes. Lives were trajectories and also endlessly conical. Spiraling up or down, Miles didn't know. And it didn't matter. They touched each other. His daughter would climb soon, and he would want to tell her the story of the *fantôme* of Fatma, the story of a boy

and sister abducted by traders and transported over foreign land-
scapes, a boy who escaped, a boy who'd been in war, a boy drawn up
into the hand of fate.

Perhaps the boy always intended to leave the spires before the
Harmattan came. Perhaps he needed that time to gather strength for
the journey ahead, for his assault on the fortress that held his sister.
Perhaps he needed binoculars. Or perhaps his story did not take that
route.

Miles watched his daughter tug at the stuffed tiger. He thought of
a boy in the Sahel. One day the boy counseled a girl with small
stones not to pass where the mamba snake had its lair. He climbed
and fell. He died and found himself on the end of a rope—a boy
who had forgotten and then remembered.

LYDIA PEELLE

Fine Arts Work Center in Provincetown

THE STILL POINT

In Thunderbird, Illinois, I get to thinking the world is going to end. During the day it's cotton candy and caramel apples, the Howler and the Zipper, the looping sound track of the carousel. But at night, when I'm stretched out in the back of the truck on the outskirts of Camper City, trying to sleep in the bowl of quiet left by five hundred people gone home sunburned and broke to their beds, the feeling sneaks in and sits down square on my chest: These are the last days. It's all going to break up. It's like I'm eavesdropping on the secret that history has been whispering to itself all along: the punch line, the trick ending, the big joke. I curl up alongside the wheel well wondering why I'm the only one who hears it. Then it's morning, the sun burning through the windows, the truck hot like a greenhouse, and I slide out barefoot onto the grass for another slow drag around the sun.

Across the aisle, Dub leans out the door of his camper, shading his eyes and squinting in my direction. "Hurry it up, man. Hurry your ass up," he shouts. "They're calling for rain today."

He steps out of his camper like he's lowering himself into a pool, gripping the doorframe and easing himself down on one leg, then the other. It takes a while for him to wade his way over. I pull off my T-shirt and crack my neck. The morning is hot and damp as the inside of a dog's mouth. All around us, Camper City wakes up slow. Generators hum, people light their first smokes of the day, piss out the door. The Haunted House woman puts on the radio and steps out to do her exercises under the awning of her RV, bouncing in a tank top, touching her toes. Everyone struggles to maintain something of a routine. Me, every morning I remind myself where we are. Now: Illinois. I say it out loud, to make it official.

By the time Dub makes it over he's sweating and puffing, his mouth a deflated O. He presses a hand to my back window to steady himself. "Get a move on," he wheezes. "We'll get an early crowd. Rain in the afternoon. They're all at home right now, glued to the Weather Channel, changing their plans. I guarantee."

Dub is always guaranteeing the unguaranteeable: the weather, the whims of people, the quality of questionably constructed merchandise. A born hustler. Me, I couldn't sell a drowning man a life jacket. We could get no business at all, for what I care. I'd just as soon sit at my table and watch the crows tear around above me, wondering what the hell set down in the center of their field. But still, I'm pulling on a shirt, lacing up my boots. Illinois. Really it's just another sky, another field, another morning, another sea of faces to come, blank-eyed, slack jawed, hands on wallets, not as much to see the spectacle as to take something away from it to put up on the shelf.

"Coffee?" Dub jerks his thumb back at the camper, jowls swaying. I nod and slam the tailgate shut. Five months, four thousand miles,

Dub's coffee's been slowly hollowing out my gut. He is a friend, or at least constant as one.

"Christ, it better hold," he shouts on his way back to the camper, shaking his finger at the sky. "I sure as hell can't afford a slow day."

Twenty minutes later, the coffee cranking through me, I head up to the Porta-Johns on the midway. Up here, things are slow to creak into gear: The carnies fold tarps, run patchy safety checks on rides, shout to one another in English, Spanish, Portuguese. Sodas are plunged into ice at the concession stands, hot dogs are eaten for breakfast, no buns. The old man in the cotton-candy stand wearily starts his centrifuge spinning and shakes his cartons of pink sugar. Ed the Giant Steer, led out of his tent so that it can be flea bombed for the second time in two weeks, sways on his stilt legs and groans, yanking his lead in his handler's palms, diving for the grass. A heavy roll of ADMIT ONE tickets is dropped in the dust and rolls to a stop at my feet. No one looks up when I pass. I might as well be just another faceless customer, passing through. The outfit is watertight. Us hucksters, relegated to the side strips, we're nothing but gulls following a fishing boat, swooping in to snatch the leavings.

Most of the vendors down on the back side are already at their booths, counting out money, listening to radios. Yawning, sleep still burning off, looking only half ready for the droves. I nod to the few I know: Indian Jim, who sells five-dollar sunglasses and isn't Indian in the least; Ronnie, the kid, sizzling on pills even at this hour, with his dream catchers and blown-glass beads on cords. They nod back, eyes hard. I stop at the wing stand to say hello to Kathy. She leans out on the counter with her hands clasped in front of her and smiles big and blank, like she's waiting to take my order.

"Cole, baby," she says.

"Good goddamn morning," I say.

Kathy's hair, as always, is done in two braids, a hairstyle she must have outgrown forty years ago. No makeup yet, which makes a big difference. She's wearing a low-necked T-shirt covered with sequins that catch the light and send it sparking all over the place. I can see the tops of her breasts, brown and cooked-looking. Whenever I see them in the light of day, I can't imagine how I ever find comfort there.

"Think the weather will hold?" she says. Her bracelets jangle as she waves toward the sky. I squint up at the clouds, making out like I'm studying something she can't see.

"Yes," I say. "Guaranteed."

She laughs, too loud. "You getting into anything tonight?" Next to her deep fryer, turkey drumsticks and wings are lined up, ruddy and stoic-looking, like they're steeling themselves for the hot oil. Dinosaur Wings, they call them. There's a pterodactyl on the sign in the window: BOB AND KATHLEEN DENNIS. PROUDLY SERVING YOU.

"What's today?" I say, though we both know it makes no difference. Every day is the same. Every night, the same clamor to erase it.

She thinks for a minute, her lips moving, counting back. "Saturday," she finally says, flipping a braid over her shoulder, triumphant.

"One more day. Tomorrow we go."

"Where?" she says with a sigh. "I don't ask anymore."

"West. Over the river." For weeks I've been looking forward to it, crossing the river, thinking things will be different on the other side. But as soon as I say it, all my anticipation fades, the way a trout loses color when it's yanked out of the water.

"Come by the bus this afternoon and see me," she says and winks, then swipes at the counter with a rag and turns to the crackling fryer. "Bob takes over at four."

When I get down to my table, Dub's already in his tent across the way, refolding and restacking T-shirts. The tent is packed with them, most XL or larger, stiff with silk-screened designs: women in confederate flag thongs leaning across the hoods of Ford and Chevy trucks, bloody-fanged pit bulls in studded collars, Uncle Sam with his middle finger extended above an American flag and the message THESE COLORS DON'T RUN. A Nam buddy left him a warehouse full in his will. Dub's been on the road three years now, says he'll quit when he sells them all. But I don't know. There's a point of no return, I'm beginning to think, and Dub may have passed it several thousand miles back.

Since spring I've been traveling. West. Already the highway has become the one true thing, towns only stopovers, names on signs. Certain smells, clouds, movements of trees will once in a while feel exactly like home. Shadows will fall on the road in such a familiar way that I get disoriented and think I'm back in Virginia, headed down to the farm, where everything is still as it once was, and a certain sort of peace will come over me. Then the light shifts and it all shatters.

I pull out my boxes, roll up my tarp, and set up my table: blue glass medicine jars, tin toys, old coins, moldy old tools. Wherever I go I'm always knocking on farmhouse doors, offering to clean out old couples' sheds and barns. All I need is some bleach and a wire brush, and people will pay fifty bucks for an old milk pail, a Radio Flyer with a broken axle. ANTIQUES, my sign says. Dub is always pointing it out to people, laughing. "Antiques? He sells junk. I sell trash." But business is generally slow. I'm lucky enough to get Dub's runoff, wives who wander over while their husbands are clawing through piles of T-shirts, debating blond or brunette.

I hear Dub shout my name and look up, wondering what now. "Looky here!" he's saying. He's standing in the door of his tent, waving me over. In his hand I see something hanging from a chain, glinting. When I get over there he holds it out against his palm for me to see: a girl's necklace, a tiny gold heart, nearly swallowed up in his beefy hand.

"Where'd you get it?" I say, suspicious.

He taps the side of his nose. "Found it on my way over here. Sniffed it out." His eyes are glassy from the heat, his forehead glistening. He's got half a pound of shrapnel in his left calf and thigh. Walking, standing—everything takes its toll. He pulls out a folding chair and sits down heavily, grunting. "Hell," he says, grinning like a dog. "I think it's worth something, too." He grabs my hand and pours the chain into it. "Go on, man. Take it. Sell it."

I look down at the little heart. Why not? Everything else on my table is borrowed, begged, stolen from the dead. When I go back and lay it down among the old campaign buttons and souvenir penknives, it might as well be a relic of someone long gone from this world.

Six months ago, my twin brother Clay's comic books were the first things I sold. The house and pastures went to a development company after two days on the market, every penny paying for my mother's new apartment in the center with round-the-clock care. Her mind, by then, was as twisted and looped as a tattered curtain in a dark window. It was up to me to clear out the house. Clay's room, fifteen years after his death, was exactly as he'd left it, untouched for nearly as many years as he'd been alive. Opening his door stirred up the dust that had settled on his absence, made it gleaming, glaring, new again. It was another day before I could bring myself to go in, and even then I moved around like a trespasser, as if any minute he might appear in the door. I found the comic books boxed up carefully, chronologically, under his bed. A brittle piece of notebook paper fluttered to the floor as I lay on my stomach to pull them out, left over from the days when we fought over everything: *Hands off,*

Cole! But that money kept me going for months, bought me the truck, got me miraculously, against all odds, out of Virginia—*Spider-Man, The Fantastic Four, Green Lantern, Atom Man.*

And the people come, as they always do. In spite of the heat, the humidity, the exhaust-colored sky, they come dropping coins and car keys, yanking kids along by the wrists, eating funnel cake with their eyes on the Ferris wheel. Their dogs locked in hot cars. I sit behind the table and watch them, the same faces making the rounds, hell-bent like they're searching for something. It's always the same, everywhere. I watch boys and men clamor in Dub's tent, T-shirts in their fists, throwing their money at him. I hear the clang of the bell at the TEST YOUR STRENGTH booth, the shouts of the barkers, hollers from the rickety Tempest, screams from the Gravitron every time the floor drops away. The bleeps and buzzes and techno bass beats of the games. Eyes pass over my table and move on, looking for something bright and plastic and new. A hot-air balloon rises on the horizon, hovers red and stark against the steel gray sky. People stop to point it out to one another, causing traffic jams on the paths. Something about it makes me uneasy. It looks like it has come to judge us.

No one has stopped at my table by the time the smells of lunch start to waft over: corn dogs, sausage and onions, Dinosaur Wings. At night, the smell is deep in Kathy's braids. Bob doesn't want her anymore, or at least that's what she told me. He spends hours in the wing stand after closing, trying to teach himself guitar. Kathy sits in the giant bus and waits for me. I come because there's nowhere else to go. She has an easy laugh, the optimism of youth. Bob's missing two fingers. He curses the stubs when he plays, the chords muted and muddy. The bus is parked so close behind the stand that sometimes, in bed with her, I can hear him. I pull the blanket over our heads and try not to listen. When I listen, I start to sink through the dark depths toward the pointlessness of it all. Why does he bother? At his age, what's the use?

Last night, I left the bus late, ended up at the grandstand, where most of the crowd had gathered for a beauty pageant. It was part of some festival going on in conjunction with the fair: the Corn Festival, the Harvest Festival, the Illinois Pride Festival, I don't know what. The girls, in their elaborate dresses, all looked incredibly earnest and downright scared, as if this was the most important event of their lives. The winner cried as they crowned her, touching her frothy pink dress and piled-up hair. The sash they looped over her shoulders read MISS HOPEWELL COUNTY. She twisted it in her fingers as she stepped to the microphone and gave a speech about her brother in the army. *We never know when the enemy might strike,* she said, feedback crackling. *It could happen right here in Thunderbird. That's why I'd like to take a moment of silence for our boys over there. They remind us all to follow our dreams and never give up.* The heads in the grandstand all nodded, and after a round of applause there was a minute or two of an almost sacred quiet. Out there, on the edge of the crowd, I tried to direct my own silence toward the common cause, but all those grave, unmoving faces only made me feel more invisible and alone.

Afterward the winner posed for pictures, biting her lip between smiles. As she turned and waved to the crowd, she moved like all the country girls I know: trying to fold in on herself, trying to tuck away her broad muscular shoulders like wings. I thought about the girls Clay and I ran with in Virginia, girls who seemed to hold the answer to a question we hadn't yet learned to ask. Clay was the one they liked, though we were as near identical as two people could be. The only difference was that he had half an inch on me, a birthmark on his right shoulder, and a heart so big all the girls thought he was in love with them. He'd take them all out driving, that nightmare summer of the accident, the summer we turned sixteen. The age this girl must be, the age I last felt whole.

I saw her again, late, past midnight. The rides shut down, the games closing up, most people gone home, I walked out into the field, far out where I could turn and see the midway lights from a distance. Already thinking about packing up the truck, slamming the tailgate shut on everything I owned. At night I like to do this, imagine the field once we've left it: the deer coming out of the woods, noses working over crumpled napkins, the foxes creeping out onto the trampled paths, sawdust scattering in the wind. It's usually a comfort, knowing the field will recover without a trace of us, just days after we're gone. But there's a danger to picturing a place without you in it. After a while you can start to feel like nothing at all.

When I walked back up toward Camper City, I went past the grandstand again, empty now. By the bleachers I happened to notice the teddy bear. It was bright orange, a prize off a game, glowing a little in the dirt. It reminded me of something, and I almost bent to pick it up, but then I heard them. A scuffling like animals, a hollow sound as she banged against the bleachers. When I peered into the darkness it took a few seconds for me to make sense of it. She'd changed out of her pink dress and into a pair of jean shorts, which were pulled down around her knees. But she was still wearing her sash, crooked now, flapping like she was unraveling. He was behind her, hands in her hair, yanking her head back a little with each thrust, his big white T-shirt billowing. I stood there and watched the whole thing, nothing but a pair of eyes. It was over fast. When he let go of her she didn't move for a moment, stayed there hanging on the support strut of the bleachers, then slowly bent down and picked up the bear and tenderly brushed off the dirt. I stepped into the shadow of a ticket booth as he turned and zipped his fly. I couldn't see his face, but I recognized the shirt immediately. It was one of Dub's—THE HUNTER'S NIGHTMARE—a deer at the wheel of an ATV with a rifle strapped across its shoulders, a dead man in camo tied to the back.

Five months on the road and already I've seen too much. Too much to feel any shred of hope for the long-gone world. I feel the burden of it all clattering behind me, slowing me down, like cans tied on for a honeymoon. Sometimes I wonder why it hasn't all burned up or broken down already. Sometimes it makes me want to lie down right where I am and just let the grass grow over me.

The sky, by two, is yellow and angry. There's a general wash of worried murmurs in the crowd. Mothers peer up at the bloated clouds, clutching raincoats; old men mutter and tell their wives they're ready to go home. Little kids run shrieking down the path, oblivious. I sell a chipped butter crock to a blue-haired, heavy-faced woman with white plastic shopping bags strung along her arms like buoys. "What'll you all do if it rains?" she asks, swinging her head toward the midway, bags rustling. She widens her eyes in concern, as if she can think of no more terrible a fate. I look up, ready to be through with these people, put Thunderbird in the rearview as I tear off down the road. "Same thing as you," I say, snapping the money box closed. "Get wet."

It is only a legend, of course, the Thunderbird. A myth the settlers stole from the Indians to scare little boys out of venturing too far from home. But they told the story enough times that they started to believe it themselves. Started whispering the terrible *what if*s, started to keep an eye on the sky. Always watching for the dark shape in the trees that might be waiting to swoop down and carry their children away. A hundred years ago, two traveling men pulled into town with the proclamation that they had captured the beast, that they had it alive and caged in a tent, to be viewed for two bits admission. When the crowd gathered, one of them went around collecting money, working the people up, describing the creature's great ferocity, the size and crushing strength of its talons and beak. And then just at the moment before the unveiling, the other one came running out from behind the tent, screaming, *It's escaped! Run for your lives!* And in the pandemonium that followed, they packed it all up quick and took off for the next town. Dub told me the story, doubled up with laughter. *You'd think that would have put an end to it,* he said. But every year there are one or two more sightings. I can imagine it, a glimpse of a wing or a passing shadow, the shuddering near miss of catastrophe.

I'm thinking about those two travelers, telling the same story to town after town, crowd after crowd, how after a while, the faces and the story must have blurred, so they no longer knew what was hoax and what was truth. I'm ready to take a break, clear my head, walk away for a while, when a group of teenagers comes careening down the path and slides to a stop in front of Dub's tent. Three boys in low-slung jeans jab a pink cloud of cotton candy in one another's faces, laughing and bumping into people. With them, in tight jeans and a tank top, Miss Hopewell County, still in her sash and crown, is giggling and slapping at their arms, trying to get in the middle of it all. She looks over and catches my eye, flashes a smile. I look down and grind my fist into my thigh. Sixty-six thousand miles an hour, the earth whips around the sun. While girls like this brush their hair, call their friends, believe that it all revolves around them. Suddenly she's in front of me, shimmering in the heat, still with that center-of-the-universe smile.

"Hey," she says.

"Hello," I say through my teeth. I can see the top of her bra as she leans over the table, lacy white, expectant.

"Cool," she says, reaching to touch an old pillbox hat. Up close, her face has a blank innocence, like a field ready for the plow. She probably still thinks that one of those boys is going to sweep her off her feet, carry her away from here. Someone has most likely assured her that the world is hers for the taking.

Suddenly she gasps. "My necklace," she says, her hand flying to her throat. She looks up at me with big blinking eyes. "Where'd you find it?"

I look over her shoulder at the boys, who seem to have tired of their game and are standing around like cows in a field, looking mutely at the horizon. I wonder which one wrapped his fingers in her hair last night, leaned her up against the bleachers. Which one might do it tonight. A meanness comes over me.

"What are you talking about?" I say, not looking back at her.

"That's my locket. I lost it last night. I've been looking for it all day." *All day.* She says it with a suffering sigh, as if a day was an interminable amount of time, as if we lived on a giant planet that turned infinitely slowly around the sun. Under my clothes, all the humidity of the air collects, trapped, heating up.

"What a coincidence," I say, "that I've got one just like it. I've had this one for months." My face burns. Sweat breaks. I squeeze my hands together behind my back, fighting the urge to pull off my shirt.

"But it's mine," she says, trying to laugh. I can see she's decided I must be teasing her. She's a little drunk, lining her words up carefully, like she's placing them on a tightrope. "Here," she says, reaching for it. "I can prove it." I find myself grabbing her hand and pushing it back from the table. Startled, she jerks it away.

"It's forty-five bucks," I say. Willing her, just willing her, to go away.

"But it's mine. If you look—"

"Forty. I can go as low as forty." I wipe sweat from my face with the back of my hand. I'm wet all over now, drenched like I've fallen in water, my clothes clinging to me, sweat running down my face. "Afraid I can't go any lower than that."

"It's mine," she says again, but quietly, dazed, with the voice of a little girl. Suddenly I can see her bedroom, in a brick ranch on the edge of her daddy's cornfield. Her mother closing the drapes and turning on the lamps every afternoon at five, though the sun is still throwing wild light across the corn. I feel a wave of sympathy. She must think it will never change.

She turns and looks back at the boys. "Who are you, anyway?" she says with her head turned, her voice filling with tears. But it's clear I've won. Without looking back, she goes over to the boys and disappears into the pack as they slouch up toward the midway.

The inside of my mouth, fingertips, toes, everything's buzzing, ringing, like I've just come crashing back down through the atmosphere. As soon as they're out of sight, I lay my hand flat over the necklace, close my fingers around it, and slip it in my back pocket.

On the drive in, I stopped at a historical marker, just to break up the numbness, the unbroken fields along the road. It was a plaque about the Hopewell people, who thousands of years ago lived on this land and built ceremonial earthworks, great burial mounds filled with pottery and tools. And there it was across the field, the mound, nothing spectacular about it at all. I got out of the truck and walked over, thinking it might be more impressive up close. There were daffodils growing along the sides of it, and a beer can had rolled down from the top. I picked it up and stood there and tried to feel some sense of the sacred, of the permanence. But I felt nothing, just the late blankness of an August afternoon, a plane droning overhead. Then, as I stood there flexing the can under my thumb, the loneliness of the ages suddenly grazed past—the shards of clay and bits of stone, the bottles and cans of countless teenage parties, the boxes of coat hangers and reading glasses and safety razors that I am always hauling out of other people's attics—all the things people leave behind, and how they really can tell us nothing, nothing about a life lived, nothing about an entire civilization that disappeared from the face of the earth. I pictured some future race, trying to make sense of what will be left of us, all of our precious treasures sad and useless in the rubble and ruin. It flashed past with a ringing in my ears, left me staggering with irrelevance. Then I let the beer can fall and walked back to the truck, the miles still ahead stretching out before me like a staircase that leads to nowhere.

The rain starts at four. Slow, just a drizzle, and people duck under shelter to wait it out, not wanting to go home. Eventually they venture back out, holding plastic bags over their heads. Umbrellas bloom in the pathways. The Mexicans come down from the midway and shake straw over the churned-up ground, kick at the power cords, giving one another dark, dubious looks. The Ferris wheel keeps turning in the grizzled air. Someone hits the jackpot up at B-52 Breakdown, the lights flash and the sirens wail, and everyone freezes for a minute, their faces full of alarm, as if the unthinkable has happened. They laugh nervously when they realize their mistake, take another bite of their hot dogs, keep on making the rounds.

All afternoon I've been slipping my hand into my back pocket, pressing my thumb against the point of the necklace's heart. Just to feel the dull prick, just to be sure it's still there. I keep searching the revolving faces, hoping and dreading to see her streak by. Her tight jeans would be soaked now, her hair wet, the white satin sash flashing behind her. I wonder if she would stop again. I'm waiting for her to stop again. *You don't want it,* I would say.

But after a while I start to get cold, my jeans heavy and wet, the rain feeling like it's seeping through me. I roll the tarp out over the table and go over to Dub's to wait it out. It's crowded in the tent, warm with bodies. I drop into the folding chair in the corner and watch them jostle one another, grabbing for shirts, and lift one off the pile closest to me. THE HUNTER'S NIGHTMARE. My stomach clenches.

"Hey, Dub," I shout across the chaos. "Where'd you get that necklace?"

"What necklace?" he calls back, looking up from his cash register, handing someone their change.

"Come on," I say, no patience for this.

He ignores me, stuffing half a dozen shirts in a bag. The deer on the shirt looks up with a near-human face. I hold it halfway up. "How can you sell this garbage?" I say loud, trying to turn some heads. Dub, unfazed, looks over. "I don't have to," he shouts over the din. "It sells itself." Several customers' eyes widen when they see the shirt in my hand and they elbow their way over to get a better look. I let it fall back down on the table and push my chair back. Dub makes his way over and grabs it. "Made in Malaysia, man. Only the finest." He throws it to a fat ten-year-old, whose face jiggles when he catches it. "Come on, Cole, where's your sense of humor?"

"I think I lost it somewhere back in Ohio," I say.

"Under the bleachers," he says. "But now I'm giving away all my secrets."

I go back to my table and hang around another half hour, not knowing what else to do. The rain keeps coming, falling in big, heavy drops, and it must be apparent to even the most optimistic that it's not going to stop. A distant clap of thunder sounds. The crowd is steadily thinning, and finally I give up on it. I pack up my table, wrapping things haphazardly in newspapers and rags, throw it all in my crates. I see Dub shoo a pack of boys out of his tent, and they pull up the hoods of their sweatshirts and head doggedly back up to the midway, determined, like soldiers. He stands at the door with his palm stretched out and makes a face at me that says he's quitting, too. "I got a pocket full of dead presidents," he shouts. "I ain't complaining."

I shove my crates under the table, throw the tarp over the whole thing. I'm ready for the warmth of Kathy's bus, the sterile, off-the-lot smell of it, the huge leather couch that slides out from the wall at the press of a button. As I head up the paths, I see that by now the only people left on them are teenagers. The only ones willing to get soaked to the bone for one last go on the Tempest or Zipper now that there are no lines. They're still eating hot dogs, funnel cake off soggy paper plates. I reach into my pocket, touch the necklace, and wonder if she's gone home. Home to the solid brick ranch beside the cornfield. A stillness inside, as her family sits together in the living room, listening to the storm. Grateful for their lightning rod and foundation. As I pass the wing stand, I hear Bob practicing his chord progressions. "Goddamn it all," he says. "Damn it to hell."

Kathy is waiting for me in the bus. She's got the news on the big wall-mounted TV, sound down low, a strained look on her face. When I duck inside, the weatherman is pointing to a red pixilated mass that's moving in fits and starts across a map of the state. She looks up at me and rearranges her face into a smile. "Just a summer storm," she says, reaching up to touch her earrings. "Nothing to worry about." She sounds as if she's trying to convince herself. Clicking off the TV, she pats the space beside her on the couch. "Look at you," she says, her voice changing when I don't sit. "Rough."

I walk back to the bedroom and lie down on the water bed without taking off my muddy boots. I hear her get up and start to make coffee. The rain comes in waves on the roof. It sounds like a hell of a lot more than a summer storm. It sounds like a wrathful sea.

"You're not sleeping in that truck tonight, Cole, baby," she calls back, running the water, opening the cupboards, banging around. It all sounds so forcedly cheerful that my mood darkens like a burnt-out bulb.

"Got any other ideas?" I say to the wall. "Think Bob will mind if I shack up here?"

She's quiet, then says, "You could get a hotel."

The thought of driving into Thunderbird, past all those lighted houses in the rain, navigating the inevitable strip, finding the chain motel with its Shriner's candy machines in the lobby and brochure rack of local attractions—it leaves me with a black hole of loneliness deep in my center.

"Cap's tight," I say, probably too quiet for her to hear. "There's worse things."

She comes in with two mugs of coffee, her rings clinking against them, squeezing sideways through the narrow door. She sits on the edge of the bed, sending a little wake rolling under me. A water bed in a bus, of all the things. She says she likes it, sleeping while they're moving, the little currents comforting, like the womb.

I know there's a part of Kathy that believes this bus will keep her young. That if she and Bob only keep moving, the odometer will spin on it, not her. As little kids, Clay and I thought that if you could just manage to keep your feet off the ground long enough, the world would revolve underneath you, and you'd come down in a different place than you left. We would take turns with a ruler, jumping as high as we could. Later we were fascinated with our grade school textbook's explanation of the speed of light. A story of twin brothers. One travels in a spaceship to distant galaxies, returns to find that while he has not aged at all, his brother is an old, old man. There was a cartoon illustration of the two of them face-to-face, an exclamation point in the air between them, the one who stayed behind with a beard like Rip van Winkle. Clay and I discussed these things often, up past our bedtime, whispering in the darkness of his room. Atomic forces, galactic maps, the theory of relativity. His voice electric with excitement, my mind tripping over itself, trying to keep up with his.

I reach into my back pocket. "Present," I say.

Kathy takes the necklace from me, gingerly, between her finger-tips. She turns it over and over, her lips tight. "Where'd you get this?" she finally says.

"Doesn't matter," I say and cross my arms behind my head, feeling suddenly expansive. "It's for you."

She looks at me, one thin eyebrow raised, then slides a painted fingernail along the edge of the heart. It springs open like a door. Inside, there's a tiny picture of a baby, a red-faced newborn in a blue cap with a pinched, wrinkled face. We both look down at it, silent. The picture is small, no bigger than my pinky nail, but it suddenly feels as if there are three of us on the bus.

Snapping it shut, she hands it silently back. I take it, avoiding her eyes, and shove it deep in my pocket, as deep as it will go, wishing that it would disappear. I close my eyes and see her grip on the bleachers, imagine the necklace swinging with each of his thrusts until it fell to the ground. A baby. It could be anyone, of course. A nephew, a cousin, an old picture of her brother, the one gone off to war. There's something tragic about it, the picture. But maybe it's just that look that newborns have, when it's hard to tell if they're alive or dead. I can feel Kathy watching me, waiting.

"You know that's someone's treasure," she finally says.

I keep my eyes shut and nod. Or the baby could be hers. No hope, then, of escape. Parked him with her mother the weekend of the fair so she can pretend for a day or two that she's free.

"I don't get you, Cole. What are you doing here? You've got your whole life ahead of you. You should make a home for yourself. Settle down."

"I like the road," I say, opening my eyes. Looking up at the close ceiling, the faux marble panels and light fixtures, the words ring as hollow in the bus as they do inside my head.

She sighs. "But don't you ever think about the future?"

"I don't think about next week."

"Well, you live your life like that, Cole, baby, and one morning you'll wake up and it will have passed you by. Like that," she says, and snaps her fingers. "Believe me." I shift and look up at her, hovering above me, her eyes sad and heavy. A sudden rush of rain pounds the roof, and a worried look passes over her face. No matter how far or how fast she travels, Kathy will grow old. She *is* old. I can see the wrinkles breaking through her thick makeup, the gray hair in her braids. The sagging flesh under her arms, gravity's toll.

She leans over as if to kiss me, but instead tries to fluff the pillow behind my head. In the penumbra of her smell, warm and soapy, I feel like I'm being pushed down through fathomless depths, weighted with lead. The bed sloshes underneath me. The narrow walls of the bus feel close and final as a casket. I jerk my head away from her and swing my feet onto the floor. The rain falls heavy, with the sound of tearing pages. In the lulls I can hear Bob's uncertain chords, his curses and false starts. I stand up on shaky legs, sick to death of other people's tragedies. To be carried away by a giant bird. There could be worse things. Everything and everyone on earth growing smaller and smaller, as all of it fell away.

"I've got to get out of here," I say.

Kathy sits up and slides her hands between her knees, trying to smile, to smooth it over. "Baby," she says, reaching out, and I step away, knocking into the flimsy closet door and sending a cascade of clothes out onto the floor. The rain roars on the roof. "Where on earth do you think you're going?"

The wind rips the door of the bus out of my hand as I dive out into the pounding rain. Pulling the collar of my T-shirt up around my neck, I duck my head and start to run down the empty path. Shouts and the beep of backing trucks on the midway pierce the thick sound of the torrent. But none of it has been broken down yet, the rides still up, the Ferris wheel looming above the crouching booths and trailers. Along the strips, figures in raincoats load up pickups, tires spin in the mud. I run away from it all, out toward the dark field. The wet grass grabs at my legs, slowing me down, but I keep running until I'm at the tree line, and I turn and look at the carnival, a somber city in the distance. When I pull the necklace from my pocket and let go, I expect it to be carried away on the wind. Instead it drops to the ground like an anchor, and I have to grind it into the mud with my boot to be rid of it. I want it never to be found again. Buried. Lost for good.

I'm the one who stayed. The brother with the beard. Clay reached escape velocity fifteen years ago, out on the dark road. I'm starting to think he was the lucky one. I stop, lean down on my knees, try to catch my breath, let the rain hammer me. The rain-swept field is desolate as the open sea. Virginia. Even if I were to turn around, drive east a thousand miles, turn on the old road and down our driveway, I'd walk up a front path that leads to nothing, the house torn down months ago to make room for the new neighborhood that is rising up relentlessly in the pasture where we spent our afternoons. Just Clay, me, and the old oak trees. And now the trees are gone, too.

This is Illinois, I say, to steady myself. *My feet are on the ground.* I crouch there, repeating it, until the rain stops. It stops abruptly, as if I've somehow willed it to, and in its place comes a thick, strange stillness, as if the palm of a giant hand has flattened over the field. Everything stands still, everything—the grass, the leaves, the sky. I stand and look up, the towering dark clouds frozen. Clay had another favorite theory. If you could go up in a plane and travel around the equator at exactly eight hundred miles an hour, the speed of the earth's rotation, the sun would appear to hang still in the sky. There you would be, no past, no future. As long as you could keep up your speed. *But,* he'd say, frowning. *But there's a rub.* It would be an illusion. Down on earth, the sun would be rising and setting, the clocks ticking away. Life would carry on without you.

Headlights come at me across the field. It's a cop car, bumping and straining over the uneven ground. The window rolls down as it pulls alongside me. Without stopping, a bull-faced sheriff leans out into the still air, jerks his thumb back up toward the road, mistaking me for a straggling reveler. "Son," he says, "we've got a tornado warning in effect. We've sent everybody home."

Let it come, I think, running back up to the midway. Let it rip through. Let it wipe the field clean. Let it carry all this away. Up on my strip, my table stands alone, the tarp blown off my boxes, everything soaked. Dub's tent is gone, the only thing left an overturned folding chair. I can see a steady line of rigs leaving Camper City, pulling out onto the road, headed for god-knows-where. The rain starts again, all at once, pounding, and then the wind, picking it up and slashing it around. What I said to Kathy, about liking the road. That was a lie. The road—what it really is—eight lanes of grinding semis barreling west with spent uranium, east with old-growth timber, hauling shit-caked cows and microwave dinners, feeding the frenzy of the country—it all moves too fast. Lately I've been thinking we'll just spin off our axis and out into the center of space. Hell. Thunderbird, Illinois, might be the first to go.

I run up the deserted paths of the midway, where rides and booths have been forsaken, left to the mercy of the wind. Flatbeds sit parked at abrupt angles next to the rides, some partly dismantled, some still standing, the wind whistling through scaffolding. Paper plates, cups, drumsticks spill out of overturned trash cans. A balloon caught on the side of the Haunted House beats itself against the wall, as if trying to break free. A loosed tarp swoops toward me on furious wings. I duck and it flings itself on down the path. I run past the Ferris wheel, where the plywood clown that kids must be as tall as to ride has toppled over and lies sideways, grinning, in the grass. The wheel shudders and groans. The carriages rock, glow in a flash of lightning. The wind shoves me along from behind. My heart takes over, pounding, shouting from my chest. *Get out of here,* it shouts when I look up at that swaying wheel. *Get out of here,* it shouts, and the moaning steel struts of the Gravitron and Tilt-a-Whirl and Zipper all shout it, too. Stumbling, I run through the rain for the remains of Camper City, for the truck, no idea what I'll do when I get there. Pull out on the road and try to outrun it, lock the doors and watch it come. Either way, I've got nowhere to go.

But then I round the back loop, and see them. A ragged pack of boys, weaving through the abandoned booths. They're passing beer cans, trying to light cigarettes in the whipping wind. They must have hid when the cops came through, first brave, then reckless, defying the lightning. Now they're swaggering through the rain, invincible. And ahead of me, up on the carousel, girls in wet T-shirts sit astride the still horses, passing a bottle in a wet paper bag. The horses' nostrils flare, eyes and manes wild, legs flung out, suspended in midflight. Behind them, all of the sky is gathering itself up at the horizon, bloodred, feathered, gathering up. The wind seems to hover above us. "Look!" I yell, pointing, but my voice is snatched away by the wind. The Ferris wheel groans, lamenting. "Get out of here! Go on!"

But none of them even notice me. The girls cackle, their hair plastered to their faces, their eyes black with smudged makeup. The boys strut over, swing themselves up onto the horses, shake the rain from their hair. They're all laughing, shouting, singing, celebrating as if they know something no one else knows. As if on the other side of that terrible horizon there's a new world coming when this one goes, a world where everything lost will be restored, and everything made whole. One of the girls, dark-eyed and wasted, sees me and reaches out, saying something I can't hear over the din, and I strain to make out her lips. *Come on,* she's saying, *come quickly, come, come—*

CONTRIBUTORS

WILL BOAST grew up in England, Ireland, and Wisconsin. His fiction has appeared in the *Southern Review* and *Alaska Quarterly Review* and is forthcoming in *Glimmer Train* and *Mississippi Review*. He is currently at work on a novel and a memoir.

ERIN BROWN served for two years as a Peace Corps volunteer in Togo, West Africa. She received her MFA from the University of Virginia, where she was awarded the Henry Hoyns Fellowship. Her fiction and nonfiction have appeared in *Open City,* the *New York Times,* and *Northwest Review.* She is currently at work on a novel.

KEVIN A. GONZÁLEZ was born in San Juan, Puerto Rico. A graduate of the Iowa Writers' Workshop, his stories have appeared in *Playboy,* the *Virginia Quarterly Review, Indiana Review, Best New American Voices 2007,* and *Best American Nonrequired Reading 2007.* He is also the author of a chapbook of poems, *The Night Tito Trinidad KO'ed Ricardo Mayorga* (Momotombo Press, 2007). Currently, he is the Carol Houck Smith Fiction Fellow at the University of Wisconsin–Madison, where he is working on a novel.

BAIRD HARPER holds an MA from the University of Montana and is a recent graduate of the School of the Art Institute of Chicago's MFA program. His fiction has appeared in *Cairn, CutBank,* and *Tin House.* He is currently finishing a novel and a collection of short fiction.

OTIS HASCHEMEYER was a Wallace Stegner Fellow at the Stanford Creative Writing Program. His work has appeared in the *Sun,* the *Alaska Quarterly Review, Iodine Poetry Journal, Barrow Street,* and other journals. He has recently won the Jeffery E. Smith Editor's Prize from the *Missouri Review.*

ANASTASIA KOLENDO was born in the south of Ukraine. Her mother's family is from a small village at the foot of the Urals. Kolendo has an MFA from Boston University and lives in Austin, Texas, with her husband. They are hoping to get a dog.

NAM LE was born in Vietnam and raised in Australia. His debut collection of stories, *The Boat,* was published by Knopf in 2008. He has received the Pushcart Prize, the Michener-Copernicus Society of America Award, and fellowships from the Iowa Writers' Workshop, the Fine Arts Work Center in Provincetown, and Phillips Exeter Academy. His fiction has appeared in venues including the Best American Nonrequired Reading series, the Best Australian Stories series, *Zoetrope: All-Story, A Public Space,* and *One Story.* He is currently the fiction editor at the *Harvard Review.*

SHARON MAY was born in California of mixed American and Iranian ancestry. Her stories have appeared in *Best New American Voices 2008,* the *Chicago Tribune, Tin House, StoryQuarterly, Other Voices, Manoa, Concert of Voices: An Anthology of World Writing in English, A Stranger Among Us: Tales of Cross-Cultural Collisions and Connections,* and elsewhere. She has received the Robie Macauley Award, the Julia Peterkin Award, and a Wallace Stegner Fellowship at Stanford University. She is coeditor of *In the Shadow of Angkor: Contemporary Writing from Cambodia* (University of Hawai'i Press, 2004). She recently completed a story collection and is working on a novel set in Cambodia.

The son of Holocaust survivors, LARRY N. MAYER grew up in the Marble Hill section of the Bronx and graduated with honors from P.S. 7 and J.H.S. 141. His first book, *Who Will Say Kaddish?: A Search for Jewish Identity in Contemporary Poland,* was published by Syracuse University Press in 2002. A teacher of at-risk high school students, he has written about his experiences working at alternative and group home schools in the South Bronx, Roxbury, Boston, Cambridge, and Lorain County, Ohio. At present, he teaches creative writing and "Representations of the Holocaust" at Washington State University while pursuing his MFA in fiction at the University of Idaho. His current novel-in-progress, "A Love Perfect Sleeping: The Misadventures of Campy Metzger," is a high-energy romp through the 1960s that explores the issues of assimilation, love, and spiritual dispossession within three generations of one nutty family in what has now become a fading world.

Born in Iran and raised in Boston, MEHDI TAVANA OKASI is now an MFA student at Purdue University, where he also holds the editorship of *Sycamore Review.* He is simultaneously working on a collection of stories and a novel.

LYDIA PEELLE lives in Tennessee. She is a recent fellow at the Fine Arts Work Center in Provincetown, and her fiction has appeared in numerous journals as well as *The O. Henry Prize Stories: 2006, Pushcart Prize XXXII,* and *Best New American Voices 2007.* She is at work on a collection of stories.

SUZANNE RIVECCA is a former Wallace Stegner Fellow in Fiction at Stanford University, where she currently teaches. Her fiction has appeared in *Best New American Voices 2008, New England Review, StoryQuarterly, Fence,* and others. She was the Alan Collins Scholar in Fiction at the 2007 Bread Loaf Writers' Conference.

JACOB RUBIN received a BA in literature from Harvard College and an MFA in fiction from the University of Mississippi. He is currently making a documentary about the author Barry Hannah and working on a novel.

THEODORE WHEELER worked on this story as a graduate fellow at Creighton University and as a Jakobson Scholarship winner at the Wesleyan Writers Conference. His short fiction has appeared in *Boulevard* and *GSU Review.* Wheeler lives in Omaha with his wife, Nicole, is finishing a collection of short fiction, and has begun work on a novel.

PARTICIPANTS

American University
MFA Program in Creative Writing
Department of Literature
4400 Massachusetts Avenue NW
Washington, DC 20016
202/885-2973

Antioch Writers' Conference
P.O. Box 494
Yellow Springs, OH 45387
937/475-7357

The Banff Centre for the Arts
Writing Studio
Box 1020, Station 34
107 Tunnel Mountain Drive
Banff, AB TIL 1H5
403/762-6269

Binghamton University
Binghamton Center for Writers
P.O. Box 6000
Binghamton, NY 13902-6000
607/777-2713

Boise State University
MFA Program in Writing
1910 University Drive
Boise, ID 83725
208/426-1002

Boston University
Graduate Creative Writing Program
236 Bay State Road
Boston, MA 02215
617/353-2506

Bowling Green State University
Department of English
Creative Writing Program
Bowling Green, OH 43403-0215
419/372-8370

The Bread Loaf Writers' Conference
Middlebury College—P&W
Middlebury, VT 05753
802/443-5286

Brooklyn College
MFA in Creative Writing
2900 Bedford Avenue
Brooklyn, NY 11210-2889
718/951-5195

Brown University
Program in Literary Arts, Box 1923
Providence, RI 02912
401/863-3260

Chapman University
Department of English and
Comparative Literature
1 University Drive
Orange, CA 92866
714/997-6750

Colorado State University
MFA Creative Writing Program
English Department, 359 Eddy Hall
Fort Collins, CO 80523-1773
970/491-6428

Columbia College
School of Fine and Performing Arts
Fiction Writing
600 South Michigan Avenue
Chicago, IL 60605-1996
312/663-1600

Columbia University
Writing Division, School of the Arts
2960 Broadway, 415 Dodge Hall
New York, NY 10027
212/854-4391

Cornell University
English Department
Goldwin Smith Hall
Ithaca, NY 14851
607/255-6800

Emerson College
Writing, Literature, and Publishing
120 Beacon Street
Boston, MA 02116
617/824-8500

Fine Arts Work Center in
Provincetown
24 Pearl Street
Provincetown, MA 02657
508/487-9960

Florida State University
Creative Writing Program
Department of English
Tallahassee, FL 32306-1580
850/644-4230

George Mason University
Creative Writing Program
MS 3E4, English Department
4400 University Drive
Fairfax, VA 22030
703/993-1180

Georgia State University
Department of English
38 Peachtree Center Avenue, Suite 923
Atlanta, GA 30303-3083
404/413-2000

Grub Street
160 Boylston Street, 4th Floor
Boston, MA 02116
617/695-0075

Hamline University
MFA Program
Graduate School of Liberal Studies
1536 Hewitt Avenue
St. Paul, MN 55104-1284
651/523-2047

Indiana University
Department of English
Ballantine Hall 442
Bloomington, IN 47405-7103
812/855-9539

The Indiana University Writers'
Conference
Ballantine Hall 464
1020 East Kirkwood Avenue
Bloomington, IN 47405-7103
812/855-1877

Johns Hopkins University
The Writing Seminars
3400 North Charles Street
Gilman 136
Baltimore, MD 21218
410/516-6286

Johns Hopkins Writing Program—
Washington
1717 Massachusetts Avenue, NW,
Suite 104
Washington, DC 20036
202/452-1123

Kansas State University
Department of English
108 English/Counseling Services
Building
Manhattan, KS 66506-6501
785/532-6716

The Loft Literary Center
Mentor Series Program
Suite 200, Open Brook
1011 Washington Avenue South
Minneapolis, MN 55415
612/215-2575

Louisiana State University
MFA Program in Creative Writing
Department of English
260 Allen Hall
Baton Rouge, LA 70803-5001
225/578-5922

Loyola Marymount University
University Hall
1 LMU Drive, Suite 3800
Los Angeles, CA 90045-2659
310/338-3018

The Michener Center for Writers
University of Texas at Austin
702 East Dean Keeton Street
Austin, TX 78705
512/471-1601

Mills College
Creative Writing Program
5000 MacArthur Boulevard
Oakland, CA 94613
510/430-3309

Minnesota State University, Mankato
Department of English
230 Armstrong Hall
Mankato, MN 56001
507/389-2117

Mississippi State University
Department of English
Drawer E
Mississippi State, MS 39762
662/325-3644

Naropa University
Program in Writing and Poetics
2130 Arapahoe Avenue
Boulder, CO 80302
303/546-3508

New Mexico State University
Department of English
Box 30001/3E
Las Cruces, NM 88003
505/646-3931

The New York State Summer Writers
Institute
815 North Broadway
Skidmore College
Saratoga Springs, NY 12866-1632
518/584-5000

New York University
Graduate Program in Creative Writing
Lillian Vernon Writers House
58 West 10th Street
New York, NY 10011
212/998-8816

Northwestern University
Master of Arts in Creative Writing
School of Continuing Studies
405 Church Street
Evanston, IL 60208-4220
847/491-5612

Ohio State University
Department of English
MFA in Creative Writing
451 Denney Hall
164 West 17th Avenue
Columbus, OH 43210-1370
614/292-2242

Pennsylvania State University
MFA Program in Creative Writing
117 Burrowes Building
University Park, PA 16802
814/865-0009

Purdue University
MFA Program in Creative Writing
Department of English
West Lafayette, IN 47907-2038
765/494-3740

Roosevelt University, Chicago Campus
School of Liberal Arts
430 South Michigan Avenue
Chicago, IL 60605-1394
312/341-3710

Rosemont College
MFA in Creative Writing
1400 Montgomery Avenue
Good Counsel Hall, Room 101
Rosemont, PA 19010
610/527-0200 Ext. 2994

Saint Mary's College of California
MFA Program in Creative Writing
P.O. Box 4686
Moraga, CA 94575-4686
925/631-4088

San Diego State University
MFA Program
Department of English and
Comparative Literature
San Diego, CA 92182-8140
619/594-5431

San Francisco State University
Creative Writing Department
1600 Holloway Avenue
San Francisco, CA 94132-4162
415/338-1891

San Jose State University
Steinbeck Fellows Program
Department of English and
Comparative Literature
San Jose, CA 95192-0202
408/808-2067

Sarah Lawrence College
Graduate Writing Program
1 Mead Way
Bronxville, NY 10708-5999
914/337-0700

The School of the Art Institute
of Chicago
MFA in Writing Program
37 South Wabash Avenue
Chicago, IL 60603-3103
312/899-5094

Sewanee Writers' Conference
123 Gailor Hall
735 University Avenue
Sewanee, TN 37383-1000
931/598-1141

Sonoma State University
MA in English with Concentration
in Creative Writing
1801 East Cotati Avenue
Rohnert Park, CA 94108
707/664-2140

Southern Illinois University at
Carbondale
MFA Program in Creative Writing
Department of English
Faner Hall 2380, Mail Code 4503
1000 Faner Drive
Carbondale, IL 62901
618/453-5321

Stanford University
Creative Writing Program
Department of English
Stanford, CA 94305-2087
650/725-1208

Syracuse University
Program in Creative Writing
401 Hall of Languages
Syracuse, NY 13244-1170
315/443-2173

Taos Summer Writers' Conference
Department of English
MSC03 2170
University of New Mexico
Albuquerque, NM 87131-0001
505/277-5572

Temple University
Creative Writing Program
Anderson Hall, 10th Floor
Philadelphia, PA 19122
215/204-1796

Texas A&M University
Creative Writing Program
English Department
College Station, TX 77843-4227
979/845-3452

Texas State University–San Marcos
MFA Program, Creative Writing
Department of English
601 University Drive
San Marcos, TX 78666-4616
512/245-7681

Texas Tech University
Creative Writing Program
Department of English
Box 43091
Lubbock, TX 79409
806/742-2501

University of Alabama
Program in Creative Writing
Department of English
103 Morgan Hall
P.O. Box 870244
Tuscaloosa, AL 35487-0244
205/348-5065

University of Alaska, Fairbanks
Creative Writing Program
English Department
P.O. Box 755720
Fairbanks, AK 99775-5720
907/474-7193

University of Arizona
MFA Program in Creative Writing
445 Modern Languages Building
P.O. Box 210067
Tucson, AZ 85721-0067
520/621-3880

University of Arkansas
Program in Creative Writing
Department of English
333 Kimpel Hall
Fayetteville, AR 72701
479/575-4301

University of California, Davis
Graduate Creative Writing Program
Department of English
One Shields Avenue
Davis, CA 95616
530/752-2281

University of California, Irvine
MFA Program in Writing
Department of English and
Comparative Literature
435 Humanities Building
Irvine, CA 92697-2650
714/824-6718

University of Cincinnati
Creative Writing Program
Department of English & Comparative
Literature
ML 69
Cincinnati, OH 45221-0069
513/556-5924

University of Colorado at Boulder
MFA in Creative Writing
Department of English
Campus Box 226
Boulder, CO 80309-0226
303/492-1853

University of Denver
Creative Writing Program
English Department
Sturm Hall
Denver, CO 80208
303/871-2266

University of Florida
MFA Program
Department of English
P.O. Box 117310
Gainesville, FL 32611-7310
352/392-6650 Ext. 225

University of Houston
Creative Writing Program
Department of English
R. Cullen 229
Houston, TX 77204-3015
713/743-3015

University of Idaho
Creative Writing Program
Department of English
P.O. Box 441102
Moscow, ID 83844-1102
208/885-6156

University of Illinois at Chicago
Program for Writers
Department of English M/C 162
601 South Morgan Street
Chicago, IL 60607-7120
312/413-2239

University of Iowa
Program in Creative Writing
102 Dey House
507 North Clinton Street
Iowa City, IA 52242
319/335-0416

University of Kansas
MFA Program
3114 Wescoe Hall
Lawrence, KS 66045
785/864-2516

University of Massachusetts, Amherst
MFA Program for Poets and Writers
Department of English
130 Hicks Way
Amherst, MA 01003-9269
413/545-0643

University of Memphis
The Writing Program
Memphis, TN 38152-3510
901/678-2651

University of Michigan
MFA Program in Creative Writing
Department of English
3187 Angell Hall
Ann Arbor, MI 48109-1003
734/936-2274

University of Minnesota
MFA Program in Creative Writing
222 Lind Hall
207 Church Street
Minneapolis, MN 55455
612/625-6366

University of Mississippi
MFA Program in Creative Writing
English Department
Bondurant Hall C128
Oxford, MS 38677-1848
662/915-7439

University of Missouri–Columbia
Creative Writing Program
Department of English
107 Tate Hall
Columbia, MO 65211-1500
573/884-7773

University of Montana
Creative Writing Program
Department of English
Missoula, MT 59812-1013
406/243-5231

University of Nebraska, Lincoln
Creative Writing Program
Department of English
202 Andrews Hall
Lincoln, NE 68588-0333
402/472-3191

University of Nebraska, Omaha
MFA in Writing
6001 Dodge Street/WFAB 310
Omaha, NE 68182-0324
402/554-3020

University of Nevada, Las Vegas
MFA in Creative Writing International
Department of English
4505 Maryland Parkway
Las Vegas, NV 89154-5011
702/895-3533

University of New Mexico
Graduate Program in Creative Writing
Department of English Language and
Literature
Humanities Building, 2nd Floor
Albuquerque, NM 87131
505/277-6347

University of New Orleans
Creative Writing Workshop
College of Liberal Arts
Lakefront
New Orleans, LA 70148
504/280-7454

University of North Carolina at Greensboro
MFA Writing Program
P.O. Box 26170
Greensboro, NC 27402-6170
336/334-5459

University of North Dakota
Creative Writing Program
English Department
P.O. Box 7209
Grand Forks, ND 58202
701/777-3321

University of North Texas
Creative Writing Division
Department of English
P.O. Box 311307
Denton, TX 76203-1307
940/565-2050

University of Notre Dame
Creative Writing Program
Department of English
356 O'Shaughnessy Hall
Notre Dame, IN 46556-5639
574/631-4799

University of Oregon
Creative Writing Program
144 Columbia Hall
P.O. Box 5243
Eugene, OR 97403-5243
541/346-0509

University of Pittsburgh
Creative Writing Program
English Department
526 Cathedral of Learning
4200 Fifth Avenue
Pittsburgh, PA 15260-0001
412/624-6506

University of San Francisco
MFA in Writing Program
Program Office, Lone Mountain 340
2130 Fulton Street
San Francisco, CA 94117-1080
415/422-2382

University of South Carolina
MFA Program in Creative Writing
Department of English
Columbia, SC 29208
803/777-4203

University of Tennessee
Creative Writing Program
Department of English
301 McClung Tower
Knoxville, TN 37996
865/974-5401

University of Utah
Creative Writing Program
255 South Central Campus Drive,
Room 3500
Salt Lake City, UT 84112
801/581-7131

University of Virginia
Creative Writing Program
219 Bryan Hall
P.O. Box 400121
Charlottesville, VA 22904-4121
434/924-6675

University of Washington
Creative Writing Program
Box 354330
Seattle, WA 98195-4330
206/543-9865

University of Wisconsin–Madison
Program in Creative Writing
English Department
6195F Helen C. White Hall
600 North Park Street
Madison, WI 53706
608/263-3800

University of Wyoming
MFA in Creative Writing
English Department
P.O. Box 3353
Laramie, WY 82071
307/766-2867

Vermont College of Union Institute
& University
MFA in Writing Program
36 College Street
Montpelier, VT 05602
802/828-8840

Virginia Commonwealth University
MFA in Creative Writing Program
Department of English
P.O. Box 842005
Richmond, VA 23284-2005
804/828-1329

Virginia Tech
MFA Program
323 Shanks Hall
Blacksburg, VA 24061
540/231-6501

Washington University in St. Louis
The Writing Program
Campus Box 1122
One Brookings Drive
St. Louis, MO 63130-4899
314/935-5190

Wesleyan Writers Conference
Wesleyan University
294 High Street, Room 207
Middletown, CT 06459
860/685-3604

West Virginia University
Creative Writing Program
Department of English
P.O. Box 6269
Morgantown, WV 26506-6269
304/293-3107

Western Michigan University
Graduate Program in Creative Writing
Department of English
Kalamazoo, MI 49008
269/387-2572

The Julia and David White
Artists' Colony
Interlink 232
P.O. Box 526770
Miami, FL 33152
www.forjuliaanddavid.org

Wisconsin Institute for Creative
Writing
University of Wisconsin–Madison
Department of English
Helen C. White Hall
600 North Park Street
Madison, WI 53706
608/263-3374

Wright State University
Creative Writing Program
Department of English
3640 Colonel Glenn Highway
Dayton, OH 45435-0001
937/775-2196